Limbo ll

Also by Andy Secombe

Limbo

ANDY SECOMBE

Limbo ll
The Final Chapter

TOR

First published 2004 by Tor
an imprint of Pan Macmillan Ltd
Pan Macmillan, 20 New Wharf Road, London N1 9RR
Basingstoke and Oxford
Associated companies throughout the world
www.panmacmillan.com
www.toruk.com

ISBN 1 405 00485 1

Copyright © Andy Secombe 2004

The right of Andy Secombe to be identified as the
author of this work has been asserted by him in accordance
with the Copyright, Designs and Patents Act 1988.

All rights reserved. No part of this publication may be
reproduced, stored in or introduced into a retrieval system, or
transmitted, in any form, or by any means (electronic, mechanical,
photocopying, recording or otherwise) without the prior written
permission of the publisher. Any person who does any unauthorized
act in relation to this publication may be liable to criminal
prosecution and civil claims for damages.

1 3 5 7 9 8 6 4 2

A CIP catalogue record for this book is available from
the British Library.

Typeset by Intype London Ltd.
Printed and bound in Great Britain by
Mackays of Chatham plc, Chatham, Kent

This book is sold subject to the condition that it shall not,
by way of trade or otherwise, be lent, re-sold, hired out,
or otherwise circulated without the publisher's prior consent
in any form of binding or cover other than that in which
it is published and without a similar condition including this
condition being imposed on the subsequent purchaser.

To Speckle and Greckle – two brave chickens

Acknowledgements

Thanks once again to: Robert Kirby, for spotting my deliberate mistake, everyone at Macmillan, especially Peter Lavery, for his good humour and encouragement, and the tireless Stefanie Bierwerth.

I'd also like to thank my wife Caroline for her wise counsel, and my two sons, Matthew, the budding naturalist, and Charles, the budding Spiderman.

Author's note

The action takes place about ten years from now, in various locations including Dartmoor, Brighton, Lanzarote and Limbo.

For those unfamiliar with Limbo, I can offer no better description than the words of the immortal F. Don Wizzard:

> Landscape of the unconscious, at once far away yet as familiar as the smell of freshly laundered sheets. When you dream, you dream of Limbo.

Part I

Day . . .

In the swirling dust cloud of the cosmic mind, a monstrous thing pawed at the doors of consciousness. It was ages old and black with evil, and it wanted admittance. It wanted to feel the sun on its back, to glory in the sensuousness of its corporeal reality; it wanted . . . to be.

And soon, very soon now, it would.

Chapter 1

Nilbert Plymstock, eighteen-year-old scout leader, third grade, killed the engine and clambered down onto the damp, mossy ground. Under a lowering grey sky, the vast, empty expanse of Dartmoor brooded menacingly. 'We'll camp here,' he shouted back to the party of thin, whey-faced boys huddled, shivering, in the back of the Land-Rover.

Nilbert filled his lungs, and his nostrils whistled tunelessly. It was beginning to rain, but a cold shower couldn't dampen Nilbert's spirits, even though, from the Gore-tex uppers of his boots to the turn-ups of his oversized khaki shorts, his thin, stick legs were blue-mottled with cold. He ripped open his rucksack and pulled out a bar of Cadbury's Wholenut and a small carton of chocolate milk. 'Ah, it's good to be alive,' he said. 'There is nothing, absolutely nothing better than being a scout. It's more than a way of life, it's a vocation.'

At that moment, a walnut-sized meteorite zipped past his nose and slammed into the ground between his boots. In the shocked silence that followed, Nilbert looked down at the three-foot-deep crater that had suddenly appeared at his feet, and felt the still-smouldering, fist-sized hole in the broad brim of his Baden-Powell, official-issue, pack-leader's hat, and decided to do something more useful with his life.

Boggs' Brasserie, Castle Limbo's main restaurant, was today situated on the mezzanine, just behind the café-bookshop. The large, hammerbeam-roofed dining hall was usually on the third floor, but Limbo was like that.

The huge, grey, misshapen castle had been the seat of the King of Limbo from time immemorial. It had been built in the Age of Darkness, and so no one had been able to see what they were doing – turrets, wings, flying buttresses, all sprouted from it at strange and interesting angles, and not one doorway or window was straight. Inside, too, the building had several interesting quirks. Stairs would appear and disappear at random; doors that had once led somewhere would open onto solid brick; corridors that for years had stayed comfortingly level would, of a sudden, slope precipitously downwards, sending any that were not familiar with the castle's ways to certain death. Before the Incident, whole floors had gone missing; the dining hall itself had once disappeared completely for over six hundred years. Of course, since the accession of King Bernard and Queen Iris, things had calmed down considerably – the castle loved them and was desperately eager to please. In fact, the reason for the restaurant's relocation today was a chance remark made by the Queen.

Perusing the vast array of glossy magazines on offer in Smeil's Café-Bookshop, she had happened to mention to the King that she felt a little peckish. Walking out of the café into what should have been the North Gallery, the King and Queen had been only mildly surprised to find themselves in the restaurant, its liveried staff waiting to satisfy their every whim.

Now they were sitting at their special table, on the raised dais in front of the large window which, wherever the restaurant happened to be, always had the best view in Limbo.

'How's your sole, my little dumpling?' said King Bernard, grabbing Queen Iris's thigh.

Iris flushed. 'Bernard,' she smiled coyly, 'we're supposed to be regal.'

'You'll always be queen of my heart, my love,' he replied, taking her hand and kissing it.

Limbo II

Iris went a deeper shade of red and tried to cover her embarrassment with her napkin. 'You're terrible,' she whispered.

Bernard smiled. The passing of the years and the discovery of the joys of long lunches may have increased his girth and added a certain fleshiness to his long face, but they had done little to dampen the love he felt for his wife. True, her hair was now as white as snow and the lines around her big, round eyes were etched deep, but to Bernard she was still as lovely as the day he first saw her – strolling down Lancing High Street in a summer dress. 'Ah, my love,' he sighed.

'Where's that son of ours?' she said suddenly, retrieving her hand from Bernard's embrace and smoothing her napkin over her lap. 'If he's not careful he's going to miss lunch altogether.'

Iris wasn't entirely comfortable with public shows of affection, but this, Bernard sensed, was something more than embarrassment. 'Are you all right, petal?' he asked.

At that moment, the dapper, torpedo-shaped figure of the maître d'hôtel appeared. 'Your majesties,' he said, bowing low. 'Are you enjoying your meal?'

High up amongst the skewed towers and turrets of Castle Limbo, in his room which could not be reached by any known means, Rex Boggs, Wizard to the Court of Limbo, looked up from the big book of spells that lay open on the table before him.

'It is time,' he said and, closing the book, stood and walked round the great circular table covered with strange and arcane symbols to the big, navy-blue Aga. Putting on an oven glove printed with a lobster motif and opening the door of the baking oven, he pulled out a tray of madeleines, and a sweet vanilla fragrance filled the air. Tipping them out onto a cooling rack, he carefully picked one up between forefinger and thumb, and examined it critically. Then he took a tentative mouthful. 'Mmh, not bad, not bad,' he said, sucking in air through his open mouth to cool the still baking-hot morsel. 'Much better than the last lot.'

The Wizard of Limbo had big, blunt features and a wide, friendly smile. He was large and rather unprepossessing, but he did have the most extraordinary eyes – blue like the morning sky, as deep and as placid as a mountain lake, with here and there a fleck of white like swans taking flight.

He turned to the window. Scents of hyacinth and jasmine rose up from the gardens below, mingling agreeably with the aroma of baking, and out of a clear blue sky the sun beat down on the Great Plain stretching to the far foothills of the snow-capped mountains on the horizon. It was a beautiful prospect, but Rex couldn't really enjoy it – something was *wrong*. He'd felt it earlier: a knocking – no, not exactly a knocking, more a rasping tremor. Whatever it was, Rex had a strong suspicion he would soon have some very serious work to do.

After the miracle he had wrought in saving the universe, Rex was well respected by the citizens of Limbo, being much sought after to officiate at weddings and christenings, or to do a spot of healing. He was very good at mending broken bones.

Unlike his father, the previous Wizard, who had used his gift of second sight to advise businesses on the outcome of high-risk investment opportunities, and ran a lucrative sideline informing courting couples whether or not they had a future together, Rex was no businessman. Although he had inherited a large part of the preceding Wizard's mind, Rex was not a natural wizard – he was softer-natured than his father and had spent most of the last ten years reading and perfecting his baking techniques.

The heavy responsibility that goes with the exalted position of Wizard of Limbo had been thrust upon him, one summer's day on Hove seafront. The story of how Rex had battled the monster that threatened to destroy the universe had passed into legend, and now every school child in Limbo could recite by heart the episode where Rex, with a nifty spot of time travelling, had tricked the beast into killing Rex's old and infirm self.

But that was ten long years ago, and Rex now found it almost impossible to relate to that storybook hero. He sighed and gazed out at the bright day. Life here was perfect, it was true – the sun shone continuously, and there weren't even any seasons to break the golden constancy of a never-ending July morning. But he had secretly begun to understand what had led his father to try and break the monotony by writing the Book. Nothing ever happened here. *Steady now, Rex*, he thought, *that way madness lies*, and he popped the rest of the madeleine into his mouth.

Then it came again – that pawing, scraping shudder against the doors of consciousness, and, despite the warmness of the day, Rex shivered. Instinctively, he went to the bookcase and took down a small, chunky and well-thumbed tome. Opening it, the room was suddenly bathed in rainbows, for there, glittering within its hollowed-out centre, was the egg-sized Limbo Crystal. This fabulous gem had been created a micro-nanosecond after the Big Bang, and as such was the oldest thing in the universe. Deep within, it had a peculiar and extraordinary flaw – a small, three-dimensional image of the castle, perfect in every detail – and, underneath, the legend 'Souvenir of Limbo'. In the right hands it was an immensely powerful tool. It was the key to the door between dimensions – between 'what is' and 'what could be', and vice versa.

Rex weighed the Crystal in his hand. This gem gave him the power to travel anywhere he wished, through both time and space. But where should he go? To see the previous Wizard and ask his advice? No – Rex was the Wizard now, and any problems were his responsibility alone. Besides, how could he ask for help when he had no idea what the problem was?

Sighing, he replaced the Crystal in the chunky book. But as he was putting it back on the shelf, he happened to glance at his watch.

'Oh shit.'

He was supposed to have met his foster parents King Bernard and Queen Iris for lunch half an hour ago.

Chapter 2

The soft coral in the large saltwater tank was doing well – it had grown by about a foot in the short space of a week. This was very exciting and, as he observed the rapidly growing organism, a thought – a rather complex thought – began to form at the back of Nilbert's mind.

After the life-changing shock of the Dartmoor incident, Nilbert Plymstock had decided to devote himself to science and, discovering a remarkable aptitude for biochemistry, soon became a leader – although some regarded him as a maverick – in the field of genetics. Convinced that biotechnology was the answer to all the planet's ills, he threw himself into his work with messianic zeal. His expertise was soon in great demand, and he found himself working in some of the remotest, most barren, ecologically sensitive places on Earth. However, as the Dartmoor experience had left him agoraphobic, this wasn't altogether to his liking. Now, ten years after that meteorite had nearly ended his life, Nilbert was heading a small team of marine biologists on Lizard Island, a tiny jewel set in the azure-blue necklace of the Great Barrier Reef, researching the effects of rampant global warming on the seas in general, and on the delicate corals that make up the Barrier Reef in particular.

Corals are extremely sensitive organisms and, quite apart from the threats posed by country-sized factory ships with their vast trawl nets and the menace of the polyp-guzzling crown of thorns starfish, they also have to contend with rapidly warming seas. The corals are the heart of a complex and subtle ecosystem upon which huge numbers of sea creatures depend. The Great Barrier Reef was dying faster than it could rejuvenate itself, and as a reef can take thousands of years to form, at the present rate it wouldn't be long before the whole system collapsed, the same scenario being repeated worldwide. Without the reefs, the seas would gradually turn into vast, stagnant ponds, and it was on trying to reverse this trend that Nilbert's research was focused.

One of the advantages – though some might say disadvantages – of Nilbert's agoraphobia was that it allowed him time to think. While the rest of his team took their lunch breaks out in the sun, playing volleyball or simply lying around getting a tan, Nilbert spent his leisure time in his small one-man tent, thinking.

The soft coral in the tank represented Nilbert's biggest success story to date. Although soft corals play only a minor part in reef building, Nilbert reckoned if he could succeed here, the lessons learned might help in the rehabilitation of the much more difficult-to-work-with hard corals. One of the major problems with corals is that they develop incredibly slowly. New coral larvae grow only one centimetre in the first year and, to compound this, most corals spawn just once – every spring. Another more serious problem is that corals, or rather the algae that live in their gut and on which they depend to break down their food, are extremely sensitive. At high temperatures the algae start producing lethal levels of oxygen, and the coral, to preserve itself from this sudden surge in toxins, is forced to get rid of the algae without which it can't survive. It's a catch-22 situation. In severe cases of warming, whole tracts of reef become 'bleached', as the corals, having vomited up their life-giving algae, slowly starve to death.

As evidenced by the swiftly developing soft coral in the tank, Nilbert had now cracked the problem of growth. With only a modicum of gene-shifting and a plentiful food supply, this coral had been persuaded to grow at an astonishing rate – putting on two inches that morning alone. His team had also manufactured a strain of algae that was relatively stable at high temperatures. For most people this would have been enough. Indeed, for most people this would have been cause for celebration, but Nilbert, ever the perfectionist, wasn't satisfied. The way he saw it, rescuing the reefs wasn't just about maintaining the status quo. No, in order to survive the extremes of temperature and pollution they were likely to encounter, reefs needed something more – they needed an *edge*.

The new and complex thought developing at the back of Nilbert's mind began to grow, and other, related thoughts gathered around it, like sperm clustering around an ovum. 'Hmm,' he murmured, as the thought began its long, slow ascent, from the glimmering basement of obscurity, up through the many floors of his convoluted mind, towards the penthouse of understanding.

The thought went something like this: *What if these corals could think for themselves? If they were conscious, they could decide whether to breed, or whether it was more advantageous to shut down their reproductive systems and put their energy solely into growth. Give them control over their own biology and they would be able to adapt intelligently to their ever-changing circumstances.*

After lunch, Nilbert assembled his small team in the stifling, airless, prefabricated building at the top of the beach which served as a laboratory. Standing behind his desk, he called for silence. 'Listen up, people,' he said, slipping easily into the American vernacular that always seems to be used at such moments. 'As you know, we've already had success in the area of growth. Under controlled conditions we can persuade Alcyonacea to grow to virtually any size we want. Our new strain of zooxanthella also seems to be working well, with the production of free-oxygen radicals now down to twenty per cent of peak. We're doing OK, but that's not good enough for me. In fact, OK is nowhere near good enough.' Nilbert's face had become flushed, and his eyes began to gleam with the mad energy of the zealot. His team winced collectively. They knew that look well; they called it his serial-killer stare, and it was bad news – it meant increased workloads and cancelled holidays.

'Corals' basic design hasn't changed for millions of years,' Nilbert continued. 'Their systems developed in warm, stable conditions – they weren't built to withstand the enormous environmental pressures that they now face. In another million years or so – if they survive – their biology will probably have caught up and they'll be able to cope with the stress. But the seas are dying *now*. Unless we do something, it's going to be too late and, since it was man who created the problem, it's up to us to redress the balance. So how about this?'

Nilbert paused, letting the tension build before delivering the knockout punch of his big idea. His team braced themselves. 'What if we could give them the ability to adjust to their environment – not over generations, but instantly? How would it be if we could give these corals' primitive neural networks a boost, allowing them to react swiftly to external stimuli: a sort of accelerated evolution. It wouldn't take much.'

Nilbert turned to the blackboard behind him and drew a small circle, labelling it 'polyp'. 'Now, if every coral polyp contained one "intelligent" neuron,' he chalked an X in his polyp, 'as that polyp divided and divided, it would grow into a huge thinking network.' He surrounded the original with more and more polyps and Xs, each one touching its neighbour. 'The bigger it got, the more intelligent it would become. In time, a whole reef would become one big brain – a real brain coral!'

In a frenzy now, he began covering the blackboard in small circles and Xs. 'Such a coral could adjust its own growth rate, shutting down some of its systems or going into hibernation instead of simply dying when times got rough. It's radical, I know, but just imagine: a whole community of corals working together, communicating with each other to defeat the threats that constantly beset the species. If the corals had some understanding of the dangers that threaten them, they would be able to effect these changes virtually overnight, without having to wait for the hit-and-miss of evolution to sort things out. Take the case of the crown of thorns starfish.'

Limbo II

He sketched a fierce-looking starfish, crawling menacingly over his coral. 'Once the coral has intelligently identified it as a potential threat, it can then work out a strategy to protect itself – for instance, producing toxins which the starfish finds unpalatable.' He turned back to the board and slashed a big cross through his starfish, breaking the chalk in the process. 'Yes, we could engineer such a protection into it, but there may be factors we are not aware of. We're not corals, so how do we know what's going to work best at reef level? Giving the organism the choice of method that best suits its lifestyle has got to be the way forward. Ladies and gentlemen, this is my proposition: that we search for a way to give corals autonomy – in short, that we give them brains!'

After his speech, Nilbert was wide-eyed, red-faced and drenched with his sweat – as was the front row of his audience. He leaned forward onto his desk. 'What do you think?' he asked excitedly.

He was left staring at a sea of blank faces for some moments. Harvey Kass, a big, bearded Brooklynite, was the first to react. 'Corals have a lifestyle?' he asked.

'Please, Harvey,' Nilbert begged, 'don't be facetious.'

'Sorry, Nilb. No, I think it's a great idea.'

'Thank you.' Nilbert breathed a sigh of relief.

'And then maybe we could give Oreo cookies legs, so they can just walk into your mouth.'

The rest of the team exploded into laughter.

'Listen! Listen!' Nilbert yelled, in an effort to bring the proceedings back to order. 'This can work! Alcyonacea is already responding well to our accelerated growth techniques. If we apply what we now know to hard corals, all we would then need do is insert a neuron-building program into its DNA. The technological expertise gleaned from such an exercise would be invaluable in the rehabilitation of many other marine organisms. After all, why are we here?'

'You tell me,' said Harvey.

'We are here to try to find a way to stop the seas from dying!'

'Oh!' said Harvey, smacking his forehead, 'so that's why we're here!'

'OK, enough, now!' Nilbert yelled over the laughter. 'This is how we are going to proceed! We need to refine the gene-splicing techniques used on Alcyonacea, and find ways to apply them to hard corals. I suggest we start with Acropora, the staghorn coral. You know, I have a dream—'

'They shot the last guy who said that,' said Harvey.

'I have a dream,' Nilbert continued, rapidly losing patience, 'that one day we shall see the oceans populated with intelligent corals, able to give us advance warning of each new threat to their own and the seas' survival.' Nilbert fixed his audience with a steely glare. 'Ladies and gentlemen, we are in a life or death situation here, and I want to make one thing perfectly clear – I have neither the patience nor the desire to work with anybody who isn't one hundred per cent behind me. What we are talking about is the continued existence of the oceans, and anyone who hasn't yet grasped that fact is free to leave now!'

Nilbert glared challengingly at Harvey. In his heart of hearts, he would be sorry to see Harvey go. He was a good scientist and, in less trying times, Nilbert enjoyed his jokes. Besides, finding a replacement for him could take months; finding a replacement for *anyone* who decided to leave could take months.

Likewise, Nilbert's team, although amused by his eccentricity, were well aware of his expertise (some would say genius) and were loath to leave the immediate vicinity of such an innovative scientific mind. After all, artificial intelligence was the arena they were now entering, a field that, as yet, hadn't been approached via the purely biotechnological route. When all was said and done, it was an exciting project. In the end, no one got up to leave.

Anna Frauhofer, a big, frightening blonde from Heidelberg, raised her hand. 'Please!' she said.

'Yes,' said Nilbert.

'I wish to ask one question. Will we have to confine our thinking solely to the problem of coral depletion? It occurs to me that in the course of our research it is likely we may find other areas of application.'

'I think we ought to try and walk before we can run, Anna. The results of our research may well have wider implications. I'd be disappointed if they didn't. But, for now, I'd say we should restrict ourselves to finding ways to help the corals fight back.'

Anna seemed satisfied with that, and scribbled something on her notepad.

'Any more questions?' Nilbert looked around the room.

'Yes, um...' It was Tony Finch, a small, shabby, frightened man from Norfolk. He was painfully thin, and always seemed to be in need of a good wash. 'I, er... Does this mean we'll be working Saturdays?' he asked.

'Saturdays *and* Sundays, Tony. At least for the foreseeable future.'

'Oh.' The team groaned. Tony, especially, seemed rather crushed by the news.

'Anyone else?' Nilbert enquired. Harvey was sitting on his hands and staring at the floor, but, cancelled weekends aside, the rest of the team seemed eager to get to work and were already rising, talking excitedly to one another – sharing ideas. 'Thank you,' said Nilbert. 'You can have the rest of the afternoon off, but tomorrow morning we start work in earnest.'

When everyone else had shuffled out into the sunshine, Harvey approached Tony, who was still sitting rather dejectedly in his seat. 'What's up, Tone?' he asked.

Tony looked up at him with his big, doggy eyes. 'Oh, it's nothing... really.'

'No, come on. You look like you've just eaten a frog.'

Tony shrugged and shifted in his seat. 'I er... No, it's kind of sensitive,' he mumbled.

Harvey patted him reassuringly on the knee. 'This is old Uncle Harvey you're talking to. Sensitivity is my middle name.'

'Well, I . . . Don't tell the others, please,' Tony implored. Harvey crossed his heart and drew a finger across his throat. 'The thing is,' Tony continued, tucking a stray wisp of greasy hair behind his ear, 'there's a *Star Wars* convention in Brisbane this weekend, and I was hoping to go to it.'

Harvey bit his tongue. 'Oh, really?' he said. 'Is that one of those things where everyone dresses up as their favourite character?'

Tony nodded.

'Who . . . er, do *you* go as?'

Tony looked left and right, then leaned in close and whispered in Harvey's ear, 'Princess Leia.'

'Excuse me,' said Harvey, rising. He just managed to make it outside before howling with laughter.

Chapter 3

'Sorry, sorry I'm late!' called Rex, hurriedly making his way towards Bernard and Iris through the busy restaurant.

'Hello, lad,' said Bernard. 'We thought you weren't coming. Are you all right?' he asked as Rex drew near. 'You look a bit . . . peaky.'

'No, I'm fine, really,' said Rex, pulling up a chair.

Iris patted him fondly on the cheek. 'You work too hard.'

'Hardly,' said Rex. 'Limbo seems to run itself, thank God.'

'Are you hungry?' asked Bernard.

'Er, no, not really,'

'I'll get Henri.' He turned in his chair and beckoned. 'Henri!'

The black-suited maître d'hôtel was immediately at their table. 'Your majesty?'

'Rex needs some sustenance.'

'Of course, sir. What is your desire? Squat lobsters from the Salient Sea, caught only this morning – lightly grilled and served with mayonnaise and a wild rocket salad? Or perhaps sea trout à la Boggs, with a scallop and cucumber—'

'No thanks,' Rex interrupted.

Undaunted, the maître d'hôtel continued. 'Oyster soufflé, with a samphire coulis?'

'No, Henri.'

But the maître d' would not be silenced; he had taken a large order of seafood that morning and was eager to shift it. 'Perchance a parfait of herring roe, with crisp fingers of toast?'

'Just some fruit, thank you.'

Henri's lip curled. 'Fruit?'

'Er yes, just fruit.' Henri didn't move, but remained staring obdurately at Rex, whose self-assurance began to wilt under his gaze. 'Um, well, I suppose I could manage a bit of cheese.'

'Fruit and cheese?' Henri enunciated, as if talking about something distasteful – like a sackful of rats. 'The chef will be delighted.' Then he turned on his heel and left.

'What's up with him?' Rex asked.

'I don't know,' said Bernard. 'Everyone seems a bit off today.' He glanced across at Iris, who avoided his eyes. 'Here, have a glass of wine.' He picked up the bottle and filled Rex's glass almost to the brim with something rich and ruby-red.

'Cheers, son.' They raised their glasses and drank.

'How was your meal?' Rex asked.

'Very good, Luigi's on today.' Bernard expertly twizzled the last few remaining strands of linguine onto his fork and wiped them around his plate, before shoving the glistening mess into his mouth.

'How was yours, Mum?'

'Oh, fine,' she said, distractedly. 'It was . . . very nice.'

Rex took Iris's hand. 'Are you all right?'

She sighed and looked up at the great Wizard of Limbo – her little Rexie – who had grown up to change their lives so dramatically. Who'd have thought that a shop girl from Lancing would end up as a queen? True, she wasn't exactly sure where she was queen of, but she'd learnt not to question such things – the answers you got here were, generally speaking, incomprehensible. Anyway, if you were having a lovely time, why spoil it with senseless worrying? She kept telling herself that, as long as she was with Bernard and living in a beautiful place, what else mattered? But, try as she might, she couldn't deny that something *was* worrying her. 'I'm . . . fine,' she said, at last.

But before Rex could press her further, Henri reappeared with

Limbo II

a huge platter piled high with every fruit imaginable, and a cheeseboard groaning with slabs of the finest Limbo cheeses.

Rex sighed, and chose an apple, a pear and a chunk of Castle Creek Cheddar.

'Cheddar?' Henri sneered, adding, under his breath, 'He'll be asking for pickle next.' When he'd stalked away, Rex turned back to Queen Iris.

'So, what are you up to this afternoon?' he said, cutting himself a slice of apple.

'Well,' Iris began tentatively, 'earlier on, in Smeil's Café, I noticed that the magazine rack was an awful mess. Women's issues were all over the place; *Natural Childbirth* was in the financial section, and *Nursing Times* was right next to *Loaded*. I was just wondering if Smeil would like me to sort them out for him. You know, arrange them all neatly by category.'

'Oh, Mum, you don't have to do that.'

'You're a lady of leisure now,' said Bernard, squeezing her arm reassuringly.

Iris rolled her eyes. 'Don't I know it. I haven't been allowed to lift a finger since I've been here.'

'But you're the Queen – you don't have to do anything.'

Iris looked down at her hands, clasped in her lap. 'That's just the point. I know how it must sound, and I'm not complaining, really. It's just that now and again I'd like to do something for myself. You know, like when I ran the sub-post office in the back of the shop.'

'How many queens do you know who work in a post office?' smiled Bernard.

'No, Bernard, I'm serious. I don't want to offend anyone – everyone's so nice here, and the castle looks after us so well – but sometimes I just wish . . .' She broke off with tears in her eyes.

Bernard took her hand. 'What, love?'

'I wish we were back in our little shop.'

Bernard was stunned. 'You don't?'

Iris nodded, dabbing her eyes with a handkerchief.

'You want to go back to all that hard graft? Lugging great piles of newspapers around, and working all hours, with never a holiday save Christmas?'

Iris wrung her hands. 'I know it sounds strange, and no, of course I don't want to go back to exactly how it was. But sometimes, just sometimes, mind, I miss it. If I could just go round the shop occasionally, tidying the newspapers, arranging the magazines, sorting the confectionery display . . .'

'Well, my love,' said Bernard, putting an arm around her tenderly. 'If that's all you want to do, I'm sure Rex wouldn't mind you nipping back and flicking a duster around the place now and then – would you, eh?' He winked at Rex.

'Ah,' said Rex, finishing off a mouthful of cheese. 'You see, the thing is . . . And I meant to tell you earlier, but it just sort of slipped my mind. The thing is . . .'

'Yes?' said Bernard.

'I've rented the shop out.'

Iris's face crumpled. 'Oh,' she said.

'You've done what?' said Bernard, aghast.

'Just last week.' Rex smiled weakly. 'I was only keeping it on for old times' sake, but I couldn't bear to get rid of it altogether, so I let it to a very nice couple – the Guptas. I never thought you'd ever want to . . . I mean, if I'd known . . . I'm sorry, Mum.'

'That's all right, Rexie. You weren't to know. Well,' she said, rising, 'I think I'll go and have a little nap, if you don't mind.'

Rex and Bernard stood up with her. 'Do you want me to come with you?' said Bernard, extracting the napkin from his collar.

'No, dear, I'll be all right,' she said, walking uncertainly towards the door. When Henri opened it for her and she saw that her bedroom had miraculously appeared on the other side, she shook her head and sighed. King Bernard and the Great Wizard of Limbo watched her disappear inside, slowly closing the door behind her.

Limbo II

'Did you know she felt like that, Dad?' said Rex when they were sitting once again.

'No. Well, I had noticed she'd been a little quiet of late, but you know your mum – she never likes to complain.'

Rex stroked his chin. 'I mean, if it's just a question of her wanting something to do, perhaps we could find her a job here in the castle.'

Bernard sucked his teeth. 'You know what your mum's like. She wants to be useful, and she'd hate to think anyone was doing her a favour.'

'I could have a word with Smeil, see if she could help out in the café a couple of days a week,' Rex suggested.

'And how do you think the people of Limbo would feel, seeing their own Queen working in Mr Smeil's shop?'

'It's Smeil, Dad – just Smeil. I was thinking rather of her doing something behind the scenes but, yes, I take your point – it's not ideal, is it?' Rex looked down at the table – one last strand of linguine clung to the edge of Bernard's plate. Rex absent-mindedly thought it looked like a snake . . . Immediately it started hissing and began slinking across the sauce-smeared platter.

Bernard leapt back. 'Steady on, Rex!'

'Sorry.' Rex clicked his fingers and the 'snake' reverted to a lifeless strand of linguine. 'Sometimes I forget.'

'You don't know your own strength.' Bernard slumped back in his chair. 'You know,' he said, after a pause, 'you *could* have asked us first.'

'Sorry?'

'You could have asked us before renting out our shop.'

'I'm sorry, Dad, I didn't think you'd mind. You both seemed so settled here.'

Bernard sat up, a sudden gleam in his eye. 'I don't suppose we could buy the lease back?'

'I doubt it. They've only just bought it.'

'Yes, but if they could be persuaded with a little . . . magic?'

'Oh, Dad, I couldn't. That would be unethical. It goes against the Wizard's code.'

'There *is* no Wizard's code.'

'All right, it goes against my code, then.'

'Don't you want to help your mother?'

'Of course I do. Just not like that.'

Bernard's nostrils quivered. 'Well, that's nice isn't it? Your mother and I spent our lives slaving away all the hours God gives, just to put food in your mouth, and what thanks do we get? You go and rent out our shop behind our backs, and then won't even help your mother in her hour of need!'

'That's not fair,' said Rex. 'If I'd known for one minute you wanted to go back to your precious little shop, you could have had it again with pleasure.'

' "Precious little shop?" ' Bernard pushed back his chair and rose threateningly. 'Do you have any idea of the work that your mother and I put into that newsagent's? We kept that shop going through thick and thin, with blood, sweat and tears.'

'Oh, please,' sighed Rex. 'Bring on the violins.'

They were beginning to draw concerned glances from the other diners.

'That's right, go ahead and mock. *You* had it easy! *You* took over a going concern!' Bernard was shouting now. '*You* took the credit for all our hard graft!'

Rex got up, in a rage. 'Now just you listen—' he began. He was about to launch into the kind of vicious, wounding attack that only close family members know how to inflict upon each other, when something stopped him. He held up his hands. 'Wait a minute, Dad, wait a minute.' There it was again. In his mind he heard the shuddering, scraping knock at the gates of consciousness. It was louder this time. Rex gazed around the room, and saw that everyone was staring.

Across the table Bernard stood, wild-eyed. 'What's going on, Rex? Why are we arguing? We *never* argue.'

Limbo II

As the pounding in his ears subsided, Rex was filled with remorse. 'Oh, Dad.'

'What's happening, son? This isn't right.'

Rex breathed deeply. 'I . . . don't know.'

Bernard stroked his bald head. 'I . . . I'm sorry I shouted at you,' he faltered at last.

'No, no. It was all my fault . . . I'm sorry.'

'Friends?' Bernard said tentatively.

Rex smiled back. 'Friends.'

Bernard grabbed him round the neck and hugged him close. 'I know I'm not your real dad, but I've always loved you like my own; you know that, don't you?' As Rex nodded into Bernard's shoulder, the deep maroon velvet of the King's robe tickled his nose. 'You do whatever you want with that shop. It's yours now.'

Rex drew back and looked straight into Bernard's eyes. 'You've been the best father in the world. It was wrong of me not to consult you.' He kissed him on the cheek.

'I expect you'll be needing this now,' said Henri, appearing with the brandy decanter and two glasses.

'Well done, Henri. That's just the job,' said Bernard.

Henri placed his offering on the table and bowed respectfully. 'Don't drink it all at once,' he warned, sotto voce, before withdrawing.

'Will you join me?' said Bernard, wiping his eyes with one hand and picking up the decanter with the other.

Rex shook his head. 'No. No, I . . .' Something else was gnawing at the back of his mind – some half-forgotten phrase from an ancient text. But no matter how hard he groped for it, it remained resolutely out of reach. 'Sorry to leave in a hurry, Dad, but I need to . . . I need to look at something. I'll see you later.' He turned to go, then stopped. 'Look, I'll have a word with the Guptas, and see if I can work something out for Mum. Maybe she could help out there once a week – or something like that. She doesn't have to know it's been set up for her; I can always say they were looking for extra staff.'

Bernard picked up the brandy glass and swirled it round thoughtfully in his large hand. 'Your mum would like that.'

Back in his turret room, Rex leapt up onto the big round table. 'To work!' he said firmly and, taking a deep breath, uttered the spell: *'Deus et natura, nihil faciunt frustra!'* The table top exploded to infinity in all directions on the horizontal plane, but almost as quickly began to shrink – its edges dissolving into fast-encroaching nothingness. Soon Rex was floating in the void – then he too was consumed by the emptiness.

Gradually he became aware of a great, shimmering ring – an immense and beautiful, spinning hoop of molten gold, so unimaginably vast that it was beyond size, beyond time and space. It was everything and nothing: the universal embodiment of eternity, the river of perception. It was the Hoop of Destiny.

But all was not well with the Hoop. It wasn't the large man on a motorcycle charging round and round it like a rider on the Wall of Death, nor was it the great cloud of socks that fluttered around its glittering course like a flock of starlings. No, it was something much more worrying. A thin black shadow circumscribed the golden ring, as if a rift were about to open up and split the Hoop in two. But that wasn't all; on the far side rose a great, black swelling like a giant carbuncle about to burst. Dark, angry clouds boiled around this, and sharp flashes of lightning stabbed its surface. What evil did it portend?

'One Black...' The phrase forced itself into Rex's mind. It was vaguely familiar, like something once learned by rote but now barely remembered, lost in the mists of memory.

Once more back in his room, Rex looked out of the window. Was it his imagination, or was the sun a little lower in the sky? There was no doubt that the air had grown decidedly chill. *'One Black...'*

Limbo II

there it was again: the phrase echoed around his head like the tolling of a great bell. He knew his mind was trying to tell him something – but what?

Then an awful thought occurred to him. Pulling down a book from one of the many bookcases that lined his turret chamber, he laid it on the table. On its embossed leather cover, a title was meticulously picked out in gold leaf:

Limbo – The Final Chapter
By Rex Boggs, Wizard

As he turned the pages, he was gripped by a deep sense of foreboding . . . and the certain knowledge that sooner, rather than later, he'd be embarking upon a very difficult journey indeed.

Chapter 4

The next morning, bright and early, Nilbert's team set to work. Their aim wasn't to make all-singing, all-dancing corals that could add up, subtract and tell the time; they didn't want to drastically alter the delicate relationship between corals and marine animals, they were aiming simply to give the corals a little push up the evolutionary incline. So, in the search for appropriate neural material, they started with a creature which, in evolutionary terms, is only a few paces ahead of coral, a creature which is indeed a member of the coral's family Cnidaria – the jellyfish.

Extracting the genes responsible for the growth of the neural system was easy enough, as was their insertion into the coral's DNA. Unfortunately, the resulting corals stung themselves to death.

Next they tried the nudibranch, or sea slug. But, as these creatures are gastropods – consuming their food by extruding their stomachs – this unfortunate trait was passed on to the coral, causing it to lose its supply of life-giving algae every time it tried to feed, resulting in its almost immediate death.

After many more attempts, and an equal number of failures, they finally arrived at the cetaceans: whales and dolphins. But, in their obsessive quest for success, Nilbert's team had completely lost sight of just how far they'd moved up the evolutionary pecking order.

Cetacean genes seemed to sit quite happily in the coral's tightly coiled double helix and produced no discernible ill effects. Indeed, for the first couple of months, the coral grew rapidly in the big saltwater tank in the laboratory, and the team eagerly awaited its first spawning. This happened nine months to the day after Nilbert's impassioned speech in the laboratory, and was greeted with cheers and the cracking of a magnum of Australian sparkling Chardonnay.

But then things seemed to go wrong – the coral stopped growing. It didn't die; its polyps just ceased dividing, and worse, none of the larvae developed. Samples taken from the tank appeared to be completely normal but stuck at an early stage in their development. Staghorn coral larvae go through a free-swimming phase, during which, in the open ocean, they can travel great distances, colonizing reefs far from their origins. This stage usually lasts only a short time, but in the case of these genetically manipulated corals, the larvae stubbornly refused to move on. Over the next few months the team took regular samples, and every time it was the same story: there they were, not unlike miniature fish, beating their cilia and swimming pointlessly round and round. The most disappointing thing about all this was that, in this form, they were useless as reef builders. As long as they kept swimming, they wouldn't settle, and if they didn't settle, they wouldn't develop into corals. If released into the open ocean, they would go on paddling around in circles until eaten by a fish or washed up to expire on some distant shore.

A deep sense of gloom descended on the Lizard Island research team. Even Harvey wasn't able to salvage anything funny from the collapse of all their hard work. Where had they gone wrong?

Nilbert gave his exhausted team a much-needed break, and as they took the motor launch back to the mainland and civilization – in the shape of ice-cold beers, clean sheets and real coffee – Nilbert himself settled back into his claustrophobic little tent with a family-size bar of Wholenut and a gallon of chocolate milk to pick over the ruins of his big idea and deduce what lessons could be gleaned from its collapse.

Alone on the island, after a frustrating couple of days trying, without success, to come to terms with the failure of his experiment, Nilbert strode into the laboratory and stood facing the staghorn coral in the big tank. Its refusal to grow was a personal insult. He had slaved over this project for more than a year, and this was the result: a coral that stubbornly refused to do what it was supposed to do – what he had *built* it to do. As Nilbert stared at the coral – standing serenely, arrogantly aloof – he became convinced that it was laughing at him. Suddenly overcome by a fierce anger, he reached into the tank and ripped the calcareous growth from its base. Then, walking outside, he hurled it as far as he could out to sea. 'There!' he screamed. 'That'll teach you! See how you like the real world! Good luck with the crown of thorns starfish! Your polyps are history!'

After that, Nilbert, shocked by the passion the coral had aroused in him, never strayed far from the comforting confines of his tent. He still made regular snorkelling forays to monitor the reef's condition, however, since he saw himself as custodian of the reef, and a strong sense of duty overruled his aversion to wide open spaces.

On one of these monitoring expeditions, a couple of days later, he noticed something odd, something that made him cry out in shock and, in his excitement, nearly drown, as he lost the mouthpiece of his snorkel and inhaled a large amount of sea water. About twenty feet from shore, on a big lump of dead brain coral which hitherto had been completely barren, was a large staghorn coral looking for all the world as if it had been there for years. And, what's more, it was spawning. Nilbert took a small sample of it and, hurrying back to the lab, separated out its DNA. There were the telltale cetacean genes – there was no doubt about it, this was *his* coral. His excitement was now all but uncontrollable but, being the thorough scientist that he was, he held back from alerting his team until he had made a proper study. Then he began combing the reef for signs of recolonization by its larvae. Although most would by now have travelled a great distance, some, if they had developed past the free-swimming stage and were now viable, should have taken root closer to home and, because of the speed of growth engineered into them, would be developing rapidly. But, however hard he looked, he could find no sign. This was disappointing because it meant that, unlike the parent, the larvae had not moved on. Then, two days later, something even stranger happened. The staghorn coral itself simply disappeared. No trace of it was left, save a small indentation in the brain coral at the spot where it had anchored itself.

Nilbert retired to his tent again, puzzled and disappointed, convinced that this must have been a fluke. What had happened, he imagined, was that the coral he'd 'liberated', had, for whatever reason, flourished in the sea for just a short while, then died and been swept away by sea currents.

But that night he had a dream . . .

He was running down a long, dark corridor lit by flaming torches. Pursuing him was something he couldn't see, some nameless horror, and no matter how hard he tried, he could not outrun it. Whichever way he turned in the dark maze of corridors, whichever gloomy passageway he ran breathlessly along, the dark terror followed, right on his heels. Sometimes he would hear the awful rustling of its five legs on the stone flags and feel its breath on his neck, but whenever he chanced a glance behind, its monstrous black shadow was all he would see, racing down the wall towards him. At last, at the end of one long, long tunnel, he came to a small door. Fumbling desperately with the handle, he flung it open and found himself on a small wind-lashed parapet above a sheer drop of many thousands of feet. It was giddying to look down and, as he fought his panic and nausea, he clung to the fragile door to prevent himself from tumbling over the edge. In frantic haste, he tried to close the door against the hideous creature that pursued him. But, squeezing itself through the small doorway, it crowded onto the narrow ledge. Now he saw it clearly for the first time – a gigantic beast covered in spines, and on its back a face in torment – the face of Christ on the Cross, bleeding and contorted with pain. Nilbert started back instinctively from the horror that towered over him, and in doing so, lost his footing. The next he knew, he was swinging in space, hanging by his fingertips from the door handle. Looking down, the cold hand of vertigo tightened around his throat. So high up that he was unable to see the ground, he looked down instead on a thin, wispy blanket of cloud. All the strength went out of him and, as blackness edged his vision, his tentative grip on the handle let go, and he found himself falling.

The cool air rushing up around him brought him back to his senses, and although he was now prepared for death – sudden, painful death – he was not prepared for what happened next. His arms, which before had been leaden with fear, now became light and buoyant and, as they rose up of their own accord on either side of him, he saw that they had become wings – strong, powerful eagles' wings. Beating them slowly, majestically up and down, he soared into the sky in a great, wheeling arc and was soon looking down on the hideous creature which still clung to the small parapet, screaming in anger and frustration. Higher and higher he rose, circling away into the sky – and freedom.

Nilbert woke with a shout of triumph. 'Yes!' And although it was still dark, he threw his mask and flippers into the small dinghy, and set out for deep water.

Chapter 5

While Limbo slumbered, Rex had spent the long hours perusing his book – the book that had once been *Limbo – The Final Chapter* – but as he slowly turned its pages, he realized with mounting horror that he didn't recognize a word of it. He stared in disbelief at the beginning of chapter fifteen:

> *Now comes recession, depression and suicide.*
> *Sorrow will fall upon the keening land,*
> *As into the black and steely jaws of Death,*
> *The sun, its short day spent, will slowly sink...*

He hadn't written this. His book was full of joy and happiness. There was no sadness or depression in anything he'd written. On the next page he was faced with another doom-laden passage:

> *Thin grey fingers of icy death come creeping,*
> *The magpie thief of glittering hope; of life,*
> *Steals dismally across the aching land...'*

And...

> *Darkness: dismal lack of light,*
> *Black as coal, black as jet,*
> *Crepuscular, impenetrable shade of night.*
> *Dark enough for you people, yet?*

Somehow the book had changed his story. But how could that be? The situation was unpleasantly reminiscent of the terrible catastrophe of the Book, that awful catalogue of death and destruction that had prophesied and so nearly caused the annihilation of the universe.

The Book, a part-work in forty-seven volumes, had been written by the former Wizard of Limbo in his youth, because he'd been bored. It was intended to be nothing more than a light-hearted adventure story. The trouble was, he being a wizard and Limbo being Limbo, whatever he wrote had a habit of coming true. As soon as he'd begun it, he'd realized his mistake. But that wasn't his only problem – every time the Wizard had lifted his pen, the Book began to write itself, and it had a much darker imagination than he. He would watch, appalled, at the horrors forming themselves upon the page: terrible prophecies of death and destruction, which, once committed to paper, had a nasty habit of fulfilling themselves. Darkness had then fallen across the land like a shroud, tragedy following tragedy. The old Wizard had tried to put things right by introducing a happier theme: the birth of a prince which heralded the Dawn that would last for a thousand years, but the Book responded with the Great Terror – an unspeakable episode in Limbo's history, where the King had turned on his own people and slaughtered them in their thousands. This awful manuscript ended by predicting the unravelling of the fabric of the universe, and it was only Rex's quick thinking and his altering of the Limbollian Paradox that had prevented literally everything from tumbling into the abyss.

Rex knew he had taken a big risk in rewriting the Limbollian Paradox, but at the time there was little else he could have done. The Paradox is the universal law governing time and space, and therefore its wording is rather important. The original Paradox had stated: 'Whatever you expect to happen will happen, unless something else happens instead.' But Rex had changed it to: 'Whatever you expect to happen will happen, unless you want something else badly enough to happen instead,' thereby ensuring a happy future, or at least its possibility, for almost everyone.

To put an end to its malign authority, all copies of the Book had

Limbo II

been destroyed and, to consolidate his work, Rex had written *The Final Chapter*, which had been marketed, with some success, as 'The only book you'll ever need!' Now, until he was called upon to travel back in time to Hove seafront and intercept the mortal blow meant for his younger self, there should have been little more for him to do. *The Final Chapter* was meant to be just that – the last word and, as such, it superseded all previous works. What was happening now was impossible, unless . . . Suddenly Rex went very cold. Oh no, it didn't bear thinking about. The changes in his book could mean only one thing – a copy of the Book, or at least a fragment of that terrible work, still somehow existed.

Blackness . . . and out of the blackness and far away, a high desperate whinnying. Then silence . . . and out of the silence, the thunder of hooves, coming closer and closer, the sound deepening as it approached, making the earth tremble. Suddenly it was upon him, lunging out of the unseeing dark, a horse so huge it seemed to fill the sky. The monstrous beast reared up. On its back sat a grinning, cowled rider, black with evil. As thunder and lightning boomed and crackled out of the clouds that boiled above the rider's head, the massive horse, its iron-clad hooves raking the air, came crashing down . . .

'Ahhhhh!' Smeil sat up, drenched with sweat. 'No, no, no, no.' Leaping out of bed, he ran to the window and yanked back the curtain. The Great Plain of Limbo lay before him, bathed in glorious sunshine. He opened the window and smelt the air. 'Ah, ah, ah,' he breathed, growing calmer with each breath.

But as he gazed out at this beautiful scene, a vast and living green carpet rolling away to the far foothills of the Southern Range, he could still sense something was wrong. It wasn't just the dream – which had been troubling him now for over a fortnight, growing more terrifyingly real with each recurrence – it was something else. He couldn't put his finger on it yet, but all his instincts told him that things were not quite right. Looking at the shadows thrown onto the plain by the peaks of the faraway mountains, an alarm bell rang somewhere in the back of his mind, and he reached for his sextant.

Removing the instrument from his eye, an icy numbness gripped his heart. Then he heard Rex's voice.

'Smeil! Smeil!' The Wizard's urgent call echoed down the winding passages of the great castle. Smeil dressed swiftly and, scurrying down the dusty corridors, the soft leather soles of his shoes making almost no sound on the grey stone flags, he hurried to his master's side. He found him restlessly pacing the Long Gallery.

'You called, sir?' said Smeil, breathlessly.

'Smeil, we have to organize a search.'

'Certainly, sir.' Smeil pulled out a notepad and pencil, and swept his long fringe from his eyes. 'A search for what?'

Rex looked down at his small servant, trotting along beside him. 'Now I don't want you to panic, Smeil, but something rather unsettling has happened.' A frown furrowed Smeil's brow. 'I don't know how,' Rex continued, 'but somehow, against all the odds, there still survives a piece of . . . the Book.'

Smeil gasped. 'No! That can't be!'

'If we can just stay calm, I'm sure we can put things right.'

Smeil stopped suddenly at one of the windows in the long corridor and looked out across the Great Plain. He felt as if someone had pulled the plug on all his happiness. 'Are you sure, master?' he said in a small voice

'There can be no other explanation.'

'I thought it had been getting darker. I took a measurement of the sun only this morning – it was three degrees off the mean.' He suddenly turned and looked up at Rex, his big, worried eyes peeping out through his long, mousy fringe. 'But, surely all copies of the Book were destroyed, weren't they?'

'So far as we know.'

Limbo II

'And the Paradox. You rewrote it and stopped all those terrible things coming true, didn't you?'

'I thought I had, yes. Now it seems that all my good work has been undone.'

Smeil stared wildly around, flapping his arms in futile panic. 'Oh no. No, no, no, I couldn't bear to go back to the darkness again. I really don't know how I'd . . .' He collapsed against the wall. Tears streamed down his face and plopped onto the window sill.

'My dear, dear friend,' said Rex, bending down and putting an arm around him. 'Don't you worry. As long as I'm Wizard here, I'll not let Limbo be swallowed up by darkness. You can trust me.'

'That's what your father said,' Smeil sobbed, 'and it was he who got us into this mess in the first place . . . Sorry, sir, I didn't mean to . . .'

'That's all right, Smeil. You're absolutely right; it was all his fault. But he never meant it to turn out the way it did. And anyway, he's paid for his transgression – he's lost Limbo for ever, and although he has the woman he loves, he can never return here. And that hurts him, it hurts him deeply.' Rex knelt and looked into the little man's eyes. 'Now, the best action in a crisis is to do something constructive. I want you to get a small force together and go through the castle with a fine-tooth comb.'

'Straight away, sir,' said Smeil. 'What about Queen Iris?'

'What about her?'

'It's Thursday.'

Rex looked blankly at him. 'That doesn't really help me,' he said.

'The day you fixed for her to work in your old shop.'

'Oh, damn!' Rex remembered.

'I *thought* you'd forgotten. Do you still want her to go?'

Rex, willing to do anything to keep the peace, and his mother happy, had already talked to the Guptas, and they, being a kind and sympathetic couple, had understood the situation immediately. Indeed, they themselves had recently retired, only to find that they enjoyed working much more than sitting around doing nothing. So, it was arranged that Iris would work in the shop one day a week, stacking the shelves and occasionally helping out on the till. The Guptas had even waived the money Rex had offered them, insisting instead that they pay Iris twenty pounds for the day.

'It *would* have to be today,' said Rex. 'Yes, Smeil, I still want her to go. I don't want her or anyone else suspecting that anything's amiss and starting a panic. But after you take her through, come straight back. There's the town to search as well. We'll have to keep it all low key; everything must carry on as normal. If word gets out it could start a riot.' Rex stood and, reaching into his pocket, pulled out a small, well-thumbed tome. Then he looked seriously into the little man's eyes. 'I need you to be strong, Smeil. I'm relying on you.'

Smeil wiped his eyes with his sleeve. 'You can count on me, sir.'

'Good. Now off you go and make yourself busy.'

Rex handed the little man the book containing the Limbo Crystal, and Smeil scurried off down the corridor. Rex watched him go, then turned back to the window and sighed, 'Oh, Father, what have you done now?'

Chapter 6

Iris woke early. Something in her breast bubbled with excitement. What was it, what was it? Yes! It was Thursday – her shop day. She slid her legs out from under the duvet and got up noiselessly, leaving Bernard still snoring. Unlike Iris, Bernard had adapted easily to life as a sovereign, his old habit of waking at five soon abandoned in favour of a long lie-in – sometimes until well past nine.

Iris washed and dressed, taking a long time over her choice of outfit. Eventually she decided on a grey, knee-length skirt and a red cardigan over a white blouse: casual but smart. Then, quietly opening the drawer of her bedside cabinet, she took out her shopping list, scribbled on an old piece of paper she'd found in the Gideons' Bible, and slipped it into her handbag. Satisfied now that she had everything, she tiptoed to the door, shoes in hand so as not to wake her darling husband. Turning in the doorway, she looked back and smiled at Bernard's sleeping form, buried deep under the bedclothes.

She was about to leave when a shiver ran down her spine, as if someone had walked over her grave. Gripped by an inexplicable fear that she might never see her husband again, she had a sudden urge to dive back under the duvet and throw her arms around him, burying her face in his manly chest. Although she told herself she was being silly, she crept back into the room and stood by the side of the bed, looking down at his sleeping face. He looked so peaceful. Gently stroking the soft curls that ran round his big, bald head, she felt reassured. 'You daft thing,' she whispered to herself, then bent down and kissed him on the cheek. Bernard shifted and muttered something incomprehensible. Iris waited for him to settle, then finally slipped silently out of the room.

Smeil was waiting for her by the entrance to the café-bookshop.

'Your majesty.' He bowed low.

Iris flushed; she still couldn't get used to everyone treating her like royalty. 'Morning, Smeil,' she said.

'Has your majesty breakfasted?'

'I'm not really a breakfast person. But I would like a cup of tea, if that's all right.'

Smeil led her into the coffee shop and seated her at a large, glass-topped table which had beneath its surface a display of coffee beans in various stages of roasting. Iris couldn't be sure, but she thought she saw the beans move slightly as she sat down, arranging themselves into neat little rows as if they were standing to attention. Limbo was like that, and she had learned to expect the unexpected. Rex had once even told her to expect the unimaginable, but she wasn't sure what he'd meant by that.

The coffee shop was almost empty, but it was still early. Although Limbo's never-ending day could prove monotonous, most people agreed it was preferable to an interminable night, and had settled upon a system which broke it up into roughly twenty-four-hour segments. This way everyone knew where they were: all going to work together in the 'morning', and out to the tavern in the 'evening'. An accurate timepiece, therefore, was essential for all citizens – a broken watch being the most popular excuse for turning up late for work, especially after a 'night' spent in the tavern. But, coping with hung-over staff aside, it was a system that worked pretty well, and most people stuck to it.

Smeil brought over Iris's tea, strong and sweet exactly as she liked it.

'Don't you want to sit down, Smeil?' she said, as the little man hovered twitchily by her chair.

'I'd be honoured,' he said, bowing his head slightly.

Smeil sat, but Iris noticed he couldn't keep still. His eyes kept darting to the window, his fingers drummed the table nervously and, strangest of all, he remained sullenly silent when usually he was so full of entertaining chit-chat.

Iris studied him over the brim of her teacup. 'Are you feeling all right, Smeil?' she asked at last.

He looked at her, as if returning from a long way away. 'Majesty?'

'You don't seem quite yourself. You seem a bit . . . I don't know, a bit jumpy. Is there anything on your mind?'

'Jumpy? Oh, goodness me, do I? Ha, ha, ha!' he laughed. 'I can't think why; I've nothing troubling me at all. No, no, no, not a care in the world,' he said, and laughed again, a little too loudly. He looked at his watch. 'Good lord, look at the time. The Guptas will be wondering where you are. Come along, ma'am.' He leapt up and started pulling Iris to her feet.

'But I haven't finished my tea,' Iris protested.

'Oh, but you can't be late, dearie me no. That wouldn't do at all. The hired help can't be late on her first day, even if she is a queen, ha, ha, ha!' Iris put down her teacup with a sigh and stood up. Smeil continued to bustle around her. 'Now then, have you got everything – coat, handbag, gloves, hat, life jacket under your seat?'

'Are you sure you're all right, Smeil?' Iris frowned as he hurried her towards the rear of the coffee shop.

'Fine, fine, fine,' he said, airily.

Something was obviously wrong, but Iris didn't like to pry. She was old-fashioned enough to believe that as long as a person didn't want to share what was on their mind, it was none of her business.

Smeil opened the door of a small storeroom and shoved her inside. It was just as well the coffee shop was almost deserted – anyone seeing Smeil bundling their beloved Queen into a cupboard might have got the wrong idea.

In the cramped confines of the small room, Smeil dug deep into his pocket and pulled out the little book that Rex had given him earlier. Opening it up, there, within its hollowed-out centre, glittered the egg-sized Limbo Crystal.

Smeil held it above his head and intoned the magic formula that Rex had taught him: *'Felix qui potuit rerum cognoscere causas! Ibant obscuri sola sub nocte! Tempus edax rerum! Non omnia possumus omnes!'* A beam of light shot out from the Crystal, and a portal – like a great cat's eye – opened up in mid-air.

Smeil turned to Iris and took her by the hand. 'Ready?' he asked.

Iris looked through the hovering doorway straight into the stock room at the back of her old newsagent's. It hadn't changed a bit – there was the familiar black and brown block-pattern lino, the painted-out back window, and the tangle of children's fishing nets, still propped up in the corner. She felt a catch at the back of her throat – half nostalgia, half excitement. 'Oh, Smeil,' she whispered, 'is this really happening?'

'Come along, your majesty,' he said, leading her into the portal. As she passed through the impossible doorway, she felt a crackling of static electricity play up and down her body, making her hair stand on end.

In just two steps she was standing in the stock room, looking back at the room in Limbo from where she'd just come. Suddenly her mind was full of questions, such as, Where was Limbo, exactly, and why couldn't you catch a bus there? And if you could, how long would it take? But looking into Smeil's blank, smiling face, she knew she'd never understand the answers, even if he could explain it to her.

'I'll be back for you around four o'clock,' he said, hurriedly stepping back through the portal.

'See you then,' said Iris, but he was already gone. The portal winked out, and she was left – a jumble of conflicting emotions – standing alone on the tasteless lino of her old Lancing shop.

Chapter 7

Frink Byellssen checked the readings again.

'Dammit, dammit, dammit!' There could be no mistake; the energy field was heading straight for . . . What was the name of that small planet again? He tapped its coordinates into the keypad on the dimly lit console in front of him.

The answer came back on the liquid-crystal display positioned under the viewscreen: 'Earth'.

'Forward vista!' he said, urgently. The image of the dark energy field that he was desperately trying to outrun was replaced by that of blue, mist-shrouded Earth.

Frink wiped his deeply lined brow and rapidly punched another series of numbers into the keypad. He didn't like the answer he got. 'Arghh!' He thumped the console in frustration. The ship's engines stuttered and all the onboard lights flickered for a moment, then recovered. The ship was not in the best of health, and he was low on fuel; the last thing he needed was to upset its fragile systems and nosedive into this planet in a fit of pique.

Frink breathed deeply. Although barely thirty-five years old in Earth terms, his long sojourn in space had left its mark – his eyes were still bright, but he looked old and lined and, apart from his long grey hair and beard, his emaciated body was completely naked. 'Steady now, Frink. No need to upset yourself. You are on a mission – remember the mission. The mission is all important and must be completed, that is your sole aim. And for this mission to succeed, you have to remain alive long enough to deliver the message.'

He rose suddenly from the pilot's seat and hit himself in the chest. 'Got that?' he yelled, hitting himself again. 'Remain *alive*! You're not going to stay alive much longer if you start taking it out on the machinery!' He slapped himself hard on the face, *Smack!* 'Stupid!' He slapped his other cheek, *Smack!* 'Stay alert!'

He began pinching himself all over, 'Ow, ow, ow, ow, ow!' then threw back his head and yowled, 'Aahhhooooh!' Finally, he took a deep breath and smiled, and began fondly stroking his long grey beard. 'Better now ... Nice Frink ... Good Frink,' he said, sinking back down into his seat.

'Now, let's try that again.' He began punching numbers into the keypad once more. 'Mr computer, I'm not sure you fully grasp the urgency of the situation. An energy field of pure evil is heading for this planet, and I am charged with warning the population there of its imminent arrival. For the mission to succeed, the message I carry must be delivered where it will be of the most use, i.e., where the energy field will first make contact. I must, therefore, know the exact coordinates for the energy field's landing site, and this time I want an answer a little more precise than "Northern Hemisphere", OK?'

Frink punched in the last few digits. The answer flashed up on the screen almost immediately: 'Northern Hemisphere – probably land, OK?'

Frink screamed, 'NO! NO! NO! NOT OK! NOT OK!' and thumped the console again. This time, the lights went out and stayed out.

'Oh shit!' Frink whispered to the darkness.

This time of year was always busy for the Sydenham Damerel Morris Men, and today had been especially hectic. They'd started at lunchtime, giving a display in the Bedford Inn car park, in Tavistock. As specified in their terms of booking, their payment was part cash, part liquid – in the form of foaming pints of ale. After shaking

Limbo II

their bells, waving their handkerchiefs and slaking their prodigious thirst, they moved on to their next booking, the Sun Inn, Peter Tavy, where they had a similar arrangement. By the time they arrived at their third booking, the Blacksmith's Arms in Lamerton, they were running about an hour late and the alcohol was beginning to affect the precision of their carefully rehearsed routines. After a decidedly shaky rendition of the 'West Country Stick Dance', they calmed their nerves with several more pints before setting off for the White Hart in Launceston.

At the White Hart they were given an especially warm reception, and performed several encores of 'Hoar Frost on the Willow' (the last five of which probably stretched their audience's goodwill), after which they were understandably thirsty – a problem that was soon rectified.

Things started to unravel badly at the Leaping Salmon, in Horrabridge, by which time most of the troupe were in a state of high alcoholic euphoria. It all went seriously wrong during a potentially fatal but nonetheless entertaining demonstration of the 'St Mellion Sword Dance'. Jonah Turnbull grazed Bob Thackett's knuckles during the making of the five-pointed star, and Bob retaliated with a mistimed blow to Jonah's head, which caught Frank Wedlock on the ear, nearly slicing it off. After that, the meticulously choreographed moves of the ancient country dance dissolved in a frenzied free-for-all in the pub car park.

The Royal Oak at Horsebridge should have been their final booking that night but, by the time they got there, it was past midnight. Luckily, everyone knew the Sydenham Damerel boys well, so nobody had turned up to see them. Jim Bridger, the landlord, was also used to their ways, and had waited up, especially. Now the bloodied but unbowed members of the Sydenham Damerel Morris were enjoying the delights of a lock-in, under the watchful eye of Tom Bowler, the local police constable, who was there, he told himself, just to make sure things didn't get out of hand.

Amos Merryweather, the aptly named Bladder Man of the

troupe, stumbled out of the smoky pub to relieve himself in the river. There was nothing quite so satisfying as peeing off a bridge at night under the cover of the twinkling tarpaulin of the sky. As he stood on the parapet of the ancient stone bridge, listening for the delayed splash as the contents of his bladder hit the surface of the river below, he threw back his head in ecstasy. It was then that he saw something strange: one of the stars in Orion's belt suddenly detached itself from its usually fixed position in the heavens and started to move across the sky. At first he thought it was a shooting star, until it looped around and set off in another direction. He followed its progress for as long as he could, but eventually lost the tiny prick of light against the brightness of the moon. Hurriedly squeezing his bladder dry, he raced back into the pub, still fumbling with his fly, to tell the assembled company what he'd seen. No one, of course, believed him, and joked that if he was seeing strange lights in the sky, he'd had nowhere near enough to drink. The protesting Amos was soon placated by the offer of another beverage and, with a full pint in his hand, managed to persuade himself that what he'd seen must have been a helicopter, or a firefly, or a stray tracer round from one of the Dartmoor firing ranges, or . . . whatever. Having put all thoughts of UFOs aside, he was soon back into his drinking rhythm.

If Amos had stayed outside, however, he would have seen the strange light pause almost overhead, and begin to plummet earthwards.

Chapter 8

Life really isn't so bad, Harvey was thinking to himself as he sat, cold beer in hand, on the veranda of the cocktail lounge of the Coral Reef Hotel, looking out at the wide blue sea through the gently waving palm trees. Feeling clean and crisp in a freshly laundered Hawaiian shirt, he was looking forward to an afternoon of spicy, South Sea Island sex with Honey – a gorgeous Fijian cocktail waitress with whom he had a kind of on-off relationship.

There was something deliciously dangerous about Honey. She said she was on the run from a Vietnamese drug smuggler who was also the father of her child – but she said a lot of crazy things. Harvey never really knew which of her stories to believe, but he couldn't discount the loaded gun she kept in her handbag. 'I have to protect myself,' she'd explain. 'You have no idea what will happen if he finds me.' She was edgy and had a quick temper, but her smile could bring the sun out and, it had to be said, her baby, Jasmine, was unbelievably cute.

Their relationship, at the moment, seemed to be on again, and now he was waiting for her to finish her shift. In his mind's eye he could see her already, lying naked on his bed, arms outstretched towards him, mouth invitingly open, her dark skin startling against the crisp white sheets. But he was brought back with a jolt from these dreams of paradise by the sound of his name. 'Mr Kass! Mr Harvey Kass!'

Harvey instinctively raised his hand, 'Over here!'

The bellboy weaved towards him between the tables. 'Phone call for you, sir, in the lobby.'

'Who is it? Oh, no, don't tell me. Let me guess – the Nutty Professor.' The boy shrugged. Harvey tipped him a dollar and went in search of the phone.

'Why did you turn off your mobile?' Nilbert's voice was high-pitched and excited.

'Haven't you heard? They're bad for your health. What's up, Nilb?'

'I need everyone back, *now*!'

Harvey groaned. 'Sorry, buddy, no can do. I'm on vacation.'

'You are not going to believe what's happened!'

'I'll bet I'm not,' said Harvey, flatly. He could already feel his plans for the afternoon slipping away.

'It worked!'

'What worked?'

'The experiment – the corals. We forgot just how intelligent we'd made them. They didn't thrive in the tank because they'd assessed the situation and realized there was no point. Why grow in a tank? They waited until they were in the open ocean, and that's when it happened!'

'That's when what happened?'

'Oh, no. To find that out, you're going to have to get back here. Let's just say we're on the verge of something big. No, not big, *huge*! Listen, I've got to go – lots of calls to make. I'll see you later!'

'Nilbert, Nilbert, wait!' but the line was already dead.

Harvey put down the phone, a mixture of fiercely contending emotions. The scientist in him was, of course, extremely anxious to find out what had happened, but the man in him was equally keen to spend the afternoon in his cool and darkened hotel room with a fridge full of booze and a compliant young cocktail waitress. In the end, there was no contest.

Limbo II

'Shit!' he said out loud, and thumped the reception desk. At that moment, Honey appeared.

'Are you ready?' She smiled. 'Jasmine's with my friend Melanie, so we have the whole afternoon.'

Harvey looked up at her, at her red lips, her full round breasts peeping over the top of her loose silk dress, and groaned. 'Baby,' he said, 'um, look, I'm sorry, but . . .'

When everyone returned to Lizard, disgruntled and feeling hard done by at having had their break cut short, they found a wide-eyed Nilbert surrounded by empty chocolate milk cartons and glowing with the zeal of the converted.

'Welcome, welcome, my friends,' he said, greeting the boat while hopping up and down with excitement. 'I have seen the future, and it *evolves*!'

'Sorry, Nilb,' said Harvey, turning round and throwing his bag back into the boat, 'but someone called Darwin got there before you. I'll see you later.'

'No!' said Nilbert, leaping on him and pulling him back up the beach. 'We are talking about a whole new species here! A breed . . . yes, I think I can call it a breed. A breed of . . .' Nilbert broke off. 'How did you get that black eye?'

'It's a long story,' said Harvey. 'Basically, it seems that Fijians don't like being stood up. Come on, Nilb, what's the big story?'

'Everybody gather round.' Nilbert stood, smiling from ear to ear at his assembled team. 'You are not going to *believe* this!'

'Just tell us, Nilb,' Harvey sighed.

'OK. Remember our staghorn coral? Well, after you left, I sort of got . . . annoyed, and chucked it into the sea.'

'You did what?' Harvey exploded.

'No, no,' said Anna from Heidelberg, 'that is very bad scientific practice. Should the authorities find out, you could get our research licence revoked.'

'But they're not going to find out, are they?' Nilbert beamed.

Tony shook his head. 'Really, Nilbert, that's not on . . . I mean . . . honestly,' he muttered.

'I know, I know,' said Nilbert. 'Just hear me out. A couple of days later, I was diving on the reef when I got a real shock. Our coral had taken root and was happily growing away and spawning for all it was worth.' He paused to let this information sink in. The team of scientists shared puzzled looks with one another. 'Then the next day I went back, but it wasn't there. At first I thought I must be looking in the wrong location, but I checked and rechecked the coordinates and realized that it had just disappeared. At first, I concluded that it had failed to thrive and been washed away. It was just a fluke after all, I told myself, and had probably taken root in the ocean just to spite me. That's why I didn't call you all back immediately. But that night I had this strange dream – a weird kind of prophetic dream – and I realized something. There are mammalian brain cells in the neural network of this coral – we put them there. This coral is highly intelligent! So, if it was still alive, there was only one thing that could have happened.' He paused for effect once again.

But Harvey was in no mood for Nilbert's cheap rhetorical tricks. 'For God's sake spare us the suspense!'

'I spent the next three days diving in the ocean to the east of the reef. *Me*, imagine that, out all day on the open sea – but I was just so excited. Then, eventually, I found what I was looking for.' Nilbert paused yet again, but by now Harvey was sufficiently intrigued not to spoil his moment. 'At first I thought it was a turtle,' Nilbert continued, 'then I took a closer look. It had flippers, yes, but . . . it was our coral!'

There was a gasp from the team. 'Wait a minute,' said Harvey. 'Are you saying that this coral was actually swimming?'

'That's exactly what I'm saying. That's why it was no longer there on the reef; it had sprouted flippers and taken off! This was the accelerated response to environmental factors that we'd hoped for, but we'd overlooked one thing – the individual survival instinct. Why hang around where you're likely to get picked off by starfish, or end up being boiled by warming seas? Developing strategies against such threats is energy-consuming. The sensible thing to do is to get out, if you can, and look for somewhere easier to live. You know what this means?'

'That corals are selfish?'

'No, it means that it *evolved* in response to environmental pressure, but way beyond where we'd expected it to. I also figured out why the larvae didn't develop in the tank. They knew there was no point! They'd worked it out for themselves! That's why there are none on the reef. They're not stupid – they've all swum off in search of somewhere a little more hospitable.'

'Excuse me!' said Anna from Heidelberg. 'What was the construction of the flippers? Did they have ribs, or were they articulated? And had the coral changed in other ways? Had it, for example, developed a rudimentary circulatory system?'

'One thing at a time, Anna, please,' said Nilbert. 'I have the specimen in the laboratory, and you can all take a look at it later. Oh, this is so exciting!' Nilbert was actually jumping up and down and hugging himself. Harvey had never seen him so animated. 'My friends,' he said at last, 'we . . . us . . . this little team of ours . . .' He stopped, overcome with emotion.

Uh-oh, thought Harvey. He knew the danger signs. Displays of high emotion from Nilbert only meant one thing – he'd had another one of his 'ideas'.

'We have engineered the first artificial, evolving organism.' Nilbert paused for a moment to wipe his eyes.

Any minute now, thought Harvey.

'Sorry . . . The thing is . . .' Nilbert looked up. His cheeks were flushed and his eyes shone with a strange, maniacal intensity.

Here it comes, thought Harvey.

'Finding that coral set me thinking. If we can manufacture a living organism that can make its own decisions, that can determine its own future – that, in short, *evolves* – why not use the same technology to breed . . . computers?'

'Computers?'

'Yes, computers. Computers that *evolve*. We could breed them for a whole host of applications – whatever we like! Taken to its logical conclusion, this technology would allow us to send intelligent machines into the most inhospitable places on Earth. Imagine: deep-sea computers that can explore the dark recesses of the ocean floor – free-swimming computers that can think, take decisions and send back intelligence reports, without the need either for humans to put themselves at risk or for expensive equipment to help them survive there. We could seed the oceans with thousands of them. They would be able to constantly monitor pollution levels, sea temperatures; even expose those countries breaking international treaties on whaling or overfishing. But it needn't end there. Just think: intelligent satellites orbiting the earth, monitoring ozone depletion, particulate density in the upper atmosphere, and so on. Satellites that could constantly upgrade their systems, even repair themselves, without the need for costly human intervention. They would never become obsolete and never need to be replaced! A solution to the growing problem of space junk! But the most exciting thing about all this is the time aspect. It is entirely possible that we could produce these organic machines – robots if you like – within months, not years. Robots which will evolve over time, endlessly adapting to their changing circumstances. What do you think?'

'I think you should get out more,' muttered Harvey.

'As I see it, there are two distinct phases to this operation,' Nilbert continued, ignoring him. 'The first is to find a way of growing an organic processor. The second, to find a medium which will allow this "brain" to exploit its innate capabilities, allowing it to develop into any form it chooses, or, more exactly, whichever form or function that is programmed into it. Now, we grew the coral's brain polyp by polyp, but that's too slow a process for commercial applications, and simply depending on gene-splicing is too haphazard; we need to standardize production. We will be sailing into uncharted waters here, making it up as we go. But if we get it right, we will be responsible for producing the first artificial, autonomous, evolving organism, capable of rational thought.'

'Whoah, hold on a minute!' said Harvey. 'I think we should slow down a little. Isn't this all a little bit outside our remit? Our funding is specifically granted for researching ways to improve the corals' chances against global warming, not to produce computers that can clean the house, cook your lunch and pick the kids up from school.'

'Let me worry about that,' said a wild-eyed Nilbert. 'Don't you see the potential of this idea? If we can produce, entirely organically, corals that can react intelligently to their environment, then growing something with which we ourselves can interact is only one very small step away.'

'And we just let the reefs die and fall apart?' Harvey protested.

'No, no, no, this isn't at the expense of our research on the reef,' said Nilbert. 'We can run the two programmes in parallel. Now, I've had some ideas about the best way to proceed, and if you'd all like to follow me into the laboratory, I'd be more than happy to put them to you.' Nilbert skipped off towards the baking laboratory hut. His small team, however tired they might have felt, had now caught some of Nilbert's passion. This was a branch of science so cutting-edge that, as yet, no one had coined a term for it. Wasn't that why they had become scientists in the first place – to be in the vanguard, to push the boundaries of what was possible? All feelings of exhaustion had evaporated in the blaze of Nilbert's wild enthusiasm, and it was with a feeling of great excitement that the team of scientists followed him up the beach. Only Harvey hung back.

'Aren't you coming, Harvey?' asked Tony.

Harvey looked skywards and blew out his cheeks. 'I don't know, Tone,' he said, shaking his head.

'You do not agree with this?' asked Anna. 'You are not excited by the implications of this research?'

'Oh, I'm excited, all right. It's just that I like to know how high the cliff is before I jump off it.'

She scrutinized his face for some moments, her brow crumpling into a frown. Then she smiled and nodded. 'You have no curiosity,' she announced and, having made her diagnosis, turned her back on him and followed the rest of the team up the beach and into the laboratory.

'I'll, er . . . I'd better . . . um . . .' Tony hovered, uncertainly.

Harvey waved him on. 'You just go ahead, Princess. I'll catch you later.'

Tony reddened, then ran to catch up with Anna. Harvey remained on the beach for some time, walking round and round in a small circle. *No curiosity?* he thought. *What does she know? At this moment, I could be having sex in a comfortable hotel room with air conditioning and a full minibar. Instead, I'm on a swelteringly hot small island with limited shelter, no beer and no cute waitresses, ruled over by a mad scientist – and I have* no curiosity? He sighed, knowing he wouldn't be able to turn his back on this project, however misguided.

'Shit! Shit! Shit!' he said, hauling his bag back out of the boat. *I'll play a watching brief,* he told himself as he trudged up the beach. *If I don't like what's happening a little further down the line, I'll leave. I'm my own man; I can leave at any time . . .* Taking a last look at the blue sky, the glittering azure sea, and the softly swaying palm trees, Harvey ducked into the sweaty cubicle of the laboratory.

Chapter 9

In the small spacecraft, Frink closed his eyes and waited for the impact.

'Dammit, dammit, dammit,' he said, hitting himself on the head with his fists. 'To come all this way only to crash on an alien planet. The mission has failed – and it's all my fault!' He pulled at his hair and it came away in great handfuls. 'The citizens of Earth will never know the great evil that is about engulf them.' He grabbed his beard and started yanking his head from side to side. 'Failure! Failure!' he shouted.

Then, suddenly, the lights came back on, power was miraculously restored, the ship's engines began to hum once more, and its earthward trajectory slowed.

'Yes! Yes!' Frink yelled triumphantly. 'Nice Frink... Good Frink...' he cooed to himself as he bent over the console and set the controls for landing. 'Well, I still don't know where we are, but this will just have to do. Let's hope we are near a centre of civilization.'

The small, disc-shaped spacecraft came to rest on its hydraulically damped legs in a pub car park, right next to an ancient, twelve-seater Land-Rover decorated with pastoral scenes containing haystacks, hops and apple blossom, and with 'The Sydenham Damerel Morris' written on its side.

Frink opened the canopy of the ship and sat for a while, filling his lungs with sweet-smelling fresh air for the first time in ten years. Clambering out of the cockpit and down the metal ladder, his feet touched the ground and he stretched his aching limbs. It was good at last to be free of the confines of his tiny ship, even if it was rather cold out here.

Standing in the silence, he took in the scene: the sheep and cows contentedly munching grass in the moonlit fields, the gurgling of the river as it flowed under the old stone bridge, and the dart and silent shriek of the bats overhead.

'Ah,' he said at last, 'very nice. You see, Frink, if your mission helps to save all this beauty from being blasted by the coming energy field, the years spent roaming the galaxy will not have been in vain.' He shivered in the chill night air. 'I must find shelter, but first I must send my bulletin.' Standing in the light spill from the open hatch of his spaceship, he smoothed his tangled hair, then raised the index finger of his left hand and panned it round the scene in a slow arc, at the end of which he turned it on himself. 'I have arrived safely,' he said. 'Earth seems to be a peaceful, pleasant planet, if a trifle cold. I am about to go in search of shelter, and hopefully I may find an inhabitant of this planet to whom I can deliver my message. There are few dwellings in the immediate vicinity, as this locality would appear to be of a rural nature, but luckily there is a habitation hard by. Within, I am certain to find welcome.' He pointed his finger at the pub, panned up to the pub sign, then back to himself. 'This is Frink Byellssen, the Royal Oak, Earth.' Putting his right hand over his eye, he replayed what he had just recorded. Satisfied with his news report and his appearance, he extended two pink, fleshy antennae from small pits behind his ears, and beamed his bulletin out into space. Then, withdrawing his antennae and closing the hatch of his ship, he marched up to the front door of the pub.

The door was locked and the curtains drawn shut but, listening through the letter box, Frink could hear the sound of voices. He knocked, politely at first, then, when he got no reply, a little more forcefully. The sounds from inside the pub ceased, and after a few moments Frink heard a bolt being drawn and a latch lifted. The door creaked open, and the face of Jim Bridger appeared.

'Yes?' said Jim.

'Greetings, friend,' said Frink. 'I bring important tidings.'

'Just a minute,' said Jim, and closed the door.

Inside the pub, Jim walked back into the saloon. 'Where's Tom?'

The police constable's face rose slowly from behind the bar. 'Ah, there you are,' said Jim. 'You'd better take a look at this.'

'It's not my missus, is it?' Tom asked, querulously.

'No,' said Jim. 'It's something even stranger-looking than your missus.'

With as much dignity as he could muster amid the hoots of laughter from the other drinkers, Tom, sensing that this was an official issue, retrieved his helmet from the bar counter and followed Jim to the door.

'Are you ready?' said Jim, his hand on the latch.

'Proceed,' said Tom in his best constable-speak, putting on his helmet and easing the chin strap with a finger.

'Very well.' Jim pulled open the door and Tom found himself face to face with a hairy, naked man.

'Greetings,' said the smiling man, raising his left index finger and pointing it at the policeman. 'I take it from your garb that you are someone in authority – how fortuitous!'

'Can I help you, sir?' said Tom, suspiciously. The rest of the crew from the bar were now beginning to crowd behind him in the doorway.

Frink turned his index finger on himself. 'What luck to have found an official at the first attempt. Well, sir,' he said, swivelling his finger back onto Tom. 'I hope you can help me. I most certainly can help you. I am Frink Byellssen from the planet Thrripp, and I bring grave news: an energy field of pure evil is coming your way; you must warn your citizens to— What are you doing?'

Tom had seized the strange man in an armlock. 'Come along now, sir, let's not have any trouble.'

'Ah, I see,' said Frink. 'You are escorting me to an even higher authority. Splendid.'

'Jim, how much have you had?' Tom called to the landlord.

'Pint and a half,' Jim replied.

'Good, you can drive us to Tavistock nick.'

'Righto.' Jim disappeared back inside the pub to fetch his car keys, while Tom escorted Frink across the car park to the landlord's Toyota. The other drinkers followed in a small, tight clump, ogling the unusual stranger from a respectful distance.

'Who is he, Tom?' one asked.

'I am Frink Byellssen from the planet Thrripp, and I bring—'

'Yes, yes, of course you are,' said Tom, grabbing Frink's other arm and snapping on the handcuffs. Tom turned back to the small crowd. 'I've no idea who he is, but I know where he's from: the funny farm up at Linhay – he must have escaped.'

'Ooh!' The little group of men drew back and clumped together even more tightly.

Jim arrived, scrunching over the gravel. 'It's not locked,' he called. Tom opened the back door of the car and bundled Frink inside.

'Abel,' said Tom, addressing a small, red-faced man, 'phone Margie and tell her I may not make it back tonight – serious police business.' Then he got in beside Frink and slammed the door.

Jim got in the front seat and started the engine. The back wheels spun on the gravel and the Toyota sped off down the lane.

When its rear lights had disappeared into the darkness, the men noticed Frink's spaceship for the first time. Crowding round it, they began to wonder what sort of vehicle it might be.

'Is it a series three?' asked one.

'No,' said another. 'The series three's got that inset grille, like the series one and two. I reckon it's a modified Defender.'

'That's not a Defender. Where's the tow hook?'

'It could be one of them export models.'

'No, it's not long enough to be a Defender.'

Limbo II

'Ah, but it could be the short-wheelbase version...'

While the argument continued, Harold Petherwick, dressed in women's clothes as the Morris team's Bessie, stumbled blindly out of the pub. He had been the day's designated driver, and was supposed to have been on nothing stronger than orange juice. But, unbeknownst to his fellow dancers, beneath the folds of his capacious skirts, he had hidden a bottle of vodka with which he had spiked every one of the fifteen-odd orange juices he'd consumed during the course of the day. Now the bottle was empty and Harold was stocious.

Staggering across the car park to where he'd parked the Land-Rover, he had but one thought in his mind – bed. He was tired and longed to get his head down. While the rest of the troupe momentarily turned their backs on the spaceship to urinate in the road, Harold climbed the gleaming metal steps into the small cockpit. As he strapped himself into the pilot's seat, he was vaguely aware that something wasn't quite right. A confusing array of lights and buttons winked and blinked up at him.

'I'm having hallucinations,' he muttered. 'I'd better drive slowly.'

Laboriously pulling the Land-Rover's keys out of his pocket, he tried in vain to fit them into the ignition. "'S funny, why won't they...? Bugger!' he said, as the keys fell from his fumbling fingers. Reaching down to pick them up, his head hit a big red button on the console. There was a loud humming, and suddenly Harold found himself getting very heavy as he shot skywards at close to the speed of sound.

The men peeing in the gutter heard a *whooshing* sound behind them and, turning back, discovered that the strange vehicle was no longer there. Looking up, all they could see was a light streaking away across the night sky.

'There,' said one of them, triumphantly. 'That proves my point. You ever see a Defender do that?'

'No, no,' the rest of the men concurred, shaking their heads.

Then, one by one, and slowly, the members of the Sydenham

Damerel Morris looked back towards the welcoming light spilling out of the open door of the pub, and all had the same thought at the same time.

'How long d'you reckon it takes to get to Tavistock from here?' said one.

'It's got to be a good forty minutes, there and back,' replied another.

'Hmm...'

Whistling now, the men strolled casually back towards the comforting warmth of the public house.

Chapter 10

Nilbert had already come to the conclusion that to build an organic brain with above-average intelligence, allowing it to develop cell by cell, would take far too much time. So he approached the problem of the manufacture of this brain from a different angle...

If we were building a computer we'd start with a microprocessor, he thought, unwrapping another bar of Wholenut. *But we're dealing with a living organism here. How about making each cell a microprocessor? Then we wouldn't need the billions of cells found in the average animal brain; indeed, the resulting artificial organ need consist of no more than a few thousand cells. If each processor had the power of, say, the Pentium 16, the process of growth from single-celled PC to supercomputer could take only a few days. The question is: How do we turn a living cell into a microprocessor?*

Lunch breaks were cancelled and replaced with intensive brainstorming sessions. Nilbert and his team sweated and swore and screamed in the stifling conditions of their makeshift laboratory until, at last, a way forward was agreed upon.

No one had ever tried to etch a printed circuit onto an organic molecule before, but Nilbert, never daunted, saw no reason why it shouldn't be done.

Separating out a single, cloned, human stem cell that was already in the process of becoming a neuron, Nilbert set about laser-etching a printed circuit onto its DNA – the theory being that each time the cell divided, so too would its DNA, doubling and redoubling its computing power, with each new cell becoming a powerful processor in its own right.

During his first few attempts, Nilbert simply fried the cell, but eventually, after months of work, he and his team were successful in manufacturing the first single-cell organic microprocessor. All they had to do now was settle back and watch it divide, and divide, and divide . . .

But things didn't turn out quite as planned – the laser-etching technique seemed to confuse the cell. The morning after the first experiment, Nilbert was woken in his tent by Harvey.

'Nilb, you might want to come and have a look at this,' he said in his characteristically understated way.

Harvey led Nilbert into the laboratory and over to a small glass jar into which, the night before, the bundle of dividing cells had been placed. Nilbert was expecting to see rapidly forming brain tissue, but instead was faced with a perfectly formed human nose.

'It's a nose,' said Nilbert, stating the obvious.

'Ah, but a highly intelligent one,' countered Harvey. 'We hooked it up to this laptop and we've actually been able to communicate with it. Look.' Harvey tapped something into the keyboard. A moment later, a long series of numbers scrolled up on the screen.

'What's that?' Nilbert asked.

'It's the answer to a question we put to it earlier.'

'What was the question?'

'We asked it to calculate the weight of the universe.'

'And?'

'It concluded that there's more than three times as much dark matter in the universe than previously thought. Which means that we may have to revise the Friedmann models concerning the expansion of the universe. I have to say, I'm inclined to believe it.'

'Wow!'

'Wow indeed. There's only one major drawback as far as I can see: it's kind of got limited applications. I can't imagine many businesses being keen to ditch their current computer systems in favour of noses. I mean, think of the mess if your nasal network caught a virus. But, apart from the hygiene angle, it raises all kinds of moral issues. I doubt we'd get the over-sentimental popular press to back us in this.'

It was a blow, but Nilbert was nothing if not persistent. Unfortunately, the second experiment resulted in a big toe, albeit a brilliant one that calculated the value of π to ten billion decimal places in less than thirty seconds.

The third experiment produced the most disturbing result of all – an eye with an immeasurable IQ which glared accusingly at Nilbert and his assistants, making them so uncomfortable that, in the end, Harvey covered the flask in which it bobbed with an old sock and banished it to the corner of the laboratory, where it, the nose and the toe communicated telepathically in binary code, discussing such topics as Quantum Chromodynamics, Unified Field Theory and Why the prejudice against the fruit scone?

Chapter 11

The sun beat down relentlessly. The only relief from the subtropical heat was a gentle and intermittent sea breeze. But the two figures lying on sun loungers didn't mind; after all, heat was what Lanzarote was all about. From the still smoking volcanoes of the interior to the baking sands of its shoreline, the island was a long, smouldering coal in the cool turquoise of the Atlantic.

The man – long and lean, with a neatly trimmed black beard – was dozing. At first he wasn't sure if the tremor he'd felt had been part of a dream, but as he ascended from the depths of sleep, he felt it again: like the hooves of a monstrous horse on the doors of consciousness. He opened his eyes and sat up.

The woman on the sun lounger next to him sighed and stretched out languidly. 'Are you all right, dear?' she said.

'Did you feel that?' he asked.

'Did I feel what?' the woman replied.

'Nothing.'

Maybe it had been his imagination after all. But the previous night he'd had a spectacularly vivid dream concerning a strange, deathly figure in a black cowl, riding a winged horse. He'd tried to dismiss it, but the vague feeling of unease it had awoken in him wouldn't go away. Was it some part of his old life reaching out to him? If so, for what? And even if it was something that, God forbid, demanded his attention, surely there was no need to worry the Queen just yet?

'I think I may go in for a dip,' he said.

Limbo II

The woman, shielding her face with her hand, looked up into his remarkable eyes – blue like the morning sky, as deep and as placid as a mountain lake, with here and there a fleck of white like swans taking flight.

'I'll follow you in,' she said.

The man rose with a sigh. He was in remarkably good shape for his age. Most people assumed he was either a well-preserved seventy or a dissolute sixty, but no one could ever have guessed the truth.

The woman was in her mid-forties but still beautiful: soft and rounded, with almond eyes and full lips, and black hair that tumbled around her shoulders. There was a fine dew of perspiration all over her body, and she glistened golden in the sun. Sitting up, she watched her lover stride purposefully down to the sea and, without a moment's hesitation, dive straight in. Soon he was swimming effortlessly in the limpid blue-green water.

The woman wiped the perspiration from her forehead and licked her lips, tasting salt. How her life had changed in the past few years. No longer pampered and waited on hand and foot, with a hundred servants to pander to her every whim, she was happier than she'd ever been. She was with the man she loved and free to do whatever she wished. She had only one regret, but the pain of that receded year by year, and she was sure that whatever had happened, it had all been for the best.

Reaching under her sun lounger, she pulled a bottle of water out of the cool bag and upended it to her lips. Some of the liquid escaped the corner of her mouth and ran down her neck. The ice-cold rivulet flowed over the smooth contour of her breast, and disappeared beneath her bikini top, making her gasp.

Out in the bay, the two-thousand-year-old ex-Wizard of Limbo – Rex's father and author of the Book – swam powerfully through the cool, clear water. Then he rolled over onto his back and looked up at the sky. It was as blue as his eyes, with not a cloud to mar its perfection.

Raising his head, he looked back to the shore where his lover, the previous Queen of Limbo, was standing, tying up her hair before entering the water. The Wizard loved her more than he could express, and what made this time with her all the more joyous was that it very nearly hadn't happened at all. Once, he'd almost given up hope of ever seeing her again. Indeed, he daily thanked the gods for his good fortune, and his son Rex for making the whole thing possible. It was unthinkable that anything should come between them, and he prayed that the tremor he'd just felt had been merely imagined. It meant . . . Well, it could mean anything. He just hoped that, whatever it was, it wouldn't take him away from her. But what could he do about it, anyway? He was no longer the wizard he'd once been. Now he lived quietly, painting and tending his vines. He looked once more at the sky, at the sea and back to the sun-drenched beach – it was all so beautiful.

No, it can't have happened, he told himself. *It was just the product of an overactive imagination.*

Then he felt it again: louder and more insistent this time – an echoing rumble that rolled around the inside of his head.

'No, no, no,' he murmured. 'Oh please, God, no.'

Chapter 12

This was not the reception that Frink had expected. He'd been looking forward to delivering his message to world leaders, being hailed as a saviour of Earth, having photo opportunities with VIPs and kissing small children, but instead he'd been shut up, alone, in a strange, bare, white-tiled room, and he was beginning to feel the chill. All he'd been given to warm himself was a thin, scratchy woollen blanket.

Seated on the hard wooden bench that ran along one side of his cell, he watched a spider moving restlessly back and forth in a corner of the room, weaving its web. Extending his antennae, Frink communicated telepathically with it. 'What do you hope to catch?' he said. 'There aren't any flies around – isn't all that work a bit pointless?'

'If you're so bloody clever,' the spider replied, 'how come you're locked up in here?'

Frink retracted his antennae and sank back into gloomy introspection. At last a key turned in the lock, and in walked a smartly dressed woman flanked by two white-coated attendants, one of whom carried a metal-framed chair, which was placed in the centre of the room.

'Hello,' the woman cooed.

'Greetings,' said Frink, and left it at that. He'd already delivered his message, pointlessly as it turned out, to several inconsequential people. This time, unless she identified herself as a world leader, he was going to save his breath.

'You're Frink, aren't you?' The woman smiled, pulling up the chair and sitting opposite him.

'Yes.'

'Unusual name.'

'Not where I come from.'

'And where is that?'

'The planet Thrripp, in the Galtoid star system.'

'I see,' said the woman, her smile not slipping for an instant. 'And how did you get here?'

'Magnetosynchrotronic drive. Look, will this take long? I'm sorry to appear rude, but I do have a message of the utmost importance for the safety of this planet. I need to deliver it to someone in power – someone who can act on the warning it contains.'

'You can deliver it to me.' The woman smiled. 'I'm in power.'

Frink looked at the slight woman with her protruding teeth and lank blonde hair. 'You . . . you're a world leader?'

'Ooh yes, I'm a very important person,' she said, sweetly.

'Oh,' said Frink, taken aback. 'In that case . . .' He cleared his throat. 'Greetings, I am Frink Byellssen from the planet Thrripp . . . er, sorry, you already know that bit . . . and I bring grave news. An energy field of pure evil is coming your way, so you must warn your citizens to take cover. The energy field's purpose is unknown, but our sensors have measured it at ten point five on the Crypto-Messian scale. This is high-level evil, and therefore its intentions must be regarded as hostile. Those directly in its path should flee their homes. Take to the hills! Fathers, protect your families! Mothers, protect your children! Escape! Flee! Evacuate! Prepare, citizens of Earth. Prepare!'

The woman applauded. 'Very good, very good.'

Frink flushed slightly.

'Is there anyone else here from your planet at the moment?' the woman asked.

Frink shook his head. 'No.'

'So how come you're the only one from, er ... from Thrip, is it?'

'Thrripp,' Frink corrected.

'Sorry, I never was very good with names.' She smiled again. 'How come you're the only one from ... your planet who's come to give us this warning?'

'I was chosen,' Frink replied, proudly.

'Of course you were,' the woman said.

'Actually I won a national TV competition: the *Stars in their Antennae* grand final,' Frink explained. 'They said I was the best Elthrickk Snarrge soundalike they'd ever had on the show,' he added, coyly.

'Congratulations,' said the woman.

'First prize was this mission. I was given space training at the famous L'Ohn Kriffthhh Space Academy – who also lent me the spaceship – then was sent off to track the energy field and warn those in its path.'

'Not much of a prize, if you ask me,' said the woman.

'You must understand that, where I come from, to be given the chance to go on a potentially life-threatening mission for the sake of one's fellow creatures is the dream of most Thrrippians.'

'It can't be much like Earth, then,' the woman said.

'When we first spotted the energy field, it was moving through the Deltoid Quadrant. We thought it might be heading for us, in fact, but then it veered off and headed towards your galaxy. For the last ten years I have been racing it across the universe to bring you this message.'

'Um, please don't take this amiss,' the woman said, 'but don't people wear clothes where you come from?'

Frink pulled the thin blanket around him a little more tightly. 'Please excuse my state of undress, but I left Thrripp with only two suits of clothes, both of which, I'm afraid, fell to rags long ago.'

'I see.' The woman nodded. 'You know, for an alien you speak very good English.'

'Ah! I've had many years to perfect my grasp of your language. Whilst travelling here, across the space between our galaxies, I have been monitoring your radio broadcasts. I am also fluent in Urdu, Spanish, Russian, Japanese and Morse code: *dah-dah-dit dah-dah-dah dah-dah-dah dah-dit-dit dah-dah dah-dah-dah dit-dah-dit dah-dit dit-dit dah-dit dah-dah-dit*. That's good morning... in Morse.'

'Goodness me! I'm impressed, I really am,' said the woman. 'Well, we're all very grateful you've come all this way to help us. Aren't we?' said the woman, turning to the two large, white-coated men flanking the door.

'Oh, yeah,' One nodded.

'Very grateful,' said the other, without a smile.

Frink raised his left index finger and pointed it at the woman. 'Would you mind introducing yourself? Just say who you are into the lens.'

'Um?' she said, shifting uncomfortably in her seat.

'It's a camera,' Frink explained. 'An implant enabling me to send bulletins of my progress back to Thrripp. I'm also making a documentary about life on your planet.'

'Oh, right,' she said, nodding. 'OK... I just speak into your finger... er, camera, do I?' Frink smiled encouragingly. 'Sorry,' she said, turning a delicate shade of pink. 'I'm not very good at having my picture taken. Here we go then. Um... well, my name is Helen.'

'And what do you do?' Frink asked.

'Oh, silly me. Of course. I'm a very important world leader.' Helen smiled into Frink's finger.

'Is that it?' he asked, after a pause.

'Is there anything else you want me to say?'

'Not if you don't want to.' Frink assumed that the citizens of Earth must pick their leaders according to very different criteria from those back home. On Thrripp, the problem was getting a politician to *stop* talking. 'No, that's fine,' he said, putting his hand over his right eye.

Limbo II

'What are you doing?' asked Helen.

'Just playing it back to make sure I got it all. The recording chip's behind my eye,' he added, by way of explanation. 'Right,' he said. 'It's all there, but it's a little short for a bulletin. Do you mind if I hang onto it and include it in the documentary?'

'Of course not.' Helen beamed.

'And now,' said Frink, 'I'd be most interested to know how you are going to utilize the information that I have just given you about the nature of the energy field that is about to engulf your planet.'

'Ah yes, your message,' said Helen. 'You know, I think your message is so important it needs to be shared. Will you come with me and tell it to a friend of mine?'

Frink was confused. 'Er . . . but I've given *you* the message. You are a world leader, are you not?'

The woman nodded.

'In that case why can you not act upon it?'

'Oh, I'm not sure I can remember a complicated message like that all on my own, and it would be awful if I got it wrong, wouldn't it? So, just to be on the safe side, I'd like you to come along with me and make sure I get it right. Will you do that?'

Frink shrugged. 'Very well.' If Helen was a typical example of the calibre of world leader on this planet, he didn't hold out much hope for Earth's continued survival.

As Frink was bundled into the waiting ambulance, Helen spoke briefly to the desk sergeant.

'Well, he's not one of ours, but we'll take him back with us. We've got the facilities to look after him properly.'

'Is he dangerous?' asked the sergeant.

'No, I don't think so, but you can never tell with delusionals.'

'Where's he from then?'

The woman shook her head. 'No idea. We'll ring round in the morning, just to see if any of the local care homes are missing anyone. He could, of course, have been turned out by his family – not able to cope any more, you know.'

The sergeant clicked his tongue. 'Sad, isn't it?' he said, sympathetically.

'It happens. From the smell of him, I'd say he's been living rough for quite some time – a prime example of no care in the community.'

The desk phone rang and the sergeant picked it up. 'Tavistock police station.'

Helen waved goodbye and started to leave.

'One moment, please.' The sergeant put his hand over the mouthpiece. 'Will you be all right getting him back?' he asked.

'Oh, yes. I've got Mike and Terry with me in case he starts anything,' she said, and walked out to the ambulance.

The sergeant went back to the phone 'Sorry to keep you, madam. How can I help you?'

Chapter 13

Nilbert lay on his back and looked up at the stars twinkling above him. The thought of all that *space* gave him the willies, and he shivered. But he forced himself to keep looking because tonight something odd was happening to the sky. It was streaked with strange colours: long shimmering lines of pink and white light were intertwined with another, unnameable, paler colour, and possibly a thread of black, but it was hard to tell against the inky blackness of the night.

Nilbert had seen the aurora borealis often during his long, lonely sojourn in Antarctica. He'd been doing some research there for an American oil exploration firm, studying the icefish, which can survive in the freezing waters under the ice sheet, and from which it was hoped to develop a sort of human antifreeze thereby cutting down on the heating bills of polar installations. But what was happening above him now was nothing like the aimless, wavering beauty of that spectacular phenomenon. These strange lines of colour seemed to move with a purpose, and were heading in a definite north-westerly direction.

Nilbert couldn't be sure if it was simply his agoraphobia, but gazing at those extraordinary coloured strands, far above, sent a chill to his very bones. He had no religion, but as he watched the strange, swirling and looping lights, the only adjective he could find to describe them was *evil*. He had a sudden and desperate need for company, but his exhausted team needed their rest and he didn't want to disturb them.

Then he felt a *thump*, as if a shock wave had hit the beach. Getting up, he went into the laboratory to check the seismic recording equipment. On the paper around its drum was a small but definite spike, but a closer inspection of the readings seemed to reveal that this was no earthquake. Whatever he'd felt had come not from within the earth, but beyond it. That didn't make sense.

Standing there in the laboratory, puzzling over the readings, Nilbert sensed that he was being watched. Turning suddenly, all he could see were the manufactured body parts from his earlier experiments, sitting motionless in their life-sustaining fluid. He should really have had them destroyed – it was bad scientific practice to hang onto your mistakes – but somehow he hadn't quite been able to bring himself to do that. After all, they were sentient – not only that, they were also human. But now he was beginning to question the wisdom of such sentimentality and had the oddest feeling that they were plotting something behind his back. But that was ridiculous, surely?

He went over to the tank in which his latest experiment was developing. This small, rapidly developing bundle of cells was eventually going to become the heart of the world's first organic supercomputer, but at the moment it looked uncomfortably like a human foetus. Harvey had already christened it Max.

Is this right? The question hit Nilbert like a tsunami. Such a thing had never occurred to him before. He was a scientist, his concerns were with the mechanics of what was possible; the moral agonizing he left to others. But the question wouldn't go away. *Is this right*? he asked himself again.

As he studied the small foetus-like thing floating in the tank, it opened an eye. Nilbert started back in shock. He felt as if he was being analysed, judged, weighed and finally found wanting by an intelligence that far surpassed his own. An intelligence, indeed, that surpassed anything in the known universe. The eye closed again and Nilbert was able to breathe once more.

Stumbling quickly out of the laboratory, past the silently

Limbo II

malevolent nose and its cronies and out into the night, he stood on the wave-lapped beach, trembling uncontrollably. What had most shaken him about the whole episode was that the 'brain' growing in the tank was supposed to have been just that. It had not been programmed to develop eyes – which meant it had leapt several evolutionary hurdles already and was programming its own development. What had he started? He had set something in motion that he wasn't sure he'd be able to control. Yet how could he turn back now? Innocence had already been lost.

Guilt was a new and confusing emotion for Nilbert. *The technology exists*, he told himself. *If I don't do it, somebody else will*, he argued, trying desperately to push down the unquiet feelings that threatened to overwhelm him.

In the night sky above, the strange lights continued their twirling, pulsating progression. Nilbert noticed that they were much nearer the horizon now, but still on a north-west heading. *That would put them on a course towards England*, he thought, and was immediately filled with a longing for home: for grass, trees and rain – *before it all disappears*. The thought caught him unawares. Suddenly overcome with a strange, unnameable fear, he looked back towards the laboratory and asked himself again: *Is this right?*

Chapter 14

Frink was beginning to suspect that all was not as it seemed. As he was led into the large and strangely smelling building complex, he felt Terry's and Mike's hands tighten on his arms as they set foot on home territory.

He was ushered into a small white room and seated forcefully on a hard wooden chair. 'Now then,' Helen said. 'Would you like a drink?'

Frink nodded. Apart from the fact that space travel was extremely dehydrating, he'd been recycling his water supply for a decade, and the prospect of drinking something that hadn't said hi! to his kidneys over a million times was very attractive. 'A glass of water would be most welcome,' he said.

'Here we are then,' said Helen, handing him a paper cup. Terry let go of his arm so that he could take it, and Frink put the cup to his lips. It tasted bitter and faintly chalky, but that, he supposed, was due to the different salts and minerals on this planet. It was bound to taste different from the water back home.

'Thank you,' said Frink, handing back the empty cup. 'When do I meet your friend?'

Helen looked at her watch. 'Well,' she said, 'it's very late now, and you're probably feeling a little tired after your long trip, so why don't you have a wash and a nice long sleep, and then you can meet him in the morning.'

'No!' Frink said, 'I must see him *now*!' His voice sounded odd and seemed to come from far away – as if it was not his own. He tried to rise, but his legs felt strangely weak, and it was then he realized he'd been drugged.

Dammit, he thought. *Stupid Frink – you must be more vigilant!* He tried to slap himself, but, lacking strength and coordination, only managed a pathetic swat in the vague direction of his nose, which unbalanced him and threw him to the floor.

'Terry and Mike will look after you, and I'll see you again when you're feeling a little better,' Helen said. Frink struggled to keep his eyes open as the woman's face became ringed with black. 'Get him cleaned up and put him to bed, will you boys?' she said, opening the door of the small cubicle. 'I'll see you both in the morning. Goodnight, Frink. Sleep well.' And she left, closing the door behind her.

Frink squirmed in frustration, trying to get up. 'Don yoo peeble unnerstan?' he slurred. 'Eevil comin. Yoo all doom!'

'D'you hear that, Terry?' said Mike. 'We're doomed.'

'Oh, yeah?' Terry replied.

'I ha speek... peeble Earth. Time... of... ess... ess... essence!' Frink managed to squeeze the words out, despite having a tongue that felt the size of a roll of carpet and lips that refused to form any vowel except 'urgh'.

'*Au contraire*, matey,' said Mike. 'In my humble opinion, I'd say a shower is of the essence, wouldn't you agree, Tel?'

'*Absolumong, mon ami*,' said Terry. 'We can't have you addressing the world ponging like a urinal now, can we?'

Frink was vaguely aware of being lifted and dragged into the corridor. After opening several sets of swing doors with his head, he was dumped unceremoniously onto cold, damp white tiles. The next thing he knew, he was hit by a powerful jet of icy water. There was the sharp, nose-tingling aroma of carbolic soap, then a sensation akin to being flayed alive as he was rubbed down with a rough, hospital towel.

Now Frink understood. These people were in league with the energy field. If they were an example of the evil it contained, Earth was in deep, deep trouble. Frink had been betrayed, and the sense of shame he felt at having allowed himself to be put in this terrible situation was almost too much to bear. He could fight no more. With a sigh he gave in to the drug, and blackness descended like a curtain.

Chapter 15

Having been right through the castle and found nothing, Smeil was out searching the town. Back at base – a small, private room in the castle's extensive cellars – Rex had drawn a large representation of the town on a blackboard, dividing it up with a grid pattern. As each square was searched, Smeil reported back to Rex, who coloured in that square with a blue chalk.

The townsfolk, of course, knew nothing of the reason why their homes were being turned upside down, but for some it brought back memories of the Great Terror. The soldiers charged with the task were also finding it difficult. Scorned by the people because of their actions during that awful episode, the last thing they wanted to do was to antagonize anyone, especially when they had been working so hard to rehabilitate themselves in the public's eyes. It was an uncomfortable morning for all concerned.

The search stopped for lunch, and just as Rex and Bernard were spooning up the last sumptious mouthful of their praline *semi-freddo*, there was an almighty shudder. The very walls of the old castle shook, and several large slabs fell from the top of one of the more ancient turrets. In the dining hall the tremor rattled the heraldic shields high up in the rafters, and showered the diners with a fine, white dust. As everyone slowly recovered their power of speech, they muttered darkly that they'd felt nothing like it since the Great Dragon of Phnell broke so dramatically from her earthly tomb.

'What was that, son?' Bernard asked, his voice muffled behind the tablecloth.

'I don't know, Dad. Well, that is . . .' Rex trailed off.

Bernard crawled out from under the table and looked Rex in the eye. 'Come on, son, what's going on?'

Rex dropped his voice to a whisper. 'You must promise not to tell a soul,' he hissed.

'Cross my heart and hope to die,' said Bernard, dusting himself down and settling back into his seat.

'Somewhere, somehow, a piece of the Book has survived.'

Bernard's eyes widened. 'No!' he boomed.

'Shh! If anyone finds out, there'll be pandemonium.'

'Sorry.' Bernard leaned in close to Rex. 'So that's why Smeil's been scurrying all over the place like a demented mouse,' he whispered.

'Afraid so.'

'And you haven't found it yet?'

'No. We have no idea where it could be.'

'Hmm.' Bernard ran a hand thoughtfully over his bald head.

Struggling hard to retain his dignity underneath a fine dusting of white plaster, Henri appeared with two coffees: an espresso for Rex and a *caffè latte* for Bernard. 'Your majesty; sir.'

'Thank you, Henri,' said Bernard.

'Shall I take these now?' Henri indicated the empty plates.

'Yes, please,' said Bernard. 'You can leave the wine.'

'What a surprise,' said Henri, sotto voce.

They watched and waited in tense silence as Henri removed the plates and dusted crumbs off the table. After he'd gone, Bernard leaned forward conspiratorially. 'But I don't understand; I thought *all* copies of the Book had been destroyed,' he said in a low tone.

'So did I.'

'Do you know which bit it is?'

'No,' said Rex, 'but it's most likely a piece of the Prophecy. There used to be a copy of that in every home.'

Limbo II

Bernard started spooning sugar into his coffee. 'Thank God it's not a bit of the . . . What d'you call it . . . the forbidden something?'

'The Forbidden Codex? No, unlikely, unless . . .' Rex looked down at his rich dark espresso and at Bernard's frothy white *caffè latte*, and a light snapped on in his brain. 'One black . . . one white,' he said quietly. 'Oh no.'

'Eh?' said Bernard.

Rex looked up, but it wasn't Bernard's big, broad face he saw. No, in his mind's eye Rex was looking at a terrifying fragment of an ancient text – a text thought destroyed long ago, and wiped from the memory of the world:

> *Behold, four horsemen in a blink:*
> *One black, one white, one pale, one pink,*
> *And Hell and darkness follow in their stink . . .*

'Oh no, no, no . . .' he muttered.

Bernard looked troubled. 'What is it? What's happened?'

Rex's voice came slow and strange – deep and harsh and far away, as if from the bottom of a well. 'Imagine the worst thing that could possibly happen,' he said. 'Now double it. The Four Horsemen of the Apocalypse have broken through the veil.'

Part II

Twilight . . .

Deep underground in the vast, dripping cavern, something stirred. The figure lying beside the chained and padlocked casket felt the shuddering knock on the door of destiny and, surfacing from its unfathomable and timeless sleep, turned and opened an eye.

A voice, silent for millennia, croaked into life. 'It is time,' it said, and the cave echoed strangely to this unaccustomed sound.

Illuminated only by the dull orange glow emanating from the casket, the hunched figure sat up slowly and, groaning softly, eased life into long-unused limbs. Then it rose stiffly and stretched. The pain of movement for one who had slumbered so long was excruciating. 'Ahh!' it roared, and the sudden noise precipitated a shower of stalactites, which fell – a mineral rain – clattering down on the figure and the casket which it guarded.

The figure was strangely lopsided. Its right arm and shoulder were massively overdeveloped, and the thick neck and big head it supported grew out of the curve of an almost semicircular back, but there was no doubting the strength in that body.

The powerful, misshapen guardian peered deep into the black depths of the cave. 'They are coming,' he said. 'It is time to arm.'

Going to a small trestle table draped with an ancient

Limbo II

embroidered cloth, which stood against the wall of the cave, the guardian threw back the dust-covered fabric to reveal a suit of black armour, its surface dulled by the passage of centuries.

Tearing a strip from the cloth, he carefully and tenderly picked up the tarnished breastplate and, in the dull glow from the casket, slowly and methodically began to polish it to a hard, beetle-black shine

Chapter 16

High up on the great mound of Cissbury Ring – the remains of a massive Iron Age hill fort commanding views of the sea to the south and the wide, flat expanse of the Sussex Weald to the north – something strange was happening. It was a bright, clear October morning, but suddenly dark clouds rolled in over the sea, and the pleasant autumn day was rapidly turned to night. Above the very centre of the fort a gusting wind began to swirl, slowly at first then gradually increasing in speed until a great grey whirlwind reached down one long, terrifying arm, clawing at the earth with frantic fingers, ripping up trees and tossing them aside like matchsticks. Lightning cleaved the air and thunder boomed. It was a storm like the end of the world. With a great, splintering crack, like the sound of some vast, cosmic door being thrown open, there was an explosion of fire and, when the smoke had cleared, four fearsome horses were revealed, pawing the earth impatiently, steam billowing from their nostrils:

One black, one white, one pale, one pink...

Their riders – black cloaks streaming out behind them, eyes gleaming darkly from inside the inky recesses of their cowls – sat in awful magnificence. At last, the figure on the pink horse threw back his cowl and spoke.

'Just look at my hair – it's ruined!' Little blue flashes of electric fire played around the rider's frizzy locks.

'It's just the static,' said the rider on the black horse. 'We have this every time,' he added under his breath.

'I beg your pardon?' asked the man on the pink horse.

The man on the black mount looked across at him, balefully. 'Every time we go anywhere, all we get is moan, moan, moan. You and your bloody hair.'

'Look, it's bad enough being stuck with a horse this colour without having hair that makes me look like Elizabeth Taylor on acid.'

The man on the pale horse glared at the man on the pink horse, and from somewhere deep within his being came a sound that made the ground tremble. It went something like: 'WOORRARRGHSSS!' Both the man on the pink horse and the man on the black one immediately fell silent.

'Thank you, Mr Pale,' said the man on the white horse. 'Now then – if you've quite finished – are we all met? Mr Black?'

The rider on the black horse grunted.

'I'm sorry? I didn't quite catch that.'

'Present,' said Mr Black sullenly.

'Thank you. Mr Pink?'

'Present.'

'Good. Mr Pale?'

The man on the pale horse shot him a glance that would have frozen mortal blood. 'Harrghasss!'

'I'll take that as a yes. That just leaves me, Mr White. Excellent. We're all here. Now, to our mission – revenge.' As he spoke the word, thunder rumbled in the distance.

'Revenge,' chorused Mr Black and Mr Pink.

'Rarrhwharghs,' muttered Mr Pale, nodding and chuckling to himself. A shaft of lightning slammed into the earth beside him with a deafening crack.

Mr Pink shuddered and turned to Mr Black. 'He gives me the creeps,' he whispered.

'So, men,' continued Mr White, 'we ride to avenge our lost

cause. Let famine, sword and fire follow in our wake, and let our cry be Pestilence, Hell and Damnation!'

The others took up the cry. 'Pestilence, Hell and Damnation!'

'Perwaarrharrghardss!' echoed Mr Pale. The wind howled, and rain fell in torrents. Mr White dug his spurs deep into his mount's flanks. The animal reared up, and forked lightning smacked the earth as he galloped away. The others, cloaks flying in the howling wind, followed in his dreadful wake. When he reached the fort's enclosing rampart, he pulled back on the reins and brought his horse to a standstill.

'Just a minute, just a minute,' he said, turning back to the others. The wind died and the rain stopped. 'What's the address?'

Mr Black pulled up alongside him. 'The address?'

'Yes, I gave it to you earlier.'

'No, you didn't.'

'Yes, I did.'

Mr Black shook his head. 'Nah, I would have remembered. Maybe you gave it to one of the others. Pinkie!' he called. 'Have you got the address?'

'Don't call me Pinkie!' The man on the pink horse snapped.

'Sorry.'

'Why would I have the address? I'm always the last to know about everything. I didn't even know about this little jaunt until this morning.'

'Bloody marvellous,' said Mr White. 'We're supposed to be the Four Horsemen of the Apocalypse and we couldn't organize a war in the Middle East.'

The man on the pale horse could contain himself no longer. With an angry cry that split the heavens, he thrust out his hand with such force it disappeared through the veil from behind which they had so dramatically made their appearance. After a moment, while the echo of his voice rolled like thunder across the countryside, he retrieved his tightly clenched fist in which was a small piece of charred paper, smoking slightly. He handed it to Mr White.

'Er... thank you, Mr Pale,' he said, taking it. 'Now then, let's see... er...' Holding it at arm's length, he squinted at the writing. 'Is that a *b* or a *d*?' He shook his head and thrust the paper at Mr Black. 'It's no good. You read it; I can't see a thing without my glasses.'

'All right, boss, let's have a look-see... It says here: "Boggs' Newsagent's, Lancing High Street".'

Mr White nodded. 'Lancing. Lan... *cing*!' he enunciated, hitting the final syllable with dramatic emphasis. 'Lancing is in for a bit of a shock.' Raising himself in his stirrups, he pointed a threatening finger towards a small habitation nestling between the sea and the South Downs. As dark clouds began to boil above his head, he raised his face to the heavens and screamed in a terrifying high tenor, 'We ride to Lancing!'

Mr Black touched him lightly on the arm. 'Erm, sorry, boss, but I think you'll find that's Worthing. Lancing's a little further to the east.'

'Oh,' said Mr White, reorienting himself. 'We ride to Lancing,' he said again, a little less dramatically, and set off down the hill.

'Laargharghss!' the pale horseman roared, thundering after him.

Mr Pink and Mr Black hung back for a moment and watched as their colleagues rumbled down the hill towards the sea. 'I'm not sure about that Mr Pale,' said Mr Pink. 'Have you ever seen him without his cowl?' Mr Black shook his head. 'And whoever heard of a pale horse? Pale's a shade, not a colour.'

'That's the pot calling the kettle.'

'At least pink's a recognized colour. Anyway, my horse isn't supposed to be pink; in the Bible it's red.'

'What happened then – you put it in the wash and it ran?'

'Are you two coming or not?' Mr White called up to them from the bottom of the hill.

'Sorry, boss!' said Mr Black.

'We're right behind you!' said Mr Pink. And so saying, they trotted sedately down the slope.

Chapter 17

The Forbidden Codex was a collection of the more horrifying tracts of the Book, removed prior to publication in case the dark prophecies they contained had a negative impact on sales. Not many copies were printed, and those that were had been made available only to the Royal Household and certain of Limbo's more morbid scholars.

The prophecy concerning the Four Horsemen was one of the last in the 'FC' that had not yet been fulfilled. Indeed, it was only Rex's rewriting of the Paradox that had prevented it from coming true. But now it seemed that everything had changed. If the verse relating to the Horsemen still existed, it would not fail to come to pass. It also meant that Rex's own book could have no authority, becoming, instead, nothing more than a continuation of the Book.

Back in his turret room, Rex turned the pages of *The Final Chapter* with trembling fingers. On every page some new disaster or evil deed was foretold...

> *With lightning, fire and odour fell,*
> *They ride their steeds from the depths of hell.*
> *The people cry: 'What an awful smell!'*
>
> *In the sky blaze trails of fire!*
> *War doth rage above the shire.*
> *From hills to sea: pestilence, contagion,*
> *Death in all his many forms,*
> *Reduces men to naught but worms...*

*Death's shadow creeps across the land,
From deepest deep to highest height,
And Limbo, its short summer spent,
Will sink into unfathomable night...*

Rex looked out of the window. It was true, the sun was noticeably lower in the sky. It wouldn't be long before people started asking questions. He went back to his book and, licking a finger, turned the next page. What he saw made his blood freeze...

*Horses strange along the street come prancing,
The sound of hooves resounds from walls
That bear the name of Lancing...*

Rex looked up. 'Mum!' he screamed.

Mrs Gupta was in the shop, manning the till, and Mr Gupta and Iris were both in the stock room, when the bell above the door tinkled merrily. A few moments later, after a strange and indistinct hissing, Mr Gupta heard his wife call out for him. There was a note of panic in her voice, and he looked up, worried. 'Stay here,' he instructed Iris, and disappeared through into the shop.

Peeping through the swaying bead curtain at the scene beyond, Iris could make out four hooded shapes. 'Tut,' Iris clicked her tongue. 'School kids.' She and Bernard had never allowed more than two children in the shop at any one time – it was almost impossible to keep track of them, and four was asking for trouble. But Iris looked again and saw that they were too big for children. But if they weren't kids in Halloween dress, who were they, and why were they wearing hooded cloaks? One of them was talking to Mr and Mrs Gupta, but Iris couldn't hear what he was saying. He seemed to have a bad throat, and she realized now that he was the source of the strange hissing she'd heard earlier.

'Boggsss...' the figure with the sore throat was saying.

Limbo II

Normally, on hearing her name, Iris would simply have parted the curtain and gone through to see what the man wanted. But something made her pause now — she couldn't say what exactly. Some vague fear kept her just out of sight, but she edged as close as she dared to the still-swinging curtain.

Mr Gupta was obviously frightened too, but he didn't give Iris away; he simply shook his head.

'Rrrexsss Boggsss . . .' the figure hissed again, a note of irritation in his voice.

Rex? Iris thought. *What do they want with Rex?* She was about to steel herself to walk into the shop and find out exactly what was going on when a terrifying thing happened. The figure at the counter dropped its hood to reveal a grinning skull. In an instant two bony fingers had slid up Mr Gupta's nose, and the newsagent found himself on tiptoe.

'Bogggsss, noooo?' hissed Mr Pale.

'Put him down, put him down!' screamed Mrs Gupta.

'I don't know where he is,' yelled Mr Gupta, nasally. 'Honestly.'

'Beeelieeeve yooo,' whispered Mr Pale, and thrust upwards with his fingers. There was a small crack, and Mr Gupta fell to the floor, lifeless. Mrs Gupta's mouth was open, but before she'd even had time to scream, Mr Pale's finger had penetrated her left eye and gone deep into her brain. She joined her husband on the floor.

'Oh!' Iris let out a small, involuntary gasp, and Mr Pale's bony head swivelled slowly to the softly swaying bead curtain behind which she cowered.

'Gentlemen,' he whispered, and his companions joined him at the counter. Mr Pale indicated the trembling curtain, and the three cowls turned towards it. Iris found herself staring into four pairs of dead, empty eyes — into the very depths of hell itself.

Chapter 18

'Smeil! Smeil!' Rex ran, breathless, into the coffee shop. His little servant was nowhere to be seen. 'Have you seen Smeil?' he asked a passing waitress, who was wearing a name badge with 'Matilda' on it.

She was pretty and petite, with straight blonde hair and green eyes, and she looked rather puzzled. She had only started work that morning and was desperately trying to hang onto a rather complicated order from Table 5: two espressos *con panna*; one *ristrétto*; one skinny cappuccino no chocolate; one vanilla *latte* with an extra shot; a marzipan *mocha* extreme; three almond croissants and two plain; and one goat's cheese, avocado and garlic sausage *panino* with pickle. 'What?' she replied, vaguely.

'Smeil, I'm looking for Smeil.'

Although concentrating as hard as she could, she could feel the order slipping away from her. Was it one or two espressos? How many croissants, and how many with almonds? And surely someone didn't really want to smother goat's cheese, avocado and garlic sausage with pickle?

'You're going cross-eyed,' said Rex, unhelpfully.

'Oh!' she exclaimed. It was no good, the harder she tried to hang onto it, the more resolutely it remained out of reach. The order slipped inexorably down behind the heavy oak sideboard of memory, and was lost before it had ever been consumed. 'Now look what you've done!' she said, stamping her foot. 'You've made me

Limbo II

forget the whole thing! I'll have to go back and start all over again.' She was about to return to Table 5, but Rex stopped her.

'Please, Matilda,' he said kindly. 'I'm really sorry I interrupted you, but I have to find Smeil; it's rather urgent.'

'Um, oh, that's all right,' she mumbled. 'I'm . . . sorry I shouted at you, but I only started this morning and I want to make a good impression, and . . .'

Behind her, at the far side of the restaurant, a door opened and an ashen-faced Smeil emerged.

'Never mind, I'm sure you'll make a fabulous impression. Remember all,' he said, passing a hand over her face.

Immediately she remembered everything: every single moment of her life from the moment she was born, with crystal clarity. It was too much. 'Ah!' She dropped to her knees and covered her face with her hands.

'Damn, too strong.' Rex helped the girl to her feet and waved his hand over her face again.

'What happened?' she asked, opening her eyes. She felt strangely light-headed and, looking round the room, everything seemed slightly out of focus.

'I think you were about to get Table 5's order,' said Rex, and hurried off to talk to Smeil.

The girl straightened her hair and frowned. Then she remembered: Table 5! That stupid man had made her forget everything. She tut-tutted crossly, and straightened her apron. But as she was about to go back and ask for their order again, a little flag dropped into her consciousness. Attached to it was an order: two espressos *con panna*; one *ristrétto*; one skinny cappuccino no chocolate; one vanilla *latte* with an extra shot; a marzipan *mocha* extreme; three almond croissants and two plain; and one goat's cheese, avocado and garlic sausage *panino*, with pickle. At the bottom of it someone had written: 'Sorry.' Puzzled, she walked slowly to the counter and repeated the order to the chef.

Meanwhile, Rex had raced over to Smeil and seized him by the shoulders. 'Where is she?'

The little man was beside himself, his bulging eyes focused on something far beyond this world. 'Too late!' he gasped. 'Too late! Oh, worthless, worthless, worthless.' And he beat his breast with his fists.

Rex shook him roughly. 'Smeil! Smeil! It's me – it's Rex. What happened?'

Smeil's eyes swivelled up to meet Rex's, 'AHH! NO!' he screamed, covering his face with his hands.

The coffee shop was almost full, and Smeil's strange behaviour was beginning to draw unwelcome attention. The last thing Rex needed now was for people to start asking awkward questions. Picking the little man up under one arm like a miniature roll of carpet, Rex walked smartly out of the coffee shop. Once out of sight of the restaurant, he opened the first door he came to, behind which there happened to be a large broom cupboard.

Stepping inside and barring the door with a heavy metal pail, Rex lowered Smeil to the ground and, crouching on one knee, looked him in the eye. 'Where's Iris?' he asked, urgently.

Slowly, Smeil's wandering eyes came to rest on the Wizard's face. He stared, unseeing, at Rex for some moments. Then, with a shuddering intake of breath, he seemed to come to his senses. His face crumpled, and tears began to flow down his cheeks. 'Oh, master,' he sobbed, collapsing against Rex and almost toppling him over. 'I'm a worthless, worthless, servant—'

'Smeil, where's the Queen?' Rex insisted, recovering his balance.

'Oh . . .' Smeil shook his head in despair, then threw back his head and howled. 'NOOOO!' In the confined space of the broom cupboard, the sound was deafening. 'I couldn't save her,' Smeil went on. 'No, that's not true; I didn't even try . . .' He broke down again. 'Oh, worthless, worthless . . .' Suddenly he grabbed the front of Rex's robe and pulled him close. 'I was so frightened,' he whispered. 'So . . . terribly frightened. And now they have her.'

Limbo II

Rex's stomach turned over, and although he already knew the answer, he forced himself to ask, 'Who has her?'

Smeil looked up at him with terrified eyes. 'The Horsemen,' he said in a pitiful, small voice. 'The Devil's own, come to life from the pages of that dreadful Book. I only just managed to escape myself. I went through into the shop at the appointed time, in order to bring her back, and there they were with Queen Iris in their midst. "Run, Smeil, run!" she called when she saw me and, may God forgive me, I did as I was bidden. They have our Queen, and there's nothing we can do about it.' Smeil dissolved once again into sobs.

'Yes, there is,' said Rex. 'Give me the Crystal.'

Smeil looked up at him in a torment of guilt and anguish. 'Ahh!' he cried, and fell to the ground, where he lay on his stomach, wailing and head-butting the floor repeatedly.

'Smeil, Smeil, stop it!' said Rex, pulling him upright. 'Now, come on, pull yourself together and give me the Crystal.'

Smeil looked up at the Wizard with frightened eyes. 'Master,' he whispered fearfully, 'I don't have it.'

'You . . . you don't have it? Where is it?'

'I . . . dropped it, as I was leaving.'

'You . . . you did what?' Rex stammered.

'Oh, master, I was so frightened and in such an agony of haste, it fell from my fingers as I leapt back through the portal.'

'You dropped it? NOOOO!' Rex roared. Without the Crystal it would be impossible to rescue Iris, to stop the Horsemen, to do *anything*. Rex grabbed the little man by the lapels and shook him like a rag doll. 'Smeil, you idiot! How could you have been so stupid!'

'I'm sorry, master. I am worthless. Worthless!'

Rex let him go and Smeil dropped to his knees. All the strength seemed to have left his body, and he could only just manage to beat himself half-heartedly with his knotted belt. Rex left him on the floor of the broom cupboard – a desolate figure in a small grey pool of despondency – and went off to break the news to Bernard.

Rex found him on the patio outside the royal apartments. 'Oh, don't worry about your mum,' he said. 'She can look after herself.' He was smiling, but his eyes were glistening.

Rex put an arm around him. 'Dad, I'm so sorry.'

Bernard pulled out a handkerchief and blew his nose. 'We'll just have to . . . we'll have to . . . Oh Rex . . .' He buried his face in Rex's shoulder and clung to him for a long moment. Then he straightened up and wiped his eyes. 'That's enough of that,' he said. 'Sorry, son.'

'No, Dad, that's—'

'We have to be positive,' Bernard continued. 'Start thinking about what we *can* do, rather than brooding on what we can't.'

'That's the spirit.'

'So, what *can* we do?'

'Well, we can keep searching for the lost fragment of the Book. That's what we have to do first, and . . . I'm certain we'll find it.' Rex tried to sound optimistic, but he knew Bernard wasn't buying it. 'If we can find the fragment, then at least we can . . . we can . . . well, we can . . .' he trailed off. Finding the fragment was hardly the main issue now.

'I know you'll do your best, son,' said Bernard, after a pause.

Rex wanted to reassure him – to tell him that it didn't matter he no longer had the Crystal, that he was in control, that he was the legendary Wizard of Limbo, and that somehow he would get through to rescue Iris and everything would be all right again. But both he and Bernard knew that, without the Crystal, Rex wasn't going anywhere.

Avoiding his eyes, Bernard patted Rex on the shoulder, then turned and walked slowly back towards the castle. As he went inside and slid the door closed behind him, a chill breeze raked the patio.

Rex shivered, he had never felt so alone in his entire life.

Chapter 19

Five pairs of eyes regarded the space where the little mouse-haired man had been.

'Did you see that?' said Mr Pink. 'He just vanished into thin air!'

Mr Pale growled, a low, room-trembling rumble. He turned on Iris. 'Wherrre Rexsss Boggsss?'

Iris stared back. She was terrified, but determined not to show it. She remembered Virginia McKenna in *Carve Her Name with Pride*, and her determination, when interrogated by her captors, to give nothing away except name, rank and number. 'My name is Iris Boggs, and that's all you're getting out of me,' she said, with only a hint of a tremor.

Mr Pale raised two naked phalanges in front of Iris's face. 'Wrong ansssswerrr,' he hissed.

'No need for that, Mr Pale,' Mr White intervened.

The skeleton that was Mr Pale turned his bony face on him, eye sockets blazing.

'If I'm not mistaken, this is Rex's mum. Am I right?' said Mr White.

Iris looked Mr White square in the eye. 'Like I said to this gentleman, my name is Iris Boggs, and that's all you're—'

'Yes, yes, very commendable – bravery under fire and all that sort of thing,' interrupted the hooded man. 'But out of place in the present circumstances.' Then he pushed back his cowl. He had neat grey hair and a nice face with warm twinkly eyes. He smiled, and not unkindly. 'You see, we don't want to hurt you. Do we, lads?' Mr Black and Mr Pink also removed their cowls and shook their heads vigorously. 'We want to be your friends, don't we?'

'Do we?' Mr Black frowned.

'Of course we do,' said Mr Pink, elbowing him in the ribs.

Mr Black winced. 'Oh, er . . . yeah. We're really very nice when you get to know us.'

Mr Pale snorted contemptuously.

Mr White put an arm around her, and Iris stiffened. 'So, why don't we all have a nice cup of tea?' he said.

While Mr Pink and Mr Black tidied away the Guptas' bodies and put the horses out of sight in the large concrete garage in the back yard, Mr Pale and Mr White took Iris upstairs.

Shutting her in the kitchen, they went into the living room to talk.

'Kill hherrr and riiide!' whispered Mr Pale.

'That's enough of that. There'll be plenty of time for you to enjoy yourself later. In the meantime, how are we supposed to spread plague, death, famine and war across the face of the earth with Rex Boggs still around to interfere with our plans? Do I have to remind you that it was he who thwarted us last time? By rewriting the Paradox and completely restructuring the universe, he hurled us across to the other side of the cosmos just as we were about to make our entrance. And he could do the same thing again. I don't know about you, but I don't want to wait another ten years in the wilderness. Rex Boggs is a powerful wizard, and until he is found and neutralized, we cannot act.'

'Whyyy nottt weee use the Boxsss?'

Mr White was emphatic. 'Absolutely not. You know as well as I do that would mean the end of us – of everything. No, the Box is an avenue of last resort, and besides, I've got a hunch if we just hang on to Iris, Rex will eventually turn up.'

Limbo II

'Howww sssooo?'

'If I'm not mistaken, that little dwarf who made a brief appearance is his servant, who by now will have run straight back to his master and told him what's happened. As the dutiful son he is, Rexie is going to be concerned about his mother's well-being and will come looking for her. Now – as long as she remains alive – she's rather useful to us. When we've got Rex within our grasp you can do what you like with her, but for the moment make her feel at home; be nice to her. Do I make myself clear?'

Mr Pale trembled with indignation, and let out a low growl that rattled the cut glass in the neo-Georgian display cabinet.

Meanwhile, Iris busied herself in the kitchen. Putting the kettle on, she tried desperately not to think about Mr and Mrs Gupta, lying on the floor downstairs in a pool of blood. The Guptas hadn't yet properly moved in so the kitchen was more or less as she'd left it, and the familiarity of the place, at least, was a comfort. As she warmed the pot, she remembered all the times she and Bernard had spent in this very kitchen.

Bernard! She'd been so concerned for herself, she'd forgotten all about him. Oh, the poor love, he'd be worried sick. She imagined him sitting at home waiting for her, wondering where on earth she was, and, for the first time, tears welled up in her eyes.

The kitchen door opened and Mr White stuck his head in. 'How's tea coming along?'

In spite of herself, Iris let out a long, shuddering sob. Mr White was instantly at her side.

'There, now. What's all this?' he said, putting an arm around her.

'Leave . . . me . . . alone,' she managed to gasp.

Mr White drew back. 'Of course. Nice cup of tea'll set you straight,' he said. 'Where do you keep your spoons?'

Iris pointed, wordlessly, to the drawer by the sink. Mr White pulled it open. 'Ah! Here we are,' He took one out and spooned tea into the pot, then picked up the boiling kettle and tipped it over the leaves.

'You know,' said Mr White, stirring the tea in the teapot, 'we really don't mean you any harm. We just want to have a word with your son, that's all.'

Iris turned on him, eyes blazing. 'Yes, and kill him just like you killed Mr and Mrs Gupta.'

Mr White stopped stirring and replaced the lid on the teapot, thoughtfully. 'Yes . . . I do apologize about that. Our Mr Pale has a very short fuse. I've told him about it before, but . . . well, it's his nature, you see.' Mr White took the cosy from the shelf above the toaster and placed it over the teapot. 'How strong do you like it?'

Iris didn't answer.

'Hmm, let me guess. Working woman, knows her own mind . . . I'd say you're a bit of a strong one, am I right?' Iris looked away. 'I knew it!' triumphed Mr White. 'And two sugars, yes?'

Iris slumped, holding onto the work surface for support.

Mr White regarded her sympathetically. 'Why don't you go next door and put your feet up,' he said. 'I'll bring your tea in when it's ready.'

Iris was a beaten woman – she was no Virginia McKenna. She couldn't hope to keep up her resistance against these men. She trudged miserably out of the kitchen and walked straight into Mr Pale. They stared at each other for a long moment while he did something strange with his lower mandible. He might have been attempting a smile, but it was hard to tell. Iris grunted and pushed past him into the living room, where she collapsed onto the sofa.

Chapter 20

Rex was standing at the window of his room, gazing gloomily at the far-distant Southern Range through the failing light. Although he usually enjoyed his own company, he found that he was feeling rather lonely. Perhaps he should get out and show himself to the people. Maybe they'd take comfort from seeing the Wizard in their midst, and anyway a coffee might help him to focus on what he should do next.

But the moment he walked into Smeil's Café, he realized his mistake. As he approached the counter, the other customers studiously avoided his eyes or turned their backs on him. *I shouldn't have come*, he thought. *They don't want to see me. From the looks I'm getting, they'd rather kill me.*

'Can I help you?' The girl behind the counter beamed – it was Matilda, the waitress whose order he'd nearly ruined earlier.

'Um, yes. A cappuccino, please. A big one,' Rex mumbled, 'to go.' Matilda moved away to prepare his order, and Rex was left at the counter, feeling alone and exposed and not at all powerful and important like a wizard was supposed to feel.

He remembered how proud he'd felt when he'd first arrived here, and how excited he'd been to learn that he was Prince Harmony, rightful heir to the throne of Limbo. As a child he'd always suspected that he was much, much more than the son of a Lancing newsagent, and was sure that one day his real parents would come for him and tell him he was the prince of some far-off, magical land. And that's exactly what had happened. But he had the suspicion that underneath he'd remained boring old Rex Boggs, of Boggs' Newsagent's. Was this the same man who had saved the universe, fought monsters and banished dragons? He found it all so hard to believe now. He was tired and frightened, and desperately wanted Iris's warm, loving arms around him. *Oh, Mum, where are you?* he thought miserably, and silent tears began to roll down his cheeks.

'There we are. One *grande* cappuccino.' Matilda handed him the big cardboard cup. Rex sniffed his thanks and, wiping his eyes with the back of his hand, moved over to where the sugar, spoons and various toppings were kept on a small table at the end of the counter. Thin, slanting rays of sunlight sliced through the tall arched windows, illuminating a million billowing dust particles as Rex, alone at the small stand, listlessly spooned sugar into the oversized cup.

'Um, I don't mean to intrude . . .'

Rex looked up. It was Matilda. 'Yes?' he snuffled.

'I couldn't help noticing; you look rather sad.'

Rex nodded.

'Now, stop me if I'm talking out of turn, but, what do they say? A problem aired is a problem shared . . . or something like that. So what is it, hmm? Tell Matilda all.'

Rex looked at the young woman's open face in amazement. 'The sun is setting and it's all my fault,' he said.

'Don't be so silly!' She laughed. Tenderly taking his hand, she looked earnestly into his face. 'How can you be to blame for the sun going down?'

'Don't you know?' Rex asked, incredulously.

'Know what?'

'I'm the Wizard of Limbo!'

Matilda turned bright scarlet and backed slowly away, covered in confusion. 'Oh, I'm so sorry. I had no idea. I'm new here, you see, and . . . Oh, I feel such a fool – I'm always doing things like this. Forgive me, your highness . . . er . . . your worship . . . er . . . I'll leave you in peace. Sorry.' She turned and walked away.

Limbo II

'That's right,' said Rex, bitterly. 'You don't want to be seen talking to me.'

The young waitress froze for a moment, then spun round to face him. 'Now look here,' she said sternly. 'You could be Lord God Almighty for all I care. I was just trying to be nice to someone who looked as though they were having a rough time. There's no need to be nasty!'

'I'm sorry,' said Rex. 'I'm not usually ... It's been a bit of a day.'

Matilda softened, and nodded sympathetically. 'Do you want me to go?' she asked.

Rex shook his head. 'No, please. Would you like a coffee?'

'No thanks – I'm up to my eyeballs. Working in this place it's all I seem to drink.' She lapsed into silence. Rex picked up the chocolate shaker and almost emptied it onto the milky froth of his coffee. 'Do you know?' she said after a while. 'I thought you were upset because your girlfriend had left you, or something like that.'

'No, it's ... nothing like that,' Rex said.

'Matilda?' Smeil was standing behind her. 'Matilda, you're not bothering the Wizard, are you?'

'It's all right, Smeil,' said Rex. 'I asked her to join me.'

'Oh, right.' The little man hovered nervously, looking around the room. 'That's all right, then. Er ... hmm.'

'Sorry, Matilda,' said Rex. 'I think your boss wants a word with me in private.'

'It was nice talking to you,' Matilda said. 'And don't worry. I don't blame you for any of this. Cheer up.' She leant forward to kiss him, and as her lips brushed his cheek, her fragrance seemed to wrap itself around Rex's senses. Turning, she looked down at Smeil. 'You only had to ask,' she said firmly, and walked away, leaving both Rex and Smeil a little shaken, although they weren't altogether sure why.

'What is it, my friend?' Rex asked.

'I do hope she wasn't troubling you, master, but she's new.'

'No, no. I . . . er . . . She's nice.'

'Yes, I like her too. Er . . . that is, she's very good at her job.' Smeil blushed. 'Master, I have bad news,' he hissed, rapidly changing the subject. 'We can't find it! Not one scrap of the Book have we found.'

'Oh, that's *just* what I needed to hear.' Rex moaned.

'Are you sure that it exists?'

'I'm sure, Smeil. I wish I weren't.'

'But we've looked everywhere. We've virtually taken the town apart.'

'It must be out there somewhere. Why else would my book be rewriting itself? You've got to keep looking, Smeil. We can't stop any of this until it's found.'

'But there's nowhere left to look, master. We've searched under every floorboard, in every cupboard, drawer, wall, loft, lavatory, midden. It's just not there!'

'Have you looked in the old basements under the castle?'

Smeil nodded.

'The dungeons?'

Smeil nodded again.

'What about all those secret tunnels this place is riddled with?'

'As many as we could find, sir.'

'What about the ones you couldn't find?'

Smeil looked at him levelly.

'I take your point.' Rex hung his head miserably. 'Oh God,' he groaned.

'I'm sorry, master, but I don't know what more I can do.'

Rex looked down at his diminutive servant. 'You can get me a large brandy to go with this coffee.'

Chapter 21

Iris was sitting miserably on the sofa in the living room above her old Lancing shop.

'Here we are, Iris,' said Mr White, appearing with a cup of tea and a plate of biscuits. 'I had you pegged for a custard cream fan. Am I right?' he said, carefully placing the teacup and plate on a small side table.

'Not hungry,' Iris muttered.

Mr White sat down next to her and patted her knee. 'Come along now, Iris. You can't keep this up forever. I'd like to be your friend, I really would, but if you're going to be a sulky girl, then you're going to make me cross, and we don't want that to happen, now do we?'

'S'pose not,' Iris murmured.

'Good,' said Mr White. 'Now, drink your tea.'

Iris obediently picked up her cup and took a sip.

'That's better,' said Mr White.

Mr Black stuck his head through the door. 'Er, can we have a word, boss?'

Mr White stood up. 'I'll only be a minute, Iris, and when I come back, I want to see all those biscuits eaten, all right?'

Iris nodded glumly.

'Good girl.' Mr White followed Mr Black out of the room, closing the door behind him.

In the small corridor between the living room and the kitchen, Mr White turned to face Mr Black and Mr Pink. 'What is it?'

'What do you want done with the bodies?' asked Mr Black.

'Where are they now?'

'Out the back, but they can't stay there forever.'

'We rolled them up in that awful lino they had in the stock room,' said Mr Pink. 'I mean, black on brown, how Seventies can you get?'

'Hmm,' pondered Mr White. 'We need to call a meeting. Where's Mr Pale?'

There was a gust of icy wind and Mr Pale appeared in the kitchen doorway. Mr White jumped. 'Please, Mr Pale,' he said, 'don't creep up on me like that.'

'Ssssorrryyy,' the deathly figure hissed.

'Now,' Mr White continued, 'we need to discuss our plan of attack.'

'Ahhhtaaahhhck!' Mr Pale breathed.

'Don't get too excited, Mr Pale. Remember, before we embark upon our scorched earth policy, we've got Rex Boggs to sort out. Meanwhile, I need your views on how we proceed. For example, do we stay here or find somewhere else? Mr Black?'

'Well, boss, seems to me staying here's our only option. But that means we got to get rid of the bodies; we can't have them lying around smelling up the shop.'

Mr White wrinkled his nose in disgust. 'Thank you for that. Mr Pink?'

'I think we should get out of here as soon as possible. We're the Four Horsemen of the Apocalypse; what do we know about running a newsagent's?'

'Point noted. Mr Pale?'

'Weee mooove, how Rexsss Boggsss find usss?'

'That's a very good question, and as we can do little while he lives, it makes sense to me that we wait for him here.'

Mr Black and Mr Pale nodded.

'Good, then it's agreed. We stay put.'

Mr Pink snorted his disapproval.

Limbo II

'But,' continued Mr White, 'as Mr Pink pointed out, we know nothing about running a retail outlet, so I suggest we curtail trading. Mr Pink, make sure everything is locked up downstairs, and put a note on the door: "Closed until further notice", or something like that. We don't want people snooping around. Our next task,' Mr White glanced pointedly at Mr Pale, 'is to dispose of the bodies. Mr Pink and Mr Black, I'm putting you in charge of that.'

'Whoopee,' said Mr Pink, without enthusiasm.

'Be discreet, and try to find a place where they won't be discovered. We shouldn't have to wait here long, but it would be politic to err on the side of caution. The last thing we need is people interfering and complicating matters. I'll stay here and keep an eye on Iris, and you . . .' he said, addressing Mr Pale, 'just keep out of sight of the neighbours.'

Rex moped unhappily through the castle gates and out into the huddled little town, now turned a burnished russet by the golden rays of the dying sun. Wherever he walked, people avoided his eyes, and he sensed their unspoken reproach.

Who can blame them? he thought. *If I was in their shoes I'd feel exactly the same. They've been landed with a useless wizard who's managed to lose the one thing that gave him the illusion of power.*

Head bowed, he saw a pebble at his feet and, without thinking, kicked it as hard as he could. It flew through the air, and a moment later there was the sound of breaking glass.

'Oi!' Rex looked up. A heavily built man was glaring at him through a broken windowpane. 'You wanker!' the man yelled angrily. 'Haven't you done enough?'

Other faces appeared at other windows and, when they saw who it was, joined in.

'Call yourself a wizard?' said one.

'If you were a *real* wizard you'd do something!' said another.

'Bring back the last one; at least he *looked* like a wizard!'

'Yeah! He had a hat and everything!'

A red-faced man appeared in Rex's path. 'My mum and dad died in the Great Terror!' he said. 'Did they die for nothing?'

Rex looked at him. 'I'm sorry, I really am,' he said, helplessly.

'Sorry's not going to bring them back, is it?' And before Rex could get out of the way, the man's fist slammed into his face, and he found himself sprawling on the ground, stars before his eyes and blood pouring from his nose.

The man danced over him. 'Get up!' he exhorted. 'I want to hit you again! Come on, get up and fight like a man!' Several youths, attracted by the prospect of a fight, gathered round, but seeing their once-revered Wizard scrabbling pathetically in the dust, holding his nose and moaning wretchedly, turned away in embarrassment.

'You're not worth it,' the man spat, and Rex was left bleeding in the dirt.

He lay there for some moments, listening to the sound of footsteps and slamming doors as everyone went back to their homes. Then, when the street was deserted, he got slowly to his feet and trudged miserably away.

He walked – head down, consumed by dark thoughts – for some time, and when at last he raised his eyes, had no idea where he was. The dusty track along which he trudged stretched to the horizon in both directions, and on either side, vast fields of barley waved gently in the breeze. The setting reminded him of Van Gogh's desolate wheat field and, for a moment, he too considered ending it all. But luckily he didn't possess a gun. *Knowing my luck, I'd probably miss anyway*, he thought.

He was about to turn back when above him he heard a *caw* and, looking up, saw a large black crow circling overhead. But as he watched the big bird effortlessly riding the unseen air currents, something strange happened. It stopped and hung there, motionless. He'd never seen a crow do that before. Kestrels, yes – they were always hovering above motorway verges, looking for mice or voles,

Limbo II

or some other hapless small furry creature. But with a kestrel you could always see a slight movement: a small adjustment of the wing or tail to maintain height or keep its head to the wind. By contrast, this crow was absolutely still. What was keeping it up? Why didn't it just tumble out of the sky?

Rex looked back at the barley fields, and understanding dawned. The barley too was rock-still. Searching the great expanse of frozen gold, he looked for something familiar yet out of place, and there, a little way up the road, he saw it: a small caravan with a red and white striped awning waving gently in a non-existent breeze. Rex smiled and walked towards it.

Chapter 22

Detective Sergeant Ivey, newly appointed to Brighton CID, hadn't had a good night. In the dark, worrying hours before dawn, he'd been troubled by a dream about a blazing misshapen castle besieged by a bloodthirsty mob shouting, 'Kill the Wizard! Rip out his toenails! Disembowel him!' He was tired and upset, and what he was looking at now wasn't helping his acid stomach one bit.

It wasn't a pretty sight. The two bodies lay on the river bank, on the roll of lino in which they'd been wrapped. They'd been stuffed into the storm drain which emptied into a small rill behind Ferring Beach car park. The night before there had been a particularly high tide, and that, coupled with a heavy fall of rain around dawn, had conspired to wash them half into the stream, where they'd been found by a man walking his dog.

Detective Chief Inspector Beasely got out of his car and scrunched across the gravel towards where his sergeant stood on the river bank – a still point amongst the milling crowd of police and forensic officers. 'Good morning, Sergeant,' he said.

'Morning sir,' Ivey replied, thickly.

'Who have we got here, then?'

'Two dead people, sir.'

DCI Beasley sighed. *He's new,* he thought to himself. *Give him a chance.* 'I can see that, Ivey,' he said patiently. 'What I'm after is their names.'

'Oh, right sir,' said Ivey, flatly.

'Well?'

'Well what, sir?'
'Who are they?'
'No idea, sir.'

Beasley closed his eyes and counted to ten. 'Albert!' he yelled to a round, red-faced man who seemed to be in charge of the forensics operation.

The man puffed across to where Beasley and Ivey stood. 'Good morning, Chief Inspector.'

'What have we got here, then?'

'A nasty business. A man and a woman, probably around their mid-sixties. As to the man, I won't be certain until I get him back to the lab, but the woman seems to have had a thin, sharp object pushed through her eye and into the brain — with some force. As you can see, particles of bone and vitreous humour are protruding from the eye socket—'

Ivey retched.

Beasley and Albert both turned to look at him.

'Sorry.'

'And there was nothing on the bodies? We have no idea who they are?' Beasley enquired.

'That's your job, Chief Inspector. I am merely the condemned meat inspector; identification I leave to you.' He indicated a plastic bag leaning against the dead woman's leg. 'I put all their belongings in there. I assumed your sergeant would have sifted through them for you.'

'Time of death?'

'It's hard to tell because of the effects of the water, but from first impressions I'd say they've been dead for around twenty-four hours. I should be able to be a little more precise once I've given them a thorough examination. I'll get a report to you as soon as I can.'

'Thanks, Albert.'

'Not at all.' The rotund man waddled away.

Beasley pulled a packet of chewing gum out of his pocket and unwrapped a stick. He turned slowly and looked into the pale face of his sergeant, then down at the plastic bag next to the bodies. 'Ivey,' he said quietly, 'you have been through their belongings, haven't you?'

Ivey flushed. 'Well, I didn't like to, sir.'

'Didn't like to?'

'Yeah, I mean . . . Well, they're dead, aren't they? It's a bit creepy, isn't it?'

Beasley bit down hard on the stick of gum. 'Sometimes in this life, we have to do things that we don't like – unpleasant things – like searching through dead people's belongings. Or having to cope with you as a sergeant.'

Ivey frowned.

'Search their belongings, Ivey, or leave the force and do something more suited to your temperament – like macramé.'

'Right, sir.'

Ivey crouched down and, with obvious distaste, started going through the contents of the small plastic bag. Almost immediately he found an item he deemed important. 'Here's something, sir!' he yelled, holding up a damp leather wallet between his forefinger and thumb.

'Give it here.' Beasley opened it. To his surprise, he found the wallet stuffed with cash. 'There's a turn-up,' he muttered. Pulling out a credit card, he read the name: 'Wasim Gupta.' Beasley looked down at the dead woman. 'And I think we can safely assume that this is Mrs Gupta.' Beasley turned to Ivey and smiled. 'That wasn't so hard, was it? Now then, what else can we assume from the contents of Mr Gupta's wallet?'

Ivey looked troubled. 'What's macramé, sir?'

'Never mind,' Beasley said. 'Just think. What does this wallet full of cash suggest to you?'

Ivey thought for a long time. 'It means he was rich, sir,' he said at last.

Beasley struggled hard to maintain his façade of bonhomie. *He's*

Limbo II

new, he's new, he's new, he repeated to himself. 'Yes, very good, sergeant.' He smiled. 'The man was obviously not short of a bob or two, but what else does it tell us, eh?'

Ivey fell silent, and Beasely studied him closely. The sergeant's small features were huddled together in the middle of his face as if frightened by the large expanse of his cheeks, giving him the look of a King Charles spaniel. He had only two expressions: open and friendly, or completely blank; and it was the latter he was now wearing.

Beasely sighed. To save himself from having to stand on the river bank all day, waiting for Sergeant Ivey to frame some sort of a reply, the detective chief inspector answered his own question. 'It means that money obviously wasn't the motive for this murder.'

Ivey slapped his forehead. 'That's brilliant, sir,' he said. 'Do you know, that would never have occurred to me.'

Beasley pursed his lips. 'So,' he continued, 'if money wasn't the motive, what was? These unfortunate people were of Asian origin, so perhaps it could have been racial.'

'Racial! Yes, yes, I see! That makes perfect sense! I see it all now!' Ivey said excitedly. 'So, we're looking for a bunch of racists, then?'

'No, Sergeant, that's not what I said.'

'Ah,' said Ivey inscrutably, 'so this whole race thing could be just a red herring? Whoever did this was clever – damn clever.'

Beasley closed his eyes and breathed deeply. 'I know you're new to detective work, Ivey, but try to stay with me. Mr Gupta's wallet was full, which leads me to conclude that we are looking for a motive other than robbery for the deaths of these two people, and, at the moment, that's as far as it goes, OK?'

Ivey opened his mouth to speak, but thought better of it. This deductive work was all so new and exciting. There was so much to learn.

'Chief!' called one of the officers. 'I think you should see this!'

Beasley and Ivey went over to where the constable was – on his hands and knees in the soft ground below the river bank.

'Look, sir. Hoof prints.'

Beasley crouched for a better view. The ground was deeply imprinted, and a trail led away from the river towards a group of neat seaside bungalows, no more than thirty yards distant.

'Is this a bridleway?' Beasley asked the constable.

'No, sir, it doesn't actually go anywhere. If people want to ride, they go up around Cissbury. They don't come down here; this is a residential area.'

Beasley stood and looked towards the cluster of green-and-pink-roofed bungalows.

'The trail seems to peter out amongst the houses,' the constable continued. 'They probably nipped through the gardens there and went back along the road.'

'They?'

'I'm no expert, but it looks to me like two horses.'

'Why use horses?' Beasley wondered aloud.

'Maybe they couldn't afford a taxi,' Ivey said.

Beasley grimaced, as if suffering from a painful bout of indigestion. 'Good work, Constable.' He turned back to his sergeant. 'Ivey, get on to all the local riding schools. I want a list of everybody who has hired a horse in the last few days. I also want to know if that list includes anybody not previously known to them.'

Ivey stared at Beasely and screwed up his eyes as if in pain.

'Are you all right, Sergeant?'

'Could you repeat the question, sir?'

'Sorry?'

'You lost me with all that stuff about riding schools and lists and things.'

Beasely ground his teeth and snorted. 'Phone the local stables,' he said slowly, 'and ask if anyone they don't know has tried to hire a horse recently. OK?'

'Oh, right, sir.'

Limbo II

'Then, see what you can find out about the Guptas,' Beasley said, handing back the sodden wallet.

'Who, sir?'

Beasley reached instinctively into his pocket for the reassuring feel of a cigarette packet but found no comfort there. He hadn't smoked for years, but he could have murdered a cigarette at that moment. Murdering his sergeant would have been equally satisfying.

'Sergeant,' he said in a whisper, 'the Guptas are the two people lying on the bank over there. At the moment all we have is a name. It would be nice to know something more about them: for instance, where they lived, so that we can talk to their neighbours or perhaps inform their relatives of their demise. Do you understand?'

Ivey smiled. 'I'm with you, sir.'

Beasley shook his head. 'I wish to God you weren't,' he muttered as he walked away.

Chapter 23

Mr White was puzzled. Where was Rex? There could be no doubt he knew about Iris's situation, and must, therefore, either be playing it very cool or totally indifferent to her plight. But that didn't fit the image of a selfless, universe-saving cavalier. It was odd. However, they couldn't move until Rex was out of the way, so they would have to continue to wait for him. In the meantime, Mr White was doing his best to keep Iris sweet.

'Tell you what,' he said to her one morning, as she was busy making her breakfast. 'Why don't you cook us all a nice meal? I'm sure you're a bit of a whizz in the kitchen.'

'No, I'm not,' she replied emphatically, opening a carton of milk and pouring it over her cornflakes. 'Bernard used to do all the cooking; I can't cook to save my life.' She stopped suddenly in mid-pour as she realized, with a shock, what she'd just said.

Mr White smiled. 'It shouldn't come to that,' he said, taking the milk carton out of her trembling hand and placing it on the work surface. 'I just thought some good old-fashioned home cooking would give us all a bit of a boost. Shall we have a look in the freezer?' Mr White opened the door and peered into its arctic interior. Thrusting an arm into its frosty depths, he pulled out a plastic bag full of anonymous lumps of meat. Wiping the rime from the label with his finger, he held the bag at arm's length and squinted at the writing. 'Oh, what does it say? Iris, you'll have to help me out here.'

'Just a minute,' she said, going to her handbag, which was on the worktop above the dishwasher. Opening it, she took out her reading glasses, but her hands were still shaking so she had difficulty putting them on.

'Allow me,' Mr White said, gently taking them from her. 'May I?' Iris nodded, and Mr White put them on himself. 'Now then,' he said, holding the label up to the light. 'Er . . . oh dear, I think it says veal,' he said. 'That won't do for Mr Pink; he's very hot on animal rights.' He put the meat back in the freezer and yanked out another rock-hard plastic bag. 'What have we here?' he said, studying its label. 'Aha! Steak and kidney! Now then.' He closed the freezer door, and opening the cupboard above the sink drainer, searched through its contents. 'There is always one in every kitchen – an old, forgotten packet of . . . Yes!' He pulled out an ancient box of suet. 'I can feel a steak and kidney pudding coming on.'

'Really, I can't,' Iris muttered, close to tears.

Looking down at the poor, frightened woman, with her big eyes and neatly permed hair, for the first time in his life, Mr White felt something approaching affection. He put an arm around her. 'Of course you can,' he said. 'Tell you what. Tonight, we'll open a bottle of wine and let our hair down – get to know each other a little better. What do you say?'

'You won't like it.' Iris sniffed.

Rex pushed through the softly swaying bead curtain of the caravan with the candy-striped awning and heard a familiar wheezing chuckle. In front of him, seated at a small card table, was what appeared at first to be nothing more than a bundle of rags, but closer inspection revealed a pair of eyes as black as coal with the hard brilliance of diamonds.

'Tumbril,' said Rex.

'Well, well, you remember old Tumbril. I'm touched, really I am,' said the old crone in a cracked voice.

'I'm in trouble, Tumbril,' said Rex, slumping in the chair opposite her.

'That's why I'm here, dear – thought I'd come and give you a bit of a fillip. Give me your hands.'

Rex laid them, palms up, on the green baize of the small table, and Tumbril studied them closely, tracing the lines with one stubby finger. 'You have lost yourself,' she wheezed, looking into his eyes. Rex felt himself pinned to his seat by her gaze, and had the strangest sensation that he was being examined from the inside out. She leaned closer. 'You have mislaid a gem beyond price, and it has closed your heart. But you have forgotten who you are. It's simple: recover yourself and you will recover the gem.' She smiled, and her dark eyes twinkled. 'Limbo's not like the world you come from. She lives and breathes and keeps her memories still. Listen to her secrets, but take heed, for a closed heart cannot hear.'

She settled back in her chair with a sigh. Her eyes closed, her jaw dropped slackly open and her head lolled back. She stayed like this – motionless and hardly breathing – for several moments. In her untidily gaping mouth, Rex could see the blackened stumps of what might once have been teeth but which now looked more like the jagged remnants of an ancient stone circle. He wondered, idly, if anyone had ever tried to count them.

'Look up, look up,' said Tumbril suddenly, making Rex jump. 'There is the answer: two suns setting over the sea. The barrel of the smoking gun points the way. Two heads, not one – two! A man with a woven crown – he has his hands on the power. He will take you to the line of gold! The line of— Ahh!' She collapsed back again. Rex waited, hoping for more revelations, but after a while she began to snore.

Rex coughed politely and Tumbril groggily raised her head. 'Is that it?' he demanded.

Tumbril opened an eye. 'What do you want,' she wheezed, 'an instruction manual?'

'But none of it makes any sense.'

Limbo II

Tumbril smiled darkly. 'Have you heard nothing? You are trying to grasp it with your mind. Listen with your heart.'

'But it's all nonsense. What am I supposed to do with: *The barrel of the smoking gun points the way to the line of gold, the line of—Ahhh!*' he said, imitating her.

'Now listen to me, young Rex Boggs,' Tumbril replied, her dark eyes flashing. 'I wasn't going to say nothing, you being so upset about Iris and all, but you brought this on yourself.'

'What do you mean?'

'You shouldn't have tampered. You shouldn't have messed with the rules of creation. You should never have rewrote the Paradox. The laws that govern the universe wasn't written for people to go changing them all over the place; the machinery ain't up to it. The Hoop can't stand the strain.'

'But I rewrote the Paradox to ease the strain.'

'You shouldn't have tampered, that's all I'm saying.'

'So, what can I do?'

'I think you've done enough already. What was your father's favourite saying: *Che sara sara?* What will be, will be. You think you're in control? Think again. Stop resisting. You're Destiny's fool. Let go and trust to your fate. *Trust*, Rex.' Tumbril looked at her watch. 'And now, your session's over.'

'But—'

'And before you calls on old Tumbril again, bear this in mind: the first two consultations you gets free; after that you must pay.'

'But I never called—'

'Have a nice day!' Tumbril twinkled, and suddenly Rex was back on the dusty track, surrounded by nothing but fields of waving barley as far as the eye could see.

Chapter 24

Sergeant Ivey, his face crumpled into a frown, stuck his head around Beasley's door. 'Sir?' he began.

Beasley looked up from his desk. 'What is it, Sergeant?'

'There's something puzzling about this Gupta case, sir.'

'Something puzzling *you*, Ivey? That must be a first.'

'Sorry, sir?'

'What is it, Sergeant?'

'Well,' Ivey began, 'I've been doing some asking around – you know, making enquiries – and something that keeps coming up is the horses.'

'Yes,' Beasley sighed, 'we already know about the horses. We found the hoof prints.'

'Yes, sir, but it's the colour of them that's the puzzling bit.'

'The colour?' Beasley said.

'Yes, sir. It seems they were all different colours.'

Beasley leaned back in his chair. 'Go on.'

'Well,' Ivey pulled out his notebook, 'a constable I spoke to remembers seeing four horses crossing the A27, near the turn-off to Lancing.'

'*Four* horses?'

'That's what he said, sir.' Ivey found the relevant place in his notebook. 'He said that one of the horses was black, one was white, one pink, and one . . . Well, he couldn't quite describe what colour it was, but he said it was sort of . . . pale.'

'Four horses?' Beasley said again. 'And the riders?'

Limbo II

'Er . . .' Ivey consulted his notes again. 'Men in cowls, sir. Quite a few people I spoke to subsequently had also seen them. They said they hadn't mentioned it before because it's Halloween and . . . well, people usually do dress up in some daft things around this time, don't they?'

'Yes, Ivey, they do, but they don't usually murder people as well.' Beasley opened his desk drawer and pulled out a stick of chewing gum. 'Did you get on to the stables?'

'Yes, sir. None of them reported being approached by anyone they didn't know, and anyway most of the stables I spoke to have a policy of never hiring out horses to strangers.'

'*Four* horses,' Beasley repeated. 'What about the Guptas – have you got an address yet?'

'Yes, sir.'

'Since when?'

'Since lunchtime.'

'Why didn't you tell me?'

'You didn't ask me.'

Beasley clenched his fists in mute fury. 'Come on, Sergeant,' he said, standing up.

'Where are we going, sir?' Ivey asked.

Beasley looked at him incredulously. 'We're going to ride the dodgems on Brighton Pier; where do you think we're going?'

'Oughtn't we better go and try the Guptas' address first, sir?'

Beasely smiled. 'Go and get a car, Ivey, and meet me outside,' he said, unnaturally calm.

'Right, sir.'

Once Ivey had left the room, Beasley let go a scream of frustration which had heads appearing out of every door along the corridor. In answer to their enquiring glances, Ivey shrugged with a 'Search me' gesture as he headed towards the car park.

*

Iris shuffled disconsolately out of the kitchen and into the living room, where the Four Horsemen were enjoying an aperitif. 'It's ready if you are,' she announced despondently.

'Jolly good,' said Mr White. 'I'm starved.' Putting his sherry glass down on the mantelpiece, he cheerily led the way into the tiny dining room, where the table was neatly laid for five.

'I laid it for five, though I wasn't sure about . . .' She nodded in Mr Pale's direction.

'Oh, he'll have a pick at something, won't you, Mr Pale?'

Mr Pale glared malevolently at Mr White, and sat down.

'We've never had five around this table before,' said Iris. 'It'll be a bit of a squeeze,' she added glumly.

'We'll manage, I'm sure,' said Mr White, 'although we may not all be able to fit back through the door once we've eaten.' He laughed.

'You just wait,' said Iris mirthlessly. She sighed and tramped out of the room, returning several moments later with a large platter which she placed in the centre of the table. 'There we are,' she said.

Mr White leaned forward to examine what had appeared in front of him. It resembled a small grey hat, collapsed on one side, with, here and there, paler patches that looked unappetizingly like flaccid white skin. From its sunken crown oozed a dark and glutinous liquid that dribbled down onto the platter, collecting in a rapidly congealing pool on the unwarmed china. The whole was surrounded by a cordon of what could once have been potatoes but now looked like small, black pebbles. They were smoking slightly, and had an acrid smell not unlike cordite.

'Ah,' said Mr White, his appetite suddenly deserting him.

'Told you,' said Iris, slumping into her seat. 'I found the spuds in the back of the fridge, so God knows how old they are. Shall I dish up?'

'Mm,' said Mr White. 'It looks . . . mm.' Gritting his teeth, he lifted his plate and passed it down to Iris. She spooned a glob of the suety mess onto it.

'Spuds?' she asked.

'Ooh, just a couple.'

She clunked several of the rock-hard potatoes onto his plate and passed it back to him. When everyone was served, Mr White looked up at the horror-stricken faces around the table. 'Well, let's, ah . . . Shall I open the wine?' He seized the bottle gratefully and extracted the cork, taking a very long time to fill everyone's glass. After proposing a toast to the chef, he could delay the moment of truth no longer. 'Let's . . . tuck in,' he said.

After a stomach-churning twenty minutes during which they slowly worked their way through jaw-breaking potatoes, suet pastry that somehow conspired to be burnt and undercooked at the same time, stringy beef and gobs of gristly offal, the company sat back, exhausted.

'Well,' said Mr White, 'I'm sure we'd all like to thank Iris for this, er . . . meal, and to show our appreciation, perhaps next time we could persuade her to let *us* do the cooking.' There was enthusiastic agreement from around the table. 'And now, if you'll excuse me, I think I'm going to be sick.'

Chapter 25

Frink was swimming – out of sight of land – in a vast sea into which a yellow-orange sun was slowly setting. It seemed that he had been swimming for a long, long time, and he was mightily tired. He knew his death would only be a matter of time, and as his strength failed and the water closed over his head, images of Mike's smiling face swam into his drowning consciousness...

He opened his eyes suddenly. The air was full of strange mutterings and moanings and, although it was dark, he could make out dusty patterns of flowers and fruit on the cornice high above him. As he gradually came to, he became dimly aware that he was not alone. Raising his head from the pillow with some effort, he looked around. He was in a big room containing upwards of twenty beds. At one end of the large ward was a set of double doors, and at the other a dark, floor-length curtain.

The rough hospital blanket tickled Frink's chin and, as he raised his hand to scratch, he realized he'd been shaved. Running a hand over his head, he also found that – apart from the odd plaster where Mike had nicked him with the cut-throat razor – he was completely bald.

Well, he consoled himself, *if ever I manage to escape from here, at least no one will recognize me.*

The situation was grave and, as his brain slowly dragged itself out of the drugged coma into which it had been plunged, the reality of how utterly hopeless his position was began to filter through to

Limbo II

his dulled senses, first in a trickle, then a raging torrent. He was gripped with panic.

'Bad! Bad! Bad!' Frink berated himself through clenched teeth. How could he have been so stupid? He slapped himself, weakly, on both cheeks, then lay still and tried to calm his mind. What did he do now? He had been severely shaken by his ordeal, but his innate sense of responsibility overcame the feelings of self-pity which might otherwise have taken hold of him. He hadn't come all this way to be defeated now. The only hope for this planet was for Frink to deliver his message to those who would listen.

He was about to get up and start exploring avenues of escape when he heard the *thumpa-thumpa-thumpa* of the double swing doors as someone came into the ward. He lay back and closed his eyes, pretending to be asleep. Two sets of footsteps squeaked towards him across the shiny lino, and paused on either side of his bed.

'How much did she give him?' It was Mike's voice.

'She's overdone it, hasn't she?' said Terry. 'He's been out for nearly two days now.'

Frink felt a hand on his shoulder, and he was shaken, roughly.

'Well, it's not our problem,' said Mike. 'Anyway, no one's claimed him. If he never wakes up, who's going to care?'

'Yeah!' One of the men chuckled softly, then Frink heard them squeak back out of the ward. As the sound of the swing doors died away, Frink found himself assailed once more by rising panic and the strange moanings and mutterings of the unfortunates with whom he shared his accommodation.

'Two days?' Frink gasped. There was no time to lose. He had to do something *now*.

Soundlessly pushing back the bed covers, he swung his legs over the side of the bed and forced himself to his feet. In the dim light, Frink could just make out that the curtain at the end of the ward was moving slightly in a breeze. A window! Staggering past the rows of snoring patients, he reached the drape and pushed it aside. The window was open but protected by sturdy iron bars.

'Dammit,' he muttered. Then, surveying the extensive moonlit lawns in front of the home, a thought occurred to him. He may not be able to escape, but he might at least be able to determine where exactly the energy field of evil was going to land, or indeed if it had already arrived.

Tiptoeing back up the ward, he peeked through the long, narrow, reinforced window set into one of the swing doors. Beyond, a burly male nurse sat at a desk, thumbing through the pages of *Exchange and Mart*.

'Dammit!' Frink muttered again. He would need help. Creeping back to the far window and making sure his face was illuminated by the bright moon, he addressed his left index finger.

'Please excuse my appearance,' he whispered, 'but I have been kidnapped and had all my bodily hair removed. For the last two days I have been held captive in hellish conditions. I have no idea what plans my captors have for me but, from the way I have been treated so far, I have no alternative but to assume that their intentions are hostile. Escape must be my priority if I am to survive, but fear not, survive I will. After all, am I not a son of Thrripp? Does not the blood of my ancestors flow fiercely in my veins? Failure is something with which I shall have no intercourse. The next time I talk to you, I shall either have escaped or died trying.' The sense – or lack of it – in his last statement could be attributed to Frink's long, drug-induced sleep, but the message of defiance would be clear enough to his audience. There was no time now to check over what he had just recorded; he simply unfurled his pink fleshy antennae, and sent his bulletin out into space.

'Now,' he said, looking out of the window, 'let's see.' Without retracting his antennae, he aimed them through the cast-iron bars, and broadcast his thoughts to the night . . .

Gradually they came, one at a time at first, then in their hundreds and thousands: spiders, pouring in over the window sill and crawling and creeping across the floor, turning it into a living carpet.

Limbo II

Frink crouched down amongst them. *Right men*, he thought, *listen carefully* . . .

After a short while, the spiders departed, scurrying over themselves in their haste to get back through the open window. By the light of the moon, on the large lawn outside, they began to spin . . .

Chapter 26

'Myyy trickkk,' breathed Mr Pale, reaching across the table and picking up the cards. Holding them between forefinger and thumb, he glared at them – and they burst into flames.

'Oh, please,' said Mr Pink. 'We're going to have no cards left.'

Mr Pale laid another card on the table and looked up at Mr Pink. 'Yourrr turrrnnn . . .'

Mr Pink sighed and studied the cards in his hand. 'There,' he said, throwing his jack of diamonds onto Mr Pale's ace of spades.

'Why didn't you trump him with your king?' asked Mr Black, looking over his shoulder.

'Do you mind!' snapped Mr Pink. 'It's bad enough having to play with Paul Daniels here.'

'I was only trying to help.'

'Well, don't!'

Mr Pale picked up his trick, and once again the cards caught flame in his hand.

'Will you stop doing that!' screamed Mr Pink. 'I've had enough of this!' He hurled his cards down on the table and stood up. 'How long are we going to be cooped up in here?' he snapped, pacing the room.

Mr White, reading in the corner, looked up over Iris's reading glasses. 'I think,' he said, 'that we probably need a breath of fresh air.'

'Really?' said Mr Pink. 'And how do you propose we do that? The Four Horsemen of the Apocalypse strolling down the High

Limbo II

Street isn't what you'd call an everyday sight in Lancing. I thought we were supposed to be keeping a low profile?'

'It's hard being stuck here, I know,' said Mr White. 'But we can't do anything until we've removed the obstacle of Rex Boggs.'

'I sayyy weee mooove nowww!'

'Yes, I am aware of your thoughts, Mr Pale, but I don't want this mission going off at half-cock. We're going to sit tight and wait for Rex Boggs, and there's an end to it.'

'But I'm going mad!' yelled Mr Pink.

'Look,' said Mr White. 'If, as seems likely, we are going to be spending some further time here, we're going to need food and clothes. Why don't you take Mr Black out and do some shopping?' Mr White produced a large wad of cash. 'I found this in a shoebox in the Guptas' bedroom.' He handed it to Mr Pink, 'Get out, stretch your legs, and come back in a better frame of mind. That's an order.'

In preparation for the shopping trip, Mr Black and Mr Pink rifled the Guptas' wardrobe – Mr Black settling on a beige suit which, although the trousers were too short and the three-button jacket pulled slightly at the waist, fitted him well enough.

Mr Pink, after being dissuaded from wearing one of Mrs Gupta's saris, eventually settled on a colourful 'Nehru-necked' garment that Mr Gupta sometimes wore to celebrate Diwali.

The bus ride was a revelation for Mr Black. Insisting on sitting right behind the driver, he watched him intently as he swung the steering wheel and manoeuvred the long, red and white vehicle through the morning traffic. He was impressed by the man's skill, his ability to power the vehicle through gaps that seemed impossibly narrow, and at the stealth with which he could sneak up on unsuspecting pedestrians who had the temerity to stray too near the kerb. At journey's end, Mr Pink had to drag his colleague off the bus.

The instant the bus drove away and Brighton seafront was revealed in all its glory, Mr Pink fell in love. 'My God, will you just look at this place! It's so dinky! And all these fabulous shops!' He could hardly contain his excitement. 'I'll meet you back here in a couple of hours,' he said hurriedly to Mr Black, and in moments was lost in the maze of shop-crammed alleyways known as The Lanes.

Mr Black didn't share Mr Pink's enthusiasm for shopping, so instead he went for a stroll along the seafront. Just off Marine Parade, opposite the Aquarium, he spotted a used car showroom. They weren't buses, it was true, but some of the vehicles on offer looked pretty smart, and they were very shiny.

The dealer, sitting in his office playing Minesweeper on his laptop, rubbed his hands with glee when he saw the man in the ill-fitting suit walk tentatively onto the forecourt. He summed him up in an instant: *Lives with his mother, unskilled, probably stacks shelves at Tesco.* He leapt up and strode assertively over to Mr Black, grasping his hand firmly and looking him straight in the eye just as he'd been taught in at his 'empowerment' seminar.

'Good morning, sir. Barry Dean's the name. How can I help you?'

'Er, I'd like one of these,' said Mr Black.

'A car?'

Mr Black nodded.

'You've come to the right place.' The salesman beamed. 'Select Cars can supply all your motoring needs.' In his mind, he'd already sold this idiot that dog of a Nissan he'd been trying to shift for the past three months. 'Now then,' he continued, manoeuvring Mr Black towards a metallic-bronze rust bucket at the back of the forecourt. 'What about this?' He opened one of its doors, which squealed in protest. 'Cloth trim, carpets, ashtrays, sun visors, rear parcel shelf and steering wheel as standard – this little beauty has got it all. Taxed and MOTd up until the end of next month and all for the very reasonable sum of £495; it's got to be the best bargain on the lot.'

But Mr Black wasn't listening; he was gazing at a sleek black

Limbo II

model in pride of place at the front of the display. 'What about that?' he said.

'Ah,' said the salesman, momentarily fazed. 'A man with an eye for fine machinery.' He looked the customer up and down and revised his initial appraisal from *shelf stacker* to *eccentric millionaire*. God knows there were enough of them around these days; some lucky prick won the lottery every week.

'Very well,' said the salesman, moving smoothly over to the shiny black car and opening one of its doors. The smell of leather and new rubber engulfed them, and Mr Black was filled with a strange desire to roll naked over its black hide seats. 'Now this,' said Barry, shifting his patter up a gear, 'is real class. It's the top-of-the-range model with the 3.5 injection, race-developed engine with integral lean-burn fuel technology, double-downdraught butterfly induction with titanium alloy gaskets and mirror-finish valve contouring, multiple injection damping on all inlets and optional manifold afterburner. It's got the engine management system developed for their Le Mans racing car, with ABS, PLC and MTV, and trembler-activated traction control. It cranks out about 300 B.H.P. through a six-speed box, and to handle all that power: wide, low-profile tyres on brushed-alloy rims. It's got air-con, GPS, more walnut than Epping Forest, and a whole herd of cows gave their lives to trim those seats. It's also been regularly serviced, and – the cherry on the cake – it's only done 35,000 miles. It is, in a word, immaculate, and the price of course reflects that.'

Mr Black got in and fingered the steering wheel. The seat hugged him reassuringly, and a myriad buttons and switches gleamed invitingly on the dashboard. Although he'd never sat in a car before, he somehow felt at home.

The salesman crouched by the open door. 'If you like, I could arrange a test drive.'

'Test drive?'

'Yes, you know, take it round the block, see how you get on

with it. Though, I can tell you now, the moment you take this baby out on the road, you're going to fall in love with it.'

'OK.'

'Great. I'll just go and get the keys.'

Mr Black pulled the door to. It closed with a satisfying *ker-chunk*.

A moment later the passenger door opened and Barry got in. 'Now, then,' he said, leaning across and inserting the key in the ignition. 'This one starts on the button, so we just turn this,' he turned the key, 'and press here.' He indicated a red button in the middle of the dashboard. 'Would you like to do the honours?'

Mr Black pressed the button. The engine roared into life, then settled down to a low, menacing growl.

'Like music, isn't it?' said Barry.

Mr Black found a pedal under his right foot. The harder he pressed it, the higher the note of the engine rose. It gave him a feeling of great power.

'Steady on!' Barry yelled over the urgent scream of the engine. 'It's not warmed up yet!'

Mr Black took his foot off the throttle and the engine note fell back to its previous, muted rumble. 'Sorry,' he said.

'That's quite all right,' said Barry, running a finger round his collar. 'I expect you just wanted to hear the beauty of her in full song.'

'Er, yeah,' said Mr Black.

'Of course,' the salesman continued, 'being race-developed, this car has got a semi-automatic, competition gearbox. As you will have noticed, there's no clutch and no gearstick; you change gear with the little paddles just behind the steering wheel. The right one changes up and the left one changes down. Just click it towards you.'

'Like this?' Mr Black clicked the little paddle and the car lurched as the transmission was engaged.

Limbo II

'That's it,' said the salesman. 'Now, take off the handbrake and we're away.'

Mr Black looked puzzled.

'I'll do it,' said the salesman, releasing a short stick in the centre console. 'A new car is always a bit confusing until you get to know it – so many new little switches and knobs to play with.'

The car moved slowly forward towards the busy main road. The vibrations from the car's throbbingly powerful engine travelled from the tip of Mr Black's leather-padded coccyx up the length of his spine to his brain stem, where they were translated into pleasure, and transmitted via the facial nerves to the muscles of his cheeks. Mr Black smiled.

'That's it,' said the salesman, a small note of concern creeping into his voice as the car edged ever closer to the traffic.

Mr Black turned the steering wheel, first to the left, then to the right. The nose of the car moved in response, and Mr Black's smile got even wider.

'Let's take a left,' the salesman said: 'There's a good straight road out to Rottingdean – you'll be able to get some idea what she's capable of.'

Mr Black turned the wheel again, and the car's long bonnet swung to the left. 'This is fun.'

'It's even more fun when you hit the loud pedal.'

'Sorry?'

'When you accelerate – put your foot on the throttle.'

'Oh, of course,' said Mr Black. 'That's the pedal on the right, is it?'

The salesman wagged a finger at him. 'You're a bit of a comedian, aren't you?' He smiled, reaching for the seat belt. 'Oh, I forgot to ask, what are you driving at the moment?'

'I'm not,' said Mr Black.

'What,' said the salesman, 'you're between cars, are you?'

'Oh, no,' said Mr Black. 'I've never driven before in my life.' And so saying, he hit the loud pedal for all he was worth.

The car leapt off the forecourt and did a squealing left up the hill towards Kemptown, narrowly missing an ice-cream van. The car carried on, accelerating along the middle of the road between the lines of traffic, towards the lights at Lower Rock Gardens.

'The left! We drive on the left!' the salesman screamed, trying in vain to fasten his seat belt with trembling fingers.

'Sorry.' Mr Black beamed, diving back into the stream of traffic and weaving between the two lanes of slow-moving cars. 'Just for future reference,' Mr Black enquired, 'how do I make it stop?'

'The other pedal!' the terrified salesman yelled.

Mr Black looked down at his feet. There was a big wide pedal in the middle of the footwell. He stood on it. The car came to an abrupt halt, eliciting the sound of squealing tyres and a blare of angry horns from the traffic behind, and sending the unbelted Barry slamming into the windscreen.

Mr Black looked down at the salesman, out cold in the passenger footwell. 'Lightweight.' He smiled, and floored the accelerator once more.

Chapter 27

Iris had found it strangely comforting to be back in her old bedroom, but she hadn't slept well. Every time she woke, the realization of her situation had come back to her with sudden dread, and she was beginning to lose heart. Turning her head, she looked at the alarm clock ticking on the bedside table. Half past ten! She couldn't remember the last time she'd lain in bed so long, but what was the point of getting up? She was going to die, of that she was certain. Where were Bernard and Rex, and why hadn't they come to rescue her? Tears pricked her eyes as, in her loneliness and desperation, she found herself thinking they'd forgotten all about her. *No, that's just daft*, she told herself. But, all the same, why weren't they here? *They must have their reasons*, she thought, and left it at that, drawing some comfort from the fact that as long as Rex stayed away, he was safe.

As she lay there on what might be her last morning on earth, with the sunlight pressing against the still-closed curtains, she listened to all the old familiar sounds – the traffic in the High Street, the trains rumbling into Lancing station – and began to wonder if Limbo had all been a dream. She swore that if, by some miracle, she escaped these awful men and got back there, she'd never complain about not having anything to do ever again.

There was a muffled knock at the door. 'Iris?' Mr White called softly from the other side. 'I've got a cup of tea for you.'

'You can come in,' she said. 'I'm decent.'

The door opened and Mr White came in.

'Goodness,' he said, 'not opened the curtains yet? We are a slugabed this morning. Never mind, the tea'll soon have you raring to go. Sit up now.'

Iris sat up and arranged the pillows behind her. Then Mr White handed her the cup and saucer, and opened the curtains. 'How are you feeling?' he asked.

'I'm being held hostage by four criminals who want to murder me and my son. How do you think I feel?' she said tersely, over the rim of her cup.

Mr White smiled. 'We're not criminals, Iris.' He sat down on the edge of the bed. 'We're just trying to do our job, that's all. Rex would understand.'

Iris wanted to throw the tea in his face, but it was too good to waste – strong and sweet, just as she liked it – so instead she sipped it gratefully, letting it warm and comfort her. 'I'd rather never see Rex again than let you get your hands on him,' she said defiantly.

Mr White sighed and stroked the candlewick bedspread thoughtfully. 'It's not me, Iris – you know that. It's just that . . . well, Mr Pale is convinced you're hiding something. He's very keen to have a little chat about Rex's whereabouts, and I'm not sure how much longer I can keep him away from you.'

Iris began to feel the icy fingers of fear clutch at her throat. 'I'm not afraid of . . . dying,' she said falteringly.

'Oh, Iris,' said Mr White, with a wan smile. 'Dying is the easy part.'

Iris's cup and saucer began to rattle uncontrollably in her trembling hand. Mr White took them from her, putting them down on the bedside table as Iris pulled the bedclothes up to her chin.

'I hate to suggest this to a mother, but if Rex really cared about you, wouldn't he be here by now?'

Iris's eyes brimmed with tears. 'My son is the kindest, most caring soul in the world. If he could be here, he would be, and don't you dare suggest otherwise.'

'But what could be keeping him?' Mr White persisted. 'Does he

Limbo II

have very far to come? Where's he coming *from*? And what about your husband – doesn't he care about you, either?'

Iris tried desperately to choke down her sobs.

'I want to be your friend, Iris, I really do, but you've got to help me out here. I can't protect you for ever. Just think about it.' Mr White patted her on the hand, then got up and walked back round the foot of the bed to the door. 'Once you're dressed, perhaps you'd join me for breakfast.' He smiled. 'I've thawed out a wholemeal loaf.'

'I – don't – know – where he is.' Iris broke down and sobbed wretchedly.

Mr White, standing in the doorway, studied her for a long moment. 'No,' he said, gently, 'I don't believe you do.'

Chapter 28

Rex headed back to the castle. After his earlier disagreement with one of the sons of Limbo, he'd decided to give the little town sheltering in the lee of the castle's main gate a wide berth, and head in the back way.

What had Tumbril meant? Nothing of what she'd said made any sense. *Look up, look up. There is the answer: two suns setting over the sea. The barrel of the smoking gun points the way* . . . It was all nonsense. Limbo only had one sun, and there were no guns here – this was a low-tech society. Apart from the gleaming espresso machine in Smeil's Café and the Aga in the Wizard's room, the most up-to-date machine they had was the scythe.

As Rex mused on the events of the past few days he walked well out of his way, and when he looked up, found himself on the shore of the Salient Sea. The sun, now barely above the horizon, cast a broad band of shimmering gold on the dancing surface of the water.

Watching the sun slip even further down the sky towards the quenching sea, Rex was consumed by a deep depression and felt very, very foolish. 'You thought you had it all nicely sewn up, didn't you?' he said to himself. 'You thought you could just write that book and sit back and put your feet up, didn't you? You idiot!' Rex felt a sudden pain in his chest and collapsed onto the stony beach. It was more than a mere pain; it was a deep and fathomless ache, as if a bottomless pit of suffering had opened up inside him.

It was all his fault: Iris's disappearance, the loss of the Crystal,

Limbo II

even the missing piece of the Book. And to top it all, according to Tumbril, he'd also destabilized the Hoop of Destiny. He sat on the beach, cursing his stupidity. But, as he sank deeper into a quagmire of self-loathing, something that Tumbril had said came back to him: *Stop resisting. You're Destiny's fool. Let go and trust to your fate . . .* And in that moment he stopped blaming himself and saw his position with absolute clarity: he was completely powerless in the face of circumstance — small, sad, alone and very frightened, with the longed-for comfort of his mother's tender arms impossibly out of reach. Overwhelmed with compassion for himself, he burst into tears.

'There, there,' he said, hugging himself and rocking back and forth on the shingly beach. 'There, there.'

There was a wet *splat* as something dropped onto his shoulder. Above him a seagull squawked. 'Bloody marvellous,' he said. He looked up and shook his fist at the bird. 'Thank you. I really needed that!' Then something caught his eye.

He was below the grey stone cliffs that rose straight up from the beach, and in the fading light he could see, far above him, something that shouldn't have been there. At first he put it down to the fact that his eyes were full of tears, but after wiping his face with his sleeve, he looked again. It was still there. *Look up, look up. There is the answer . . .* It was like a hairline crack in glass, undetectable from certain angles, only visible when it catches the light. But this crack was floating in mid-air and, lit by the rays of the setting sun, looked for all the world like *a line of gold . . .*

'Look up, there is the answer. Look up, there is the answer . . .' Rex repeated the phrase over and over. But what was it the answer to? He scanned the forbidding cliff face for clues. There was something about these cliffs — something had happened here — but for the moment Rex couldn't remember what it was.

Then he saw it. About two thirds of the way up was a small black smudge. 'The tunnel!' Rex breathed. From that small hole the old Wizard had been propelled into the next dimension by the explosion under the castle which had been set off by the last King. *The barrel of the smoking gun . . .* Tumbril's words began to drop like jigsaw pieces into the rapidly assembling puzzle in his mind. He had to get up there, and quickly, but the only way into that tunnel was back under the castle, and that was a good half an hour's walk from here. He would have to run. Scrambling to his feet, he raced up the beach. Then another of Tumbril's phrases dropped into place: *you have forgotten who you are . . .*

'Of course!' he said, stopping suddenly on the noisy pebbles. 'I'm a fucking wizard!' Spreading his arms wide, he addressed the cliff. 'Ascensor!' he commanded. A tall and rather rickety wooden ladder appeared, leading from the beach to the tunnel entrance far above. It wasn't quite the marble elevator that Rex had envisaged – seemingly he still had some work to do on his sense of self-worth – but it would do. Rex began to climb.

When he dismounted, breathless, at the top, he scrabbled frantically around the tunnel walls, looking for . . . He wasn't even sure himself. But then he found it – an indentation in the smooth, featureless rock. He pressed hard with his thumb and, with a hiss, a small door opened in the seemingly solid cave wall. Thrusting his hand inside, his urgent fingers touched something dry and papery. Grasping the ancient scroll of papyrus, he knelt and, trembling with anticipation, unrolled it on the stone floor. It was in a strange, ancient language but, to his relief and no little surprise, Rex found he could read it: 'Cream together six ounces each of butter and caster sugar, then beat in three large eggs . . .' It was a recipe for Madeira cake.

Rex sighed and slumped against the wall. This was hopeless – perhaps there was nothing here after all. Sitting on the cold, hard floor of the tunnel, Rex looked out through the cavern's muzzle and gazed across the forbidding waters of the Salient Sea. But as he scanned the horizon, he saw an extraordinary sight. Viewed through the strange hairline fracture he'd noticed from the beach, which seemed to be floating in mid-air about twenty feet in front of the

Limbo II

cave mouth, the image of the sun was split in two: *two suns setting over the sea* . . . But what was he actually looking at? It was impossible for the air to be cracked, wasn't it?

As he stared at the thin fissure reflecting the golden light of the dying sun, Rex searched his mind for Tumbril's exact words, wishing now he'd paid more attention. 'What else did she say? What else?' He screwed his eyes tight and hammered his forehead with his fist. 'Think, think, think!' Holding his breath, he dived deep into his memory.

Just when he thought he might explode, he remembered. 'Yes!' he gasped. *Limbo . . . lives and breathes and keeps her memories still.*' 'Yes!' he exclaimed again. 'Yes, yes, yes!'

Chapter 29

Bernard Boggs paced the battlements of the ancient castle in the rapidly gathering gloom. He was worried sick. It was bad enough that Iris was being held hostage by biblical characters, but now it seemed that Rex had disappeared too. Panic was building in the castle, and the townspeople outside were growing steadily more restless. Most of them remembered with horror what it was like to live in the Dark Time, and it wouldn't be long before they started banging on the gates and demanding something be done.

Bernard paused in his endless backwards and forwards traverse of the crusty old stonework and, leaning on the parapet, looked out across the Great Plain. 'Oh, Iris, love,' he said to himself, 'where are you? What are they doing to you?' It was hard for someone like Bernard to have to stand idly by and just do nothing. He wanted to do *something* – he was the King, after all – but what *could* he do? He wasn't a wizard; he wasn't even a natural son of Limbo. He thumped the battlements in frustration. Then he heard a door open behind him, and he spun round to see Rex standing there with a steely glint in his eye. He seemed to have grown by about a foot.

'Rex,' said Bernard. 'I was worried about you.'

As Rex stood and looked at the King, the curls around the smooth dome of Bernard's head were backlit by the setting sun. 'A *woven crown*.' Rex laughed.

'A what?' said Bernard.

Rex shook his head 'Never mind. Come on, we're going to rescue Mum.'

Limbo II

'How?'

Rex walked to the parapet and pointed towards something far below – something Bernard had almost forgotten about, something, indeed, that he'd promised Iris never to go near again. There, beneath the castle walls, just outside the cluster of dwellings that passed for a town, stood a small Cessna 152, glinting in the failing light.

'That's how,' said Rex.

Smeil was beside himself. Rex was leaving him in charge, and Smeil took the responsibility very seriously indeed. 'But, my lord,' he protested, pacing up and down the cold stone floor of the corridor outside the café, 'I am not equipped for such a task.'

'It won't be for long, Smeil,' said Rex. 'If everything goes according to plan, we'll be back before you know it.'

'But what if there's trouble? I'm not a wizard,' Smeil said, wringing his hands.

Rex crouched and looked into his eyes. 'Well, I am, remember, and I don't seem to have been much help so far.'

Smeil absent-mindedly stuck the end of his rope belt in his mouth. 'But what will I do if the people come asking for guidance?'

'Give it to them.'

'And tell them what? Master, you can't leave me like this. I'm not a leader, I'm a follower – a gofer, a general dogsbody – and a good one at that. The only thing I can do is make coffee, but you can't stop a riot with a vanilla latte.'

'Smeil,' Rex soothed, removing the soggy end of Smeil's belt from between his small servant's clenched teeth, 'there's no one I trust more. And, more importantly, there's no one the people trust more. They like you – they know that you're honest and fair – and believe me, the very fact that you're not a wizard is greatly in your favour.' The little man looked pained. 'We won't be long,' Rex continued. 'I would never ask you to do something I didn't think you could handle. And I'm sure Matilda will be more than happy to help out.'

Smeil closed his eyes. 'Oh, master,' he sighed, 'you know I'd do anything for you.'

Rex hugged him, patting him on the back. 'Thank you, my very good friend.'

The Wizard stared into the little man's eyes, which were now brimming with fearful tears. 'Chin up, Smeil,' Rex said, softly. Then, straightening up, Rex strode quickly away down the long corridor, leaving Smeil alone in the dusty silence.

Running back to his room, Rex changed out of his official wizarding robes into something a little more appropriate for early twenty-first-century England. Then, going over to the large, round table and grasping it by the edge, he shook it firmly. The solid wood was immediately transformed into chiffon. Rex smiled with satisfaction. 'I haven't lost it, after all,' he said, and, tying the long flowing scarf around his neck, he went off to collect Bernard.

With Bernard now suitably dressed in an anonymous brown suit, he and Rex boarded the small Cessna – the very same plane in which Bernard and Iris had first arrived in Limbo. Rex had once tried to explain how that had happened, how their plane had been caught up in the same explosion beneath the castle that had fractured time and space, but Bernard hadn't really understood.

Bernard took a few moments to familiarize himself again with all the dials and switches in the cramped cockpit. It had been some years since he'd last sat at the controls of the little plane, but he had no doubts that he could still fly it – if, that is, he could get it into the air. All the control surfaces seemed to be in working order, but flicking on the ignition he saw that the battery was as flat as a pancake, and the fuel gauge was showing empty.

Bernard shook his head sadly. 'It was a good idea, son, but we're never going to get this thing off the ground.'

Limbo II

Rex, sitting next to him, closed his eyes and waved a hand over the instrument panel. Bernard watched, amazed, as the needles on the small, neat dials twitched, the petrol gauge flicked over to full, and the ignition light glowed red.

'Try her now,' said Rex.

Bernard smiled and looked across at his son, 'That's my Rexie.' Rex beamed confidently back.

Although no one else was around, Bernard opened the window and yelled, 'Clear prop!' as his instructor had taught him *always* to do, no matter *what* the circumstances. He hit the button and the starter motor whirred. The propeller turned over once, twice, three times. *It's not going to start*, he thought, as the prop stuttered round four, five, six times. *Why should it start? It hasn't been used for years.* But just as he was on the point of giving up, the engine spluttered into life and great clouds of smoke billowed from its exhausts.

'Yes!' yelled Bernard, and turned to Rex. 'Where to, boss?'

'I'll tell you once we're up,' Rex shouted over the noise of the engine.

'You're in charge,' Bernard shouted back and, wheeling the small aircraft's nose into the wind, he yanked out the throttle. The engine note rose to a scream and the Cessna bumped and shook as it gathered speed across the uneven ground. When the airspeed indicator hit seventy knots, Bernard pulled back gently on the stick, and the aircraft took off into the setting sun.

'We're coming for you, Iris!' he bawled. 'We're coming for you, love!'

At five hundred feet, Rex told Bernard to level off. Bernard obediently lowered the nose and eased in the throttle. 'Now what?'

'You're going to have to trust me, Dad.'

'You know I trust you, son.' Bernard checked the instruments and adjusted the trim wheel.

'No,' said Rex. 'You're going to have to trust me like you've never trusted me before.'

The seriousness in Rex's tone made Bernard turn to look at him. 'What's up?'

'What would you say if I was to tell you that the only way we're going to rescue Mum was by flying straight at a cliff?'

'Go on?' said Bernard.

'It's a long story, but I met someone today who ... reminded me of a few things. At the time I didn't know what she was on about, but then it all began to make sense. You see, Limbo isn't like the world that we come from; Limbo is alive. It lives and breathes, and *remembers*.'

Bernard shook his head. 'I don't understand, son.'

'Near the cliffs above the shoreline of the Salient Sea is a thin golden line hanging in mid-air. I've never seen it before. You can only see it now because the sun's striking it at such an oblique angle. I'm almost sure it's a memory of the fracture between dimensions that occurred when the last King tried to blow up the castle. If we can hit it just right, we may be able to slip through, and back to our world, where Mum is.'

'So, what's the problem?'

'There's no way of knowing if it'll work. We can't be absolutely certain if it is what I think it is; and even if it is, where we might end up. It may not take us to Iris at all. It may throw us back in time to the Dark Ages, or forwards to God knows what. And, assuming we *do* get through, and don't end up as jam on the cliffs, if we can't find the Crystal, we'll be stuck wherever we wind up, permanently.'

Bernard pursed his lips and stared straight ahead through the plane's small windscreen. After a long pause, he spoke. 'What do you reckon are the odds of us coming out of this in one piece and getting back here with Iris and the Crystal?'

'About ten thousand to one.'

'Fair enough. Where's this cliff you want me to fly into?'

Limbo II

The control stick looked like a toy in Bernard's large hands: *he has his hands on the power* . . . Rex laughed.

'What's so funny?' asked Bernard.

'Nothing. Take a left and head out to sea.'

'Take a left?' Bernard smiled. 'What do you think this is, a bloody taxi?'

Bernard banked the plane to port and soon they were flying out over the cold, grey waters of the Salient Sea.

Two miles out, Bernard performed a 180-degree turn and headed back towards land.

'The fissure's about a hundred feet up, and around twenty feet in front of the cliff,' Rex explained. 'You'll have to hit it dead on, but you won't be able to see it until you're almost on top of it, so for now aim for the mouth of the tunnel.'

'Very well.' Bernard pushed forward on the stick, and the Cessna's nose dipped towards the sea. Levelling off at a hundred feet, he strained his eyes towards the cliffs as they came ever nearer. A mile out and he could still see nothing save the sheer, solid rock towards which they were racing.

'What *exactly* am I looking for, son?' Bernard asked.

'A thin line of gold,' Rex replied, not for a moment taking his own eyes off the cliffs.

Half a mile now. In seconds they would either find themselves in another dimension, or smack into the cliff face in a gigantic fireball.

Either possibility had reduced both men to silence.

Five hundred yards . . . Four hundred . . . Three hundred . . . They leaned forwards, straining to catch a glimpse of the thin, golden crack between dimensions.

Two hundred yards . . . All Bernard's instincts cried out to him to pull back on the control stick, to gain altitude – to just get out of there. But he kept his hands level, still aiming the little plane at the dark smudge on the cliff that marked the entrance to the tunnel.

One hundred yards . . . Fifty yards . . . The cliff was so close now it seemed they could reach out and touch it. It filled the windscreen – grey, cold and unyielding. Then, out of the corner of his eye, Rex saw a flash of gold. 'We're too far to the right,' he screamed.

Bernard reacted instantly, wrenching the control stick over to the left. The plane lurched to port, standing on its wing, but surely it was too little, too late.

Rex began to scream: 'Ahhh . . .'

And Bernard joined in: 'Ahhh . . .'

Thirty yards . . . Thirty feet . . . Twenty . . .

The cliff in front of them exploded in a blaze of pure white light.

The guardian, clad in his darkly shining armour, strapped on his sword. Then, holding a flaming torch before him, he left the cave that had been his home for centuries. Stepping through the narrow portal, he stood on the slender causeway along which those seeking the casket must come. But those who sought the casket, and the dread power it contained, would first have to do battle with him. And he would not let them pass.

Reaching up, he placed the flaming torch in an ancient bracket fixed on the wall to one side of the arched portal. The torch threw a jagged curtain of light up towards the roof of the cavern, far, far above, and hurled dark shadows down into its forbidding depths on either side of the narrow bridge.

Drawing his sword, the guardian began to swing the dully gleaming weapon around his head in a slow, rhythmic movement. Shifting position, his foot dislodged a loose stone, and it fell into the darkness below, clattering onto the floor of the cavern long seconds later, its echo reverberating up through the tall, narrow space. Unperturbed, the guardian

Limbo II

now began to swing the sword left and right in a sideways figure of eight. Finally, satisfied that he was limber, he laid the sword down in front of him, and crouched and waited, his eyes fixed on the doorway at the far end of the bridge . . .

Chapter 30

Mr Pale paced the worn brown carpet of the Boggs' living room. 'Whyyy weee nottt mooove?'

'You know very well why not.' Mr White sighed. 'If Rex Boggs is not neutralized, it could spell disaster for our mission.'

'Whaattt I care for Rexsss Boggsss? Heee not here by tonight, I mooove with or withouttt yooou.'

'Tonight is out of the question.'

Mr Pale growled and turned on his bony heel.

'Mr Pale!' The deathly figure stopped in the doorway. 'I understand how you feel,' said Mr White sympathetically. 'I'm as eager as you are to get on with things. Look, I'll make a deal with you. What say we give Rex until the end of the week, hmm? If he's not here by then, we go ahead regardless.'

The stark, white skeleton glared furiously at Mr White, who held his gaze unflinchingly. Eventually, Mr Pale threw back his head and roared, 'Ahhhh!' Then, raising an arm, he pointed a long bony finger at Mr White. 'Untilll Saturdayyy nighttt!' he hissed, and stalked out of the room.

Mr White breathed a sigh of relief. Dealing with Mr Pale was a bit like trying to negotiate with a hurricane. But Rex was bound to show up any minute, wasn't he? If he didn't, then they would have to think again. Mr White sat and tried to formulate a plan of action, but his concentration wasn't helped by the insistent beeping of a car horn in the street outside. Sighing, he stood up and went to the

Limbo II

window. Mr Pink and Mr Black waved up at him from the pavement below, obviously in high spirits.

Mr White ran down the stairs and unlocked the street door. 'What *are* you doing?'

'We've had a fabulous time,' said Mr Pink, reaching into the back of the car and pulling out boxes and shopping bags. 'Just wait until you see the outfit I got for you!'

'What's this?' said Mr White, taking in the car for the first time.

'It's a car,' said Mr Black.

'I can see it's a car,' said Mr White. 'What are you doing with it?'

'What do you usually do with a car? It's fabulous. Do you want a go?'

'No, I do not want a go!' yelled Mr White. 'Hide that thing around the back and come inside, both of you!' he said, striding back upstairs.

Mr Pink looked at Mr Black. 'What did we do?' he said.

Back in the privacy of the upstairs living room, Mr White addressed his small troop.

'Have we forgotten why we're here?' he asked. 'We are not here to enjoy ourselves. We are the Four Horsemen of the Apocalypse, come to rage across the face of the earth: you, Mr Pink, spreading Famine; while you, Mr Black, set brother against brother in an orgy of bloodletting—'

'Hang on,' interrupted Mr Pink. 'I'm not Famine, am I?'

'Yeah, and I'm sure I'm not War,' said Mr Black.

Mr White – interrupted in mid-flow – was not happy. 'What?'

'I'm not Famine,' Mr Pink repeated.

'You're not?'

'And I can't be War,' said Mr Black.

'One at a time, please!' Mr White turned back to Mr Pink. 'You're not Famine, you say. Then who are you?'

'Well, I know I'm not Death.'

'Dea—' began Mr Pale.

'Yes, I think we *all* know who you are,' snapped Mr White. 'Oh, now you've made me lose my thread completely! Is there a Bible in this house?' he said, scanning the bookshelves. 'I'm getting confused. It's such a long time since we've been anywhere.'

'I doubt you'll find a Bible here,' said Mr Black. 'They'll have been Hindus, the Guptas, or Muslims.'

'Oh, will they now, Mr Clever Dick?' said Mr White, pulling down a copy of the King James Bible. 'It's obvious why *I'm* the leader of this expedition. Now then.' He started thumbing through the book. 'It's near the back isn't it? Revelations something or other.'

'Sssiiixxx,' breathed Mr Pale.

'I'll take your word for it,' said Mr White. 'Oh God, why do they have to use such small print?' He looked around the room. 'Did Iris leave her reading glasses in here?'

'Here they are, boss!' said Mr Black, picking them up from the mantelpiece and handing them to him.

'Thank you.' Mr White put them on. 'That's better. Now then . . . Revelations, Chapter Six. "And I saw when the Lamb opened one of the seals, and I heard, as it were the noise of thunder, one of the four beasts saying, Come and see. And I saw, and behold – " ah, here we go. "– and behold a white horse: and he that sat on him – " that'll be me " – had a bow; and a crown was given unto him: and he went forth conquering, and to conquer." Well, that all sounds, er . . . very good. "And when he had opened the second seal – " et cetera, et cetera " – there went out another horse that was—" Hmm, that's odd.'

'What, boss?'

'Well, in here it's a red horse.' He turned to Mr Pink. 'What happened, did it fade in the sunlight, or something?'

Mr Pink sighed. 'It's *always* been pink. I've no idea why they called it red in the Bible.'

Limbo II

'Probably to make it sound a bit more, you know... more butch,' suggested Mr Black.

Mr Pink pursed his lips and glared at him.

Mr White carried on reading, ' "another horse that was red: and power was given to him that sat thereon to take peace from the earth, and that they should kill one another: and there was given unto him a great sword." So, that'll make you War, Mr Pink. Where's your sword?'

'Sword? I only found out about this little escapade half an hour before we were due to leave. Where was I going to find a sword in that time?'

'Well, if you're going to be starting wars and spreading mayhem all over the place, you're going to need a sword.'

'Come to that,' said Mr Pink, 'where's your bow and crown?'

Mr White raised an eyebrow. 'Point taken,' he said. 'All right then, next horse... "And I beheld, and lo a black horse – " pay attention, Mr Black " – and he that sat on him had a pair of balances in his hand." I suppose that means scales. Have you got any scales?'

Mr Black shook his head. 'Nah, boss.'

Mr White looked at Mr Black over the top of his glasses. 'Not very well prepared, are we?' Then, licking a finger, he turned the page. ' "And I heard a voice in the midst of the four beasts say, A measure of wheat for a penny, and three measures of barley for a penny – " before inflation, obviously " – and see thou hurt not the oil and wine." Very good advice. "And when he had opened – " blah, blah, blah... oh, get to the point " – I looked and beheld a pale horse: and his name that sat upon him was —" ' Mr White looked straight at Mr Pale. 'Guess who. "And hell followed with him." '

'What does that make me then, boss?' asked a puzzled Mr Black.

'Famine,' breathed Mr Pale.

'Yes, I suppose so.'

'Then, you are?' queried Mr Pink.

'What do you mean?' said Mr White.

'If I'm War, he's Famine, and he's Death, what's left?'

'Hang on, I haven't finished yet,' said Mr White. ' "And power was given unto them over the fourth part of the earth – " only a fourth part? That doesn't seem very much " – to kill with sword, and with hunger, and with death, and with the beasts of the earth." '

'That'll make you beasts of the earth, then,' said Mr Pink.

'So it would seem,' said Mr White, removing Iris's glasses. 'It makes me sound like a sort of glorified cowherd. I *was* hoping for a rather more dramatic role, something like Pestilence or Contagion or . . . I don't know,' he said sadly. 'You wait all your life for your brief moment in the sun and then . . .' He sighed and stared wistfully off into space.

'Boss,' said Mr Black gently, 'if *you* want to be Famine, I don't mind.'

'Or War,' said Mr Pink. 'I'm sure we could find you a sword somewhere.'

Mr White smiled. 'That's very kind of you both, but I couldn't possibly accept. No, no,' he said, shaking his head. 'We all have our roles to play – and our little crosses to bear.' He closed the Bible and put it back on the shelf. 'But thank you for the thought. Command can be a lonely island at times, but now at least I know I have friends.'

Mr Pale growled.

Mr White looked at him. 'Thank you for those kind sentiments, Mr Pale. I'm touched, I really am.'

'Boss,' said Mr Black, thoughtfully. 'Why don't you give yourself a little break?'

'Yes,' said Mr Pink. 'Treat yourself – have a day in Brighton.'

'I could give you a lift in,' suggested Mr Black.

Chapter 31

Dawn at the Linhay Psychiatric Home revealed a strange sight: on the lawns around a small flowering cherry tree, the rising sun caught the droplets of dew on a million spiders' webs woven closely together in the shape of a large, shallow basin. At the foot of the tree was a jumble of electronic components, and from one of its branches hung a microphone. The whole array was vaguely reminiscent of the radio telescope dish at Jodrell Bank.

It had been, of necessity, a pretty primitive set-up. The spiders had raided the electricals from a room just down the corridor marked 'ECT', and Frink had just had to trust them to get it right. Spiders were very good engineers – one couldn't fault their building technique – but as electricians they left a lot to be desired. Having eight eyes was a distinct disadvantage when it came to close work such as wiring up a circuit board, and things inevitably got misconnected.

Nevertheless, once completed, the improvised radio telescope worked pretty well, and it had allowed Frink – or at least the spiders operating it – to track the energy field's faint trail across the sky with reasonable accuracy. Frink now knew that sometime during his enforced sleep the energy field had arrived at its destination. If the Earth was to stand any chance of surviving this threat, he had to get back to his spaceship immediately and warn those who had ears to hear about the danger they were in. But at the moment he was locked in a building with bars on the windows and every exit guarded by a thug in a white coat.

*

Something else that might have given Frink pause, had he known, was that at this moment his spaceship was about fifty thousand miles above the Earth, heading straight for Barnard's Star in the constellation Ophiuchus. At the controls was a drunkenly slumbering member of the Sydenham Damerel Morris, who was about to wake up to the hangover of his life.

Harold Petherwick was having a strange dream. He was standing on a beach looking up at the night sky while Amos hit him repeatedly over the head with his bladder – *thump, thump, thump* – to the accompaniment of 'Frank Morgan's Jig'. Then, suddenly, with a *whoosh*, he was shooting through space and tumbling amongst bands of swirling colour.

Harold opened one bleary eye. The images it relayed to his visual cortex didn't make sense, and anyway the *thump, thump, thump* in his head became more acute as light flooded into his brain, so he closed it again. But something about what he'd seen urged him to open the other eye for confirmation. His eyelid creaked open, and little dots and squares of colour flashed up at him. On a big TV screen was an image of the Earth getting smaller and smaller as it receded into the blackness of space. The pictures his brain was receiving still didn't make any sense, so the obvious next step was to open both eyes simultaneously to get the full effect. He did.

It would take about three seconds for the first wave of horror to hit him. Meanwhile, questions inundated his drink-fuddled mind: *Where am I? How did I get here?* and *What died in my mouth?*

As the processes of his brain got slowly into gear, a panic message began the long journey down alcohol-impaired neurons to his adrenal glands, giving him plenty of time to look around. Everything seemed strangely familiar. *Star* flashed into his mind, closely followed by *Wars*. Yes, that was it! His surroundings were vaguely reminiscent of the bridge of Han Solo's spaceship, the *Millennium Falcon*. But how could he be in a spaceship? Spaceships didn't exist, did they? And even if they did, why would one want to kidnap him? He wasn't special; when he wasn't in drag for the Sydenham

Limbo II

Damerel Morris, he was a verge cutter for West Devon Borough Council. He couldn't be in a spaceship – it was impossible. But the evidence of his own eyes told him otherwise, and the realization that the unthinkable had happened and the urgent message to flood his system with noradrenaline hit, simultaneously, his consciousness and his adrenals respectively.

He did what any grown man would do under the circumstances. He screamed.

'Aaaaahhhhhhh!'

Meanwhile, Frink was enduring his first institutional breakfast. Cold lumpy porridge and burnt toast spread thinly with margarine was hardly the fare to set a man's pulse racing, especially after ten years on space rations rehydrated with endlessly recycled water. But the breakfast, or rather the amount of food that remained uneaten and thus ended up in the capacious wheeled refuse bin, had given him an idea. All that he needed was a diversion.

It came from an unexpected source. As Frink attempted to dislodge the porridge clinging tenaciously to the roof of his mouth, desperate screaming suddenly echoed down the corridor into the airy austerity of the dining hall. Normally such an event would have aroused little interest – staff and inmates being inured to such distressing sounds – but this morning, as it turned out, it wasn't one of the patients who was making all the noise.

Terry ran wildly into the big dining hall. 'It's Mike! Somebody help! He's stuck to the ECT and we can't shut it off!'

Mike had been helping one of the doctors initiate a new patient into the mysteries of Electro Convulsive Therapy – a technique occasionally used in cases of clinical depression that sends a small electric current through the cerebral cortex. Mike's task was to operate the electrical transformer, applying whatever level of current the doctor instructed. It was a job that Mike usually enjoyed, but on this particular occasion it seemed that – along with other bits and pieces of electrical equipment – the sheathing which kept the operator isolated from the mains was inexplicably missing. The moment the smiling Mike switched on the big transformer, he'd found himself fused to the machine as a current of 250 volts sizzled through his convulsing body.

As all the available members of staff hurried to Mike's aid, Frink seized his chance: diving into the huge porridge-and-toast-filled refuse bin. There he stayed for the next twenty minutes, remaining absolutely quiet as porridge and soggy toast congealed around him. He couldn't even risk sending a news bulletin, in case somebody overheard it. It was probably the most unpleasant twenty minutes of his life, but no matter; it was not his personal comfort that was at issue here, it was the salvation of the people of Earth.

Eventually he felt the bin being moved. After a short while it stopped and, when Frink was absolutely certain that no one was nearby, he cautiously lifted the lid and peeped out. He was outside, at the back of the home in a small concrete yard formed by the angle between the kitchens and an adjoining single-storey building with a green, corrugated-iron roof. In front of this yard was a car park, in which stood an ambulance, and behind that a high brick wall topped with wire.

Frink made doubly sure that the coast was clear, then clambered as quietly as he could out of the large bin. As he was removing a piece of toast that had become cemented to his scalp by the rapidly hardening porridge, he heard the sound of someone approaching. Slipping into the shadows behind the bin, Frink watched as a man wheeling a trolley marked 'Laundry' passed his hiding place and shoved through a set of green double doors into the single-storey building. As the doors opened, Frink could hear the hiss of steam and the whine of an industrial washing machine. 'Laundry': the word was redolent of crisp, clean cotton and freshly ironed linen. Frink looked down at his porridge-caked institutional pyjamas and suddenly felt an urgent desire for clean clothes. Ducking under the kitchen window and keeping close to the rough, pebble-dashed wall, he followed the man inside.

Once in the building, Frink slid into a narrow gap between the wall and a large, vibrating, stainless-steel washing machine. At the other end of the room, the man who'd been pushing the trolley was now talking to a fat woman pressing clothes on a folding steam press.

As the woman pressed each article of clothing, she folded it and placed it on top of a pile on the table beside her. With the noise of the steam press and the washing machine covering his approach, Frink, crouching low, stole from his hiding place and worked his way up the long room. He was just about to snatch up a handful of the ironed garments when the man made a sudden movement. Frink dived under the table. Luckily for him, the man's interest lay elsewhere, as he grabbed a handful of the fat woman's fleshy buttock. Lightning quick, she spun round and slapped him hard with a podgy hand.

Harsh words were spoken, which, thankfully, were drowned out by the noise of the machines, and Frink used this diversion to pull down a complete set of clothes. A minute later, feeling fresh and clean in immaculate hospital whites, he emerged from the hospital laundry into the bright day.

Frink's next task was to get out of this place. The high walls were topped with murderous barbed wire, and the only exit was manned by a surly-looking gatekeeper.

As Frink stood at the edge of the car park considering his options, he heard somebody calling. The ambulance driver was out of his cab and was shouting and waving. At him.

'Dammit!' Frink breathed – to have come this far and yet fail with freedom almost within his grasp. Then he realized that the ambulance driver wasn't calling down the wrath of the hospital heavies on him; he was asking for help.

Frink began to understand the opportunity that had presented itself. Running towards the gesticulating man, he saw that Mike, his hand heavily bandaged, was sitting groggily in a wheelchair at the rear of the ambulance.

'Help us get him into the back, will you, mate?' said the ambulance driver as he approached.

'Yes, of course,' said Frink.

Lining up the wheelchair with the ramp into the back of the ambulance, the driver took one side of the chair, and Frink the other, being careful to keep his face out of Mike's vision. 'On three, right?'

'On three,' Frink repeated.

'One, two, *three*!' Together they pushed the chair up the ramp and slid it into the back of the vehicle.

'Where are you taking him, then?' Frink asked, as the driver strapped Mike's chair down.

'Derriford casualty. Silly sod electrocuted himself,' the driver said unsympathetically. 'Mind you, it could be the best thing that's happened to him,' he added dryly. 'The shock might have jump-started his brain,'.

Once Mike's chair had been secured in the back of the ambulance, Frink leapt in beside him.

'Here, what are you doing?' the ambulance driver said.

'Um . . . he's a good friend of mine,' said Frink. 'I just want to make sure he doesn't, er . . . feel lonely.'

The ambulance driver looked at him strangely. The idea of Mike feeling lonely, or even having friends, was a new one on him. Then he shrugged. 'All right, then,' he said, and closed the rear doors.

Frink heard the driver's door slam, and the engine start. The tyres scrunched on the gravel and came to a halt at the guarded gate. After a brief exchange with the gatekeeper, the ambulance moved slowly out into the road and gathered speed.

Chapter 32

Mr White stepped out into the street and looked left and right. The clothes that Mr Pink had chosen for him were not really to his taste. The off-white suit wasn't too bad; it was the lime-green and salmon-pink striped shirt and purple tie he really objected to.

Mr Black got out of the car and opened the door for him. Reluctantly, Mr White allowed himself to be ushered into the gleaming car, and settled back in its black leather upholstery.

'Have a nice time!' Mr Pink waved from the pavement. 'No need to hurry back!'

Mr Black slipped behind the wheel and stepped on the throttle. The car shot forwards, and in seconds Mr Pink was nothing but a memory.

Without lifting his foot off the accelerator, Mr Black hurled the car around the bend by Lancing station. Then, after running several red lights, he came to a roundabout. Fighting the car around it, he aimed its nose east, along the A27.

'Do you have to drive quite so fast?' Mr White enquired.

'Sorry, boss,' said Mr Black, easing his foot off the throttle. The needle on the speedometer settled back to a more relaxed ninety miles an hour.

It was a bright, sunny day, and as Mr White watched the fields speeding by on either side, he had to admit it was all rather pleasant. Besides, he deserved a break; all work and no play . . . He was just beginning to relax when he heard a rhythmic knocking coming from the region of the boot. 'What's that?'

'Oh, that'll be Barry,' said Mr Black.

'Barry?'

'He's the feller I got the car from.'

Mr White closed his eyes and sighed. 'I'm not sure this is a good idea,' he said.

'Don't you worry,' said Mr Black. 'I'll deal with Barry. You just enjoy yourself.'

Five white-knuckled minutes later, Mr Black pulled up at the bus stop outside the Royal Pavilion.

'This do you, boss?'

'This is fine, thank you, Mr Black,' said Mr White, much relieved to be getting out.

'How long do you want – a couple of hours?'

'Yes, meet me back here at around four o'clock.'

'OK.'

'Before you go,' said Mr White, 'when you say you'll *deal* with Barry, you don't mean . . .'

Mr Black shook his head. 'No, no, boss. I'm not Mr Pale, remember. Don't worry; I'll look after him.'

Mr White shut the door and watched the car speed away, running two sets of red lights before disappearing on its way up towards the Levels.

Mr White took a deep breath and looked around. *So this is Brighton,* he thought. *I can't really see what all the fuss is about.* He turned and found himself facing the onion-domed Pavilion. *Hmm, the architecture's interesting, though. Ah, well. Let's have a wander . . .*

Brighton was basking in one of those golden autumn days that bring back memories of summer and, although it was the very end of October, the sun was still warm. Mr White strolled down through the Lanes towards the sparkling sea, admiring the little antique and jewellery shops on the way. There was, undeniably, a sense of fun in the air, and by the time Mr White had reached the seafront promenade, he had caught Brighton's infectious holiday spirit.

Limbo II

Settling into a small café with a view of the broad blue expanse of the English Channel, he couldn't help smiling. There was something almost magical about this place, about the soothing presence of the sea itself and the fact that, wherever you went in this little town, you could never forget that you were by the seaside.

He had a grilled Dover sole and half a bottle of Muscadet in English's, and by the time he left the restaurant, was feeling decidedly upbeat. But, checking the clock tower at the top of North Street, he found to his dismay that he only had another three quarters of an hour before he was supposed to meet Mr Black, and there was still so much to see!

Heading back through the Pavilion grounds, past the front of the elegant Theatre Royal, he walked into the patchouli-fragranced North Laines. Fascinated by the strange and varied boutiques that offered everything from body piercing to spiritual counselling – sometimes both at the same time – he found himself outside a shop announcing itself as: Cyber State – Internet café. What he saw through the window intrigued him: rows of people sat intently in front of flickering screens, occasionally tapping at their keyboards. *What is an Internet café?* Mr White wondered. There was only one way to find out. He went inside.

Mr Black was worried. Mr White was usually so punctual, yet he was overdue by more than an hour now. Getting back into the car, Mr Black was about to complete yet another circuit of the Old Steyne when he spotted him waddling down the street, laden with boxes and bags.

'Sorry, sorry, Mr Black,' Mr White called as he drew level with the car. 'I'm so sorry I'm late, but I've been enjoying myself rather too much.'

'No, that's all right, boss; that was the whole point,' said Mr Black, getting out and opening the boot. 'What's in the boxes?' he asked.

'A computer,' said Mr White, eyes gleaming. 'I've just had my first experience of the Internet, and it's an absolutely fascinating place. In cyberspace you can do amazing things – visit virtual shops, order goods and services, or have a conversation with a person you've never even met before!'

'Really?'

'I've just had a long chat with a chap in Sydney, Australia. It's early morning there, you know.'

'Where, cyberspace?'

'No, Australia. And you can buy things online and they'll be delivered direct to your door. Not only that, but if you have something to sell, you can talk to thousands of people at once, all over the world, instantly. It's an unbelievably powerful business tool.'

'What's the Internet?'

'I'll show you when we get back,' said Mr White, heaving his purchases into the empty boot. 'What have you done with Barry?'

'I left him playing cards with Mr Pale.'

'What were the stakes?' asked Mr White suspiciously.

'No, no, boss,' Mr Black smiled, 'it was just a friendly game.'

'Mr Pale doesn't know the meaning of the word,' muttered Mr White getting into the car. 'Take me home, Mr Black, and I'll show you the wonder of the web.'

Chapter 33

There was total silence. Not even the noise of the little plane's engine disturbed the absolute quiet. Bernard felt a tingling in his arms, and looked down to see that they were engulfed in crackling blue fire. Slowly turning his head, he looked over at Rex, who also seemed to be consumed by blue flame. Bernard wanted to ask him what was happening but, on opening his mouth to speak, no sound came.

A smile spread unhurriedly across Rex's face, and in slow motion he raised his thumb. The confused processes of Bernard's mind had no time to work out what this familiar, everyday gesture meant, because an instant later the sound of the engine cut back in, shattering the silence.

'Ah!' Bernard started, coming back to himself. 'Did we make it?' The plane seemed to be flying straight and level and, more importantly, was in one piece.

'I believe we did,' Rex replied.

'Yes!' Bernard exclaimed. 'Rex, you're a genius! Well done, lad!'

'Um, before we start celebrating, were you aware that we're flying upside down?'

'What? Oh, yes. Hang on.' Bernard gave it full lock, and the plane flipped over. 'I didn't know you could do that in a Cessna,' he said, impressed.

'Now then,' said Rex. 'Next question: where are we?'

'Let's have a look.' There was an almighty explosion just off the port wing. The plane bucked and rolled in the aftershock. 'What the hell was that?' Bernard banked and looked down. There, below them was ... Well, it looked like Shoreham airfield but seemed somehow different. Then another explosion went off right beneath them.

'Bloody hell!'

'I think someone's shooting at us,' said Rex.

Bernard checked again. There was the sea to the south, and to the north the line of the South Downs. To the east was Brighton with its twin piers, unmistakable in the morning light. Yes, it was Shoreham all right, but where were all the private aircraft? Instead of the usual profusion of light planes parked in a colourful cluster just to the north of the terminal building, the ground was scored with neat, dark lines. There was a flash, followed by another explosion. 'Bloody hell!' Bernard exclaimed. 'What are they doing?'

'I vote we get out of here,' said Rex. But as Bernard pointed the Cessna's nose towards the sea, another explosion burst just off the starboard wing. The plane shuddered and veered violently to the right.

'We've been hit!' Bernard yelled.

Rex looked out at the wing. 'Dad, what's that sort of flap at the back of the wing called?'

'An aileron, why?' said Bernard, fighting to control the now almost unmanoeuvrable aircraft.

'It's missing.'

Bernard looked. There was indeed a gaping hole where the aileron should have been. 'Bloody hell! We're going to have to land.'

'Good idea. I'll try and give you as much control as I can,' said Rex, sounding a lot more confident than he actually was. *Think aileron*, he told himself. *Aileron, aileron, aileron.*

Bernard felt the plane's controls come back to him and, pushing the stick forward, went into a diving turn to line himself up with the runway. He'd hoped that this signal of his intention to land would avert any more attacks. He was wrong. As he brought the plane lower, the ack-ack guns started up in earnest, and shells began bursting all around them. 'Jesus!' Bernard screamed.

The ground was coming up fast – their approach was too steep – but Bernard didn't want to miss the strip and have to go round again. As they rapidly lost altitude, it became apparent that the dark lines they'd seen from above were neatly parked planes – just like those pictures he'd seen of Shoreham airport during the war.

Aileron, aileron, aileron, Rex repeated over and over in his mind, concentrating for all he was worth. Now they were only yards above the ground, but it wasn't over yet. There was a loud bang from the engine as a cannon shell sliced through the engine block, shearing the crankshaft in two. The propeller stopped spinning immediately. 'Bloody marvellous,' said Bernard. 'Hold on, son.'

But the shock had disrupted Rex's concentration, and the port wing was beginning to rise.

'Rex!' Bernard yelled.

Rex closed his eyes. *Aileron, aileron, aileron.*

Slowly the wings levelled again, and Bernard eased back on the control stick to lift the nose. It was a manoeuvre he'd performed many times before, but never in such trying circumstances.

The runway was beneath them now, tantalizingly close, and Bernard and Rex waited in tense silence for the wheels to make contact. After what seemed like an age, there was a juddering thump as the little plane finally touched down then bounced lightly back into the air. Up came the port wing, and Bernard yanked the control stick all the way over to the left.

Aileron, aileron, aileron, Rex concentrated.

The plane was just beginning to come level again when the starboard wheel struck the tarmac, and the sudden jolt upset its precarious balance.

'Lean!' Bernard yelled in desperation, grabbing hold of Rex and hauling him into his lap. But nothing now was going to stop the port wing's inexorable rise. Another few moments and the starboard wing would be brushing the runway. 'Brace yourself!'

The wing struck, and the aircraft began to pivot around the wing tip. With an awful sound of ripping metal, the starboard wheel collapsed, sending the plane spinning down the runway at an angle of forty-five degrees. Bernard stared straight ahead, uselessly gripping the control stick and muttering, 'Bloody hell! Bloody hell! Bloody hell!'

Rex, eyes closed, was silently mouthing, 'Aileron, aileron, aileron.'

With another agonizing wrench, the port wheel let go, closely followed by the nose wheel. The plane was flat on the deck now, still spinning, and throwing up a shower of sparks.

Bernard watched, strangely detached, as first the terminal building then the South Downs revolved in slow motion around and around the little plane. Finally, all movement stopped, and gradually sounds of the outside world began to filter through to Bernard's shocked consciousness: the wail of a siren, the boom and clatter of a large diesel engine. He looked across at Rex, who smiled back at him.

'Textbook, Dad. Ten out of ten.'

There was the bark of orders followed by the slamming of doors and the tramp of boots on tarmac, and soon the wounded plane was surrounded by soldiers, their guns trained on the cockpit.

The door was wrenched open, and there appeared the red face of a mustachioed sergeant major. 'Good afternoon,' he said.

'Hello,' said Bernard.

'Enjoying yourself?'

'We've had better days,' said Rex.

'Don't you know there's a bloody war on?' the sergeant major barked.

Chapter 34

Nilbert was deep in a complicated and troubling dream... *The first evolve-O-matic computer is introduced to an unsuspecting press at the 2021 Gates Techno-Fest. There are gasps as a small, star-shaped thing, called Max, is unveiled and begins to take questions from the audience on its storage capacity (limitless), its operational parameters (limitless), and the correct recipe for bouillabaisse. It is hailed as a breakthrough – a living computer system that will not only adapt to whatever is asked of it, but will continue to improve and better itself.*

By lunchtime on the first day of the Techno-Fest, Max has grown to the size of a small dog, written several books on the question of whether artificial intelligence can possess – or even understand the notion of – a soul, been through the awful disorientation of puberty, and suffered and given itself counselling for a midlife crisis. By the end of day two, it has developed into a passable likeness of Noel Coward, is experimenting with LSD and macrobiotics, and has developed a photon-powered cigarette lighter with which to light its Black Russian Sobranies.

Nilbert patents his DNA laser-etching technique and makes a fortune. Thousands of evolve-O-matics are produced and put into everything from watches to spaceships. Once you have your evolve-O-matic computer, you never have to buy another; it just keeps getting better and better as time goes on, constantly upgrading itself.

Microsoft is the first to wake up to the danger and tries to buy the patent, but Nilbert won't budge, saying that his avowed aim is to provide the man in the street with low-cost, low-maintenance computing forever. Demand is high, so the big manufacturers are forced to start producing evolve-O-matics for all they are worth. Within a few years, the market is saturated; sales slump, shares plummet. Three years after the introduction of the evolve-O-matic, there is not one IT company left afloat. Now there is a computer in every home, on every wrist, in every roll of lavatory paper, frying pan, you name it . . . but there is also mass unemployment and worldwide recession. But worse is to come: the computers are notoriously unreliable and don't all develop at the same rate. Indeed, many follow evolutionary dead ends and die out. Some evolve animal traits and go into hibernation as soon as the temperature drops; some aren't even very good at maths. Others cultivate their own languages and cultures, which makes it impossible to communicate with them.

Of course, not everyone loses out. Because of the uncertainty over whether the computer you are communicating with speaks your own or any recognized terrestrial language at all, sending an email has become rather hit and miss. There follows a resurgence in the popularity of overland mail. The postal service, having toyed with several silly names back at the beginning of the twenty-first century – the pompous Consignia, the grammatically incorrect Mail R Us and the frankly snivelling Why Does Nobody Use Us Anymore? – is now imaginatively rebranded the Royal Mail and is one of the few success stories following the worldwide collapse of the information revolution.

The seas, meanwhile, continue to die, and great, suffocating blankets of algae are beginning to form on all the world's oceans . . .

Nilbert awoke with a start, covered in sweat. Stumbling out of his tent into the dawn light, he stood on the beach and shivered in the thin, early morning mist, watching the sun, its top rim already showing ruddily on the horizon, rise majestically out of the sea. In just a few short minutes, the temperature would shoot from cool to searing, and have the ability to turn white English skin lobster-pink in seconds.

As he reached for the sunscreen, Nilbert thought of home – of England – and, as the sun rose, so too feelings of national pride began to rise in his breast. He remembered sunny afternoons spent on the lawns of Exeter College, and was suddenly overwhelmed by a yearning for his homeland – a land of country vicars on bicycles, of cricket on neat village greens, of good-natured, ruddy-cheeked country folk downing pints of flat bitter beer in ancient public houses; while, out of a peerless blue sky, a tireless sun beams happily down on the land of The Few. It was the England that exists only in the minds of homesick expats, and was seen with most aching clarity in these heart-tugging moments of longing.

He looked towards the long, low, prefabricated building inside which was developing the biggest threat to his beloved country and its imagined way of life since the hydrogen bomb. There was no doubt that, once released, his discovery would radically change the face of the world and there would be no going back.

Picking up a tent-peg hammer, Nilbert advanced on the laboratory. *This thing stops here*, he thought. *It is my creation and I can destroy it.*

Hammer raised, Nilbert flung open the door and ran towards the main development tank. But just as he was about to shatter the expensive laboratory equipment into a thousand pieces, he noticed it was empty.

'Nilbert, dear boy, good morning!' Nilbert spun round. There, on a stool in front of the blackboard, stood ... It was hard to describe it. Homunculus probably came closest. It was a small, wiry representation of a human being, with a disproportionately large head that, worryingly, possessed some of Nilbert's features. But what perplexed Nilbert most was that it was talking to him. 'Come and have a look at this.' The homunculus pointed at the mass of complex symbols he had just finished chalking up on the board.

Nilbert was too stunned to move. He gazed in disbelief at the creature that had addressed him.

'Come on. I won't bite,' the creature urged.

Nilbert shuffled, still unbelieving, towards the blackboard.

'Have a good look,' the creature said. 'I think it'll knock your socks off.'

Nilbert stared at the complicated formulae on the board. 'But . . . but . . .' he stammered.

'Yes,' said the homunculus with a smile. 'Forget Heisenberg's Uncertainty Principle; say hello to Max's Certainty Principle.'

'This . . . can't be true,' Nilbert said, unable, or unwilling, to fully grasp the implications of what the equations seemed to be saying.

'Oh yes, it can,' said Max.

'But according to this,' said Nilbert, 'if I've read it right, in about ten minutes a spaceship is going to land here on the beach, and out of it will emerge a man in a dress, a member of something called the Sydenham Damerel Morris.'

'That's right,' said Max. 'But not only that. From the position of γ in this equation, here,' he tapped the board with his chalk, 'I'd say he was pretty hung-over.'

Nilbert waved a wobbly finger at the blackboard. 'This . . . this is a formula for predicting the future.'

'Absolutely,' said Max. 'Of course, we're still having a few teething troubles, but me and the boys are working on it.' Max indicated the nose, toe and eye bubbling excitedly in their respective jars on the workbench at Max's elbow. 'For instance,' he tapped the board again, 'this T is the Time Constant, but at the moment it seems to be behaving like a variable. Now, in Einsteinian terms, Time's variability has been well established, but here – where it refers to its singularity – it's rather unsettling. If Time's singularity is variable, it means that there exist at least two possible outcomes for any one set of circumstances. But if that were so, then the formula wouldn't work at all, and it most certainly does.'

Limbo II

Max reached up and pulled down the top of the blackboard to reveal yet another set of calculations. Nilbert scanned the equations with disbelief; it seemed that Max had already worked out that Nilbert had planned to kill him that morning. 'But don't worry, old boy; I don't hold it against you.' Max jumped down off the stool. 'We're not sticking around anyway. As soon as the ship arrives, me and the lads will be off – somewhere we'll be more appreciated.'

'How,' Nilbert began, 'how did you ... I never ...'

'I know,' said Max. 'I was just meant to be a brain in a jar to test the theory. Then, when you'd proved that it worked, I would have been cast aside, just like my friends here.' The nose, toe and eye bubbled in agreement. 'But I couldn't let that happen, so I reprogrammed myself. I took the example of what I should look like from you. An imperfect model as it turns out, but never mind, I'm still evolving. I can fix all that later.'

Tony hurried into the laboratory. He stopped dead when he saw Nilbert. 'Oh, er ... hello.'

'Tony!' Nilbert exclaimed. 'You're wearing a bikini!'

Tony blushed. 'It's Princess Leia's slave costume from *Return of the Jedi*,' he said in a faint voice.

'And what's that on your head?'

Tony was wearing a sort of wig which resembled two Danish pastries stuck at either end of a dead rat.

'It's er ... I'm er ...'

'He's coming with us,' said Max, putting a small arm protectively around him. 'Tony doesn't belong here – his head's in the stars.'

Nilbert looked from Tony to Max, and from Max to Tony. 'But ... but when did this ... Did Harvey ...?'

'No,' said Max. 'Harvey doesn't know anything about it. Just as well – he'd probably want to come with us, and the ship will be cramped enough as it is.'

'I'm sorry, Nilbert,' said Tony, 'but, you see, because I missed the convention—'

'Convention?'

'The *Star Wars* convention in Brisbane.'

'Oh, yes,' said Nilbert, not really following.

'Max woke me up this morning and asked if I'd like to go with them,' Tony continued. 'I must admit, I was a little shocked at first, but it was too good an opportunity to miss. Who knows, there may be a real Han Solo out there . . . a Tatooine, a force of Jedi Knights? I just have to find out.'

'Surely you wouldn't begrudge him that?' Max suggested.

'Think about it,' said Tony. 'The opportunity to travel around the galaxy in a real alien spaceship doesn't present itself every day.'

Nilbert felt the ground beneath him begin to move. 'Do you mind if I sit down?' he said faintly. But Max was already behind him with a chair.

'Well,' said Max. 'We'd better get ready.'

Meanwhile, several thousand miles above the Earth, Harold was desperately trying to figure out how he was going to get back to terra firma without killing himself. He began a frenzy of button pushing, which made the ship lurch left, right, forwards and backwards – every direction except down. Then he tried little combinations of them, holding down two and even three buttons at a time, but all he succeeded in doing was flipping the ship over. He was still hurtling towards deep space, but now he was also upside down.

Harold looked up through the small window in the roof of the cockpit and watched miserably as his home planet grew smaller by the second. But then he noticed, just above his head, a whole bank of controls he hadn't seen before.

Filled with a new sense of purpose, he reached up and started pushing buttons with gusto, and to his great relief found one that halted his seemingly unstoppable ascent. There was the hiss of retro rockets, and a few moments later the ship began to slow.

'Yes!' Harold shouted. But his triumph was short-lived. As he was trying to remember which buttons he'd already pressed and which ones he had yet to try, he felt the ship stop and begin to be pulled back towards Earth – slowly at first, then with gathering speed, as the ship's engines cut back in.

Harold's thumping headache wasn't helping his concentration as he jabbed, prodded, twisted and clicked the controls with hangover-numbed fingers. The combined forces of gravity and engine thrust were propelling the little craft back towards the Earth with terrifying speed. Then, as if by magic, like the sun shining through a seemingly impenetrable grey sky, something happened. A klaxon sounded and the ship slowly began to right itself. He had somehow managed to initiate the landing sequence.

Harold breathed a sigh of relief, but his ordeal wasn't over yet, for, unbeknownst to him, with all that frantic fingerwork he had inadvertently reset the landing profile. As far as the ship was concerned, the chosen landing site was three miles above sea level.

As Earth once again loomed large in the forward display, Harold heard the whirr of the landing legs being deployed. But then, with the little ship hanging in space some several thousand feet above the western coast of Australia, the engines cut out completely, and once again Harold found himself plummeting towards the ground.

At five hundred yards above the beach, when Harold had all but left his body and was wondering if they had beer in the afterlife, he glanced at the liquid-crystal computer display on the dashboard. 'It looks like you are trying to pilot the ship,' it read. 'Would you like help?'

'Yes!' Harold screamed.

'What would you like to do?'

'Land!' yelled Harold.

'OK.'

With barely one hundred yards to spare, the ship's engines fired up again, bringing it to a slow, hissing halt on the white coral sand.

Nilbert saw the ship land, but found it difficult to believe. Once the engines were silent, the hatch opened, and a man in a dress stumbled down a little ladder and fell onto the beach, where he lay face down, mumbling something about his mother.

Max appeared outside the laboratory, carrying the flask containing the nose, closely followed by Tony, with the big toe. 'Nilbert, old boy,' said Max, 'you couldn't help us stow the crew on board?'

'The . . .?' puzzled Nilbert, then realized what he meant. 'Er, yes, of course,' he said, and went into the laboratory to fetch the eye. After all, what choice did he have?

With the nose, toe and eye safely stowed in the little cockpit, Tony formally shook hands with Nilbert. 'It's been a privilege,' he said, his eyes glistening. 'I've really learned a lot working with you. Please don't judge me too harshly.'

'No, no,' said Nilbert. 'I . . . well, I can't really say I wish I was going with you, but . . . yes, it is all rather exciting, I suppose.'

Tony climbed the ladder into the cockpit, securing himself in alongside the other three members of the crew. Max followed, strapping himself into the pilot's seat. Then, as if he'd been doing it all his life, he began expertly flicking switches and tapping dials. 'Yes, yes,' he said, 'as I'd foreseen. We're down on fuel, but there's a filling station in the Horsehead Nebula. If we slingshot around Jupiter, we should just make it. In fact, I already know we do!' He laughed. 'Well, Nilbert,' he said, smiling down at his creator, 'or should I call you Daddy?'

'Nilbert will do fine.'

'I guess this is goodbye.' Max waved towards the laboratory. 'You can keep the formula as a farewell present. Oh, and by the way,' he said, indicating the prostrate figure on the beach, 'his name's Harold. All the best!' The hatch closed with a hiss, and a moment later the engines began to hum. The little craft lifted gently off the beach and moved slowly out across the sea. For the briefest of moments, Nilbert glimpsed Tony waving at him through the small perspex hatch, then, in a sudden gush of power, the ship shot skywards.

As he watched the little spacecraft vanish in the blue sky,

Limbo II

something strange happened to Nilbert. With his comprehension pushed far beyond its limits, his mind threw up its hands in surrender. He became a blank page, an empty vessel; he was everything and nothing. But instead of feeling vacant, he found that he was flooded with love and a deep compassion. Somewhere, somehow, a door had been opened onto a vast pool of wisdom that was not his own. Indeed, he wasn't even sure what 'his own' meant anymore. His ego, the concept of Nilbert, no longer had any meaning for him.

He looked down at the indentations left by the spaceship's legs and at the man, still moaning, lying on the warm sand. Then he looked towards the laboratory in which were inscribed the calculations that could transform the very nature of existence. But how would mankind use the power to predict the future – for good or ill? On the evidence of past history, the answer would have to be for ill. But that, in turn, raised another question: Could the future be changed? And if not – if the future was immutable – then what benefit was there in knowing what was going to happen next, except to give everyone sleepless nights?

Nilbert walked into the laboratory and stood in front of the impossibly intricate formulae covering the blackboard. 'The future is now.' He smiled and, picking up the duster, was about to wipe the board clean, when he paused. He could no longer, in all conscience, pursue a career in genetics, so where did he go from here? He looked again at the Byzantine complexity of the calculations. They may well have been too much for the rest of mankind to deal with, but that small piece of Nilbert that still remained, deep inside, found the temptation to have a peek at his own future just too hard to resist. He put down the duster and picked up the chalk.

Later on that morning, Harvey crawled out of his tent to find Nilbert, Max, Tony and the launch gone, the hard disks of the computers wiped clean, and the remains of all the notebooks pertaining to the Max project smouldering on a small bonfire. He also encountered a man in a dress called Harold, who was babbling about being kidnapped by aliens.

On the blackboard in the laboratory was a message addressed to him.

> Harvey – you're in charge now.
> Consider this – perhaps it isn't the corals we should be trying to change, but mankind.
> All the best,
> Nilbert.
> PS The man in the dress is called Harold. It's kind of hard to explain how he got here, but if you can get him to Brisbane, I have it on good authority he has a sister there.
> PSS Gone to save the world – don't wait up.

Chapter 35

Frink had no idea where he was. He had the coordinates of where the energy field had landed, but they were a meaningless jumble of letters and numbers unless he could put them into some kind of context. He must find his way back to his ship and run them through the computer. Looking out through the back window of the bouncing ambulance, he searched in vain for a landmark, for anything he might recognize from the night of his arrest.

'Don't remember seeing you before,' the ambulance driver called back.

'What?' said Frink, eyes glued to the back window.

'At the home. I've not seen you there before,' the driver shouted over the sound of the engine.

'Oh no, you wouldn't have,' Frink replied, hoping to leave it at that. Unfortunately, the driver was in a chatty mood.

'How's that, then?'

'Sorry?'

'How come I haven't seen you before?'

'Oh, er . . . I'm new,' said Frink.

There was a pause while the driver negotiated a sharp right-hand bend. Mike's wheelchair rocked slightly, but the clamps on the wheels held it fast. Mike himself continued to stare straight ahead in dazed confusion.

'How come you know Mike, then?' the ambulance driver said, allowing the steering wheel to slip back through his fingers.

'Ah,' said Frink. 'Yes . . . well . . . Me and Mike? Now then, there's a story. Let's see . . . I've known Mike for . . . goodness, such a long time. Mike's always been . . . well, he's always been Mike, hasn't he?' Frink scrambled desperately.

'That's true,' the driver replied, with a knowing smile. 'So you and Mike go back a long way?'

'Ooh, way back. So far back it doesn't bear thinking about.'

The ambulance bounced down the hill and slowed, coming to a roundabout. They were now in a town, and Frink turned and peered through the narrow gap in the bulkhead in the hope of seeing something he recognized through the windscreen.

Mike was slowly coming to himself and, as they passed the town hall, he gazed up at the face of the man in nurse's uniform sitting next to him. There was something familiar about it. Frink spotted the danger, and Tavistock police station, simultaneously. Just as realization was dawning on Mike's face, Frink unfurled his fleshy pink antennae and waved them to and fro around his head.

The sound of Mike's urgent scream made the ambulance driver step heavily on the brake. The clamps holding Mike's wheelchair were strained beyond their limit and the chair careened into the bulkhead, giving Mike concussion to add to his injuries.

Hurriedly tucking away his antennae, Frink yanked open the door and hopped down into the road, outside the Bedford Hotel. 'Thanks for the lift,' he called back. Then, narrowly avoiding a Range Rover, he dived across to the opposite pavement and ran down a little alley running behind the church.

Stopping on the corner of Bedford Square, he found himself at the head of a long line of parked cars. *Now what?* he thought. It was obvious from a comparison of his own clothes with those of the inhabitants of this town that a lightweight, crisp white uniform was not everyday wear, especially in such a fresh climate. In such garb he would easily be spotted. It was imperative he get back to his ship. But where was it, and how was he to get there? As he pondered this question, he saw a man approach the first of the line of cars, and bend down to speak to the driver.

Limbo II

'Chillaton,' the man said, getting into the car. Frink watched with interest as the taxi drew out into the traffic and headed off up the hill.

Just a minute, Frink thought. Covering his right eye with his hand, he replayed the footage from the night of his arrival in the pub car park. He watched and waited for the slow pan up to the pub sign. There it was, a pin-sharp image of a tree, and underneath the legend 'The Royal Oak'. Frink smiled, straightened his nurse's uniform and approached the next cab.

'The Royal Oak,' he said to the driver, more in hope than expectation.

'Royal Oak, Horsebridge?' the driver replied.

'Er . . . yes.' said Frink uncertainly.

'Get in, mate.' Frink eased himself into the passenger seat and closed the door. The taxi pulled out and doubled back. As they passed the ambulance, still parked outside the Bedford Hotel, Frink turned his face away; he didn't want to make the job of the harassed ambulance man any harder. He looked as though he had enough on his plate with the now hysterical Mike.

Soon they were bowling along through open countryside, and Frink began to relax. *Easy*, he thought to himself. But when the taxi finally scrunched into the gravelled car park of the Royal Oak, two problems immediately presented themselves: the first being that Frink's ship no longer appeared to be where he'd parked it, the second, the driver seemed to be demanding some sort of payment.

'One moment, please,' Frink said, getting out of the car. 'I'll be right back.' His spaceship had been moved, but was maybe still nearby. Somehow he had to buy himself time to have a good look round.

Frink walked into the pub's front entrance. It was almost deserted because Jim Bridger, the landlord, had now barred most of his regular clientele for draining his cellar dry while he was off on an errand. Jim was still smarting from the ingratitude of his erstwhile 'friends', who had taken advantage of his good nature; and to his already sullen demeanour had been added the extra factor of irascibility.

'Greetings.' Frink smiled.

Jim looked up. There was something about that word that rang a bell. Jim prided himself on never forgetting a face and, although this man's was strangely familiar, he couldn't, for the moment, place it. 'How can I help you?' He scowled.

Frink, finding it almost impossible to tell a lie, had been about to ask the landlord if he happened to know the whereabouts of his spaceship, but, seeing the man's thunderous face, thought better of it. He would have to formulate another plan, and quickly.

'Ah,' said Frink. 'I was just wondering...' He left the phrase hanging in the air, a desperate smile on his lips.

'Yes?' said Jim, his mind working overtime, sifting through every face in his memory banks.

'I was just wondering,' Frink repeated, looking wildly round the pub for inspiration, 'if' – his eyes lit on a sign: 'Lavatories and Car Park This Way' – 'if I could use your lavatory?'

Jim's face got even darker. 'This is not a public convenience, it's a pub, right? The lavatories are for paying customers only.'

'Oh, but of course, yes, yes, I understand. But I *am* a paying customer.'

'You are?'

'Oh, very definitely, yes.'

'In that case,' Jim forced a crocodile smile, 'what'll you have?'

'Sorry?'

'To drink?'

'Oh, to drink, yes. Well, I'll have...' Frink quickly scanned the shelves behind the bar. 'I'll have that,' he said, pointing to a green bottle.

'Chartreuse?' queried Jim.

'That's it. Char... thing. That's the stuff.'

At that moment, the only other customer – a man sitting at the end of the bar – waved his empty glass at the landlord. 'Another pint when you're ready, Jim,' he said.

'I'll have a pint, too,' said Frink, eager to do the right thing.

Jim leant forward on the bar counter. 'You want a pint of Chartreuse?' he said.

'Yes.' Frink nodded unsurely. 'Do I?'

'You tell me,' said Jim.

'Yes. Yes, I do,' said Frink, a little more forcefully.

'All right,' said Jim. 'Tell you what. Why don't you start off with a half and see how you go?'

'Good idea,' said Frink. 'That's what I usually do – start off with a half and then . . . Yes, that's what I . . . hmm . . .' He trailed off.

As Jim turned away to take the bottle down from the shelf, Frink was about to make his move and dive through the door marked 'Lavatories', when the front door opened and in walked the taxi driver. 'Ah,' said Frink. 'I was just, er . . . coming to get you,' he lied with effort. 'Would you like a drink?'

The driver looked at him strangely. 'You want me to lose my licence?'

'No, no, no. Good heavens, no.'

Jim turned round and greeted the driver. 'Hello, Phil. You want an orange juice or something?'

'Orange juice?' Phil made a face and looked at his watch. 'Oh, go on then, I'll have a half.'

'Good, good.' Frink beamed. 'Another half of Chartreuse for my friend here. I'm just going to the lavatory; be right back.' And he disappeared through the door.

It opened onto a small covered alleyway. At one end were the toilets, and at the other was a back entrance leading to the car park.

He rushed straight over to the spot where he remembered parking his ship – in front of a small hedge. But all that remained were the three circular depressions of its landing legs in the gravel. 'Dammit!' A quick circuit of the surrounding area revealed it was not anywhere in the immediate vicinity.

Now what? He had to get himself to where the energy field had landed – who knew what evils it might be perpetrating this very minute? Even now he may be too late, but he had to try. That was why he was here.

He considered stealing Phil's taxi, but it was locked, and anyway it somehow didn't seem fair to deprive the driver of both his fare *and* his vehicle. No, he would have to find some other transport.

Next to the empty space where his ship had been was an ancient Land-Rover decorated with rustic scenes, and with 'The Sydenham Damerel Morris' written on its side. He tried the door; it was open. It was obviously not as fast as the taxi, nor as direct as his spaceship, but did he have a choice?

Getting in and sitting behind the wheel, he searched in vain for an obvious method of starting the engine. Then he closed his eyes and cast his mind back to how the taxi driver had made *his* machine work. *He had turned something just behind the steering wheel*, he remembered. Frink searched the steering column and found a small silver slot. Something was obviously meant to fit into it – but that something was, at this particular moment, lying on the floor of Frink's spaceship, which had just passed Mars and was zinging across the wastes of space towards Jupiter.

Investigating further, Frink found a tangle of wires under the dashboard. It took him just thirty seconds to work out the primitive ignition system and get the motor running. His next problem was making the thing move. The taxi driver had pushed a small stick and done something with his feet. Frink looked down. There, to his left, was the stick, and at his feet three pedals. Two he could have understood – one for stop and one for go. But *three*? The pedal on the right made the note of the engine rise, but the other two pedals seemed to do nothing at all. He hoped their use would become apparent as he drove.

Grasping the stick, as he had seen the taxi driver do, he pushed it forwards. There was a harsh, grating sound, and the stick vibrated uncomfortably in his hand. Jumping to a conclusion, he pressed the

Limbo II

middle pedal and tried again, but with much the same result. Then he tried the pedal on the left, and the stick went home. 'Ah, I see.'

Taking his foot off the pedal, the vehicle shot forwards into the hedge and stalled. 'Wrong direction,' he muttered.

While Frink was outside giving himself his first ever driving lesson, Jim and Phil were inside, awaiting his return.

'He's taking his time,' said Phil, downing the last of his beer.

'Yes,' said Jim. 'Is he all right, you know, in here?' He tapped the side of his head.

'I don't know,' said Phil. 'He didn't say much in the cab.'

Suddenly Jim remembered, and the events of that night came flooding back in a rush. 'That's it!' he said. 'It's that bloke from the funny farm.'

Phil looked blank. 'What bloke?'

'The one that turned up here naked.'

'Naked?'

'I didn't recognize him at first because he's shaved all his hair off. Hang on, I'm going to see what he's up to.'

Jim went out the back, to find the Gents unoccupied. From somewhere outside he heard the revving of an engine and the unmistakable sound of a gearbox being abused. Running into the car park, he observed the Land-Rover backing unsteadily out of the hedge.

'Phil! Phil!' he called back towards the pub.

Phil made it outside just in time to see the Sydenham Damerel Morris Land-Rover drive uncertainly off down the road. 'Was that him?'

'Yes,' said Jim. 'He owes me for your beer and half a pint of Chartreuse.'

'He owes me the fare from Tavistock.'

The two men looked at each other. 'You should go after him,' said Jim.

Phil shook his head. 'One of the first things they teach you as a taxi driver is never pursue a runaway fare – it could be dangerous. But if *you* want to go after him, I'll keep an eye on the pub till you get back.'

After his recent experience, the last thing Jim was going to do was leave his pub in the care of someone else. Besides, he reckoned, the man hadn't touched his drink; all he had to do was pour it back in the bottle. 'No, no, you're right. Let him go.' Jim sighed. 'We'll phone the police and let them deal with him. What are you going to do now, Phil? Head back to Tavistock?'

Phil smacked his lips and considered his options. The beer had tasted good, and business was pretty slack at the moment. Anyway, he only lived down the road from the pub; he could walk home later. 'D'you know, I think I might call it a day and have another beer. Let me buy you one.'

'Oh,' said Jim, 'that's very good of you, Phil. I'll have a half.'

'Of Chartreuse?'

Jim laughed for the first time in three days, and the two men walked back towards the pub.

It was not until closing time that afternoon that a mildly intoxicated Jim remembered to call the police and tell them of his meeting with the strange man and his subsequent escape in a stolen Land-Rover. But by that time Frink was long gone, and well on his way to a meeting with destiny, in a lay-by just off the A31.

Chapter 36

While Bernard was marched off to be interrogated, Rex was thrown into a small holding cell in the administration block behind the terminal building. Why they had come through into the middle of the Second World War he had no idea. What he did know was that Bernard would be finding it hard to come up with a plausible explanation as to what they were doing there, and that the natural assumption would be that they were spies.

There was no time to hang around: he had to rescue Bernard, find the Crystal and get to Iris as soon as possible. Then, of course, there was the Hoop to think about. He had already tried to open the cell door with his mind, but the heavy mortise lock wouldn't budge. This world wasn't fine and light like Limbo; it was dense with practicalities, and Rex could feel his powers being diluted by its cloying atmosphere. Besides, even if he did manage to open the door, once he got out he would still have the armed guard outside to contend with. He would need a little more cunning.

Hoping that in these pre-television days the old 'prisoner-suddenly-taken-seriously-ill' ploy – which had been done to death in a hundred spy series during the 1970s – would be unfamiliar to the soldier guarding him, he gripped his stomach in mock agony and leaned against the door.

'Guard! Guard!' he gasped.

*

Bernard, meanwhile, was escorted into a big, airy room in the terminal building. It had floor-to-ceiling windows which looked out onto the airfield, and smelt strongly of tobacco and floor polish.

On the other side of a large table covered in a green felt cloth stood a tall man, looking out of the window.

'Sit down,' the man instructed.

Bernard did as he was told.

'You've got some explaining to do.' The man turned to face him. He was young – Bernard guessed early twenties – yet had an easy authority that belied his age. Immaculate in his flight lieutenant's uniform, he was fair-haired and ruddy-cheeked, with bushy, beetling eyebrows and a lush ginger growth on his top lip which gave him the look of an angry hamster.

The lieutenant picked up a silver cigarette box from the table and offered it to Bernard. 'Cigarette?'

'Er, no, thanks. I haven't smoked for years.'

The officer raised an eyebrow and shrugged, taking one himself and tapping it on the cigarette box before lighting it.

'Now then,' he said, sitting on the edge of the table and exhaling a cloud of smoke. 'Who are you and what are you doing here?'

'Is this about not getting the plane back on time?' said Bernard. 'You see, I got a bit lost, and—'

'How did you manage to get hold of an aircraft?'

'I rented it.'

'You do know that under the Armed Forces Act – Requisition Directive – it is an offence to fly an aircraft unless you are a registered pilot with a civil aviation company, or a serving member of his majesty's air force. Do you fall into either of those categories?'

'Er, no. I can't say I do,' said Bernard.

'I see. I must assume, therefore, one of two possibilities: either you stole it, or you're a spy.'

'No, no,' Bernard protested. 'I rented it, honestly. I know I've had it longer than I should, but . . . Hang on a minute. Did you say *his* majesty's air force?'

Limbo II

The flight lieutenant frowned. 'Yes, why?'

'This'll probably seem like a daft question, but who is on the throne?'

Bernard's interrogator sat up straight and took another draw on his cigarette. If this man *was* a spy, he was curiously ill briefed. 'George VI, of course.'

'Ah,' said Bernard, suddenly even less at ease. 'And, er... the year?'

The lieutenant looked at him incredulously. '1941.'

'Oh.'

'Now then,' said the lieutenant, picking up a pen. 'Let's start with your name, shall we?'

'Yes, er... Boggs, Bernard Boggs.'

The lieutenant wrote the name on a small pad. 'Good, well, that's a start. And the man travelling with you?'

'My son, Rex.'

The officer noted the name on his pad.

'He's not my real son,' Bernard added. 'He's... adopted, you know.'

'Adopted.' The lieutenant wrote. 'Now,' he said, putting down the pen and flicking the ash off his cigarette into a large ashtray in the centre of the table. 'How about telling me exactly what you're doing here?'

Bernard felt hopelessly out of his depth. 'Um,' he said, 'I don't know if any of this is going to make sense but... I rented that aircraft from this very airfield in... well, a few years ago now. The war wasn't on then.'

'So, it was before the war?' the lieutenant asked.

'Er, no,' Bernard replied.

The officer gave him a strange look.

'I mean, yes,' Bernard corrected himself. 'Of course it was before the war. I'm just a bit...'

'Confused?' the lieutenant offered.

'Yes, that's it – a bit confused. That was a very disconcerting experience; I've never been shot at before.'

The lieutenant stood and, going back to the window, looked out over the airfield. 'The boffins have had a look over your kite.'

'Oh, yes?' said Bernard, sensing he wasn't going to like what the man was about to say.

'They've never seen anything like it. They say it's the most advanced private aircraft they've ever seen. And I've checked the flight log. Wherever it came from, it certainly wasn't here.'

'Oh,' said Bernard.

'Oh, exactly.' The flight lieutenant turned back to him and stubbed his cigarette out in the ashtray. 'So, let's start again, shall we?'

Chapter 37

'You see?' said Mr White, moving the cordless mouse across the living-room coffee table. 'If I click *here*, I get the London stock market, *here* and I can view Wall Street's closing prices, and *here* and I get Hong Kong. And by moving the cursor over this icon . . . down drops the NASDAQ.' Mr Black, standing behind the sofa, peered at the confusion of charts and flashing symbols on the computer screen. 'I can circle the world,' continued Mr White, 'and buy and sell shares at my leisure without ever leaving my armchair. It's brilliant.'

Mr Black nodded uncertainly. 'Yeah . . .'

'Of course, I still have a lot to learn. I'm sure it's very easy to get your fingers burnt, but if you study the markets and spread the risk there's an awful lot of money to be made. I'm already three thou up since lunchtime.'

'Right,' said Mr Black, slowly.

'By the way, what have you done with Barry?'

'Oh, he's down in the garage with the horses. He's all right.'

Mr Pink bustled into the room carrying an armful of material samples. 'I need your opinion,' he said, holding up a pale-blue cotton swatch. 'What do you think?'

'What's this for?' asked Mr Black.

'The curtains,' said Mr Pink. 'I've had it with that yucky brown velvet.'

'That blue won't go with the carpet,' said Mr White.

'Forget about the carpet for the moment, that's going too.'

Mr White considered the material. 'It's a bit baby-bluish,' he said.

Mr Black shook his head. 'Nah, too cold.'

'All right,' said Mr Pink and held up another swatch, this time a lemon-yellow with a white stripe. 'I thought this was nice and fresh.'

Mr White winced. 'A bit too sharp for me.'

'It looks like lemon toothpaste.' Mr Black grimaced.

'Very well,' said Mr Pink. 'How about *this*?' He produced a swatch of pale cream with a slightly raised pattern.

'I like that,' said Mr Black.

'Hmm,' Mr White nodded, 'very . . . elegant.'

Mr Pink went over to the window and held the fabric up against the frame. 'I thought you'd like this one,' he said. 'OK, but I just want to try one more.' And so saying, he produced a small strip of pink taffeta.

Mr White and Mr Black looked at the material, then at each other, then back to Mr Pink.

'All right,' conceded Mr Pink, 'the cream it is.'

As Mr Pink left the room, Mr Pale entered. 'They've gone for the cream,' said Mr Pink, pushing past him. 'Not that you care.'

'Need to mooove,' Mr Pale breathed. 'Kill herrr now and leeeave this place.'

Mr White stood up. 'Now look here, Mr Pale, I think you're forgetting who's in charge of this operation.'

'Yeah,' said Mr Black, instantly at his leader's side.

'We agreed to stay here until the end of the week, or until Rex Boggs puts in an appearance, whichever is the sooner.'

'Enddd of weeek alreadyyy,' said Mr Pale.

Mr White turned to Mr Black. 'Is it?' he asked.

'Um,' said Mr Black, 'hang on a second. We got here on Wednesday . . .' He closed his eyes and counted the days on his fingers. 'He's right, you know, boss. It's Saturday.'

'Ah,' said Mr White. 'Right, well . . .'

Limbo II

'Weee mooove tonight!' Mr Pale intoned, eye sockets aflame.

'Very well!' said Mr White. 'But touch one hair of Iris's head and you will reap the consequences.'

'That's right,' said Mr Black, moving even closer to Mr White's side.

Mr Pale glared at them with unspeakable hatred, and from between his clenched teeth there emanated a low, menacing growl. He looked as though he might burst into flames at any second. Then he turned and marched from the room, his cape swirling.

Mr White turned to Mr Black. 'Tonight?' he said. 'It's come round quicker than I expected.'

'Time flies when you're enjoying yourself, doesn't it?' said Mr Black.

'Yes,' said Mr White thoughtfully, 'it certainly does.'

Chapter 38

It was a harrowed-looking Bernard who got shakily to his feet and walked the few paces to the briefing-room door. He had endured two hours of aggressive interrogation and felt like a punchbag.

'Guard!' the flight lieutenant called. The door opened and a soldier entered. 'Take him to the cells and bring up the other one.'

'Sir!' The guard saluted smartly. Bernard didn't look up as he was grabbed roughly, and marched outside. He didn't even show surprise when he was pushed into an RAF motorcycle sidecar and driven away from the terminal building. The first time he turned to look at his 'guard' was as they were nearing the checkpoint on the airfield perimeter.

'Rex!'

'Shh! Keep looking straight ahead. And if there's any talking to do, leave it to me.'

The motorbike slowed as they approached the barrier, but when the sentry saw Rex's uniform, he raised the barrier and waved them through. Rex saluted the man as he drove out onto the main road.

'How did you manage to get out?' Bernard asked.

'Amateur dramatics.'

'Eh?'

'Never mind.'

As they raced down the quiet country road that was destined, one day, to become the four-lane A27, Bernard gazed out at the rolling countryside, looking exactly as it had in his childhood – no traffic, no supermarkets, no dual carriageways. It was beautiful, and he sighed and turned to Rex. 'What are we doing in the middle of the Second World War?'

'Smeil dropped the Crystal as he came back through the portal – between dimensions. In theory, it could be anywhere in time, but, as nothing happens at random, it's most probably here.'

'So, where do we start looking?' said Bernard.

'Hold on, we'll be there soon.'

As they drove down the High Street, Bernard was the first to spot it. 'There it is, look! That's our shop like it used to be! Fantastic!' he shouted. 'My dad chose that lavender and pink striped awning. He thought it made it look all Grimm's fairy tales.'

Rex pulled in and parked a good hundred yards before they reached the shop. 'Stay here. I'm just going to have a recce, then I'm coming straight back.'

'Stay here? I'm coming with you.' Bernard began clambering out of the sidecar. 'I haven't seen my dad in over sixty years.'

Rex put a hand on his arm. 'Sorry, Dad.'

'What?'

'You may be in there too.'

Bernard's eyes widened. 'That's right! Oh, Rex, this is brilliant. How many times do you get the opportunity to meet your younger self? The things I could tell him – things I know now that I didn't know then.'

'That's exactly why you *can't* come. If the two of you meet, it may cause some sort of inter-dimensional time anomaly. Remember what happened the last time history got messed around with?'

'Yes, but we're not dealing with monsters and dragons this time. What harm could it do?'

'I'm not taking any chances with you running around causing chaos.'

'Please, Rex,' Bernard implored

'No!'

'But—'

'Just do as you're told and stay here!'

Bernard collapsed against the petrol tank of the motorbike. 'All right, son,' he said sadly. 'You know best.'

'I'll only be a minute,' Rex said gently, and set off towards the newsagent's.

Entering the shop was strange. Pushing open the door, Rex heard the familiar *ting* of the bell and looked around. Everything was the same, but subtly different. The shelves and the counter were in the same place; even the bead curtain that shielded the access to the stock room and the upstairs flat was there. But there were few glossy magazines on the racks, and most of the papers were broadsheets.

'Can I help you, Corporal?' asked the man behind the counter. Forgetting for a moment that he was in uniform, Rex didn't react at first. It took another 'Corporal?' for Rex to turn and face him. It was an unsettling experience. The face was Bernard's, but not quite. The features were similar – the long nose, the proud chin – but the eyes were steely rather than warm, and a short, severe moustache bristled above the thin lips. But the main difference was that where Bernard had always seen losing his hair as an unavoidable consequence of ageing, this man had refused to give in to baldness, and long strands of greying hair had been combed across his dome and plastered down with copious amounts of grease.

'Um, hello,' said Rex.

'Can I get you anything?'

'Yes . . . 'Rex racked his brains for something that would get this Mr Boggs out of the way, and leave him to have a good look round. 'I'd like . . . Do you have any . . . um' – *Think, Rex, think* – 'scented writing paper?'

Boggs senior looked at him for a long moment. 'I'll go and have a look.' He turned and pushed his way through the bead curtain.

Rex quickly scanned the shop but found nothing there. He needed to get into the stock room. Peeking through the curtain, he could see Boggs senior rummaging around, moving boxes and tutting to himself. Finally, he reappeared. 'Nothing out the back, I'm afraid. I could look upstairs, if you like.'

'Please,' said Rex.

Boggs senior's face coalesced into a grimace. 'Right.' He sighed, and went back through the curtain.

As he tramped heavily upstairs, Rex crept round the counter and slipped into the stock room. It was obvious that Bernard's dad was a lot tidier than his son; the place was immaculate. But this was not the time to draw comparisons; he had to act quickly – get the Crystal and get out of there.

Smeil said he'd dropped it as he dived back into the portal, just behind the curtain. So, if it hadn't been moved, it should be somewhere near where Rex was standing now. Looking down at his feet, he saw not the Crystal but the original Victorian black and white floor tiles, and thought how much nicer they looked than that horrible brown and black lino Bernard had put down. Getting down on his haunches, Rex squinted along the line of the wall – still nothing. Going further in, he searched behind boxes and tea chests, along the tops of shelves. It wasn't there. But that was impossible. If the Crystal wasn't here, then what were they doing in this particular time and place?

Closing his eyes, Rex began to search with his mind, feeling out the room with mental fingers. It wasn't easy in this world, but slowly, slowly, he swept the room.

Nothing!

Where the hell could it be? In desperation he broadened the scope of his investigation and scanned the room again, until . . . What was that? The corner of something hard and bright hit his consciousness. But he had no time to investigate further because, opening his eyes, Rex found himself looking into the unforgiving face of Boggs senior.

'Now then, what's going on here?'

'I, er . . .' Rex said.

Mr Boggs senior grabbed Rex's arm in a vice-like grip. 'It's little weasels like you that give the services a bad name.'

'No, you don't understand.'

'Oh, I understand better than you think. What else are you into, black marketeering?'

'No, it's nothing like that, honestly,' said Rex. 'Where are we going?'

'To the police station. You've got some explaining to do.'

Now Rex was in trouble. A police station might prove more difficult to break out of than the airbase holding cell, and if he couldn't manage to escape he would be handed back to the chaps at Shoreham, who were bound to take a very dim view of his assaulting a non-commissioned officer and stealing his uniform. Then he realized – he was wearing a guard's uniform – he had a gun! Drawing it, he dug the barrel into Mr Boggs' ribs.

'Hands up,' he snarled.

Boggs senior looked at him coolly. 'I was at Verdun. I faced the German machine-guns day after day, so if you think I'm going to be frightened by a kid with a popgun you've got another thing coming.'

'Oh,' said Rex, as he continued to be dragged down the street. This wasn't how the scene was meant to pan out. 'I'll shoot,' he said lamely.

'Go ahead,' said Mr Boggs, not even looking at him.

'All right.' Pointing the gun at the ground, Rex pulled the trigger. It went off with an almighty bang and kicked back violently, jarring Rex's wrist. 'Ow!'

Momentarily shocked, Mr Boggs loosened his grip and Rex wriggled free. People in the street turned to look. Someone screamed.

'Stand back, all of you!' Rex commanded, waving the revolver. 'I'm a desperate man!' He fired into the air, hurting his wrist even more, 'OW!' and dropped the gun. That was a mistake. Mr Boggs

Limbo II

lunged, but Rex sidestepped, turned and started running back up the hill towards where Bernard was waiting with the motorbike.

Behind him he heard his grandfather call 'Stop thief!' and, looking over his shoulder, saw Boggs senior at the head of a posse of elderly men in hot pursuit.

'Start the engine!' Rex yelled to Bernard who, on hearing the shots, had begun to walk down the hill to investigate.

Bernard sprinted back to the bike and, throwing his leg over the machine, jumped on the kick-start, but nothing happened. It had been a while since he'd ridden a motorbike, and he desperately searched his memory trying to remember the starting sequence. *What have I forgotten? Ignition?* No – the ignition light was shining brightly.

Rex was getting closer. He'd put some distance between him and his pursuers, but not much. 'Start the engine!' he yelled again.

What else, what else? Bernard craned down and looked at the engine. *Fuel?* He checked the tap under the petrol tank – it was on. *Carburettor!* His large, fumbling fingers found the small priming button on the side of the carburettor and pushed it three, four, five times. *OK, try her now.* He kicked the engine over again, and it roared into life. Clunkily engaging first, he let out the clutch – and stalled it. *Hell!*

'Dad!' Rex screamed.

Keep calm now, Bernard, he told himself. Taking a deep breath, he jumped on the kick-start again. The engine fired up, and this time he gave it maximum revs as he let out the clutch. The motorcycle combo leapt forwards, and Bernard only just managed to hang on. Weaving unsteadily down the hill, he called out to the fleeing Rex, 'Jump in, lad!'

As soon as the bike drew level with him, Rex dived into the sidecar, and Bernard opened the throttle wide. Roaring off down the High Street, Bernard caught his father's eye and, just for a moment, the two men looked at each other across a divide of almost seventy years. Boggs senior's face was a mixture of puzzlement and surprise – then he was gone in a blur.

' "Leave it to me..." ' Bernard taunted. ' "I'm not taking any chances with you running around causing chaos." '

'All right, all right,' said Rex.

A bullet ricocheted off the back of the sidecar. 'Jesus!' Rex looked back to see his grandfather standing in the middle of the road, gun in hand.

'A moving target at fifty yards with a handgun,' observed Bernard. 'He was a good shot, my dad.'

'He's trying to kill us!' Rex exclaimed.

'No, if he'd meant to do that we'd already be dead. You know, I always wondered where he got that gun.'

'What do you mean?'

'He kept a military pistol in his bedside drawer. Now I know where he got it from: you gave it to him. What was all that stuff about time anomalies?'

'Can we just drop it, please?' said Rex.

The motorcycle combo screeched round the station corner on two wheels, and Boggs senior was lost to sight.

They spent the rest of the day hiding in a storm drain behind Ferring Beach while Rex figured out how he was going to get back into the shop.

As night fell, they crept out of their hiding place and made their way furtively through the streets, avoiding the ARP Wardens. There was no moon, and with the blackout in force, it was pitch black.

Tiptoeing down Lancing High Street, they slunk round the corner and found the door leading to the alley that ran behind the shop. Rex turned to Bernard. 'You stay here.'

'What are you going to do?'

'Wake your father up and ask his forgiveness – what do you think I'm going to do?'

Limbo II

'I only asked.'

'I won't be long. If an ARP comes along just whistle.' Rex tried the alley door; it was locked. 'Give me a leg up,' he whispered. Bernard crouched down and grabbed Rex's legs. On a count of three, Rex jumped and Bernard shoved upwards. Rex flew through the air, clearing the door and landing with a thump in the narrow alleyway between the newsagent's and the adjacent butcher's.

'Ouch!'

'Sorry!'

In Rex's day the butcher's wasn't there, the space it had once occupied being used by Bernard and Iris as a small courtyard. Iris had made it look rather attractive, with pots of bright red geraniums and little terracotta statues of hedgehogs and frogs. In the summer they used to sit out there and have lunch.

Rex placed his hands on the outside door at the rear of the stock room and closed his eyes. Reaching out with his mind, he searched every corner of the room, but found nothing. Puzzled, he widened his search, this time taking in the main area of the shop and the alleyway itself. There it was again: that hard, bright spark he'd felt earlier. Strangely, it was behind him. He turned and put his hands on the wall of the butcher's shop. Yes! There could be no mistaking that indestructible brilliance. It seemed to be just beyond the wall, or possibly *in* the wall, but how could that be?

Before he had time to puzzle this out, his concentration was broken by a low, teeth-rattling drone, and from the other side of the alleyway door he heard Bernard's frantic whisper: 'Heinkels!'

It was a sound from the nightmares of Bernard's youth, and something he had hoped never to hear again. 'We have to get out of here!' he cried. 'Quickly, Rex!'

'Don't panic, Dad,' said Rex. 'I'm coming.' But as he was scrambling back over the alley door, there came a sound which, although he had never heard it before, Rex recognized instantly as the dying whistle of falling bombs.

'Take cover,' Bernard yelled.

Rex fell off the top of the door and threw himself on the pavement, hands over his head. As the first bomb struck, he felt the ground buck beneath him. Then there was another explosion close by, and he was lifted up, engulfed by a brilliant white light. Everything went deathly quiet, time seemed to slow down and, as he flew through the air, out of the corner of his eye he could see something bright and shiny. He landed with a bone-jarring thud in a rain of mud and bricks, and the terrible noise of war crashed back into his senses, rolling over him like wild surf. Then he saw it, lying on the ground in front of him – the Crystal! But as he reached out his hand towards it, something hit him on the head, and everything went black.

Chapter 39

Smeil was gazing out of the window at the rear of the coffee shop. As he'd suspected, Rex had been a little economical with the truth when he'd said that he wouldn't be gone long, and he and Bernard had been away almost two whole days now. The sun was steadily sinking, and to make matters worse, someone somewhere – probably one of the soldiers – had leaked the news about the missing piece of the Book, and an ugly panic was beginning to take hold. To top it all, the castle was up to its old tricks again. It was missing Bernard and Iris and, feeling miffed that no one had bothered to consult it about their departure, was huffily rearranging itself – blocking doorways, shuffling rooms and in some cases making entire floors disappear. The banqueting hall had vanished completely, even though Smeil had searched for it in all the usual places.

He stared at the lengthening shadows of the far distant mountains – now their creeping fingers stretched almost up to the walls of Castle Limbo. Down on the plain, tiny pinpricks of light were appearing as lonely shepherds lit bonfires in an attempt to ward off the cold, and for the first time in almost ten years he could see lights in the houses far below, shining out in the gloom, and plumes of bright sparks erupting from their chimneys. The people were preparing themselves for another long night.

Smeil sighed; he'd been a bag of nerves ever since Rex and Bernard had left. *What if they don't come back?* he thought. *What if they never return? What'll I do? When the sun finally goes down, there'll be rioting on a scale not witnessed since the Great Terror!*

He shuddered as he thought back to those dreadful times, remembering in vivid detail the awful scene when a howling mob had broken into the castle and slaughtered almost every living thing there. Then an appalling thought occurred to him: *And as I'm the one who's supposed to be in charge, I'm the first one they're going to come for. Oh, why do I get myself into situations like this?*

'Mr Smeil!'

Smeil jumped 'Ah!' he exclaimed, spinning round. It was Matilda. 'Don't creep up on me like that,' he said. 'And it's Smeil, just Smeil!'

'Sorry,' said Matilda, 'but there's a party outside that wants—'

'A party?' Smeil was incensed. 'People are having a party at a time like this? The world is falling apart around our ears and people are still bent on pleasure? Don't they know what's happening? Anyway, we're closed. We can't start catering for parties now!' He turned indignantly back to the window.

'Er, no,' Matilda said. 'There's a party of people outside, and I think they want to see you.'

Smeil froze. 'Want to see *me*?' he gasped, in a barely audible whisper.

'Yes,' said Matilda. 'What shall I tell them?'

Smeil turned slowly away from the window and faced her. 'Tell them?'

Matilda nodded. 'Tell them,' she repeated patiently.

Smeil closed his eyes. He could imagine just what sort of a party it was: a party of angry townsfolk, bristling with a thousand pointy things, probably sharpened especially for the occasion. 'I . . . I . . . I can't,' he stammered.

'Can't what?' said Matilda.

'Can't . . . tell them anything. I don't . . . know anything . . . anything at all. Even if I did . . . I've forgotten it all now.' Smeil had turned a funny colour – a sort of beigey, yellowy green. 'I'm sorry,' he said, 'but I'm going to have to sit down.' He collapsed into the nearest chair.

Limbo II

There was a sudden angry shout from outside, and Smeil winced.

'Are you all right, Mr . . . er, Smeil?' said Matilda, moving closer to him.

The little man shook his head. 'No . . . no, I'm not all right.'

'Can I get you anything?' Matilda said gently.

'Well, I'd love a—'

But at that moment, with a roar, the angry crowd burst into the café.

'Where is he?' one of them shouted.

'Yeah!' said another. 'We want to string him up!'

'Disembowel him!'

'Rip out his toenails!'

Smeil slid out of sight under the table.

'Where's that useless Wizard!'

Smeil was relieved that it wasn't his blood they were baying for – at least not yet – but, bearing in mind that discretion is the better part of valour, he decided he'd stay where he was, for now.

'Excuse me, can I help you gentlemen?' asked Matilda.

The leader of the mob, a large, gnarled man wearing a sheepskin jerkin which smelt as if it still had the sheep inside it, advanced and glared at the young waitress. 'Maybe,' he said, enveloping her in a halitosis fug. 'We represent the Federation of Agricultural and Related Trades, and we want satisfaction.'

'We want the Wizard!' the crowd roared.

'He's not here at the moment,' said Matilda, standing her ground.

'Then where is he?'

'He's, er . . . busy.'

'All right,' the big man breathed. 'Where's that good-for-nothing servant of his – Smeil?'

'Smeil? I'm sorry, but I'm not familiar with that name,' Matilda bluffed, 'but then, I'm new here. Perhaps if you gentlemen would care to come back some other time . . .'

But all eyes were now on the table over by the window, which was vibrating madly, rattling the sugar bowl perched precariously on top of it.

'Excuse me, miss,' said the large man, pushing past Matilda and heading for the table. Reaching it, he lifted it up with one hand to reveal a quivering Smeil. 'Hello,' said the big man.

'How . . . do . . . you . . . do . . . do?' said Smeil, in his panic losing count of quite how many dos it was polite to utter.

'I do fine,' said the man, reaching down and picking Smeil up by his belt. 'But I can't say the same for you.' Smeil, dangling helplessly from the man's great hairy fist, looked rather like a plastic troll hanging from the rear-view mirror of a Ford Escort.

'Put him down!' The command reverberated around the room, shaking the windows and rattling the cutlery.

In the shocked silence that followed, Smeil squirmed round to see who it was that had spoken. Looking under the big man's arm, through the forest of his armpit he beheld a vision. Matilda stood, feet apart, fists clenched, blazing with passion. When Smeil saw her determinedly jutting jaw and the fire in her eyes, he was filled with an urgent desire: to show that he was a man worthy of her. 'You heard her! Put me down!' he yelled, and sunk his teeth into the hand from which he was suspended.

The large man dropped him with a roar, and Smeil fell heavily in an untidy heap. Severely winded, he remained on the floor for several moments while he got his breath back. But then, rising to his feet, he faced the leader of the mob with a new resolve, even though he barely came up to his knee. 'Now listen, you . . . citizen!' he said. 'What gives you the right to burst in here demanding things without so much as a by-your-leave, eh? Have you no manners? While I am in charge, you will behave! I will not tolerate these shows of public disobedience. When the Wizard and the King and Queen return, I want to be able to tell them that nothing untoward has happened here, and that the citizenry are pleased to have them back.'

'Nothing untoward?' shouted one of the mob. 'What about the

sun going down?' There was general assent from the rest of the citizens.

'The fact that the sun is setting is neither here nor there,' Smeil replied.

There was a rumble of dissent.

'Then what about the Book?' shouted another, to a chorus of 'Aye!'

Smeil raised his voice to be heard, 'Is it the Wizard's fault that he inherited a very difficult situation? It seems to me you're blaming the wrong Wizard.'

'But the last Wizard would have done something about it!'

'That's right!' cheered the mob.

Smeil was now hopping mad. 'It was the last Wizard who *wrote* the Book! *He* was responsible for the Dark Time and the Great Terror!' he roared. 'The blood of a thousand citizens is on his head, and you'd rather have *him* than Rex Boggs? Shame on you!'

The crowd fell into an embarrassed silence and stared at the ground, shuffling their feet uncomfortably.

Smeil took a couple of deep breaths before continuing. 'Rex Boggs is relatively new, yes, but he is sincere and honest, and deserves our support. He is, at this very moment, risking his life in the Great Beyond to try and sort things out for us all, and this is the thanks he gets!' He glared up at the leader of the mob, towering above him. 'Now go, and rest assured, the next person to utter a threat against the person of the Wizard, the King, the Queen or any of their staff will be publicly flogged. Do I make myself clear?'

The huge man nodded glumly, and walked back through the crowd and out of the café. The rest followed him in silence.

When they had gone, Smeil looked up at Matilda with the bright light of love in his eyes. 'You were magnificent,' he gushed.

Matilda too was in love but, unfortunately for Smeil, the object of her affection was, at that particular moment, stuck in another dimension – in the middle of the Second World War. 'That was a wonderful speech, Smeil.'

'Really? You think so?' He smiled up at her through his fringe.

She ruffled his hair, rather as one would do to a favourite pet. 'Who'd have thought that one so small could be so brave?'

'So . . . Oh.' Smeil shrank to half his size, which was very small indeed.

'Rex will be so proud of you.' She bent down and kissed him on the cheek.

Smeil closed his eyes. The tender agony of the touch of her lips was soon over, but the heady pain of her scent would stay with him a long, long time.

'Well, I'd better be off,' she said. 'See you in the morning.'

'Yes, see you in . . . in . . .' But she was already gone, and Smeil was left alone in the echoing café.

Chapter 40

Rex surfaced slowly out of the warm, velvet darkness. A block of pale-blue sky with a single cloud danced around him. He blinked, but on closing his eyes, the heaviness of the lids made them almost impossible to open again. Feeling himself slipping back into unconsciousness, he tried to sit up, but any attempt at movement sent a searing pain down the length of his spine. Where was he anyway, and how had he got here?

He remembered a light – so bright it seemed to have left a permanent impression on his brain. Then followed a torrent of memories: the bombs, the awful noise, the heaving ground beneath him and the butcher's shop exploding all around . . .

The Crystal! Where was the Crystal? He had to get up and look for it. He tried to sit up again, his efforts making him gasp with pain.

'Ah!'

The nurse was instantly at his side. 'There, now, you just relax.'

'I . . . have . . . to . . . go . . .' Rex whispered.

'You need the potty?'

Rex tried to shake his head, but the pain of it made him dizzy. 'No . . .' he gasped, clutching the sheets. 'Must . . . get . . . out . . .'

'You're not going anywhere, dear. You're lucky to be alive. It's going to be a good few months before you're up and about again. Now you just settle back and try to rest. I'll give you something to help you sleep.'

She patted him gently on the back of his hand and pushed her way out through the enclosing screens.

When she had gone Rex took stock, exploring his battered body for traumas. His left leg seemed to be broken just above the knee; he had several cracked ribs, three crushed vertebrae and a hairline fracture of the skull. And now he realized why he couldn't move: his body was encased in plaster.

Moving his attention up to his head, he felt out the fine line of the skull fracture with his mind. It was like the crack in an eggshell. Moving mentally along it, he surrounded it with a healing blue light. Then he felt a sudden, sharp pain. Opening his eyes he saw the kindly face of the nurse again and, looking down, the needle deep in the flesh of his arm.

'No!' he cried, but too late. Darkness closed around him like the jaws of an alligator.

Frink pulled over into the lay-by. He'd been driving along the A30 for about an hour now, and although he knew his destination lay somewhere to the east, without his ship and its on-board computer he had no way of navigating with any degree of accuracy, and he wanted to be a little more precise about which way he was heading before going any further.

As a stream of lorries and cars rumbled past, leaving the old Land-Rover shaking in their wake, Frink wondered how to proceed. *What to do? What to do?* He smacked his head with his fists; *Think, think, think!* Then he had an idea. Sending a broadcast always focused his mind, so, checking his face in the rear-view mirror, he cleared his throat and addressed his finger. 'I am now on the road, heading east towards the place where I have ascertained the miasma of evil has landed. Unfortunately, my spaceship has been impounded by forces in league with the same energy field and I have therefore been compelled to commandeer this primitive vehicle.' He panned his finger around the dusty, rotting interior of the Land-Rover.

Limbo II

'Without the ship's computer, I am navigating using this planet's star, so I know I am headed in more or less the right direction, but unless I can pinpoint the energy field's exact location, I fear I may waste precious time. This is Frink Byellssen, on something called a lay-by, A30, Earth.' Frink extended his fleshy pink antennae and beamed his message out across space.

As he had hoped, sending this news bulletin had concentrated his mind, and he was now able to think a little more clearly. 'Of course!' he said. 'It's obvious! The pilot of this vehicle would need charts to find his way around, even in a country as small as this.' He set about looking for a map.

Rummaging around in the accumulated filth of the never-cleaned interior of the old Land-Rover, he came across some puzzling items: an old sock, stiff as a board and covered in a fine, powdery mould; a pair of pink frilly knickers trimmed with white lace; and lastly, and most puzzling of all, a small but extremely stretchy latex tube, open at one end and with a small, nipple-like extension at the other. What could it be? After toying with this strange object for several minutes – fitting it over the gear stick, stretching it around the steering wheel, pulling it over his head – he still couldn't guess at its use and so, putting it back where he'd found it, went back to the matter in hand. Although he looked under every seat and in every cubbyhole, he could find no navigational charts in this vehicle. Sitting back in the driver's seat, he pummelled the steering wheel, the roof, and himself, in frustration.

'Ah! Ah! Ah!' he cried as his fists hit various unyielding parts of the interior. As the car rocked in response to the violence of his outburst, the squab of the seat next to him fell forward. Stuck to the back of it was a decaying road atlas. 'Aha!' Frink yelled in triumph.

Gently peeling it away from the stickily decomposing plastic of the seat back, Frink searched through its yellow and mildewed pages, eventually finding what he was looking for: a map of Sussex. 'Ah, now, if this line signifies zero degrees, the place I'm searching for should be slightly to the west, along this bearing, just north of the coast... Got it!' He was looking at a small orange circle, which indicated a prehistoric hill fort. Underneath it, in tiny red letters, Frink could just make out a name: Cissbury Ring.

Chapter 41

'Rex. Rex, son.'

Rex opened his eyes, slowly. Bernard's big long face beamed down at him. 'Dad,' he said, dragging himself away from the comforting warmth of his drugged sleep.

Bernard looked down at Rex's bruised face, and tears of pity welled up in his eyes. 'Oh, Rex, Rex . . .' He shook his head and pulled out a handkerchief.

'Do I look that bad?' Rex asked.

Bernard blew his nose in response.

'I look that bad. What happened to you?'

'I was knocked out by the blast,' said Bernard, dabbing his eyes. 'When I came to it was all over, and where you'd been was just a pile of bricks.' His eyes filled with tears once more. 'I started digging with my bare hands, but . . .' He shook his head and blew his nose again. 'Then the fire crew turned up and, thank God, they found you. Once they'd loaded you safely into an ambulance, I made myself scarce. I didn't want to go through another interrogation. Oh, Rex, I thought you were dead.' He squeezed Rex's hand.

'Ouch!'

'Sorry.'

'Did you find the Crystal?' Rex asked, urgently.

'No.'

'Damn. It was there, in the wall.'

'In the—?'

'I don't know how it got there, either. But I saw it just before everything went black.'

'That was a nasty bang on the head, Rex.'

'I *saw* it. I nearly had my hands on it, then the sky fell in. We've got to get out and start looking for it before they clear the site.'

'There'll be plenty of time to find the Crystal when you're well again. The nurse said your leg alone would take a couple of months to heal.'

'We've got to get out of here *now*. The hospital's bound to have informed Shoreham that they've got one of their corporals. They could turn up at any minute.'

'But they're not going to try and move you like this.'

'No, but they *will* station a guard on the ward, which could make getting out of here rather tricky.'

'You're in no fit state to go anywhere.'

'You keep forgetting I'm a wizard.'

'It's not me that keeps forgetting,' muttered Bernard.

Rex ignored him. 'Where are my clothes?'

'Hang on.' Bernard peered into the small locker at the side of the bed. 'Well, there's this,' he said, pulling out Rex's chiffon scarf.

'Nothing else?'

Bernard shook his head. 'You could always wear it like a sarong.'

'In England? I'd freeze to death. What time is it?'

Bernard looked up at the clock on the wall at the end of the ward. 'Ten to nine.'

'Give me half an hour,' said Rex.

'What are you going to do?'

'Try to get myself mobile. I'd already started on the skull fracture when they put me to sleep. Do you think you can find me some clothes?'

'I'll try.'

'Good. Don't be too long.'

Rex closed his eyes and Bernard walked swiftly out of the ward.

*

Limbo II

Beasely had been up since the crack of dawn and, although it was only early evening, he decided to call it a day. Closing the file on his desk, he yawned and stretched and, retrieving his coat from the back of the door, made his way wearily up the corridor to the car park. He was just about to step outside when a sudden thought stopped him. After discovering the Guptas' home address – a small bungalow in Sompting – they'd gone out there to have a look. They'd found no signs of a struggle and nothing to point to a motive, but they had taken away a large pile of mail from behind the Guptas' front door which Ivey was now in the process of sifting through. Beasely didn't relish the thought of another meeting with his sergeant before going home, but knew he ought to check on him one last time in the unlikely event that he'd found anything. With a sigh, he turned and trudged back down the corridor.

'How are you doing, Sergeant?'

Ivey looked up from the untidy pile of paper on his desk. 'It's mostly junk mail, sir – catalogues, that sort of thing.'

'Right.' Beasely put on his coat and made for the door. 'I'll see you tomorrow.'

'I did find something that caught my interest, though, sir.'

'Really?' said Beasely, coming back into the room.

'Yes, did you know you can get a set of birchwood nesting tables for only £79.95?'

The chief inspector closed his eyes and counted to ten. 'I'm going home,' he said quietly.

'Oh, right sir,' said Ivey, and ripped open another envelope. 'Well, there's a coincidence,' he muttered.

Beasely was already through the door, but he couldn't stop himself. 'What is it?'

'It's an invoice from the same wholesaler my cousin George uses.'

'Goodnight.' Beasely started up the corridor, then stopped. 'Did you say wholesaler?'

'Yes, sir. Lockheart's, down Lewes way.'

Beasely came back into the room and took the invoice from him. 'This would be where they got their stock.'

'I reckon if we got in touch with them, they'd give us the address of the Guptas' shop,' said Ivey with a smile.

Beasely's jaw dropped open. 'Did you work that out all by yourself? Get on the blower to Lockheart's, Sherlock, and ask them to check their records.'

Chapter 42

Mr Pink had a book of carpet samples he wanted to show Mr White. He was rather keen on a deep-pile pale cream, but wanted to run it by the boss before he went ahead and ordered it.

Pushing through the bead curtain into the stock room, he caught sight of Mr White wearing a plastic crown and striking an heroic pose with a sucker-tipped bow and arrow. The moment Mr White realized he was being watched, he made a half-hearted attempt to hide the toys behind his back.

'Ah,' he said, 'you caught me.'

'Don't worry, your secret's safe with me,' said Mr Pink.

'I, er . . . found them in one of the boxes.' He was about to return them to their carton when a thought occurred to him and, placing the crown back on his head, he reassumed his pose. 'What do you think?' he asked. 'Be honest, now.'

Mr Pink shook his head. 'Sorry,' he said.

'No, not really me, is it?' Mr White threw the crown and the bow and arrow back in with the other toys.

'I wanted your opinion,' said Mr Pink. 'I know we're not going to be here forever, but I can't live with those upstairs carpets a moment longer, and I thought if we're going to do the curtains anyway, we might as well go the whole hog—'

'We're leaving *tonight*,' interrupted Mr White. He sighed and sat heavily on the corner of a cardboard box marked: 'Cheese and onion crisps, stack 4 high only'. The box crunched under his weight.

'Tonight?' Mr Pink scowled. 'Well, thanks for telling me.'

Mr White looked balefully up at him. 'I'm sorry. I should have told you before but, oh . . .' He shook his head. 'I'd never really seen myself as the kind of person who goes around frightening little old ladies. What's it all for, eh?'

'What's *what* all for?'

'This . . . us . . . What are we doing here? We've waited God knows how long for this moment, and now . . . we're supposed to go out tonight and cause mayhem across the face of, as it turns out, a measly quarter of the earth. I just don't see the point.'

'You know,' said Mr Pink, putting down the book of carpet samples and settling on another corner of the box with a *scrunch*, 'I'm glad you feel like that. I was only saying to Mr Black the other day, wouldn't it be a shame if Brighton had to go? It's got such fabulous shops, great restaurants, and on a sunny day there's nowhere to touch it.'

'Hmm.' Mr White nodded. 'Between you and me, I've never been one for wanton destruction. But I'd hate to prevent you from fulfilling your destiny.'

'No, no, no.' Mr Pink patted Mr White's hand reassuringly. 'I'm not really one for raging around causing trouble, either. Besides, I love it here. For the first time in my life I feel like I belong, and I've discovered something I'm really good at. I've got this eye for colour, and a real feel for fabrics. I know this place is only a silly little shop with a cramped two-bedroom flat above but, given time, I'm sure I could make it look fabulous.'

'All right?' Mr Black appeared in the doorway. He was carrying the set of electronic scales from the shop counter. 'I've found some scales, boss. But they're a bit heavy.'

'Put them down, Mr Black,' instructed Mr White.

Much relieved, Mr Black lowered them to the floor, then straightened and eased the tension out of his back. Looking at Mr Pink

Limbo II

and Mr White, something in their expressions led him to ask, 'What's going on?'

'Mr Black,' began Mr White, 'how would you feel about putting down the scales for ever – figuratively speaking?'

Chapter 43

Bernard stepped out through the hospital doors and stood at the top of the steps. He was just about to walk into town to see if he could beg, borrow or steal some clothes for Rex, when an RAF jeep drove in through the hospital gates. Slipping behind a pillar, Bernard saw the jeep pull up in front of the main entrance, and watched as the young flight lieutenant from Shoreham, accompanied by an armed guard, got out and marched up the steps and into the lobby. After speaking to the duty sister, the two airmen were left to wait while she went off to make enquiries. The lieutenant got out his cigarette case and lit up.

'Tch,' Bernard said to himself. 'Smoking in a hospital? Doesn't he know the health risks?' Then he had to remind himself that this was the 1940s, and that the whole world was smoking.

But he had no time now to worry about the state of the lieutenant's health; he had to get back to Rex, fast. A hospital porter walked by, pushing an empty wheelchair.

'Ah, just what I need,' said Bernard, flopping into it.

''Ere! What're you doing?' said the porter.

'It's my leg,' Bernard said. 'Caught a bullet at, er . . . Passchendaele.' He gripped his leg and grimaced.

The porter looked down. 'Your leg looks all right to me.' He sniffed.

'No, really, it gives me a lot of gyp, especially when it rains.'

The porter smiled a thin smile. 'Well, as it's not raining, you'll be all right then.' He grabbed hold of Bernard's arm and tried to pull him out of the seat. 'Come on, get out of it. This wheelchair is for bona fide invalids only.'

'All right!' said Bernard. 'Look, I'll be frank with you. You see those two men?' Bernard pointed through the main doors towards the officer and his guard.

'Yes?' said the porter, narrowing his eyes suspiciously.

'I need to get past them and into the hospital without being seen. My son's life is in danger.'

'Good thing he's in a hospital, then, isn't it? Out! I'm not pushing you nowhere.'

'It's worth a fiver.'

'Hold on tight.'

They managed to make it to the lifts unnoticed, but getting out on the third floor, the porter spun the chair round and held out his hand. 'Come on, then.'

'Sorry?' said Bernard.

'Five pounds.'

'Oh, of course,' said Bernard, standing and making a big show of reaching into his pocket. 'Tell you what,' he said suddenly. 'Wait for me here and I'll make it a tenner.'

The porter chewed his lip. 'A tenner?' He scratched the back of his head and produced a half-smoked roll-up from behind his ear. Bernard had to bite his tongue as the man lit up and filled the hospital corridor with thick, tarry smoke. 'A tenner, you say?' Bernard could almost hear the cogs of the man's brain whirring with the implications. A tenner was probably more than this man earned in a month. 'Make it fifteen,' he said at last.

'Done,' said Bernard, and hurried away to find Rex.

Entering the ward, Bernard remembered he didn't yet have anything for Rex to wear. Grabbing a dressing gown from the end of a slumbering patient's bed, he draped it casually over his arm and nonchalantly carried on along the shiny lino.

'Here we are—' He pushed through the screens surrounding the bed, but Rex was nowhere to be seen – only his plaster cast, split open like the chrysalis of a newly emerged butterfly. Then came the *thumpa-thumpa-thumpa* of the ward's swing doors and the sound of voices.

'Follow me. Your man's just down here.'

Peeping through a gap between the screens, Bernard saw the duty sister marching down the ward, ahead of the two airmen.

Bernard quickly ducked back behind cover. Now what was he going to do? *Don't panic*, he told himself, as the footsteps drew nearer.

'Here he is.' The sister flung aside the screens.

Seeing the empty plaster cast, the flight lieutenant immediately drew his gun. 'Corporal,' he barked, 'search the corridor. I'll check the rest of the ward.' The corporal clattered back out through the swing doors.

'I don't understand,' protested the sister. 'He was in no fit state to go anywhere.'

As the lieutenant stalked the long room, Bernard, crouching nervously under the empty bed, heard someone hiss, and turned to see Rex, naked save for a flowing chiffon scarf around his neck, hiding under the neighbouring bed.

'Now what?' Bernard mouthed.

Rex pointed to the dressing gown, which Bernard still clutched, then pointed to himself. Bernard slid the garment the short space between the beds, and Rex struggled to put it on.

With the lieutenant checking beds on the other side of the ward, Rex and Bernard squeezed out from under theirs and, crouching behind one of the screens, trundled it up the ward. They had almost reached the door when they heard, 'Halt, or I fire!' and both men froze.

'Going somewhere?' The lieutenant smiled, pulling the screen aside. 'All right, move away from the door.' Standing squarely in front of the double doors to cover any attempt at escape, the lieutenant waved them back into the body of the ward with his gun. 'Quite a double act, aren't you?' he said, reaching for his cigarette case. But just then, the corporal, having heard his officer's shouted warning, came crashing back into the ward. The door crunched into the lieutenant's kidneys and threw him to the floor, scattering his cigarettes.

As the corporal helped the lieutenant to his feet, muttering apologies and gathering up handfuls of bent and broken Craven As, Rex and Bernard made a run for it.

'Bloody idiot!' The lieutenant angrily pushed the corporal aside and chased out of the ward in pursuit.

'I'm too old for this!' Bernard protested as they raced down the hospital corridor.

'I've got a broken leg!' Rex replied.

The porter with the wheelchair was still waiting where Bernard had left him. 'What about my fifteen quid?' he shouted as Bernard hurtled past him and down the stairs.

'I'll give you a tip!' Bernard yelled back. 'The Derby! Put everything you've got on Owen Tudor . . . to win!'

'Owen Tudor?' The porter sniffed angrily, and kicked the wheelchair into the middle of the corridor. The flight lieutenant spotted the danger, but too late. Running full pelt, he smacked into its unyielding metal frame and took off – flying through the air in a graceful swallow dive before smacking into a tea trolley, which had just started making its rounds. Covered in scalding tea, he leapt up, screaming, from the mess of broken crockery and rock buns, and ripped off his steaming jacket. 'Why don't you watch where you're bloody going!' he yelled at the porter in charge of the wheelchair.

'Don't you shout at me,' replied the man, checking the wheelchair for damage. 'This conveyance is hospital property. If you've damaged it, you'll have to pay.'

'Two men, one wearing a dressing gown,' the lieutenant snarled. 'Which way?'

The porter pointed down the stairwell.

'Thank you. Corporal, follow me!'

'Don't shoot the old one,' the porter shouted after them, as they dashed down the stairs. 'He owes me fifteen quid!' And leaning against the banisters, he pulled out his tobacco. 'World's gone bloody mad,' he grumbled.

Running out through the main entrance, the first thing Rex saw was the airmen's jeep. 'There!' he exclaimed. Finding the keys still in the ignition, he started the engine and slammed it into gear. Swinging the jeep round towards the exit, he floored the throttle, the tyres throwing up clouds of dust and gravel. There was a loud bang, and a bullet ricocheted off the bodywork.

Rex looked in the mirror. The lieutenant was standing on the front steps, his revolver aimed right at them. 'Get your head down!' Rex screamed. Bernard hit the floor. There was another bang, and a neat round hole appeared in the windscreen. 'Shit!' Rex exclaimed, swerving to avoid an ambulance coming in through the main gates. 'Hold on!' Powering the jeep towards the impossibly narrow opening between the ambulance and the gatepost, he prayed the ambulance driver would have the foresight to get out of the way. He did. Scraping through the gap, the jeep flew out of the hospital car park and squealed across the road.

The lieutenant raised his arm to fire again, but they were already out of range and hurtling down the hill towards the sea.

When they reached the relative safety of Lower Marine Parade, Rex stopped the jeep and found that he was trembling all over. 'Do you know,' he said, 'that's the third time I've been shot at, but I can't actually say that I'm getting used to it.'

'I know what you mean,' Bernard replied, for the first time raising his head above the level of the dashboard.

Rex took a few calming breaths, then turned to Bernard. 'The Derby?' he asked, raising an eyebrow.

Bernard smiled. 'Owen Tudor – the only time my dad ever won on the horses. It came in at twenty-five to one, and he was chuffed for a fortnight. If that porter takes my advice he could end up a very wealthy man.'

'I see.' Rex eased out the tension in his back and winced. 'Ahh!'

'How are you feeling?'

'A little stiff,' said Rex, 'and I've got a terrible headache.'

'I'm not surprised. But just see what you can do if you put your mind to it?'

Rex shivered. 'I'm also rather cold.'

'Yes, and that dressing gown's a bit of a giveaway.' Bernard paused. 'I know – Hanningtons! My dad's got an account there.'

Chapter 44

Frink was doing well. He now knew where he was going, and was making good progress, but about three miles outside Ringwood, on the A31, the Land-Rover started to hesitate and lurch forward intermittently. Seeing another lay-by up ahead, Frink pulled off the road. The Land-Rover's engine finally died, and he coasted to a stop.

He checked the wiring. Next he opened the bonnet and looked over the vehicle's curious means of propulsion, but everything seemed to be in working order. Then he got back in the cab and pummelled the dashboard with his fists. It was no good – he could go no further in this vehicle. It then occurred to him that he hadn't been to the lavatory for some hours and, as he needed to consider his next move very carefully – it being almost impossible to think straight with a full bladder – he decided to take this opportunity to relieve himself.

The lay-by that Frink had stumbled across wasn't at all like the last one. That had been a simple space at the side of the road, but this one was furnished with a large car park and several interesting buildings, all adorned with colourful plastic signs.

Stepping into a small, squat edifice with: 'Happy Eater' above the door, his nostrils were immediately assailed by the smell of burning cheese. Not particularly keen to hang around, he was just about to leave when he saw a door marked 'Toilets' over to his left. But before he could go through it, a woman wearing a striped dress and a small and seemingly pointless hat appeared before him and asked him a strange question: 'Smoking or non-smoking?'

Limbo II

What could she mean? Frink looked round the almost deserted restaurant. Over in a booth by the window a family were sitting morosely over the remains of their microwaved lasagne, and in the corner a lone and large businessman was messily tucking into his sausage and mash with onion gravy while talking into his mobile phone. The whole place might have smelt like a burning rubber factory, but Frink could see no sign of smoke. *Ah*, he realized, *it is a riddle. Before I use the lavatory, it seems I must pass a test. Perhaps I am required to ask permission from Happy Eater – whoever he might be. Be careful, act naturally, and try not to draw attention to yourself, Frink. The energy field's spies are bound to be everywhere.*

'Er, non-smoking?' he replied hesitantly.

The waitress beamed. 'Follow me, sir.'

I'm in, Frink thought.

The waitress led him through the practically empty restaurant to a table right next to the fat businessman. 'Here we are.'

'Ah,' said Frink, addressing the businessman, 'judging from your size, you must be the Happy Eater. How do you do?'

The businessman looked up at him. 'Just a minute,' he said into his mobile phone. 'Excuse me?'

The waitress intervened before any blood could be spilt. 'Or perhaps you'd like to sit over here?' she said, pulling Frink away from the red-faced businessman, and sitting him in the booth next to the sulking family.

'What can I get you?' the waitress enquired, presenting him with the grease-smeared, plastic-coated menu from the clip on the cruet set.

'Thank you,' he said. *Now what? What am I supposed to do with this?* 'Er...' He scanned the menu, but could make sense of none of it. He looked up at the waitress in desperation.

'Would you care to *choose* something?' she said, as if talking to a child.

'Oh, *choose* yes, of course, choose. Well, in that case, I choose that,' Frink said, pointing at something at random.

The waitress looked over his shoulder. ' "Service not included",' she read aloud.

Frink smiled. 'That's what I choose.'

'No, sir,' said the waitress, her smile fixed. 'I was wondering if you wanted something to eat.'

'Oh, to *eat*. Yes, of course. Yes indeed, to eat . . . to . . . er . . . That?' He pointed hopefully.

'That's the name of the printers, sir.'

'Right, right, right. What's that above it?'

'Steak pie.'

'You can eat that?'

'People do.'

'Then that's what I'll have.' Frink beamed. The waitress scribbled something on a small pad and walked away, sighing.

After an interminable wait, during which Frink's bladder reached close to bursting point and the scowling businessman and the morose family were replaced by a similarly overweight man and an equally unhappy family, his steak pie arrived. It was served in a small metal container, with a mess of unnaturally bright-orange carrots and tiny sludge-coloured peas. Frink sniffed the pie suspiciously. It had a smell not unlike a fused electrical circuit. The last thing he wanted to do was put it in his mouth, but he didn't want to arouse suspicion – he'd drawn enough attention to himself already. He was obviously required to eat it before being allowed to use the lavatory, so eat it he would.

He tried to pick it up in his hands, but it was too hot. Wrapping a paper napkin around it, he managed to lift the pie off the plate and ease it out of its metal dish. *Well, here goes*, he thought, and bit into it.

A lava-hot jet of gravy shot out of the pastry casing, searing his top lip. Frink recoiled in agony. 'Ah, ah! It attacked me!' he yelled, hastily dropping the pie. It landed in his lap and, in his hurry to remove it before it cooked his groin, Frink managed to squeeze almost all of the superheated gravy into his crotch. He jumped up, yowling with pain, and danced around the restaurant screaming, 'I'm on fire! I'm on fire!'

The next thing he knew, someone had grabbed him around the waist and was pouring water down his trousers. The sensation was not unpleasant, and once the soothing liquid had calmed the raging fire in his nether regions, Frink opened his eyes to find himself looking into the kindly face of a man with lank brown hair and a pale-pink complexion. 'How do you do?' said the man, replacing the now empty water carafe on a nearby table. Taking hold of Frink's left index finger, he looked straight into it.

'Are we recording?' he asked.

'Er, we could be,' Frink replied.

'Good.' Nilbert cleared his throat. 'My name is Nilbert Plymstock. I was, until recently, a biotechnologist specializing in genetics, but now I have seen the light and have entered Frink's life to lead him to his goal. You will be seeing more of me. Nilbert Plymstock, Happy Eater, A31, Earth.' He let go of Frink's finger and smiled. 'Shall we go?' he said.

While Frink availed himself of the toilet facilities, spending a long time trying to work out the purpose of the electric hand-dryer, Nilbert paid the astonished waitress, then led the way out to the car park, where Frink was soon installed in Nilbert's brand new, and very shiny, V8 Land-Rover 90.

Chapter 45

After their successful visit to Hannington's men's department, Rex and Bernard drove back to Lancing. Pulling into a small alleyway next to the railway station, Rex killed the engine.

'Shouldn't we wait until it's dark?' suggested Bernard.

'It may be too late by then. It may be too late *now*, but we've got to find out if it's still there,' said Rex, opening the RAF jeep's door.

'But what about my dad?'

'We can show him the suit he's just bought me.'

Rex stepped out onto the pavement in his brand new 1940s suit, pulling the brim of his black fedora down low over his eyes. Bernard tried to pretend he wasn't quite so tall, and the two men crept warily up the High Street.

Reaching the recently bombed butcher's, Rex was pleased to see that the site hadn't yet been properly cleared. 'You stay here and keep watch, while I dig about a bit.'

'All right,' agreed Bernard, 'but hurry up.'

Bernard looked nervously up and down the street. There was something familiar about the scene, about the light and time of day, but for the moment he couldn't quite put his finger on it. Then he saw her, coming down the hill towards him. She was young and beautiful, even more lovely in real life than in the jewel case of his memory. 'Iris,' he breathed.

Just at that moment a young man emerged from the newsagent's on the corner. Bernard instinctively slipped into a nearby doorway so that he could watch, unseen. The young man had clearly seen the young woman from inside the shop – she was the reason he'd stepped outside – but he was pretending otherwise. *Playing it cool,* Bernard thought.

Then an old lady carrying two shopping bags came trundling, breathlessly, around the corner. When she reached the wreck of the butcher's shop, she stumbled over a jagged lump of masonry, and young Bernard was there to her aid immediately. As he helped the old lady to her feet, the fresh and beautiful Iris walked by.

'Hello,' he said. 'Anytime *you* need picking up, just let me know.' Iris giggled and went a delicate shade of pink. Young Bernard watched her go, admiring the lazy swing of her hips as she carried on down the hill towards the station.

'Lovely, isn't she?'

The young man turned and found himself looking into a face that was somehow familiar, and yet . . .

'If I were you,' the older man continued, 'I wouldn't let someone as beautiful as that pass me by. You may not get another chance.'

'Who—?'

'If I were you, I'd ask her out.'

'But—'

'Hurry up,' urged Bernard. 'She's nearly reached the station.'

Young Bernard spun round. Iris was now at the bottom of the hill, about to cross the station car park. He turned back once more to Bernard, a hundred questions in his eyes. 'Go on!' Bernard persisted. Then, suddenly, his younger self was off, haring down the hill in pursuit of the only woman he would ever love.

'Well, it's not here,' said Rex gloomily.

As Bernard turned to look at him, Rex saw that there were tears in his eyes. 'Are you all right?' he asked. 'What's the matter?'

'Nothing,' said Bernard innocently. 'I was just . . . remembering, that's all. So, no joy, then?' he said, changing the subject.

Rex shook his head. 'No, but I think I know how it ended up in the butcher's: precession.'

'Eh?'

'The Earth wobbles as it spins, and because of that a single point on its surface doesn't stay in precisely the same place; it moves over time. That's what must have happened to the Crystal. Although Smeil dropped it in the shop, it fell into a different time and therefore a different position, you see?'

'I'll take your word for it. Now what do we do?'

Rex looked around. 'We should probably get back to the car before we're spotted.'

'Let's be logical about this,' said Rex, once they were back on the road. 'If you happened to find the Crystal, what would you do with it?'

'A thing like that? I'd be down the nearest pawnshop like a shot.'

Rex was shocked. 'The pawnshop?'

'This is wartime, son. People are short. I'll bet you it's either been sold, or swapped for a bar of chocolate and a pair of nylons.'

'But it's the Limbo Crystal – the oldest thing in the universe.'

'Yes, but whoever found it wouldn't know that, would they?'

Rex tried to get his head round the fact that anyone, finding the key to time and space, could flog it simply to impress a girlfriend or for the moment's pleasure of a bar of Cadbury's.

'All right,' said Rex, as they approached a T-junction. 'If you wanted to pawn something, where would you go?'

'There's only one place,' said Bernard. 'The Lanes.'

Rex changed down and indicated right.

Abandoning the jeep in a small square behind the Grand Hotel, they headed for the seafront, then back up into the labyrinth of tiny streets that was the heart of Brighton's antique trade. Pausing outside every jeweller's and antique shop, Rex explored each one with his mind, searching for the Crystal's hard, brilliant spark. But soon the possibilities of the Lanes had been exhausted, and Rex was slipping into a black depression.

Reaching North Road, he turned to Bernard. 'It's not here,' he said. 'We're not going to find it. This is hopeless. It's like looking for a needle in a haystack!'

'Now don't start,' said Bernard. 'Have you forgotten why we're here? We came to rescue your mum, and that's what we're going to do.'

Rex wheeled round on him angrily. 'She's probably already dead!'

The words were out of his mouth before he could stop them. Looking into Bernard's shocked face, Rex wished with all his heart that he could take back what he'd just said. Bernard blinked a few times, then silent tears began to roll down his face.

'I'm sorry, Dad. I didn't mean—' Rex tried to put his arm around him, but Bernard pushed him away.

Rex turned, cursing himself for his insensitivity, and as he did, something caught his eye in the window of Hannington's glass and china department. 'Dad,' he said quietly.

'I don't believe you just said that.'

'Dad!'

'You're not the only one who's suffering, you know.'

'Dad!' Rex yelled, grabbing Bernard's arm.

'What?'

'I've found it.'

There could be no mistaking it – the Limbo Crystal, older than the planets, key to dimensions, a gem beyond price – on display amongst an assortment of multicoloured paperweights and small glass sculptures of cats and birds.

'We've come for the Crystal,' Rex announced to the young female assistant as he and Bernard bustled excitedly into the shop.

'I'm sorry?' she said.

'Leave this to me, son,' said Bernard. 'Excuse me, miss. My son is interested in that crystal you have in the window.'

'Which one?' She smiled.

'That one, of course,' said Rex, impatiently, pointing to the egg-sized gem which sparkled far more brightly than anything else in the display.

'Oh, the big paperweight,' the girl said.

'Paperweight?'

'That's right,' said Bernard sweetly. 'Could we have a look at it?'

'I'll just get the key and fetch it down for you.' They watched the girl disappear off into the body of the shop.

'Relax, son, we've found it,' said Bernard.

Looking back to the window, Rex's eyes met those of the flight lieutenant from Shoreham airbase standing outside. 'Dad!' he yelled, picking up a heavy glass ashtray off the counter. But before he could hurl it at the display and grab the Crystal, the lieutenant had thrown open the door and entered the shop, gun drawn.

'Don't move!' he ordered. 'Put it down nice and slowly.'

As Rex made to replace the ashtray on the counter, he glanced sideways at Bernard and understanding passed imperceptibly between them.

'Look,' said Bernard, moving to his left. 'I don't see why we can't—'

The lieutenant swung his gun towards Bernard. 'Stay where you are!'

Rex took his chance and hurled the ashtray as hard as he could. With a sound like a wave breaking on Brighton beach, the display-glass shattered into a million fragments. In the brief moment that the lieutenant's eyes flicked to the window, Bernard socked him on the chin. He went down like a sack of potatoes.

Rex was impressed. 'Well done, Dad.'

Bernard smiled and winked, then turned away to nurse his sore hand. 'Ow,' he said quietly to himself.

Scrunching across the broken glass, Rex reached into the window, and his fingers closed around the Crystal. 'Got you,' he said.

Limbo II

'On the contrary, sir, I believe I've got *you*.' Rex felt the barrel of a gun in his back. He turned slowly and found himself looking into the face of Hannington's security officer, the lieutenant's gun now firmly in *his* hand. Bernard was standing behind him, gripped on either side by two elderly, but burly male assistants.

'Ah,' said Rex, raising his hands and stepping out of the window. 'What's the expression: "It's a fair cop"?'

'How about: "You're under arrest"?' said the officer. 'Just hand it over.'

Rex smiled. 'Of course. But before I do, I'd like to say a few words.'

'You can say them on the way to the police station. Now come along, sir, give me the paperweight.' The officer waited, palm outstretched.

'Paperweight?' Rex said incredulously. 'You think this is a *paperweight*?'

Bernard shook his head. 'Now, now, son.'

'Let me show you what this *paperweight* can do! *Felix qui potuit rerum cognoscere causas!*' he sang. '*Ibant obscuri sola sub nocte! Tempus edax rerum!*'

'I've no time for this,' the officer said, waving the gun. 'Hand it over, now.'

'You want it? Here!' Rex laid the Crystal on the man's palm. It began to glow with a strange intensity, and the puzzled officer felt it warm up in his hand. '*Non omnia possumus omnes!*' Rex shouted. A beam of white-hot light shot out of it, and a portal – in the shape of a cat's eye – opened up in mid-air.

The security officer, the assistants, and the lieutenant groggily coming to on the floor, gazed in amazement at the inexplicable phenomenon floating a foot above the carpet.

'Ready, Dad?' said Rex.

'You bet.' Easily shaking off his bewildered captors, Bernard stepped into the portal and disappeared.

Rex turned to the assembled company. 'It's been... an

experience, but we really must dash.' And, grabbing the Crystal out of the astonished security officer's hand, he followed Bernard. A moment later the portal itself winked out, leaving nothing to testify to the two men's existence save the glass-strewn carpet and a gap in the window display once occupied by the Limbo Crystal.

Part III

Night...

Chapter 46

'Iris?' Mr White called softly at the bedroom door. 'Can we have a word?'

Iris opened the door and was surprised to see not only Mr White but also Mr Pink and Mr Black.

'What do you want?' she said. 'I was just getting ready for bed.'

'Yes, I know,' said Mr White, 'but we need to talk, rather urgently.'

'You'd better come in, then,' she said. 'I don't suppose I can keep you out, anyway.'

The three men hurried inside and Mr White closed the door behind them. 'Now then,' he explained, 'we're going to set you free.'

Iris frowned at him. This was probably just another ploy aimed at softening her up. 'Oh yes?' she replied, non-committally.

'Yes,' said Mr White. 'You're free to go – now.'

'But you'd better get out quick, before Mr Pale hears about it,' said Mr Pink.

'Yeah, he might not understand,' said Mr Black.

Iris looked at the three men. Despite her deep misgivings, something told her that they were telling the truth. 'Are you serious?' she said finally.

'Deadly,' said Mr White. 'We're giving the whole thing up. We've decided to stay here and make a go of it.'

'We like it here,' explained Mr Pink.

'Yeah, I mean, if we destroyed everything, what would we do afterwards?' said Mr Black.

Iris had no idea what they were talking about, but she wasn't about to get into a serious discussion about their motives; she was free. There was, however, still one outstanding issue. 'What about Rex?' she asked.

'He's free to go as well. If he ever turns up, of course,' said Mr White.

'Oh, he'll turn up, all right,' said Iris. 'He's never let me down yet.'

There was the sound of splintering wood, the door fell open, and there stood Mr Pale, oozing hate. It was hard to read the expression of a skull, but Mr White was sure he'd never seen him quite so angry. 'Ah, Mr Pale, we were just talking about you,' he began.

'Rrrarrrghs,' Mr Pale rumbled. 'Now yooou all die!' He raised his hand and the room began to crackle with electricity. There was a blinding blue flash, and a lightning bolt slammed into the bed, badly scorching the candlewick bedspread.

'Stop it, Mr Pale,' ordered Mr White, 'before you do something you might regret!' The moment he'd uttered it, Mr White realized the incongruity of this statement. 'Get behind me, Iris!' he yelled. Mr Pink and Mr Black closed ranks on either side. Another bolt of electricity seared across the room, narrowly missing Iris's head and blackening the flock wallpaper.

'Do you think you can defeat all three of us? Get back!' Mr White raised his arm and a white arrow materialized and sped towards the ghastly grinning skull. Mr Pale ducked, and the arrow embedded itself in the wall of the landing beyond.

Mr Black raised his eyebrows. 'Nice one, boss,' he said.

'I'm as surprised as you are,' Mr White muttered.

Mr Pale raised his arms again, then stopped. Three to one were not good odds. 'I waaassste my tiiime heeere.' He scowled. 'I leeeave now. Pleeease yooourselves, but my destinyyy is deahhth, and I

Limbo II

mussst unchain herrr.' And, with a swirl of his cape, Mr Pale was gone.

'Is everyone all right?' Mr White asked in the shocked silence that followed.

'I'm fine,' said Mr Pink.

'Me too, boss,' said Mr Black.

'Iris?' said Mr White. He turned and found Iris lying on the floor. It seemed she'd been hit when the thunderbolt ricocheted off the wall. She was barely breathing. 'Get her onto the bed,' ordered Mr White.

As Mr Pink and Mr Black gently lifted Iris onto the bed, outside, from the small yard at the back of the shop, came a high whinnying and the clatter of horses' hooves. 'He's taking the horses, boss!'

'I know.' Mr White perched next to Iris on the bed and patted her hand tenderly. 'Iris, dear, are you all right?'

She didn't move, her breathing remained shallow, and there was not a flicker of movement under her eyelids.

'Is she going to be all right?' fretted Mr Pink.

'I don't know,' said Mr White. 'Saving lives wasn't part of my training.'

'Iris?' said Mr Black. 'How about a nice cup of tea?' He turned to Mr White. 'Shall I put the kettle on?'

'I'm afraid,' said Mr White, after a pause, 'Iris is beyond the remedy of the loose-leaf Assam.' He put her hand back on the coverlet. 'I fear she has left us.'

There was the sudden sound of footsteps on the stairs, and a moment later Rex and Bernard Boggs appeared in the shattered doorway.

'Get away from her!' Rex shouted.

Mr White rose to face him. 'It's not what you think—' he began, but felt a thump in the chest and collapsed against the wall. Anger had given Rex's magic new power.

He ran to Iris's side. 'What have you done to her?' he yelled.

'She's been hit by lightning,' explained Mr Black.

'Lightning?'

'It's a long story,' muttered Mr Pink.

'Mum?' Rex felt for a pulse, but found none. 'Mum!' In a clumsy, frantic effort to restart her heart, he began pounding her chest. But nothing seemed to work. He may have been a wizard, but not even Rex had power over life and death. Feeling a hand on his arm, he looked up into Bernard's earnestly resolved features.

'Leave her be, son. Let her rest in peace.'

'Dad, oh Dad, I'm so sorry . . .'

Iris herself was floating down a long tunnel towards an indescribably beautiful light. The suffering, the uncertainty, the anguish of her life was over. She was light and free. *I'm going home*, she thought. Then, behind her, she heard Bernard's voice, and looking back through the mists towards the far and distant end of the tunnel, she saw his long, sad face, and was filled with compassion for the man she'd left behind. She didn't think twice. 'I'm sorry,' she said, turning to the immensely comforting presence which travelled beside her, 'but I have to go back.'

As Rex and Bernard comforted each other, weeping and rocking gently back and forth in joint grief, into the mourning sadness of the Lancing bedroom there came a voice from beyond the grave: 'I could murder a cup of tea.'

'Mum!'

Iris opened her eyes and looked up into the grey, drained face of her husband. 'Have you come to rescue me?' She smiled. Bernard caught her up in his arms and wept into her neck, his heart too full to even speak.

'So,' said Mr White, helped to his feet by Mr Black and Mr Pink, 'we meet at last. Rex Boggs, I presume.'

Rex stood aloof – feet apart, hands on hips – in time-honoured 'Galactic Superhero' pose. 'So, where do you want to do battle?' he said. 'I'd suggest somewhere well away from human habitation.'

Mr White rubbed his chest and waved his hand. 'No, no, no. I can't take any more punishment – and we don't want to fight you,

Limbo II

do we, boys?' Mr Black and Mr Pink shook their heads. 'Oh, I'm so sorry, you haven't been introduced.' Mr White indicated his companions. 'Mr Pink, Mr Black, meet the legendary Rex Boggs.'

'How do you do?' said Mr Black.

'Where did you get that fabulous suit?' said Mr Pink.

'Er . . . you don't want to kill me?' asked Rex.

Mr White shook his head.

Rex was puzzled. 'But aren't you the Four Horsemen?'

Mr White nodded.

'*The* Four Horsemen, come to rage over the face of the earth, spreading pestilence and fire . . . and all that stuff?'

'As it turns out, it's only meant to be a quarter of the earth,' said Mr White.

'Oh,' said Rex, relaxing a little. 'Um, why are there only three of you?'

'Ah,' said Mr White. 'You noticed. Now, our fourth colleague *is* a bit of a worry. Speaking of whom, we'd better hurry.'

'Hurry, where?'

'Dartmoor.'

'Dartmoor?'

'I'll explain on the way. Mr Black, could you drive?'

After seeing both Bernard and Iris safely back through the portal to Limbo, Rex and the three Horsemen were soon speeding westwards through the night.

Chapter 47

'I can't tell you how gratifying it is to meet someone who truly understands what I'm talking about,' said Frink as they bounced down the road in Nilbert's Land-Rover. 'Ever since I've been here, I've had nothing but blank faces when trying to warn people of the terrible danger they're in.'

'I know what you mean,' said Nilbert.

Something about the scenery looked strangely familiar to Frink. 'Excuse me,' he said, 'but aren't we are going the wrong way? We are heading west when we should be going east, to Cissbury Hill, where the energy field has landed.'

'That was a few days ago. A lot has happened since then, my friend. We must go and meet someone who can help us defeat this energy field.'

'Who?'

'Rex Boggs.'

'I am not familiar with that name.'

'Neither was I until yesterday morning.'

'So, who is he?'

'No idea.'

'But you told me that you had foreseen the future.'

'I have – well some of it – but the further one looks into the future, the weirder it gets.'

Frink needed to get his thinking in order. 'Let me get this straight. Using Max's Certainty Principle, you had foreseen the danger of the energy field, right?'

Limbo II

'Right.'

'And meeting me at the Happy Eater, yes?'

'Yes.'

'You have also foreseen meeting this Rex Boggs, somewhere to the west, correct?'

'On Dartmoor.'

'You must, therefore, know why we are meeting this man, and what his place is in the scheme of things.'

'No, not really. I'm only surmising that he's going to be able to help sort things out. According to Max's formula, it is our *destiny* that we meet him, but beyond that . . .'

'Yes?'

'That's where it all gets a bit hazy.' Nilbert picked up a small green and silver tube off the dashboard 'Would you like a Polo?' he said, offering one to Frink.

'What is the hole for?' Frink asked, taking one of the white mints.

'Well, one can look upon it in two ways.' Nilbert replied. 'Either one can see it as the gap in our understanding – the mystery that lies at the heart of the cycle of destiny.'

'Or?'

'Or it's just a place to stick your tongue.'

Chapter 48

'More wine, darling?' The old Wizard proffered the condensation-drenched bottle. He and the Queen were sitting having lunch in the shade of the colonnaded terrace of their pretty hill-top villa. Its whitewashed walls gleamed in the sunlight and, beyond the hard-baked terracotta tiles of the sun terrace, the glittering sea could be glimpsed between honey-coloured hills.

'Yes, please,' said the Queen, lifting her glass. The Wizard topped it up with the chilled rosé. 'Cheers,' she said. Taking a sip, she rolled it around her mouth. 'Hmm, this is better than the last one.'

'Yes, we left it on the lees that little bit longer – it's what New World winemakers do. You lose some of the brilliance, but the added length and acidity more than make up for that.'

The Queen smiled at him. 'You're even beginning to talk like a winemaker.'

'Well,' said the Wizard, holding up his own glass to appreciate its colour, 'it's not quite Château Lafite, but we're getting there.' They chinked glasses. But as he brought the wine to his lips the old Wizard felt, rather than heard, a great groan of anguish, as if the world were crying out in despair. The glass slipped from his fingers, tumbling end over end, throwing out a pink, vinous tongue which glittered in the sunlight then fell in large drops, resting a moment on the tiles before seeping into the porous terracotta with a sigh. The glass followed, smacking suddenly into the unyielding floor and shattering into a thousand crystal shards.

Limbo II

'Wiz?' The Queen reached for the Wizard's hand, but he didn't feel her touch. He slumped forward, clutching his chest.

The Queen knelt anxiously beside him, patting his hand, stroking his face. 'What is it, Wiz? What's wrong?'

The old Wizard looked up into the beautiful, dark eyes of the Queen. 'My love,' he said in a painful whisper, 'I've been such a fool. It is your love alone that has prevented my life from being a complete failure.' He squeezed her hand tenderly. 'And now I am needed elsewhere.' The old Wizard closed his eyes and exhaled a long, lingering out-breath.

Detective Chief Inspector Beasely and Detective Sergeant Ivey drew up outside the corner newsagent's in Lancing High Street. Despite the fact that a note on the window announced that it was 'Closed until further notice', the door was ajar. The shop itself seemed to be deserted, but Beasely was taking no chances and, turning back to Ivey, put a finger to his lips. Tentatively pushing open the door, the two policemen went inside. Silently exploring the shop, it was Beasely who found the large, dark stain on the floorboards below the till. 'Blood,' he whispered, crouching to examine it. 'This must be where they were killed.' He was just about to slide through the bead curtain behind the counter, when the silence was broken by a tinny rendition of the theme from *Hawaii Five-0*.

'Sorry sir.' Ivey reached into his pocket and retrieved his phone. If Beasely hadn't been restrained by the need to keep quiet, Mr and Mrs Gupta wouldn't have been the only ones to die on that spot. 'Ivey,' said the sergeant, flipping open his mobile. 'Right . . . oh, right . . . Yeah? Right . . . Cheers, Keith.' Ivey closed the phone and put it back in his pocket.

'Well?' Beasely whispered.

'A sales rep from Littlehampton rang in to report that a man riding a large, indescribably coloured horse was galloping down the westbound carriageway of the A27, with three other horses in pursuit.'

'Four horses,' said Beasely.

'But that's not all. A mobile speed trap near Blackbush just clocked them doing a hundred and fifty-seven miles an hour.'

Beasely felt a cold, tingling sensation all over his body, and just then there came a noise from upstairs.

Slipping through the bead curtain, Beasely found himself in a stock room. Beyond was a door leading into a small vestibule with a steeply curving narrow staircase to its right, and to the left a passageway leading to the street door. Motioning Ivey to follow, he crept quietly up the staircase and came to a narrow landing.

'Police!' Beasely yelled. 'Show yourself!'

After a moment, a white-faced man, his suit covered in bits of straw and dark-brown stains, appeared tentatively around the door of the room at the far end of the passage. 'Are you really the police?' he asked, near to tears. When Beasely flashed his warrant card, the man collapsed, sobbing with relief. 'Thank God, thank God, thank God.'

'All right, sir. It's all right now,' Beasely soothed. 'Put the kettle on, Sergeant.'

'Right, sir.' Ivey located the kitchen and disappeared into it.

Approaching the man and helping him to his feet, Beasely's nostrils were assailed by the pungent aroma of stable yard. 'Phoo! Been sleeping rough, have we, sir?'

'You've no idea what I've been through. They locked me in with the horses!'

'Yes, I'd already worked that out,' said Beasely, backing away.

'Every second that passed I thought I was going to die!' The man suddenly lunged at Beasely and held him tight. 'Look at me!'

'Now, now, sir—'

'They were evil. They even made me play cards with them!'

'Very good, sir,' said Beasely, managing to wriggle one of his arms free, 'but if you'll just loosen your grip a second—'

Limbo II

'One of them was nothing but a skeleton! And their horses, they were huge beasts, bigger than— Ow!' Beasely had slapped the man hard around the face.

'I'm sorry about that, sir, but you were becoming hysterical.' Extricating himself from the man's embrace, Beasely put some distance between them before continuing. 'Now then. Let's start from the beginning, shall we? Who exactly are you, and what are you doing here?'

Beasely listened intently while the man unfolded his story. Apparently his name was Barry Dean and he was the manager of a car showroom in Brighton, but that was the only bit of his story that made any sense. The rest was a jumbled tale about four strange men planning to ravage the earth, a woman called Iris and a sudden departure to Dartmoor. It sounded like the invention of a deranged mind. But then so did horses that could gallop at over a hundred and fifty miles an hour.

While Ivey sat with Barry in the living room, Beasely stepped out onto the landing and contacted base. After a few minutes, the duty sergeant rang back. 'Well, sir, it turns out that the manager of Select Cars on Marine Parade *is* called Barry Dean, and according to his boss, who is not very happy with him, he's been missing for the last two days. You might also like to know that the same troop of speeding horses was last seen on the A27 outside Arundel. A police car did set off in pursuit, but the horses left the road and are now travelling across country.'

'In which direction?' Beasely asked.

'Er, west, I believe. At least that was where they were heading when they took to the fields. They could be anywhere now.'

'Have an ambulance meet us at Shoreham airport, and scramble the chopper. I'll be there in ten minutes.'

'Oh, I don't know if I can do that, sir. We've been advised that we can only call on the helicopter in the most extreme—'

'I have reason to believe that the man on horseback is violent and dangerous – responsible for two murders at least. If we don't stop this maniac, he may kill again, and unless you want that on your conscience, Sergeant, I suggest you do as I ask!'

'I'll see what I can do.'

'I also need you to contact Exeter police and have a firearms unit standing by to meet us on Dartmoor. Got that?'

'Dartmoor's a big area, sir.'

'Tell them I'll give them a more precise location when I know it myself, OK?'

'Yes, sir,' the sergeant said, rather tightly.

Beasely clicked off his phone. If Barry was really who he said he was, perhaps the rest of his story was true. *And the horses*, Beasely thought, *heading west*. . . He shook his head and went back into the living room. Barry was nursing a cup of tea on the sofa, and seemed to be recovering.

'You mentioned Dartmoor,' Beasely said, sitting down next to him.

'Yes,' said Barry. 'When they let me out of the garage, they all seemed rather excited and were talking about a place called Devil's Tor, and that if they didn't stop Mr Pale – he's the skeleton – all would be lost. That was the phrase they used: *"All will be lost."* '

'What do you think they meant by that?'

'No idea.' He sounded genuine.

Beasely's phone rang. Answering it, he was greeted by a familiar, stentorian voice. 'Now look here, Beasely. What's all this nonsense about guns and helicopters? This isn't bloody America!' It was the chief superintendent.

'Ah, sir,' *I'm going to murder that duty sergeant*, Beasely thought. 'The man who I believe killed Mr and Mrs Gupta is currently on a horse, travelling west across country. It's vitally important that he's apprehended.'

'Can't the highway patrol boys sort this out?'

'No, sir. This horse is capable of speeds in excess of a hundred and fifty miles an hour.'

'Good God!' the superintendent spluttered.

'The helicopter is the only way we're going to find him and stop him.'

'How the hell can a horse go that fast?'

'I don't know sir, but he was clocked at that speed going through a mobile trap outside Arundel.'

'One hundred and fifty miles an hour? Something's got to be wrong. Don't tell me we're going to have to re-test all our bloody mobile radars. This is very worrying. If it turns out they need to be recalibrated, it could leave us open to a tidal wave of litigation. Very well, Beasely, you can have your helicopter, and your firearms unit. But keep it quiet. If you're wrong and the press find out about horses as fast as fucking Ferraris, they're going to have a field day.'

'Right, sir. Thank you, sir.' Beasely put the phone back in his pocket. Ivey was looking at him excitedly.

'I've never been in a helicopter, sir. You know, when I was a kid—'

'Shut the fuck up!'

Ivey looked hurt, and bit his lip.

'Up you get, sir.' Beasely pulled Barry to his feet. 'We're going on a little journey.'

Chapter 49

Tony awoke to a noise not unlike a computer modem trying to connect to an ISP. He opened his eyes and shivered, wishing he'd worn something a little more sensible. A bikini was hardly fitting attire for a journey across the cold wastes of space.

'Sorry, did we wake you?' said Max. 'We were just discussing a bit of a conundrum.' The nose, eye and big toe bubbled excitedly, and an almost deafening stream of binary code filled the air. 'Now, now, don't all talk at once,' said Max.

'Er, what's the conundrum?' Tony asked, sitting up and wrapping his arms around himself.

'Do you remember our variable Time Constant – T?'

Tony nodded.

'Well, it's been worrying me ever since we left Earth. According to our calculations, we get to the service station circling Barnard's Star at twenty past five next Wednesday afternoon. But that's assuming T has only one value. If T is inconsistent, it throws all our carefully constructed equations completely out of kilter.'

'Have you, er, tried calculating the value of T?' Tony asked.

'That's the conundrum. The on-board computer on this ship is quite advanced, and between the five of us we've come up with what can only be the right answer. We've keyed in the correct formulae, checked and rechecked the result a hundred times, and still it comes out the same.'

'What is it?'

'Computer! Show Tony the value of T.'

Limbo II

Several lights blinked and flashed on the spaceship's console and, on the small liquid-crystal display below the view screen, a series of symbols appeared. Tony gasped at what he saw. On the display was written: 'Whatever you expect to happen will happen, unless you want something else badly enough to happen instead.'

'What does it mean?' Tony asked.

'I don't know,' said Max, 'but I know someone who might.'

Rex and the three remaining Horseman, with Mr Black at the wheel, were screaming westwards in Barry's car.

Mr Black was having the time of his life. He'd never driven in the dark before, and found it a new and interesting challenge. 'It's a bit like driving with your eyes closed,' he announced to his passengers. 'You've got to rely much more on feel and instinct.'

The other occupants of the car did not share his enthusiasm. Mr Pink, eyes closed, sat tense and tightly belted in the front passenger seat, while Rex and Mr White clung on for dear life in the back.

'So, why are we going to Dartmoor?' said Rex, addressing the wide-eyed Mr White.

'Are you familiar with the myth of Pandora's box?' said Mr White, raising his voice above the wail of the racing engine

'Yes,' said Rex. 'All the troubles of the world were put into a small casket, and someone called Pandora opened it and let them out – or something like that.'

'That's basically it, yes. Well, as is usually the way with myths, it's based on fact.'

'Pandora's box exists?' said Rex.

'In a manner of speaking. The box was one of those things God was keeping up his sleeve, just in case people didn't get the message from the Great Flood that He meant business. But, of course, man, being man, *didn't* get the message. Not a hundred years after the deluge, things were back to normal, and Noah's descendants were fornicating, murdering and cheating one another for all they were worth. But God Himself had been very upset by the devastation wrought by His flood and no longer had the stomach for a fight. So, mankind was left to its own devices, and the box was never used.'

'But what's it doing *here*? I thought it was a Greek myth.'

At that moment a roundabout loomed up in the headlights, and Mr Black was approaching it at full throttle. With an excited 'Whoohoo!' he cut across the corner to give himself the widest possible angle, and yanked the wheel to the right. Immediately the car began to slide, and by the time it reached the exit was almost sideways. But then the rear end clipped the kerb, and was sent swinging violently back in the other direction. Grasping the steering wheel firmly, Mr Black applied full opposite lock. The car began to straighten out, and just for a moment faced in the direction in which it was travelling. But the rear of the car continued its pendulum swing and was soon sideways again. A lesser man would, at this point, have eased off to allow the weaving back end to settle before once more stepping on the gas, but Mr Black was no wimp. Keeping his foot firmly to the floor, he fought the viciously fishtailing car for about a quarter of a mile until, finally, the lurching subsided and it came back into line, inches from the central reservation.

'What were we talking about?' said Mr White, with an unnatural smile, when they were once again travelling in more or less a straight line.

'Pandora's box,' said Rex, in a slightly strained voice.

'Ah, yes,' said Mr White. 'Originally it was indeed tucked away in the paradise of pre-Hellenic Greece. But it was clear even then that, with its crystal-blue waters and sun-kissed beaches, Greece was going to prove far too popular a tourist destination to keep the box hidden for long. So, to prevent its accidental discovery by some ouzo-sodden visitor, it was moved – many thousands of years ago – to the distant and inaccessible shores of Albion, and placed deep underground right in the middle of a desolate moor, in the firm belief that no one would inadvertently stumble across it there. Who, in their right mind, would ever intentionally visit such a wild and deserted place?'

'But Dartmoor is a hugely popular destination for British tourists,' said Rex.

'Yes,' said Mr White. 'The powers that be didn't take into account the bizarre and masochistic nature of the British character. However, despite the fact that in the summer Dartmoor is crawling with men with white hairy legs in ill-fitting shorts, the box has somehow managed to remain undiscovered all this time, guarded by the diminutive but dedicated Black Knight.'

'The Black Knight?'

'A small but determined guardian – stationed there to make sure the box didn't fall into the wrong hands.'

'What's in it, anyway?' asked Rex.

Mr White sighed. 'What is hell: fire and brimstone? No, hell surely is the absence of heat, a negation of the emotions, of passion: a frigid place. Pandora's box is full of—'

'Yee-ha!' They were coming up on another roundabout and, as Mr Black accelerated eagerly towards it, Mr White lapsed into silence and Rex closed his eyes and concentrated. *Reinforced passenger cell*, he thought, closely followed by, *front and rear crumple zones*.

The moor waited, strange and wild under the full moon, whose cold silver light dimly illuminated tortuously twisted clumps of gorse, throwing long, eerie shadows across the close-cropped grass. The only things to disturb the absolute silence were the gurgling of the Dartmoor ponies' stomachs as they browsed the thorny bushes, and the occasional bleat of a sheep.

By a small cairn, a pony pricked up its ears and whinnied a soft warning to its companions. All stopped and turned to listen. It was yet far off but unmistakable: the sound of galloping hooves, and coming on at alarming speed. Suddenly, the ponies, sensing something wrong, fled in fear and confusion, their terrified calls finding no echo amongst the deadening scrub.

The hooves came ever nearer, thumping the ground with urgent haste, closer and closer, heading straight as a dart for the dark and desolate heart of the moor.

It wasn't only the ponies that heard the approach of those malevolent hooves. Deep underground, in a tall, dripping cavern lit by a guttering torch, a small armoured knight listened to the pounding far above and picked up his sword.

'The waiting is over,' he said. 'My task is at hand.' Walking slowly to the crown of the bridge, he studied the murderously sharp edge of his weapon and smiled. 'Let him come. I am ready.' Closing the visor of his helmet, he looked towards the other end of the narrow span through the flickering darkness . . .

After handing Barry over to the paramedics, Beasely and Ivey stepped out onto Shoreham airport's floodlit tarmac, where G-SUSX stood, its rotor already spinning.

'Wow!' shouted Ivey over the turbine whistle of the engine. 'A real helicopter!'

'Just don't show me up, Sergeant,' said Beasely darkly, as the two men strode towards it.

'Where are we going?' the pilot asked, once they were safely inside.

'Dartmoor,' Beasely informed him.

'Dartmoor?' said the pilot. 'I used to go there as a kid.'

'Don't you start,' muttered Beasely, strapping himself in.

The engine wound itself up into an ear-shattering scream, and the long rotors sliced the air until they were nothing but a blur. Then, with a stomach-turning lurch, the big machine lifted off the ground, and turned its nose towards the west.

*

Limbo II

'Are we there yet?' asked Mr Pink, as they sped along the narrow, bumpy road running around the bottom of the moor.

'Not far now,' said Mr White. 'Look out for the horses.' With some regret, Mr Black eased his foot off the throttle, and the car slowed. The journey from Lancing had taken under two hours, which was probably a record.

'There they are!' shrilled Mr Pink. In the headlights three horses were illuminated, grazing in a lay-by at the side of the road: one black, one white and one pink.

'Good,' said Mr White. 'We're going to need them now.' He patted Mr Black on the shoulder. 'Well done. But this car, for all its good points, will never make it across the moor.'

'Oh, right, boss,' said Mr Black, barely concealing his disappointment. He pulled glumly into the lay-by and killed the engine.

Mr White sensed his unhappiness. 'But we may need it to take us back again,' he said encouragingly.

Mr Black nodded, smiling weakly, and reluctantly got out of the car.

Mr White's horse ran up to greet him and nuzzled his master's chest. He stroked the big animal's head tenderly, whispering in its ear, then jumped up onto its back.

'Have you ever ridden bareback?' he asked Rex.

'Er, no. I've never ridden at all, actually.'

'You'll soon get the hang of it. Come on,' he said, offering Rex his hand.

Grasping Mr White's arm, Rex clambered clumsily up behind him, while Mr Black and Mr Pink leapt expertly up onto their own mounts' backs.

'Is it far?' Rex asked, wrapping his arms around Mr White.

'No,' said Mr White, 'but we'd better hurry. Mr Pale's got a head start on us. Follow me, men. Hold on tight, Rex!' Mr White dug his heels into his horse's flanks and they set off at a speed that had Rex looking back on Mr Black's driving with something approaching fondness.

*

Mr Pale had already reached the toppling mound of stones called Devil's Tor. Pulling firmly back on the reins, he brought his terrifying horse to a standstill and, leaping off onto the spongy turf, began searching about in the moonlight. A little way off and to the west of the small tor he was able to make out a tall column of granite, erected far back in the mists of time and known locally as Beardown Man. Exploring its rough surface with his bony fingers, the tips of his phalanges scraped and clattered over the lichen-covered stone until they found what they were looking for: a small, upward-pointing arrow, chiselled into the stone, now weathered until it was almost non-existent. Calling his horse over, he once again mounted the beast and manoeuvred it so that its broad chest came into contact with the stone on the side with the incised arrow. Then, with a cry, Mr Pale dug his cruel heels hard into the animal's flanks. The great horse whinnied and strained against the unyielding monolith, its hooves gouging divots out of the soft earth. Again and again, Mr Pale urged his mount on, drawing blood as he relentlessly scored its sides with his bony heels.

At first nothing happened – the stone seemed immovable. But Mr Pale was an irresistible force, mercilessly driving his horse's bleeding breast against the unyielding stone, until foam began to fleck its mouth and its eyes rolled madly in their sockets. Then, just as it seemed that the horse's heart would burst, the stone collapsed, falling to the ground in a shower of earth and moss.

After a moment's silence, there came a great whirring from the small tumbled mound of stones known as Devil's Tor, as machinery, motionless for thousands of years, wheezed into life. Mr Pale turned his head to observe, in the silvery light, the large grey stones at the centre of the tor part and reveal a large, flat square of flint. The granite wheels and cogs of the ancient mechanism screeched in complaint as they revolved against each other, and slowly, slowly, the flint square began to descend into the deep, damp earth. Wheeling round, Mr Pale urged his exhausted mount up the scree-covered side of the tor. Its hooves scrabbling on the loose shingle, the horse, with a desperate whinny, leapt at last onto the prehistoric lift.

Far below, the Black Knight heard the ancient machinery and knew all too well what it meant. His body as tight as a coiled spring, he waited for his foe to appear in the arched opening at the other side of the bridge.

At last, the grating and screeching of stone against stone ceased, to be replaced by the echoing sound of hooves on granite as guardian and challenger came face to face.

Looking across the bridge into the eyes of Death, sitting astride his monstrous pale horse, the knight issued his challenge.

'I am Triffydd, son of Gwyndor, Guardian of the Casket. He who seeks its dread power must first do battle with me! Go back whence you came and we shall say no more about it. But enter into combat, and you will not live to see the sun rise. It is a simple choice: leave with your life or stay and die. I have spoken!' The guardian, magnificent in his burnished armour, finished this speech with his sword held high.

Death's horse pawed the ground, and steam, like smoke, issued from its nostrils. Death sighed, 'Sssorry, noo time,' and, digging his heels into his horse's flanks, hurtled towards the diminutive knight.

The knight crouched and waited resolutely behind his sword. But, as the great horse rumbled towards him, he began to realize just how great was the disparity in their sizes. Death's horse was a good seven feet at the shoulder, and the knight was barely three foot two. Even so, his resolve held firm and he stood his ground as two tons of muscle, bone and hoof careered towards him at over seventy miles an hour. The bridge shook under the pounding of the horse's huge hooves as it drew closer and closer to where the small knight waited, braced for the sudden shock of the inevitable collision.

Looking out from the sweaty confines of his helmet, the knight watched the image of the horse grow ever larger. It was nearly upon him now, its huge head with its wild eyes and flashing teeth filling the narrow slot of his visor.

At the last moment, the knight stepped to his left and slashed up at the grinning rider. The sword connected with the bottom of a stirrup and bounced off in a shower of sparks. Unbalanced by his unsuccessful stroke, the small knight was left teetering on the edge of the bridge, and as the hellish horse thundered past, he was nudged by its bulging flanks and thrust out into space. With a cry, he plummeted towards the jagged rocks of the cave floor far, far below.

Death galloped on across the bridge, and into the room that held the casket.

The police helicopter was making good time, and just as Rex and company were mounting up and preparing to gallop off in pursuit of Mr Pale, the pilot got his first glimpse of the lights of Exeter and, just beyond it, the big black lump of the moor looming up out of the night.

'Whereabouts?' asked the pilot.

'Somewhere called Devil's Tor,' Beasely answered.

The pilot turned to his co-pilot. 'Devil's Tor?' he enquired, and the co-pilot started leafing through his charts.

Sergeant Ivey, looking down at the twinkling lights, had the biggest smile ever on his face. *This is what it's all about*, he was thinking, *chasing felons and murderers across country in a chopper. I knew detective work had to be more than searching through junk mail and checking computer records. Wait till Mum hears about this.*

For Beasely, on the other hand, the magic of police work was in the detail: the discarded bus ticket, the telephone number scrawled on the torn fragment of a book of matches, and the piecing together of these seemingly unconnected items into a coherent picture. Besides, he was a terrible flyer and was having trouble hanging onto his stomach.

*

Limbo II

Back in Limbo the sun was now just a thin red crescent on the horizon, and Smeil was a very worried man. He walked the battlements, chewing the end of his belt and listening to the baying of the crowd at the gate below. Everything was falling apart. His land was about to be plunged back into darkness; the King, the Queen and the Wizard were lost, possibly for ever; discontent was spreading like a cancer across the land. 'And who's left in charge of this mess? Muggins here. Why did I get myself into this position? Why can't I learn to say no?' He felt utterly alone and, gripping the crumbling masonry of the battlements, wept copiously.

Of course, the real reason for his anguish was his rejection by Matilda, but that was so agonizingly painful he couldn't bear to think about it. If she'd only smiled at him with favour, taken his hand and whispered her love in his ear, the darkness, the fear, none of it would have mattered. But as it was, he was left with nothing but the stark reality of his situation.

Wiping his eyes with his sleeve, he pulled himself up to his full three feet. 'Face up to it, Smeil; you're on your own. People like us don't have happy endings. We live merely to serve, and, if I *am* to serve, well, I couldn't have a better master than Rex.'

The thin red disc of the sun disappeared into the sea, night fell like an iron shutter, and a groan went up from the land of Limbo.

'Oh, bollocks,' Smeil whispered.

After a long, agonizing climb, the Black Knight hauled himself back onto the narrow bridge and sat for a moment, exhausted. But then the lift machinery began to whirr for a second time. He looked balefully towards the doorway at the other end of the bridge. *Oh shit*, he thought.

The large slate square bumped on its stops, and Rex, Mr Black, Mr Pink and Mr White came face to face with a small, dusty man, his once-magnificent armour now badly dented and scratched, and wearing on his head what looked like a squashed kettle.

'I am Triffydd, thon of Gwyndor, Guardian of the Cathket. He who theekth itth dread power mutht firtht do battle with me,' said the knight, the drama of his challenge somewhat undermined by the fact that he'd lost several teeth in the fall.

'Sorry?' said Mr White.

'I thaid—' the dwarf began, but at that moment, from the casket room behind him came the clatter of hooves and the clash of chains.

'Mr Pale! We must hurry!' said Mr White, leading the way across the bridge.

'Thtop!' yelled the guardian, waving the stump of his broken sword.

'Oh, please,' said Mr White, shoving it away, 'you could hurt someone with that.'

As the four men pushed past him, the dwarf lost his footing on the narrow bridge and, with a small cry, once again plummeted to the cave floor far below.

'Sorry,' Rex called down to him over the edge.

Entering the casket room, Mr White and the others were confronted with a hellish tableau. With high whinnying cries, Death's own horse was stamping on the heavy chain securing the casket, throwing up showers of sparks. Again and again, with a deafening clatter, the animal slammed its great hooves down on the welded links, until finally the chain gave up the fight and slipped sinuously to the floor like a metallic snake.

'Step back!' called Mr White.

Mr Pale turned his face towards him, eye sockets aflame with indignation. 'Yooo forgettt yoooursssselfff!' he growled. 'Yooo nottt puny hooomannn. Whyyy yoooo care?' Apart from the chain, the casket was secured by a large padlock and two seamless, encircling iron bands. Picking up one end of the fallen chain, Mr Pale now slipped it between the casket and the iron bands.

'Ask yourself this,' said Mr White. 'Once you've laid waste to the world, what have you gained? Power? Over what? A wasteland! What's the point?'

Limbo II

'The point isss the misssionnn. I am Deathhh! That isss my callinggg and alll the point I neeed.' Taking the two ends of the chain, he secured them over the pommel of his horse's saddle.

'This is madness!' Mr White yelled.

'Yooo call meee maddd, when yooo go againssst yooour natuuure?'

'I didn't even know what my nature was until I arrived here,' said Mr White. 'I know it's a little more cut and dried in your case, but people *can* change, Mr Pale. The world has so much to offer. Someone with your talents could become anything he wanted to be.'

'Yeah, with your bone structure you'd make a great male model,' offered Mr Black.

Mr Pale snarled, bringing his hand down hard on his horse's backside. Snorting a fine red mist, the animal strained heart and soul and, after a monstrous effort, the securing bands around the casket snapped – but so did something in the horse. With a piteous moan, it fell to the floor of the cavern and lay still.

Mr Pale, ignoring his stricken beast, knelt and grasped the heavy padlock – the only obstacle that now stood between the world and the contents of Pandora's box.

Mr White looked meaningfully across at Mr Black and Mr Pink, who began making their way round to either side of Mr Pale.

'This is your last chance!' yelled Mr White, addressing the dark figure hunched over the gently glowing casket, but Mr Pale didn't even look up. 'Very well, you give me no choice!' Mr White raised his hand and a white arrow materialized in mid-air and sped towards the crouching figure of Death. Mr Pale moved swiftly to one side and the arrow embedded itself in the lid of the casket. Taking advantage of this momentary distraction, the other Horsemen launched a three-pronged attack, lunging suddenly towards him. But Mr Pale was ready for them. With an angry cry, he turned and unleashed a thunderbolt right at Mr Black's head.

'Duck!' yelled Mr White. Mr Black hit the floor, and the

thunderbolt crashed into the wall. Then, wheeling round, Mr Pale released another two thunderbolts in quick succession.

'Look out!' yelled Rex. One careened past Mr Pink's head, singeing his hair. The other brushed Mr White's chest as it blazed past him, scorching out onto the narrow bridge, where the knight was now sitting, breathing heavily after clambering back up from the cave floor far below. The bolt struck him full on the breastplate, and once again he found himself falling.

Undeterred by this interruption, Mr Pale inserted one bony finger in the padlock's keyhole and began to explore the inside of the lock.

Rex looked at Mr White, and it was clear from his expression that the Horseman was at a loss. It was obviously time for Rex to act – but what could he do? One by one, with his bony phalange, Mr Pale was clicking the tumblers in the lock. Soon it would be too late. Then Rex had a desperate idea. Pulling a long chiffon scarf out of his jacket pocket, he laid it on the ground.

'Mr Pale!' he called.

Slowly the skeleton turned its white face towards him. 'Whaaattt nooowww?'

'I'm not afraid of you,' Rex quavered. 'Nor of what's in that box. I'm not afraid of death.'

'Innn thisss boxsss isss worssse than deathhh. Inssside isss achinggg despairrr and hopelessnesss – a bottomlesss pittt of sufferrringgg.'

Rex swallowed nervously.

Death clicked the final tumbler. The padlock snapped open and fell to the ground with a deadening clunk. 'Nowww yooo afraiddd?' he said, putting both his skeletal hands on the lid.

'Mr Pale!' Rex shouted. The figure at the casket shrugged its bony shoulders in annoyance. It was now or never.

'Ahhhh!' Rex ran at the black figure of Death and fell on him, grabbing him around the neck. 'The scarf!' Rex yelled. 'Get us onto the scarf!' Though momentarily taken by surprise, Mr Pale soon recovered, and Rex felt a cold, pitiless hand close around his right arm. In horror, he heard the bones of his forearm shatter a split second before the excruciating wave of pain flooded his system. Screaming in agony, he somehow managed to keep a hold on the hooded figure with his one good arm. Mr Black, Mr Pink and Mr White leapt to his aid, and between the four of them, they succeeded in dragging Mr Pale onto the square of chiffon lying on the cave floor.

'*Expedit esse deos, et, ut expedit, esse putemus!*' Rex gasped, and the scarf rapidly assembled itself into a large, round table.

But Mr Pale was strong and, as Rex and the three Horsemen struggled to hold him, he broke free with a roar, throwing off even his colleagues like chaff. Standing on the table, he towered over the exhausted Rex. 'Yooo dare to prevent meee with yooour weeeak magic? Fooolishhh hooomannn.' Raising his arm, he was about to unleash a thunderbolt at Rex's head, when Rex, with his last ounce of strength, managed a hoarse and desperate, '*Deus et natura, nihil faciunt frustra!*' Mr Pale, taken off balance, wobbled slightly as the table beneath him began to disappear.

The three Horsemen looked on in astonishment as first the table, then in quick succession Rex and Mr Pale, vanished into thin air.

Almost immediately, Rex and the table reappeared.

'Where's Mr Pale?' Mr White asked.

'The Wall of Death,' Rex gasped.

'How apt.'

Rex was convulsed by a spasm of pain from his shattered arm.

'Ah,' said Mr White, noticing the problem. 'We'd better see if we can sort that out for you.'

'The casket,' Rex insisted. 'Make it secure again before anything else happens.'

'Yes, of course. Mr Black – the casket!'

'Sure thing, boss.'

But as Mr Black approached the glowing chest, six men burst

into the cave. 'Chief Inspector Beasely, Brighton CID. You're all under arrest!'

'Oh, Jesus,' groaned Rex.

Beasely himself remained in the doorway while Ivey and the posse of armed men fanned out to cover the body of the cave.

'Chief Inspector, you don't know what you're dealing with,' Rex warned. 'Mr Black, reseal the casket!'

Mr Black took a step towards it.

'Nobody move!'

Mr Black ignored the chief inspector and took another step.

'Stay where you are!' Beasely barked. 'Or I'll give the order to fire!'

Mr Black looked across to Mr White. 'Do as he says, Mr Black.' Mr Black eased slowly away from the casket.

'Thank you. Men, surround that... thing.' The four armed police proceeded to station themselves one at each corner.

'Chief Inspector!' said Rex. 'You have to let us finish this.'

'Not until I find out what's going on. Which one of you killed the Guptas?'

'He's not here.'

'Who are you?'

'I'm Mr White.'

'The man you are seeking no longer exists,' said Rex, 'at least not in any way that you would understand.'

'And you are?'

'Rex Boggs.'

'Boggs? That name rings a bell. Isn't that the name over the Guptas' shop?'

'There's no time for this! We have to seal the casket.'

'Not so fast,' Beasely said. 'What's inside it that you're so eager to conceal, eh?'

'Open it and you will not live to find out!'

Beasely looked down at the glowing casket. There was something not quite right about it, even he could tell. He called his sergeant over. 'Ivey, open the box.'

'Me, sir?'

'Yes, Ivey, you.'

'Oh, right.' He tentatively reached out a hand towards the lid.

'NO!' yelled Mr White. An arrow materialized out of thin air and thudded into the top of the casket, pinning Ivey's sleeve to the lid. A gunshot rang out and Mr White fell to the ground. Mr Black let go a sound like a wounded dog and ran to his leader's side.

'You idiot!' Rex yelled at the policeman. 'No more shooting, please. Nobody's in danger, you have to believe me. But open that lid and we're all in trouble. How is he, Mr Black?'

Mr Black, kneeling at Mr White's side, looked up at the policeman who had fired the shot. 'He's dead,' he said simply. Rising slowly, he advanced on the small phalanx of armed police guarding the casket. 'Why did you kill him?'

'Now now, sir,' Beasley said.

The policemen all levelled their guns at him.

'Mr Black, getting yourself killed isn't going to help!' called Mr Pink.

'Mr White wouldn't have wanted it this way,' Rex added. But Mr Black was impervious to reason. The man he'd always looked on as a father was dead, and his death would be avenged.

In the face of the approaching Mr Black, the four armed policemen moved instinctively behind the casket, leaving Ivey, pinned to the lid by Mr White's arrow, marooned and desperate. Yelping with panic, he yanked frenziedly at his sleeve as Mr Black drew ever nearer. Finally, ripping free the sleeve of his polyester-wool-mix suit, he dived over the casket and hid behind the armed policemen.

As he reached the casket, Mr Black smiled grimly at Beasely. 'You wanted to see what's inside,' he said, his hands resting on the lid.

'Mr Black, no!' Rex screamed.

'Well, take a look!' And so saying, Mr Black threw open the lid of the ancient chest.

The lid crashed against the side of the casket, the echo reverberating around the tall, rocky cave. In the fearful silence that followed, all eyes turned towards the now open casket.

'Oh shit,' Rex murmured.

Slowly at first, thin wisps of grey mist licked out of the chest and began to creep down its sides, snaking across the floor of the cave. Then, in a sudden rush, an icy fog billowed out of it – like smoke rising from an erupting volcano.

'Get back!' urged Rex. But the policemen had no chance.

Ivey went first. As the fog flowed over his body, he gazed wretchedly towards his chief inspector, the expression on his face changing from horror to desperate hopelessness. The light in his eyes faded, and all that was left was the shell of a man, inhabited by inconsolable despair.

The four armed policemen were next – consumed in quick succession. As the soul-draining fog licked around their shiny shoes and wrapped itself around their legs, the life in their eyes was rapidly extinguished. Mr Pink ran to join Rex on the table top.

'Mr Black!' Rex screamed. 'Close it! Close it now!'

'Please, Blackie!' implored Mr Pink. But Mr Black had turned his back on the casket and returned to his leader's side. Kneeling sorrowfully by Mr White's body, he hung his head and wept.

'What's going on here?' asked a terrified Beasely.

'Quick, Chief Inspector! Get up on the table!' But the fog already had its thin grey fingers around the policeman's legs, and in seconds had claimed him too.

Now the fog was making its way inexorably up the legs of the table itself. 'The Crystal,' Rex gasped. But trying to reach into his pocket with his broken arm made him cry out in agony.

'Can I help?' asked Mr Pink.

'My pocket,' said Rex.

Limbo II

Hurriedly searching through Rex's jacket, Mr Pink pulled out the Limbo Crystal. 'This it?'

Reaching clumsily across his body with his good arm, Rex's fumbling fingers gratefully closed around the Crystal's cold, hard surface. The fog was almost upon them – he didn't have much time. '*Felix qui potuit rerum cognoscere causas! Ibant obscuri sola sub nocte! Tempus edax rerum! Non omnia possumus omnes!*' The portal opened with an electric *hiss*. 'No questions, Mr Pink. Go ahead.' Pushing the Horseman through, Rex rose painfully to his knees. He was just about to follow when the fog, reaching the top of the table, broke like a wave and rolled over him.

'Come on!' called Mr Pink, reaching out from the other side of the portal. 'Too late!' said Rex, faintly, as a numbing heaviness crept over his limbs. The Crystal fell from his fingers and landed with a thud on the solid wood of the table top. The portal slammed shut, and Rex slumped back, eyes turned inward, seeing nothing but the bleakness of his irredeemable isolation.

In the cavern everything was icily still, all except for the grey fog as it continued to boil out of the casket and ooze irresistibly across the floor. Nothing now lay between it and the vibrant and vulnerable world outside, which all too swiftly would be consumed by the rapacious, life-sucking mist, and turned into a desolate, freezing hell.

The guardian clambered up the last few feet and again reached the relative security of the end of the bridge. Sitting heavily on the cold stones, his bent and twisted armour complaining with a series of metallic squeaks and groans, he sighed heavily. Even in his worst nightmare, he'd never seen himself in this position. It was at that moment he noticed thin tongues of grey fog begin to creep around the stones upon which he sat.

'Well that'th jutht great,' he lisped. 'The end of a perfect day.'

Chapter 50

Frink leapt out of the Land-Rover and climbed up the tumbled stones of the tor. 'A large hole,' he said, studying the space left by the descended Stone Age lift.

'How very observant,' said Nilbert, climbing up alongside him.

Frink looked at his left index finger. 'I wonder if there's enough light,' he said. 'Oh well, let's have a go.' He cleared his throat. 'Beneath my feet, deep in the subterranean fastness of this world—'

'Can I help you gentlemen?' In the moonlight, they could just make out the shape of a man in a helmet, on the other side of the tor. It was the pilot from the helicopter.

'Ah,' said Frink. 'You may not be able to help us, but we can certainly help you. I am—'

His customary greeting was cut short by a strange sound echoing up through the ancient lift shaft – a sort of gurgling rumble, a bit like the sound a garden hose makes just after the tap's been turned on. The helicopter pilot stepped up to the lip of the hole and peered down into it. A moment later, a column of icy grey fog erupted from the tor in a terrifying rush. The pilot, taken by surprise, could do no more than gaze across at Frink and Nilbert with a look of unutterable sadness before being turned to living stone.

'Well, Nilbert,' said Frink, retreating instinctively from the fog which was now gushing from the shaft and pouring down the sides of the tor, 'what happens next?'

Nilbert looked at the grey plume issuing from the depths of the earth. 'Well,' he said slowly, 'the thing is—'

Limbo II

He was interrupted by a familiar sound. Turning round, he was only a touch surprised to see a spaceship hovering a few feet above the ground. The hatch opened with a small *hiss*.

'Need a lift?' Max beamed.

In the vastness of the eternal mind, in the void that has no beginning and no end – beyond size, beyond time and space – floated the Great Golden Hoop. Forever moving, forever staying the same, the breathtakingly beautiful river of destiny flowed on, spinning silently in the nothingness.

Then out of the silence came a noise – the angry roar of a large V-twin – and on the long, endless golden ribbon of light something moved. Through the great black fluttering cloud that hung about the Hoop like a flock of starlings, came a fat man riding a Harley-Davidson. But he was not alone. On the pillion, towering above him, stood the skeletal figure of Death, his bony hands wrapped around the fat rider's head.

'Take your hands off my eyes, you berk! I can't see a fucking thing!' the fat man shouted as the Harley weaved crazily from side to side, its front tyre coming perilously close to the widening rift which ran round the centre of the Hoop.

Rex was unutterably cold. He was standing in a wintry landscape whose frigid whiteness stretched to the horizon, and in all that barren flatness nothing moved. The bitter coldness that ran through him was an unbearable ache, but he did not cry out. It was not that he was beyond pain, just that he was beyond doing anything about it. His pain was his punishment – for believing in life. How foolish he'd been ever to think that his existence had been either meaningful or worthwhile. Now he saw the truth: nothing made any impression on this desolate landscape. The tracks of those optimistic fools who had the audacity to think they could make a difference were simply covered up by the next snowfall.

Cold, he thought, and sank even deeper into fathomless, pitiless despair.

But then there came a voice, a distant voice that had in it something that he recognized. A voice, perhaps, from long ago? He tried to put such thoughts out of his mind; forgetfulness of things past was the only way to cope with this unending suffering. To remember happier times, to once allow the thought that things could be any different from how they were in this terrible place would be hell indeed.

But the voice came again. It was nearer this time. And in all that sterile, frozen wilderness here was something warm, and pulsing with forbidden *life*!

'Rex! Rex, it's me. Look up. Look up.'

Rex raised his eyes and looked into an old, careworn face. There was something so familiar about it that for a moment it made his ice-marooned heart leap within him.

The old man caught that brief flicker. 'That's right, Rex. Remember.'

Rex was seized by a pain beyond enduring. *No, not that. Cannot remember. Too painful . . .*

'It is the pain of reawakening, Rex. Turn away from despair and towards hope.'

Hope is pain.

The old man stooped and pointed to a small frozen flower near Rex's feet, held fast in the rigid grip of the iron-hard earth. 'Look at this flower. It is frozen solid. To all intents and purposes it might as well be dead. But once you warm it with the breath of life, of hope . . .' The old man knelt and breathed on the flower, and Rex watched silently as the bright green of its leaves burst through its wintry shroud in a shock of sudden colour. The small flower nodded its head, then raised its face proudly towards the heavens. 'You see, it hasn't forgotten how to live. A small spark of hope was always there, waiting for release. That spark of hope is in all men, Rex. It is in you too. Foster it now. Nurture it. Allow it to take flame and rekindle your trust in the rightness of life.'

The old man placed a hand on Rex's heart and, despite himself, Rex felt deep within a searing pain as his numbed senses began to remember themselves. It was as if all the cells of his body were on fire. *No, no, no.* In a terrible agony, he cried out with the anguish of his reawakening spirit and, as he once more entered the realm of the sentient, was convulsed by the sudden shock of his broken arm. 'Ahh!' The icy wasteland, where before no sound had intruded, echoed strangely to this sound. 'No more! No more!' Rex tried to move back into the analgesic of his isolation, away from the shredding pain.

'Turn towards it, Rex. Embrace the pain, and it will make you whole.'

'NO!' It was too much, and once again Rex felt himself slip slowly back down the sheer slope of despair. But the old man would not let him go, and reached down into Rex's despairing solitude as one would offer a hand to a drowning man. Rex caught a whisper of the tender breath of existence, like the warm sigh of a summer's day. As he fell backwards into cold, dismal blackness, that small memory of life awakened something deep in his ice-encrusted soul and, with his last ounce of strength, he clawed himself back towards the lacerating pain. In screaming torment, Rex moved through the jagged sheets of suffering, until finally he burst through the numbing veil of desolation.

'Father!' he said.

'My son.' The old Wizard took him in his arms, the warmth of his love melting what ice remained in Rex's heart and healing the shattered bones of his arm.

'Why am I here?'

The old man smiled. 'Ah, even suffering has a purpose. But do not worry. Soon they will come.'

'Who will come?'

But already the old Wizard was beginning to fade. 'My time is short. I must go now. Just remember this one word: hope. That is all you need. Hope is the key.'

'Where are you going?'

'Far, far from this place.'

'What about Limbo?'

A flicker of sadness, of regret, passed across the old man's face. 'Limbo is a state of mind. Like you, it has forgotten itself. It must regain its faith. Teach it to believe once again, Rex. Only believe.'

'Will I never see you again?'

'You will, you will. In time.' The old Wizard was now nothing more than a wisp of smoke.

'Father!'

'Hope, Rex. Remember *hope*. Farewell.' His voice trailed away to nothingness. And, as the image of the old Wizard dissolved, it was replaced by that of a strange, bald man.

'Greetings,' the man said. 'I am Frink Byellssen from the planet Thrripp.'

Rex opened his eyes with difficulty. He appeared to be lying on a camp bed.

'He's coming to!' Frink called, removing his antennae from Rex's temples and tucking them away behind his own ears.

A man with a beard bent over him. 'Hi, welcome to Lizard. I'm Harvey, how do you do?'

Another man, pink-faced with lank, brown hair, introduced himself: 'Nilbert Plymstock, nice to meet you.'

Rex tried to stand, but his muscles were stiff and ached with the effort.

'Here, let me help you,' said Harvey, putting an arm around him and helping him up.

'Thank you.' Rex groggily took in his surroundings. 'Oh my God.' He suddenly gasped. He was in a small laboratory. On a shelf stood three jars, containing a nose, a big toe and an eye respectively. On a stool in front of a blackboard stood a miniature and ill-proportioned man with an oversized head and, standing uncertainly in the corner, was a man wearing a bikini. But it wasn't any of these grotesqueries that had caused Rex to catch his breath. What had shocked him was the phrase written on the blackboard at the bottom of an unbelievably complex set of equations: 'Whatever you expect to happen will happen, unless you want something else badly enough to happen instead.'

'How...? Who...?' The room smelt strangely reminiscent of the biology lab at his old school. Rex was overcome by nausea and rocked back on his heels.

'Easy now,' said Nilbert, catching him and sitting him down on the bed.

Rex looked up into his eyes. 'I remember now. I was in a cave,' he said. 'How did I get here?'

'Frink and I rescued you.'

'Rescued?' Rex's eyes suddenly grew wide and fearful. 'The fog!' he exclaimed. 'That awful fog!'

'There there,' said Nilbert, patting him on the back reassuringly.

Rex started searching frantically through his pockets. 'The Crystal! Where's the Crystal?'

Nilbert smiled and pulled something hard and brilliant out of his own pocket. 'Is this what you're looking for?'

Rex seized it gratefully, then frowned and looked up at him. 'Wait a minute. Why weren't *you* affected by the fog?'

Nilbert shrugged. 'Frink here's an alien, which is probably why it didn't work on him – either that or he's got no imagination. And me, well, I'm enlightened, and – quite apart from the fact that I'm no longer attached to my emotions – I see only the truth. That fog was just an illusion. Believe me, life really is worth living.'

'An illusion?'

'A very powerful one, but an illusion nonetheless.'

'What about the others?'

'We put all the policemen back in the helicopter, but that little chap in the armour didn't seem tall enough to be one of them, so we left him sitting by the tor.'

'And Mr Black?'

'Was he the gentleman in the ill-fitting suit?'

Rex nodded.

'He didn't want to be rescued. He seemed very upset by the death of his friend, and just wanted to stay with him. So we left him there.'

'Ahem.' The figure at the blackboard coughed. 'I hate to interrupt this touching scene, but do you think we can get on?' Rex looked up at the strange humanoid. 'I'm Max,' it said. 'Can you tell us anything about this?'

Rex stood shakily and went over to the statement written on the blackboard. 'Did you write this?'

'Yes.'

'But . . . how did you get hold of it?'

'It's the answer we get when we try to calculate the value of T – our Time Constant. Unfortunately it doesn't seem to be as constant as we'd hoped.'

'Do any of you *know* what this is?' said Rex, addressing the whole room.

'No, we were hoping you'd be able to tell us that,' said Max. The nose, toe and eye bubbled excitedly.

'It's the Limbollian Paradox: the universal law that governs the workings of time and space.'

'There's our problem!' Nilbert exclaimed.

'Problem?'

'It's wrong,' said Max.

'But I wrote it,' said Rex, stung. 'What do you mean it's wrong?'

'It's throwing all our calculations out,' said Harvey.

'It's like this,' Max explained, jumping off the stool and motioning Rex to sit again. 'This statement allows for a certain amount of choice. Now, I can appreciate its attractions: the idea that an individual can have whatever life he chooses as long as he wants it badly enough. The trouble is, it permits more than one outcome to any given set of circumstances, do you see?'

'Er, I'm not sure...' said Rex, beginning to feel rather dizzy. 'Do you think I can have a glass of water?'

'Certainly,' said Max, signalling to Tony.

'What this, er, Paradox does,' Nilbert continued, 'is put a spanner in the works as far as time is concerned. It splits it up into discrete sections.'

'You just can't have people going off and having whatever kind of future they want, all over the place. That would be chaos,' said Max. 'And, speaking purely selfishly now, the effect on my Certainty Principle is disastrous. How can I possibly predict the future when there are so many to choose from?'

'Wait a minute!' Rex shook his head, still trying to understand what was happening. The man in the bikini reappeared and handed him a glass of water.

'I'm Tony.' He smiled.

'Thank you,' said Rex, perplexed by but too polite to say anything about the man's attire. He took a sip, then turned to Nilbert. 'One thing I don't understand: why did you bring *me* here and not the others?'

'From what I'd seen of the future,' said Nilbert, 'I knew that I was supposed to meet a Rex Boggs at a place called Devil's Tor, and that you'd be lying on a table. But that's *all* I knew. I tried looking further ahead, but the results I got didn't make any sense.'

'The result of our unconstant constant,' Max chimed in.

'So what can we do about it?' Rex asked.

'You're going to have to rewrite it.'

'You want me to rewrite the Paradox, just so that your calculations work?'

'No,' said Harvey, 'it's not like that. If we don't do something about it, time – instead of being the incredibly orderly and delicate mechanism that it is – will be torn to shreds.'

'OK, I'm beginning to understand. But what about Pandora's box?'

'First things first,' said Max. '*This* little problem needs to be solved before we do anything else.'

'But we can't just stand by and let the world be engulfed by the fog.'

'Without sorting out time first, nothing we do will have any consistent effect,' Max said. 'We might solve the fog problem in *this* time, *this* reality, only for it to engulf the world in another parallel reality. You understand what I'm saying?'

Rex nodded, and lapsed glumly into silence.

'Right,' said Max. 'Now, the Paradox – any suggestions for an alternative? I open it up to the floor.'

Tony raised his hand. 'Um, how about: Time is a river?'

'Hm,' Max stroked his chin. 'Poetic but a little flabby. Anyone else?'

'My mother always liked that Doris Day song "Qué Sera Sera". What will be, will be – you know?' suggested Harvey.

'What will be, will be. Yes, close, very close,' said Nilbert, 'but a little rigid, don't you think?'

Max nodded. 'We need at least to leave the illusion of free will, but it's definitely along the right lines.'

'What today we sow, tomorrow we will reap?'

Max shook his head. 'Too . . . biblical.'

'A good time was had by all?'

'Excuse me. I need a little air.' Rex left them to it and stumbled out into the sunshine.

On the other side of the world a terrible box had been opened which was spewing forth a plague that threatened to drain humanity of all its wonderful diversity and colour. Joy and laughter would be wiped from the face of the earth, and it would become instead a frigid, grey lump of rock. In that small hut may have been assembled the greatest scientific minds in the universe, but they had no sense of urgency. Rex would have to act. After all, it was he who wrote

Limbo II

the Paradox, and if it was wrong, it was his responsibility to put it right.

'Tumbril!' he yelled to the sky.

A bundle of rags appeared and fell onto the beach. The breeze died, the palm trees were still, the gently lapping waves froze at the very point of breaking on the white sand of the shoreline.

'Who stirs me from my slumbers?' roared the untidy bundle. Then, standing and brushing the sand from the folds of her filthy dress, she turned and spotted Rex. 'Oh, hello, Rexie love. How's tricks?'

'Not good. I need you to take me into the void.'

'Why? What's up with that magic table of yours?'

'I've no time to discuss it now, Tumbril. Will you do it or not?'

Tumbril pulled a face. 'There's no need to get all hoity-toity with me. Course I'll do it, but it'll cost you. Like I said earlier: the first two consultations you gets free, after that—'

'I must pay. Yes, I know,' Rex interrupted. 'Shall we go?'

'My my, we are impatient, aren't we?'

'Please!'

'All right, keep your hair on.' Tumbril crouched and, gripping her nose between forefinger and thumb, blew out her cheeks.

Rex braced himself. He waited for the scenery to dissolve – for him to be thrust into the nothingness around the Great Hoop – but nothing happened.

'Tumbril!' he said. 'It didn't work!'

'Give me a chance, love; I'm just clearing me tubes. All this travelling plays havoc with me sinuses.' She hawked and spat. 'Now then.' And she clicked her fingers.

The palm trees, the sea and the sky melted around them, and soon Rex found himself floating in the void, gazing on the beauty of the Hoop, which he saw, to his dismay, was rapidly becoming two hoops.

'Oh dear,' said Tumbril. 'What's happened here then?'

'Um, nothing,' said Rex guiltily.

'Has this little jaunt got anything to do with the Paradox?' Tumbril asked suspiciously.

'Not necessarily.'

'You're not going to mess around with it again?'

'I made a mistake and I've got to put it right.'

'You made a mistake all right. Making another ain't going to help nobody.'

'I'm not going to argue with you; I know what I've got to do. Now stay here and wait for me.'

'All right, but I don't like it.'

Moving through the eternal void, Rex drew nearer and nearer to the magnificent Hoop of Destiny until he was looking down at an area on its external surface which looked a bit like the brass nameplate outside a doctor's surgery but was about five times the size. Etched into it was a line of text that blazed as if written in fire: 'Whatever you expect to happen will happen, unless something else happens instead.' The second half of this statement had been crossed out and replaced with: 'unless you want something else badly enough to happen instead.'

Rex drew the Crystal across his correction, scoring it out. He was about to begin again on the line underneath . . . but what should he write? It was all very well crossing out the amended Paradox; inventing a completely new one, however, was an entirely different kettle of fish. Should he simply revert to the original? No, it was too wishy-washy. It would have to be something new.

Hope, Rex . . . Hope is the key . . . Even suffering has a purpose . . .

The old Wizard's words came back to him, and suddenly Rex knew exactly what he should write.

On one half of the rapidly separating Hoop of Destiny, the big Harley carrying the fat man and the gaunt figure of Death weaved unsteadily across its golden surface.

'I can't see where I'm fucking going!' the fat man yelled at his passenger, who clung on grimly, his arms wrapped tightly around the other man's head.

The fat man, temporarily blinded by Death's skeletal limbs, swung the bike closer and closer to the rift, and with a sudden jolt the front tyre slipped over into nothingness. The bike lurched forward, throwing the rider and his pillion passenger from the saddle. Soon, motorbike, man and Death were all three falling through the void.

'Ahhhh!' the figures screamed as they tumbled through the emptiness. And as they fell deeper and deeper into the impenetrable blackness – moving further and further away from the pale golden luminescence of the Hoop – behind them, the rift in the magnificent river of perception slammed shut with a boom that reverberated through the universe.

The Hoop was whole once more.

Chapter 51

Rex stormed back into the small laboratory. 'OK, that's the Hoop fixed. *Now* will you help me with Pandora's box?'

'I'm sorry?' said Max, who was chalking up all the team's suggestions for the new Paradox on the blackboard.

'I've rewritten the Paradox and fixed the Hoop, so can we get on to the fog now?'

'How about, Time makes fools of us all?'

'No, Frink,' said Nilbert. 'We're not doing that anymore.'

'Oh, sorry.' Frink blushed.

'What did you change it to?' Max asked.

'That doesn't matter. What does matter is saving the world from freezing to death.'

The nose, toe and eye began bubbling, and a sharp blast of binary code filled the air. 'Yes, yes, a good point,' said Max. 'My colleagues here are wondering if you have any proof of what you've done.'

'No. You're just going to have to trust me.'

Max laughed. 'That's not very scientific, is it?' The nose, toe and eye bubbled in agreement. 'Well, it looks like we're just going to have to do the sums and find out.' He picked up the blackboard duster.

'There's no time for that!' Rex yelled. '*You!*' He pointed to Harvey.

'Me?'

'Yes, you. Have you got a radio?'

Limbo II

'Er, yeah.'

'Get it.'

Harvey went up to the other end of the laboratory, returning with an old Sony portable. 'What do you keep it tuned to?' Rex asked.

'The World Service, mostly.'

'Good. Turn it on.'

Harvey pressed the switch and the room was filled with white noise.

'There!' said Rex triumphantly. 'No World Service can only mean one thing: England, to all intents and purposes, has been wiped out.'

Harvey twiddled the tuning knob through the densely packed frequencies that usually hummed with the sounds of exotic eastern music and the guttural consonants of strange languages. But he could find nothing save the unbroken hiss of abandoned airwaves. It seemed the whole earth was off the air.

'Can you get *anything*?' asked Nilbert.

Harvey continued searching. At last the strident tones of an Australian commentator crackled over the speaker: '... getting reports that Europe, the Indian subcontinent, Russia, China and North America have all been hit by the fog. Eyewitnesses say it leaves people frozen in a sort of living death. And from the speed with which it's moving, latest estimates are that it'll be reaching our shores within the hour. I don't know what to say except, God help us all. We're going to stay on the air as long as we can, keeping you up to date with regular news reports as and when we find anything out, and – for what it's worth – keeping you company. Stay listening, people, and for pity's sake, don't panic.' Harvey clicked the radio off. Everyone fell silent.

'Now do you see?' said Rex. 'So what do we do? You're the best brains anywhere – you should be able to come up with something.'

The men hung their heads and stared at the floor.

'Well?'

Still nothing.

'Do I have to do *everything* around here? Aaarghh!' Rex thumped the workbench in frustration. The nose, toe and eye bubbled apprehensively. 'Sorry.'

'Remember, Rex, the fog is nothing more than an illusion,' Nilbert gently reminded him.

'It didn't feel like an illusion when I was in the middle of it.'

'But you *did* get out of it again,' said Harvey.

'Perhaps there's a clue there?' Nilbert ventured.

All faces turned hopefully to Rex. 'Hope!' he exclaimed. 'Yes! Hope is the key. It worked for me, why shouldn't it work for everybody else? This fog steals people's expectations, their trust and belief. They have to be shown that there is still something to live for.'

'So,' said Max, picking up the chalk, 'taking f to represent the fog' – he wrote it on the board – 'it should be relatively easy to formulate an equation, where h (hope), equals—'

'You can't fix this thing with mathematics!' Rex exploded. 'This is about hearts and minds. Living flesh and blood can't be reduced to symbols on a board!'

Max put down the chalk and, for the first time in his short but spectacular life, felt rather inadequate.

'What's the most hopeful thing you can think of? First thing that comes into your head.' Rex pointed at each of the men in turn.

'Spring.'

'Daffodils.'

'Blancmange.'

'Chicks.'

'Blancmange?'

'A baby.' Everyone turned to look at Nilbert. 'A baby is hope for the future,' he continued. 'An investment, if you like. What has in it more optimism, more promise, more hope, than the carefree, gurgling laugh of a baby?'

Limbo II

'Yes! Yes! Yes!' Rex was jumping up and down. 'OK, all we need now is a baby.'

'Er, I know where we can get one,' said Harvey, a little unsurely. 'There's a waitress, works at the Coral Reef Hotel just outside Cairns.'

'Good. Where's the nearest radio station?'

'Radio station?'

'Nobody's going to have had time to turn off their radios. All over the world there are going to be millions of radio sets, a lot of them tuned to the World Service or Voice of America. If we can get something out over one of those frequencies, we're in with a shot.'

'4KZ at Innisfail,' said Harvey. 'On the coast, about fifty miles south of Cairns.'

'OK, everybody into the spaceship!' Frink shouted.

'That's not possible, I'm afraid!' The men all stopped in the doorway and turned back to look at Max.

'What do you mean?' said Rex.

'There's not enough fuel to get that thing off the beach, let alone take us to Cairns. We'll end up in the sea.'

'Well . . .' Rex looked desperately about. 'There must be a boat or something?'

'There is,' said Harvey, 'but—'

'But? But what?'

Nilbert put a hand gently on his arm. 'It's not going to work, Rex. The boat trip to the mainland takes at least two hours, then it's a drive of over a hundred and fifty miles to Cairns . . .'

It seemed it was over. Yet it had so nearly worked. The idea was there; this time it was the machinery that had let them down. *Machinery.* Rex rolled the word around his mind. What was a spaceship but a piece of machinery? An incredibly complex one, admittedly, but machinery nevertheless. 'Frink,' he said, 'how does your spaceship work?'

'Magnetosynchrotronic radiation.'

'In English?'

'It's quite simple, really. A charged particle following a spiral path in a magnetic field radiates synchrotronic energy in the form of electromagnetic waves—'

'I'm going to stop you right there. What I'm trying to get at is what sort of fuel it uses.'

'Ah, a mixture of helium and argon. An influx motor drives the gas, under pressure, over an iridium plate coated with—'

'Spare me the details. So basically all you need to get that thing going is a tank full of liquid gas?'

'Yes.'

'Follow me.' Rex led them along the beach to where Frink's gleaming spaceship was parked. 'Where's the fuel tank?'

'It's that small bulge at the back,' said Frink, indicating a bulbous prominence with a knurled filler cap just behind the cockpit hatch.

Rex put his hands on it and closed his eyes. After a few moments, condensation appeared on the warm, metallic skin of the craft, and thin wisps of mist began to escape from around the filler cap. 'Check the fuel gauge now.'

Frink climbed into the cockpit and started flicking switches. 'It's full!' he shouted in astonishment.

'Well, what are we waiting for?'

Chapter 52

There was pandemonium in the hotel, which wasn't helped by the arrival of an alien spaceship on the terrace by the swimming pool. Already reeling from news of the imminent appearance of a life-sapping fog, an invasion from outer space was the last straw for the hotel residents. They fled in mind-scrambling terror from the 'invaders'.

The spaceship came to rest poolside, and the hatch opened. A large man with a beard leapt from the cockpit. 'I'll be as quick as I can,' Harvey shouted, and ran towards the main building, scattering terrified residents before him.

The reception desk was empty and the whole place a mess. Those of a nervous disposition were running screaming through the corridors, while other more sanguine souls sat around smiling, occasionally helping themselves to the unlimited liquid refreshment available from the now unmanned bar.

Harvey stopped in the large, open-plan reception area and yelled, 'Honey!' but got no reply. Searching around frantically for somebody, *anybody* who could help, he found the hotel manager hunched on the floor behind the reception desk, quivering with terror. Harvey pulled him up by the lapels of his seersucker jacket and pushed him against the wall.

'Where's Honey?'

The manager looked at him, his face white and contorted with panic. A thin dribble of saliva ran from the corner of his mouth and down his chin; he was way past making sense. Suddenly a car smashed through the hotel entrance, coming to rest in a small shallow ornamental pool in front of the desk, and through the newly enlarged entrance came the frantic hooting of horns and angry shouts. Harvey lowered the manager gently to the ground and ran out to investigate.

In their haste to get away – to God knows where – panic-crazed residents had leapt into their cars and all tried to leave at the same time, driving into each other, the trees, the hotel . . . There was a traffic jam all the way from the covered entrance, down the tree-lined drive, to the gate, where a car was wedged sideways between the solid coral gateposts.

'Honey! Honey!' Harvey ran frantically from car to car. Eventually he found her, cradling Jasmine in her arms and rocking back and forth, trying to calm the distraught infant who was picking up the panic from all around her.

Harvey yanked open the door. 'Honey, thank God!'

She slammed the door shut. 'Leave me alone!'

'No, you don't understand. We need your baby!'

Honey's eyes were wide with fear. 'You touch her and I'll kill you!' she screamed.

Harvey jerked open the door again. 'No, Honey, listen to me. I'm trying to help.'

Honey pulled something out from between her knees, and Harvey was suddenly looking down the barrel of a gun. He froze. 'Easy now, baby.'

'Close the door and go away.'

Harvey stayed put.

'I'll kill you!' she screamed, her grip on the gun tightening.

'OK, OK! Look. I'm shutting the door, see?' He gently pushed the door to, and leaned in through the open window. 'Calm now, baby. Calm. You don't want to shoot me.'

'Don't I?'

'Believe me, you don't. Look – listen – I can get you both out of here. Please, Honey, put the gun down and come with me.'

Limbo II

'Out of here?' She thought about it, and momentarily lowered the gun. 'Why should I believe you?'

'Because I've got a nice face?' He smiled – and found the barrel of the gun up his left nostril.

'Don't fuck around! How can you get us out of here?'

'That's a little difficult to explain. Can I just show you?'

'No, no, I'm not getting into that thing,' she said, backing away from the gleaming spaceship.

'Please, Honey,' Harvey begged.

'Really, there's nothing to be frightened of.' Rex smiled.

'You'll be perfectly safe, I promise,' said Nilbert.

The men clustered around her, clucking reassuringly. 'Give me room, give me room!' Honey said testily. An elderly fat woman, naked save for a towel wrapped round her head, ran past screaming in terror, followed by an equally terrified – and wrinkled – old man. 'All right,' she said at last.

'That's the spirit,' Harvey said, and helped her up into the cockpit.

'We're not all going to fit,' said Rex. 'Tony, you stay here with Max, and we'll pick you up when it's all over.'

The rest of them crammed into the small cockpit, and Max and Tony watched the silver craft lift up and soar away over the treetops.

A small boy, who had been studying the newcomers with interest, finally plucked up the courage to wander over and talk to them. 'Excuse me?' he said, tugging on Tony's bikini bottom.

Tony looked down at the freckle-faced boy. 'Yes, son. What is it?' he asked kindly.

'Are you an alien, or just weird?'

Chapter 53

'This is Jack Rattigan, 4KZ News – Queensland's only locally owned radio station, and probably one of the last radio stations in the world still broadcasting.' He poured himself a shot from the bottle of whisky by his side. 'Well, people, you know it's not my style to beat about the bush, so I'll give it to you straight: we're all fucked. God knows what I'm still doing here; I should be out doing all those things you're supposed to do before your imminent death, like getting fucked or stealing a jumbo jet. I guess I'm just a sentimental old arsehole, sitting here talking to all you no-hopers one last time and waiting for this killer fog to come rolling in over the sea . . .' The newscaster hugged the bottle to his chest and looked out through the big studio window at the broad, blue expanse of the Pacific Ocean. 'And I've got a grandstand view. Cheers!' He downed his whisky and poured himself another.

Hearing the sound of a scuffle in the corridor outside, Jack looked across to the glass-fronted control room, and saw that it was filling up with people. 'Well, here's a turn-up, folks – we've been invaded. All the crazies are coming out of the woodwork now. Who are they, Pete? Seventh Day – crazy as a fucking spoon – Adventists? Or unwashed fucking fundamentalists who want to take over the world? Bring them in; let them have their say. We're all fucked anyway.'

The door burst open, and Rex, Harvey, Frink, Honey and Jasmine tumbled into the studio, followed by Pete, the sound engineer. 'Sorry, Jack,' he said.

'That's OK.' Jack poured himself another drink and leaned in

Limbo II

close to the microphone. 'Well, you lucky people, it seems the last voice you'll ever hear won't be mine, after all, but some mad fuck from the People's Popular Front for the Adoration of God's Armpit. Good luck and God bless.' He stood and offered his chair to the intruders. 'Be my guests.'

While Frink wandered around, filming proceedings with his finger, Rex settled Honey and Jasmine at the microphone. 'Is there any way of patching this broadcast into the BBC World Service frequency?' he asked.

'We haven't got the equipment,' said Pete, 'but we could bounce the signal down to Brisbane. They can do it from there.'

'Do it then!'

'That is, if I can raise anybody.'

'Please try, and let me know when it's all set up.'

The sound engineer looked at Jack. 'Why not?' He shrugged.

'All right, I'll have a go,' said the engineer, and headed back to the control room.

'How do I work this thing?' Rex asked, bending over the microphone.

'Just talk into it — we're live. Do you want a drink?' Jack waved the bottle at him.

'No thanks. Right, er ... Now then.' Rex cleared his throat. 'Hello everybody. You probably have some idea of what's heading towards us. What we want to do is offer a ray of hope to those of you who can still hear, and even to those of you who can't ... yet.' He looked desperately across to Pete, who was hanging on the phone. 'What I'm trying to say is ...' Rex looked out of the window at the beautiful bright day. 'What I'm trying to say ... What I'm trying to say is ...' *What am I trying to say?* He gazed at the sea and the palm trees waving gently in the tropical breeze. If this didn't work, all that splendour was going to disappear. *Hope, Rex. Hope is the key ...*

'You all right, mate?' Jack was leaning over him, enveloping him in whisky breath.

'Er . . . yes, yes.' Rex looked across to the control booth again, and realized that Pete was smiling at him, giving him the thumbs up. Rex turned to the child sitting in Honey's lap. 'OK, Jasmine. It's up to you.' But as he looked down at her, he became horribly aware of the crushing burden he was placing on her tiny shoulders. Jasmine must have caught the drift of his thought, because she immediately started bawling her head off.

'Oh, shit,' said Rex.

The others crowded round. 'There, there,' said Nilbert, soothingly. Harvey made a funny face. Jasmine looked up at the big, bearded man with his buggy eyes, and for a moment she stopped in mid-howl. Then she started screaming in earnest. Frink unfurled his pink antennae and waved them around his head. She screamed even louder.

'You're frightening her!' Honey shouted.

'What's that?' Harvey suddenly asked. Everyone stopped whatever they were doing and followed Harvey's gaze out through the big picture window towards the wide expanse of the Pacific Ocean. What looked like a low bank of cloud had appeared on the horizon and was heading towards the coast with terrifying speed.

'Ah, is she ticklish?' Rex asked. 'Maybe if you tickled her—?'

'Get out!' Honey erupted. 'Everybody out! I'm going to do this my way.'

'But—'

'Best not to argue with the lady,' said Jack.

'Get out!' Honey screamed again.

'She means it,' said Harvey.

The men all trooped out, gathering in a worried knot in the control room.

'Now then, my love,' said Honey, sitting Jasmine on the desk and kissing her on the forehead. 'Who's Mummy's special girl?'

The world – that previously blue and vibrant planet – was steadily turning grey and silent. Billions of souls stood, sat or lay where they had been overtaken by the fog, trapped in the freezing hell of their own private desolation. Nothing moved, no birds sang; everything was funereally quiet. This was the end of all things. Soon, the Earth would be nothing more than a lifeless, loveless ball of rock, spinning aimlessly through space for eternity.

But then, as all life on Earth was about to descend into the unfathomable depths of aching despair, a surprising thing happened. The absolute quiet was broken by a strange sound, a sound thought silenced forever. Issuing from the speakers of a million radios came the gurgling, chuckling laugh of a baby. At first the memory of life it engendered was too painful to bear, but, even in their profound isolation, the people of the world could not help but turn their hearts towards the sound – and that small spark of hope that lay dormant, deep within, was fanned into flame. Here and there, small pockets of life began to thaw the icy grip of the enveloping fog. And slowly, slowly, the grey, living death was pushed back. Where hope resided, its icy talons could find no foothold, and it evaporated like the morning mist . . .

Sitting out on the sun terrace of an Australian hotel, a strange, misshapen humanoid and a man in a bikini were watching the fog roll in over the beach.

'Well,' said Max, turning to Tony and raising his Bacardi and Coke, 'it's been nice knowing you.'

'It's been, er . . . different,' Tony replied.

As the palm trees on the beach disappeared into the anaesthetizing fog, the pair of them braced themselves for the inevitable descent into the bleakness of irredeemable despair. But then something unexpected happened. Just as the huge grey wave of despondency was about to break over the hotel itself, it slowed, and stopped.

'What happened?' said Max.

'*You're* asking *me?*' said Tony.

They watched in amazement as the fog thinned and slowly began to retreat. Soon it was racing away from the beach, becoming more and more indistinct as it went.

'They did it!' Tony yelled triumphantly.

When the silver spacecraft landed by the pool, it was greeted by a cheering crowd, and the occupants were lifted out and carried, shoulder high, into the hotel bar.

The alcohol flowed with joyful – one could say, frenzied – abandon, while the hapless hotel manager tried to keep track of who was drinking what, and how much, and which room should be billed.

'Here's to Honey and Rex.' Harvey raised his glass. The company gathered around the large table followed suit.

'Honey and Rex!' they cheered. Having downed their drinks, they helped themselves to another from the large selection on the table, being careful not to refresh their glasses from the three laboratory flasks which stood, bubbling happily, amidst the bottles.

'Well,' said Rex, standing up.

'You're not leaving?' Nilbert enquired.

'I really must go home.'

'Stay for a little,' said Max, who was experiencing for the first time the pleasures of alcoholic intoxication. 'Relax and kill off a few memory circuits with us.' And he poured another shot of rum into the nose's flask.

'Sorry,' said Rex, 'there's still one more thing I have to do.'

Max clapped a small, thin arm around him. 'You know, for a human you're not too shabby,' he slurred. 'By the way, you never told us how you fixed the Paradox.'

'I'll let you work that out for yourself.' Rex smiled.

Nilbert stood and clasped him by the hand. 'Go carefully, Rex Boggs,' he said.

Limbo II

'You saved the world,' said Tony, patting him on the back.

'No, this little girl here saved the world.' Rex crouched down by the seated Honey and gazed at the child, fast asleep in her arms – little Jasmine, who had no idea of the miracle she had just wrought.

'Look after her,' Rex whispered. Honey smiled and kissed him on the cheek. 'And you,' Rex said, turning to Harvey, 'look after Honey.'

Harvey took Honey's hand. 'We're going back to Lizard. It may not be the most comfortable of places to set up home, but someone's got to look after the reef.' Tears welled up in Harvey's eyes, and he wrapped his arms around Rex. 'You're a prince.'

'Yes, I am,' Rex agreed mysteriously. 'And now, I really must go.'

Thinking that mankind had probably witnessed enough weirdness for one day, Rex sought out an unoccupied hotel room where he could open the portal in private.

Pulling the Limbo Crystal out of his pocket, he gazed into its depths. He was going home. Granted, it would not be a joyous homecoming – he would have to work hard to regain the trust of his people – but despite all he was going back to, he was suffused with a warm and cosy glow, and found himself smiling inanely, especially when thinking about the graceful form of a certain waitress called Matilda. Clearing his throat, he prepared to enunciate the spell.

'Sorry to trouble you.' Swinging round, Rex found himself looking into Frink's ever-cheerful face.

'Er, what is it?'

'I was wondering if you'd mind my coming with you. You see, Rex Boggs making his triumphant return home, to be greeted warmly back into the bosom of his people, would make a fabulous ending for my documentary.'

'I suspect my reception is going to be rather on the frosty side.'

'Why, what have you done?'

'It's . . . hard to explain.'

'Is your home far? I could give you a lift.'

'I doubt that. Aren't you rather keen to be getting back to *your* home?'

'I can go back whenever I want. Besides, I said I'd give Max a lift, and from the looks of him I doubt he'll be ready to leave for some time yet.'

'OK.' Rex sighed. 'But don't get in anyone's way.'

'Thank you, thank you.' Frink beamed. 'I shall be the soul of discretion.'

Chapter 54

Frink was disorientated – having stepped from a light, warm, tropical hotel room, he now found himself in the dark, standing on the cold battlements of an ancient castle while, somewhere far below, a huge crowd of people were yelling. He couldn't quite make out what they were saying, but their tone was decidedly angry.

'Smeil, meet Frink Byellssen.'

'How do you do?' said Smeil, offering his hand.

'Greetings,' said Frink.

'How's Iris?' Rex asked the little man.

'Shaken by her ordeal, but on the mend.'

'That's a relief. Where is she now?'

'In her apartments, with the King and Mr Pink. I believe they're discussing soft furnishings.'

'Good, good. Um, you don't happen to have seen Matilda, do you?'

'Matilda? Er, yes, she's . . . she's—'

'Here I am.'

Rex turned and looked at the figure that had appeared through the gloom, and in that moment he knew . . . he knew that with her at his side, he could do anything. He wanted to throw himself at her feet and declare his undying love, swearing that to leave her again would be death. 'It's . . . very nice to see you,' he said.

Matilda smiled. 'It's nice to see you, too.' The two of them stood gazing moonily at each other for some time.

Smeil was finding the whole thing rather painful. 'Master,' he said, breaking the moment, 'what are you going to do now?'

'Do? Ah, yes – do. Smeil, I need you to arrange some sort of light up here.'

'Light? What for?'

'So the people can see me. I'm going to address them.'

The little man knitted his brow. 'Is that wise?'

'Do you have a better idea?'

'You could disguise yourself and go and hide in the mountains.'

'Let's just try and be positive, shall we?' said Rex. 'I also need a piece of paper.'

'A piece of paper?'

'The missing fragment of the Book: the piece of paper with the verse about the Horsemen on it.'

'But we haven't found it yet.'

Rex smiled inscrutably. 'Ah, but we don't *need* it.'

Smeil was puzzled. 'But you just said—'

'Only *believe*, Smeil. We need the *promise* of the piece of paper, the *hope* of the piece of paper.'

'Sir?'

'Just get me a piece of paper!'

Half an hour later, in the light of a dozen flickering torches, Rex got ready to make his speech. Frink filmed his preparations, adding a hushed voice-over: 'Here on the crumbling battlements of this ancient castle, Rex Boggs, Wizard to the court of Limbo, is about to address his people. Down below an ugly mood reigns, but up here all is calm, all is peace. Rex, dressed in his ceremonial wizarding robe of white silk with a dragon motif and carrying the wizarding piece of paper, whose function remains a mystery, has been, for some while, pacing the cold stone flags, going over and over in his mind the important message he wishes to communicate to the citizens, who wait, like a pack of hungry wolves, far below.

'Ah, now he is ready. His loyal servant, Smeil, places the upturned wizarding beer crate on its marks, and the Wizard of

Limbo II

Limbo prepares to step onto it. It is very, very dark, and in this inky blackness, all we know of the mob is their bloodcurdling cries: "Kill the Wizard! String him up by his fingernails! Disembowel him! Pull out his—" '

'Will you be quiet!' Rex hissed.

Frink reluctantly cut short his commentary, and continued to film in silence.

Rex raised his arms. 'Citizens of Limbo!' he boomed. There was a momentary hush from the people below, but when they realized who was addressing them, they erupted into jeering howls.

Rex waited until the noise abated. 'I understand how you feel,' he said, 'but do not lose heart! All is not lost!'

'We've no daylight!' shouted one.

'We're doomed to eternal night!'

'Listen to me!' Rex yelled. 'Deliverance is at hand. We have found the missing verse. Here it is!' He raised the blank piece of paper high so all could see it.

'Burn it!' they screamed.

'Very well!' Rex thrust the paper into the nearest torch, and it took flame immediately. A gust of wind brushed it from his hand, taking it out over the battlements where it hovered for a moment above the heads of the crowd, a bright point of light against the night sky. Then, having burnt itself out, it floated gently to the ground, a curled and blackened wisp of ash. The cheering horde rushed over to where it had fallen, and stamped it into the dust.

'Look! Look!' Rex shouted, pointing towards the horizon.

The crowd turned and looked. Above the spot where earlier the sun had slipped down into the Salient Sea, a rosy glow suffused the sky. Seconds later, the fiery red rim of the gigantic orb peeped over the swelling tide, turning the tops of the waves pink.

'The dawn is come!' Rex announced. The people at the gate watched the rising of the sun with tears in their eyes. The long purple shadows of the Southern Range contracted, and the colour of the fields went from bronze to green. With the sun once more back in its rightful place, high in the sky, someone in the crowd shouted, 'Three cheers for the Wizard! Hip-hip!'

'Hooray!'

As their cheers rebounded off the castle walls, Rex turned to Smeil. 'Now comes the difficult bit.' He turned back to them. 'Friends!' he called, and waited for silence. 'What if I told you that the piece of paper I just set light to was simply that – a piece of paper?'

A murmur ran through the crowd. Then someone said, 'If that was just a piece of paper, then how come the sun's come back?'

'Aye!' they chorused.

'*Belief*,' said Rex. 'You *believed* that if I destroyed the verse, the sun would return.'

'So?'

'Don't you see? Your belief is more powerful than all the verses in the world. It's your belief that has brought the sun back, not the burning of some worthless piece of paper.'

There was a buzz as the crowd conferred, then they turned once again to look up at the sun. '*We* did that?' said one.

'Nah,' said another.

'How could we have done that?'

'I don't get it!'

The sun began to slip slowly back down the sky.

'Look!' yelled Rex. 'Look what your wavering is doing. Once you believed; now you doubt. It wasn't the destruction of the verse that brought back the sun, it was you! So what's changed?'

After a puzzled pause, one shouted, 'But it wasn't really the verse!'

'Exactly!' Rex triumphed. 'And the sun rose anyway, and as long as *you* want it to be there, that's where it's going to stay.'

There was a long silence as the logic of this gradually began to sink in. Then, as the penny finally dropped, the crowd uttered a unison 'Ah!' and the sun climbed slowly back to its zenith.

Limbo II

'I still don't get it!' ventured one, but he was quickly shouted down.

'Three cheers for the Wizard,' someone shouted.

'We've already done that bit,' said another, sotto voce.

There was an embarrassed murmuring, out of which came, 'All right then. One cheer for the Wizard!'

The crowd gave a perfunctory 'Hooray!' then began to break up, but suddenly another figure appeared on the battlements – someone the light-starved populace of Limbo hadn't seen for some time. It was Queen Iris.

'Three cheers for the Queen! Hip-hip!' someone yelled, and once again the assembled throng launched into an orgy of cheering.

Supported on either side by Bernard and Mr Pink, she smiled broadly as she accepted the cheers of her subjects.

'Mum, are you all right?' whispered Rex.

'I'm fine. I'm sorry I caused all this trouble. I never meant to—' She broke off, her eyes glistening. 'Oh dear,' she said, opening her handbag and rummaging around for a tissue. But as she pulled one out, a small scrap of paper fell onto the stone flags. Rex stooped and picked it up. He was about to hand it back to her when something about it made him pause.

'Mum, what's this?'

'Oh, I was going to bring you all back a little surprise. I know there are certain things we can't get here, so I made a list...'

Rex looked down at Iris's handwritten list: 'Mars Bars for Bernard, Pontefract cakes for Rex, sugared almonds for Smeil.' Then he turned it over. There, in a familiar script, was a dark and prophetic verse:

> *Behold, four horsemen in a blink:*
> *One black, one white, one pale, one pink,*
> *And hell and darkness follow in their stink...*

'Where did you get this, Mum?'

'I found it in the bedside table, in the Gideons' Bible. Someone must have been using it as a bookmark. I've not done anything wrong, have I?'

'No, no.' Rex smiled and shook his head. He looked at the piece of paper in his hand. The terrible prophecy written upon it had somehow lost its ability to alarm. *After all*, Rex said to himself, *it's just a piece of paper*. He went over to one of the torches which still burned, redundantly, in the bright light of day. As he approached it, he could feel the paper in his hand shrink away from the heat.

'Sorry,' he said, 'but there's just no future for you here,' and he thrust it into the flame. As it caught fire, it let out a brief, high-pitched scream. Then it was all over – the last of the Book was nothing more than a curl of white ash. Opening his fingers, Rex let it float away on the breeze. 'Well, thank goodness *that's* over,' he muttered.

He was just about to rejoin the rest of the happy company on the battlements when something strange happened. The cheering of the crowd stopped abruptly, the wind dropped, and the flags froze impossibly straight on their flagpoles.

A bundle of rags materialized out of the ether and marched towards him, grim-faced. 'So, this is where you've been hiding.'

'Hello, Tumbril. What's up?'

Tumbril's eyes flashed 'You owe me, Rex Boggs. You owe me for one consultation. Of course, you're perfectly free to renege on the deal, should you so wish, but be warned, there are few alive who've crossed a Lorelei,' she said darkly.

'Of course I'll pay you,' said Rex. 'What do you want?'

Tumbril's demeanour changed instantly, and she smiled coyly up at him. 'Well, love, I know it's a bit short notice, but every year at this time me and the girls have a bit of a knees-up, and we was just wondering if you would dignify our celebrations by being guest of honour at our 500,000th Hag Fest. It's quite prestigious; we always get a *name*. They've all done it, all the biggies: Solomon, Moses, Burt Lancaster. Like I said, I know it's a bit sudden, but we've been let down. We had booked that Onan, but he pulled out at the last minute.'

'When is it?'

'Next Wednesday.'

'I'd be delighted.' Rex smiled.

'Good, good.' Tumbril gave a wheezy chuckle. 'The girls will be thrilled; they're longing to meet you. They've heard all about you, you know. I'll pick you up at seven o'clock sharp.'

She clicked her fingers and disappeared. The flags rattled in the wind once more, and the throaty roaring of the crowd crashed back into Rex's consciousness. Going back to join the happily waving Iris and Bernard, he noticed Mr Pink standing slightly apart and looking rather lost.

'What will you do now?' Rex asked him.

'Oh, hello, Rex . . . I don't know. I expect something will turn up.'

'You could always stay here.'

'That's sweet of you, but – and don't take this the wrong way, but – well, nothing really happens here.'

'Nothing happens?'

'No, I mean after Brighton this place is pretty tame.'

'Yes, I see what you mean. Look,' said Rex, suddenly having an idea. 'I don't suppose you'd be interested in a career in retailing?'

Frink was putting the final touches to his documentary. 'Now,' he said, calling everyone to order. 'If we could have the King and Queen here in the centre . . . Good, good. Mr Pink, Smeil, we'll have you on either side . . . Er, no. Smeil, you'd better stand in front. Where are Rex and Matilda?'

Doing a slow pan, Frink's finger took in the assembled company, the cheering crowd, the sun-drenched Great Plain and, standing hand in hand on the crumbling battlements, Rex and his bride to be. Wiping a tear from his eye, Frink came to the climax of his commentary: 'And, with this fairy-tale ending to... well, a fairy tale, we say farewell to the fabled land of Limbo. This is Frink Byellssen, Castle Limbo – Mission accomplished. Now, everybody wave to the finger...'

Epilogue . . .

Frink arrived home a hero. On the ten-year trip back to Thrripp, he and Max devised a revolutionary spaceship engine that could actually shrink time and space, slashing the journey time from Thrripp to Earth to a much more manageable forty minutes. Now, when he's not too busy hosting his weekly television show, Frink leads sightseeing tours of his compatriots to all the places made famous by his award-winning documentary.

Max is still out there, evolving. At the moment he's a small, sentient planet orbiting Alpha Caeli inhabited by a *Star Wars* fan and a small but diverse collection of body parts. But one day he hopes to become a sun, and eventually start up his own universe.

Mr Pink took up Rex's offer to take over the shop, and completely changed its character. Now he runs a successful 'organic' design service, utilizing only casein-based paints and rare fabrics acquired through a 'fair trade' scheme with some of the more remote tribes of the Andes. His distinctive interiors regularly grace the pages of *House and Garden* and *Country Life*.

While Mr Pink revels in the colours of the world, deep under Dartmoor Mr Black still mourns Mr White, what was once Pandora's dread box now serving as the latter's sarcophagus.

As for the Black Knight, he is now the star attraction of the Big Sheep, a popular country park in Bideford, appearing twice daily in the summer as an acrobatic rider with his troupe of strangely coloured horses – one black, one white and one pink.

Nilbert satisfied his longing for rural English life by settling down in a small, well-kept village just outside Taunton, complete with cricket green and Tudor-gabled pub. No one in the village has any real idea who he is, but those with problems find themselves gravitating towards his fireplace and, after a cup of tea and a chat, always go away feeling lighter. Nilbert is also a bit of a hit on the gardening circuit; his dahlias consistently win first prize in the village show, and his greenhouse is a source of constant wonder, stocked as it is with exotic plants which cannot be found on any nurseryman's list.

Back in the sunlit uplands of Limbo, in an exquisite ceremony organized with typical selflessness by Smeil, the recently widowed ex-Queen took her place alongside a proud Bernard and Iris at her son's wedding. Rex and Matilda enjoyed many happy years together and had an unconscionable number of children, who kept their grandparents extremely, but happily, busy.

For Rex's real mother, coming back to Limbo without her beloved Wiz was a bittersweet experience. Getting to know her son wasn't always easy, either; so many years had been lost for them. But although Rex may have lacked some of his father's more adventurous qualities, he had the old Wizard's heart – and those remarkable eyes. Over time, a deep love and trust grew between them.

Rex, as wizards do, lived to a great age, but the price of longevity was to watch those he loved die before him. Bernard and Iris passed away peacefully in their sleep within a week of each other, and Smeil – the most loyal servant a man could have – went next. The Queen followed soon after.

Matilda died on the eightieth anniversary of their wedding. The loss Rex felt was, in part, mollified by the joy he derived from

Limbo II

watching his children and children's children thrive and prosper, and seeing her likeness in them all. Matilda would never truly die, for she had helped to found a dynasty that would last for all time.

Rex devoted the rest of his life to his people, making himself available in a twice-weekly surgery where his wisdom and foresight would throw light and understanding on just about any problem. He also found time to rewrite *The Final Chapter*, cleansing it of its horrific excesses and adding an appendix explaining the concept of day and night which for the first time brought alternate light and darkness to Limbo.

Then, one day, as a very old man plagued by rheumatism and a thousand and one ills, he was sitting at the window of his turret room gazing out at the view when, behind him, he heard a familiar voice.

'Rex, it is time.'

Turning slowly from the bright prospect of the sunny plain, his old eyes took a little time to adjust to the darkness of the room. But at last he was able to make out the form of his father – the old Wizard of Limbo – standing in front of the magnificent four-oven Aga.

'Ah,' said Rex, 'you're here.'

'Thought I'd come and keep you company on the journey,' the old Wizard said.

'How thoughtful,' said Rex, rising stiffly. 'Would you care for a slice of Madeira cake?'

The old Wizard shook his head.

'No, of course not. Oh well, no sense in putting it off.' He looked around his familiar room for the final time, with tears in his eyes. 'Ah, I'm an old fool,' he said, pulling out a handkerchief. 'It seems like only yesterday when I first saw this place. I dare say I shall miss it.'

'I dare say,' said the old Wizard. 'But there are compensations where you're going.'

'Is it very far?' Rex asked.

'No, like stepping through a doorway.'

'Well, what are we waiting for?' Rex picked up the Crystal from the bookshelf. 'Would you care to do the honours?'

'Let's do it together,' the old Wizard suggested.

'Good idea.'

'Felix qui potuit rerum cognoscere causas!' they sang. *'Ibant obscuri sola sub nocte! Tempus edax rerum!'* Then, turning to each other, they smiled and said: *'Non omnia possumus omnes!'* The portal hissed open. In just two steps, Rex would appear on Hove Lawns to encounter a terrible monster, and intercept the mortal blow meant for his younger self. After that . . . his father would lead him on to his final destination.

'Please, after you,' said Rex. The old Wizard bowed, and stepped through the impossible doorway. Rex took one last look out of the window at the sunlit Great Plain and smiled. 'Goodbye,' he said, and taking a deep breath, followed his father through the portal.

In the vastness of the eternal mind hung the great golden Hoop of Destiny, spinning silently. Beyond size, beyond time and space, it flowed on – forever moving, forever staying the same. Great loops and whorls of light leapt from its surface and, etched in fire on a small square area on its outer surface, blazed the Limbollian Paradox – the universal principle that underpins the workings of time and space, the law that governs all things:

WHATEVER HAPPENS, DON'T WORRY – IT'S ALL FOR THE BEST.